Praise for Steph Swainston:

'Thoughtful, exuberant, incredibly inventive, funny but never whimsical or mannered . . . Honest-to-god unputdownable'   China Miéville

'Steph Swainston's writing is as elegantly superior to most other fantasy as a samurai sword is to a flint dagger'   Richard Morgan

'An uncompromisingly classy act'   *Guardian*

'A more original sort of fantasy'   *Time Out*

'A wildly imaginative novel that suggests [Swainston's] a novelist about to take fantastic fiction somewhere entirely new. Bracing'   *SFX*

A hugely entertaining, smart and passionately rendered novel'
SciFi Now

'A stunning fantasy . . . The setting is impeccably realised, with a deftness of touch and a genius for description . . . In fifty years' time, people are still going to be reading this book and talking about it the way we talk about Gormengast'   George Walkley, *Ink Magazine*

'A joy to read, it is bursting at the seams with ideas'   SF Site

'A rare combination of the grim, the bizarre and the hilarious. And somehow it all works'   Emerald City

D1150011

FAIR REBEL

Steph Swainston

This edition first published in Great Britain in 2017 by Gollancz

First published in Great Britain in 2016 by Gollancz
An imprint of the Orion Publishing Group Ltd
Carmelite House, 50 Victoria Embankment,
London EC4Y 0DZ

An Hachette UK Company

1 3 5 7 9 10 8 6 4 2

A CIP catalogue record for this book
is available from the British Library.

ISBN 978 0 575 09752 0

Typeset by Deltatype Ltd, Birkenhead, Merseyside

Printed in Great Britain by CPI Group (UK) Ltd
Croydon, CR0 4YY

MIX
Paper from
responsible sources
FSC® C104740
FSC
www.fsc.org

www.stephswainston.co.uk
www.gollancz.co.uk

To Brian

No wind ever shakes the untroubled peace of Olympus

– Homer, Odyssey

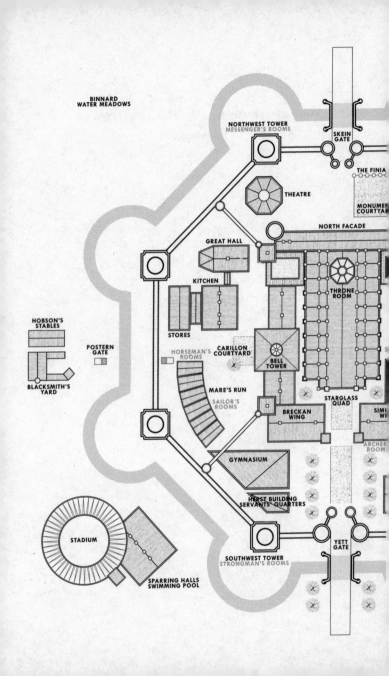

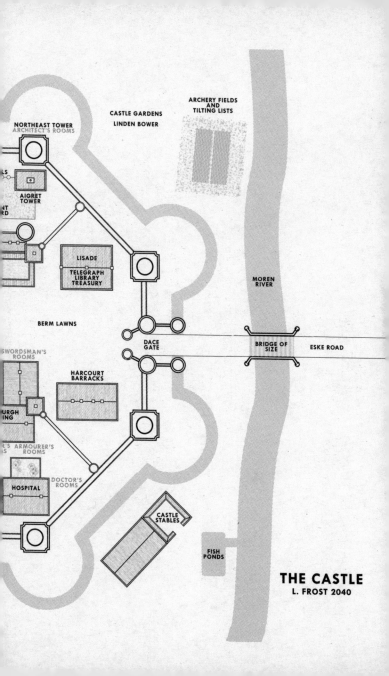

NORTHEAST TOWER
ARCHITECT'S ROOMS

CASTLE GARDENS
LINDEN BOWER

ARCHERY FIELDS
AND
TILTING LISTS

AIGRET
TOWER

LS

NT
RD

LISADE

TELEGRAPH
LIBRARY
TREASURY

MOREN
RIVER

BERM LAWNS

DACE
GATE

BRIDGE OF
SIZE

ESKE ROAD

SWORDSMAN'S
ROOMS

HARCOURT
BARRACKS

URGH
ING

R'S ARMOURER'S
S   ROOMS

DOCTOR'S
ROOMS

HOSPITAL

CASTLE
STABLES

FISH
PONDS

THE CASTLE
L. FROST 2040

CHAPTER 1

A Grave On The Seashore

The smoke rising from the pyre was blowing into tattered, hazy scrims as it drifted out to sea. We stood in a loose arc around it, and I was at the very end of the line, staring numbly at the flames. Every figure in the arc wore black: to introduce any colour into this day would be sacrilege. Across from me, the rising heat distorted Saker's face. He had one hand over his mouth and the other in his greatcoat pocket.

The pyre was built from hundreds of musical instruments. Guitars of various kinds, flutes and oboes, now reduced to skeletons by the flames, surrounded the harpsichords inside like a palisade. Fire crackled up from stacks of burning violins and cellos; the tortoiseshell was peeling back off a hundred harps like fiery wings; bassoons and clarinets were aflame within their silver wire. And on top of it all, in the centre of intense heat and billowing smoke, stood Swallow's rococo grand piano, on which her body lay.

Swallow Awndyn was just a black, charred shape now, with flames pouring around her, hugging her tightly, and the smoke lifted up from her and drifted out to sea.

My wife, Tern, was crying silently, pressing a silk handkerchief to her nose and mouth. I put my arm around her waist and brought her close. She was warm and yielded to me, softened by grief. To my left the arc of mourners wound behind the pyre. The heat haze rippled their figures; they seemed to sway. They had footprinted the dry sand around them into peaks and troughs, over which shadows chased and ebbed.

I recognised some of the mourners: musicians from two National Orchestras, virtuosos from the Royal Academy, singers from the Hacilith Opera, and a few very big names in blues and jazz. They had cast their instruments onto Swallow's pyre as if vowing their music would die with her, and now all eyes were on her last appearance. The depth of their loss was immeasurable. They were heartbroken, and so was I.

I felt inside my shirt collar for my Castle pendant, ripped it off and turned the sunburst on its gold disc between my fingers, then hurled it into the flames. Tern squeezed my arm.

Fire played the whole orchestra at once; it curled and roared within the piano's casing. Pings resounded as the strings snapped. Fire poured around the necks and split the ivory pegs of the guitars, burst the membranes of the drums with squeals and booms. It flickered long fingers over the holes in the piccolos, licked its forked tongues into their tubes – each one became a chimney gushing smoke and tips of flame. Swallow took all these instruments with her into death.

The piano bier gave a crack and its middle fell in. Great black braids billowed up and some of the women half-turned away from the flames, from the sight. I could no longer tell if they were crying or if their eyes were running from the smoke. The form atop the piano had gone; it had fallen piecemeal into the mahogany shell. A few breathed sighs of relief. Eventually the fire began to burn down into embers and the smoke lessened, spinning into clouds and carrying Swallow far out to sea. A bell tolled nine in the town behind me, doleful and low and, without a word spoken, the funeral party started to break up. Even the smoke was now thinning. Goodbye, Swallow, I thought. Goodbye.

Saker turned from the others and walked away over the hard, corrugated sand to the edge of the ocean. Foam-edged wavelets were licking in, hissing to a halt, then another pushed in, lapped over the top and curled its knuckles on the sand. They touched his boot toes and, after a while, lapped around them.

Parallel planes of the sea and the identical sky receded to meet at the horizon. Seldom ripples coming in on the limp sea moulded the chill sand. The mourners were silently returning to the town, leaving tracks slate grey and scuffed against the pale cream of the long strand.

Tern nodded to me. 'Let's go and see him.'

We joined Saker at the water's edge. He didn't look round, he knew who it was. 'It's over,' I said.

'I know.'

'Everyone's going back to the house.'

'They can wait.'

We walked on a little way up the beach, not looking back to the pyre or the mourners, though I could still smell that smoke. Here and there flat black pebbles were embedded in the sand. Saker stooped and collected an armful, ignoring the brine soaking into his sleeve.

'She loved the sea,' I said.

'Hmm.'

Straight shafts of sunlight shone through silver-rimmed holes in the cloud cover. Their beams struck the ocean and set it sparkling.

'I saw you throw your pendant into the fire,' Saker said at length. 'That was a nice touch.'

'If Swallow couldn't be part of the Circle I scarcely want to be, either.'

'It's not our fault the Emperor wouldn't let her in,' Tern said. 'We did all we could.'

Saker said, 'I loved her, you know.'

'We know.'

'I really did love her. It was not some act. I was overwhelmed by love for her. I would have given everything. And now ...' He stopped and stared out to sea.

'You're not to blame for this,' I said.

'No.' He sighed. 'It didn't surprise me, when I heard the news. It doesn't surprise me that she would ... kill herself. We should have predicted it, that Swallow would kill herself. We should have seen it coming.'

'Yes.'

'Unlike Raven. He didn't have to jump. But Swallow ... dear Swallow ... drinking poison – well, anyone can understand.'

'I don't think so,' said Tern.

'No? Did you think she would continue to make music? Happily for us, for the world? Given the number of times the Emperor rebuffed her? Given the amount she was kicked around and buffeted by the world? Do you think it all comes out spontaneously just for your enjoyment? Do you think it would still flow if we continued to ignore her needs and treated her so badly?'

'She had reward and acknowledgement,' I said. 'Everyone loved her music. We knew she was the best.'

'*She* knew she was the best. That was the problem. She wanted to use it and join the Circle. She wanted to be immortal. How could she ever be happy while the Castle stands there and the Emperor won't let her in?'

'She couldn't be content,' I said.

'She's at peace now,' said Tern, and then, 'Oh, god, I'm sorry.'

Saker took one of the flat stones he had collected and skimmed it over the water, punctuating the silence. Flick ... splash, splash, splash. Again: flick ... splash, splash, splash.

'She had *one* aim,' he said. '*One* ambition, *one* desire. Her only determination was to join the Circle and it burnt her up from the inside out. Poor Swallow. It was a white heat so powerful that everything she did was bent towards joining the Circle.'

'For god's sake, Saker,' I said, piqued. 'It doesn't matter now.'

'The Emperor should have let her in because she was a genius musician and now we have lost all her music. The music she would have written if she was made immortal.'

Flick ... splash, splash, splash, splash.

'He should have let her in because she suffered so much. Days and waking nights. No mortal has ever been as tortured with so great a desire to become immortal. And San thinks that's no reason!'

'It would be against his law.'

'He could have made an exception.'

'No,' I said. 'He has to follow his own rule.'

'He could change it!'

'Anyway, many mortals are driven mad by not being able to gain a place in the Castle.'

'Swallow wasn't mad.' Flick ... splash, splash, splash, splash. 'And most of all he should have let her in because doing so would change the Castle. There *was* space for her music.' Flick ... splash, splash, splash. 'There *is* a place for art. Not just cannon and gunpowder. Not just the sabre-swingers that San makes his slaves.'

'I resent that.'

'But you must admit it.' He weighed one of the smaller, sea-wet pebbles in his hand. He turned slightly sideways and: flick: splash, splash, splash, splash, splash, splash, splash.

'That's seven,' said Tern eventually.

'Oh, I can do a hundred and eight. There are people out on Tris right now saying, "What the fuck was that?" '

'Come back to the house, Saker. It's all over.'

He sighed and sent another stone skipping on the trail of the last. 'The Emperor said no and she killed herself. What else could she do? Drink poison. She suffered in life so much: how she must have suffered in death. Did she suffer, Jant?'

'I don't know what drug she took,' I admitted.

Flick ... splash, splash, splash.

'The smoke is clearing,' I said.

'Yes, and the house has opened to view,' said Tern. 'Eleonora's waiting.'

Saker straightened up, folded his arms and looked out in the direction of the line of expanding concentric rings his last skipping pebble had made. 'The tide's coming in.'

'Yes.'

'It will take away the ash.'

'Yes.'

4

'And the wind will scatter the rest.'

'Ye—'

'It always will, you know. For ever. No matter what happens.'

'It'll be gone by nightfall,' said Tern.

'Poor Swallow.' His voice cracked and he hid his face in his hand. Again we waited, Tern and me, until he emerged. 'This is how the Castle treats talent.'

'*Musical* talent.'

'Any art that matters.'

I agreed. We've made ourselves like Insects, to fight them, and without humanity we are no better than them. But still I thought this was a poor way for the King of Awia to behave.

'Eleonora wants to see the house,' said Tern.

Saker pulled himself together, and wiped his hands on his sleeves to brush off the sand. 'Jant. Go tell Leon we'll meet her at the house. We'll walk there. All right?'

'All right.' I kissed Tern, then turned and half-padded, half-splashed over the water-filled corrugations, then crunched on the dry sand, past the lines of seaweed. I slip-stepped up the slope, paused on its crest at the edge of the road, and looked back.

Tern and Saker were now two small figures, Tern in a long, black skirt and Saker in a mourning suit, walking past the smouldering pyre with the strand ahead of them, the sea the colour of pumice and the sky the same opalescent grey, to the terracotta manor house on its grassy promontory at the head of the beach.

The Queen of Awia's coach waited patiently on the road, the coachman on his seat in a capecoat, and six glossy sable mares standing in harness with funeral ostrich plumes on their heads wafting in the breeze.

Eleonora Tanager must have been watching me stamping the sand off on the road, because as I approached the coach door opened and its white eagle coat of arms swung wide revealing a moiré silk interior. She leaned out, in black but still sporty: a shaped jacket cinched at the waist and with the same pert practicality I've come to expect from Saker's wife.

'Jant,' she said. 'I'm so sorry for your loss.'

'The world's loss,' I said.

'She was lifted up in the smoke. I bet she'd have liked to fly.'

'Spare me that bullshit.'

She shrugged and smiled diplomatically. I said, 'Saker and Tern will meet us at the house.'

'I see ...' She patted the seat opposite. I climbed in and shut the door. The horses' hoof-falls blurred into one as we rolled off smoothly, leaving sand grains blowing across the cobbled road.

Inside, was just me and Eleonora, with her fawn-brown eyes, her severely short hair, rounded breasts still high and firm; she's athletic and looks younger than forty, tight trousers, top boots and leering smile. She leant forward and I shuffled back uncomfortably. 'Saker's taking it badly, the silly sod.'

'What do you expect?'

She pinned me with a glance. 'We have much to do. His mind must be on this sale.'

'I hear you won.'

'Of course we won!' She laughed. 'Nobody could outbid the crown of Awia!'

Not only did Swallow die intestate but she had mortgaged the whole manor. It was no longer hers. She'd mortgaged it to the Bank of Hacilith, which last week had auctioned it and Saker and Eleonora had reached out and bought it, at which point the newspapers went so crazy I flew down from Lowespass to see what was happening.

'Do you know how much she mortgaged it for?'

'Jant, the Bank won't say. It's an *extraordinary* sum of money, none of which remains. *None*. It's nowhere to be found, and there are no accounts. Well, only sketchy ones.'

'I knew Swallow was feckless, but ...'

'She was completely irresponsible. Who knows where the money went? Everyone says she was bad at managing Awndyn.'

'She only cared about music,' I said.

'Yes. Doubtless it went on that. Funding aspiring musicians. Elaborate stage designs. Or maybe she frittered it away writing another symphony while the harvest went untended.' Eleonora eyed me shrewdly and continued, 'So we're closing the deal and in an hour Awndyn will be ours.'

I could picture her in her favourite armour – as if she was wearing plate even now. 'We've achieved a lot,' she said. 'Saker and me have united all the manors of Awia. We own four out of six, and now we're buying Awndyn, so we have a Plainslands manor too. And two healthy children. It's not been a bad fifteen years' work, don't you think?'

'Not bad at all,' I said glumly.

'Awia will never have to ask for help again.'

'Well,' I added, 'Congratulations.'

'Cheer up, Jant. The world goes on.'

She leant her cheek on the window, looking up the road as it began a slight curve, following the bay. Her breath misted on the glass. 'Look! Gypsy carriages. Why don't they move?'

I pushed down the window and leaned out, though it put me too close to her for comfort. Sure enough, the road ahead was blocked by a line of Litanee wagons. The Litanee had arrived early in the morning and helped to build the pyre. They'd been waiting all this time at a quiet distance and now they were harnessing their horses and starting to drive away, but unhurriedly.

'They're here to pay their last respects,' I said. 'They liked Swallow.'

'Oh.'

'She was kind to them. She wanted to learn their music.'

'Oh, I see.'

They politely gave way to each other, manoeuvring their wagons, and with the clop of hooves drove on in a troupe. The wagons were covered in colourful paintings: apple trees, hayricks and sailing boats, but they were too distant for me to tell their tribe. Each had a black canvas stretched over the roof: their sign of mourning.

'They'll be gone in a minute,' I said.

We started up again, but now we were at the rear of their procession, so we followed them along the coast road while the uneven roofs and tall red chimney stacks of Awndyn Manor hove into view. We turned off onto its private road, laid in herringbone brickwork, and between the wet, sandy lawns either side, which the gypsy wheels had rutted. We stopped in front of the arched porch, and beyond the wing of the manor house, I could see the grey sky and ocean slanting away into a damp, metallic distance, the pyre still smoking.

Eleonora flung the carriage door open and, with half-spread wings, marched majestically into the house. I sighed. Awndyn manor would become hers, from the rolling chalk downland and wheat fields around Drussiter, to the pretty, chaotic town of Awndyn-on-the-Strand, its bohemian streets and sweep of beach, its miles of machair; from its red cows that fed on seaweed to its pickled herring barrels sent to the Front. From Swallow's Artists' Almshouse, to the auditorium where she conducted open air concerts, all would be Eleonora's. I didn't feel good about it at all.

CHAPTER 2

Swallow's manor house,
Awndyn-on-the-Strand, April 2039

The air in the drawing room was like old corked wine. It seemed darker in here, now it was no longer lit by Swallow's bright personality. She had truly illuminated wherever she was: every situation she enlivened, and now there was just the dark, heavy furniture and a musty smell of dried flowers.

Wittol, the manager of the Bank of Hacilith Moren, welcomed us, and straight away obsequiously ushered Saker and Eleonora into the adjoining dining hall, where documents were spread out on the table. He shut the door with an unctuous click, leaving me and Tern alone with Bunting, Swallow's Steward.

Bunting was as Awian as they come. He was in shirt and waistcoat, and had draped his overcoat on the back of the chaise-longue, under the diamond-paned bow window. His broadsword was tied into the scabbard with black crepe, and gold cord with acorn knots draped from its hilt. He toyed with them nervously. We unsettled him.

He was telling us how he discovered Swallow dead: 'I was the first to find her ... I was coming to advise her that dinner was ready and she ... she was just there, sitting in that chair.' He pointed to a great desk against the far wall. It was polished walnut, its roll top pushed back, and many small, empty pigeonholes and ivory-handled drawers circled like theatre balconies the expanse of its writing surface. Green leather, edged with gold tooling, it was matched on the seat of a chair pulled out from under the arch of the desk, and you could see the impression, where Swallow always sat. The morning sun shone through the leaded glass and cast a network of shadows over it. Atop the desk was a metronome (stopped), a rosin pot full of pens, and a coffee mug on a coaster. That was all.

'She was sitting on the chair, but resting face-down on the table, her head in her arms.'

We approached the table respectfully. The musty smell was stronger here. 'At first I thought she was asleep. She was lying on her score ...

She'd been working on that symphony all year. So I put my hand on her shoulder to wake her ... she was cold.'

He caught his breath and continued. 'She was cold and very pale. I'd never seen anyone so white. I turned her over and felt for her pulse ... nothing!'

He pointed to the mug. 'That was the poison she drank. And she must have kept writing the score while the poison acted on her because ... look ...' He picked up the sheaf of paper and sure enough you could see where her hand had begun to shake because the notes were ill-formed, and the pressure of the pen became lighter until they were just little flecks with their tails at the horizontal. Lighter and lighter, smaller and smaller, until they stopped in the middle of a phrase.

'She never stopped trying,' I said.

'She died with a pen in her hand,' said Bunting. His tone was accusatory and then he blushed. 'I'm sorry.'

Tern took the manuscript from him and studied it intensely. I was more interested in the mug. The musty smell emanated from it. I picked it up and sniffed it: inside was a dark brown residue, like coffee grinds. It was redolent of dead leaves and long-abandoned houses. I didn't know what poison it was – and because I know all there is to know about drugs and poisons, this was very disconcerting.

'Who killed her?' I exclaimed.

'It was suicide, Jant,' Tern said soothingly.

'Could anyone have put this in her drink?'

Bunting shook his head and brushed his damp palms on his backside. 'No, Comet. She made it herself.' He showed us a copper kettle in the fireplace. 'She often boiled water there and made tea or coffee. She made this the same way.'

'Could someone have come in and poisoned her drink?'

'Well ... I suppose it's possible. I was in the kitchen, so was the cook. I hadn't seen Swallow since breakfast. She demanded privacy when she composed.'

'And she didn't keep many servants.'

'No.'

'I want to question them. One at a time.'

'Jant,' Tern said. 'What are you talking about? Swallow killed herself – we know why.'

'We think we do. But I've never smelt anything like this. I can't identify it. So where did it come from? Where did she get it? ... If it *is* an infusion I suppose it might be hemlock gone stale. Look,' I said to Bunting, 'decant it into a bottle for me. I'll take it to analyse.'

Bunting ran his hand through his hair, forcing it up into sweaty peaks, and regarded me with untold misery. In the silence a clock ticked in the cloakroom. All was now passing into the hands of Saker and Eleonora: the linenfold wall panelling that smelt of beeswax, the stone-mullioned windows grouped in sixteens and thirty-twos, the plasterwork ceiling with its small pendentives, and the writing desk, against which leant Swallow's walking stick.

No fire was lit in the hearth, but the April morning was beginning to warm. Sparks of dust danced through a shaft of light, each one flashing golden, enjoying brief fame, before randomly rejoining the shadow.

'It's taking a long time,' said Bunting.

'It's a big business.'

He nodded with the carelessness of despair. 'I suppose you see a lot of mortals die.'

'Thousands,' said Tern. 'But rarely this way.' She rearranged her fur stole around her dainty shoulders, and the nets and silks of her long skirt, damp at the hem from the beach, swept the floor as she went to sit on the chaise longue.

'What was Swallow like in the last few months?' I asked Bunting.

'Bitter! Well ... ever since Thunder's Challenge she'd been bitter. More and more so until it consumed her. For a decade, Comet, she bottled her fury up inside. She was bound to kill herself ... I'm afraid ... with hindsight ... She kept biting her lip and ... her eyes glittered. I've never seen anyone so angry.'

'Quietly angry?'

'Ferociously. It scared us.'

'Did she take it out on you?' asked Tern.

'No, no. She was good to us. It was the Emperor she hated. Begging your pardon, my lady. She hated the Castle. All immortals. And then maybe she turned to hating herself.'

I was growing tired of pacing back and forth on the oak floorboards, the green Ghallain rug. After Thunder's Challenge, I should have come to visit Swallow. But the Emperor had given me so many orders I'd never had chance. And I think she wouldn't have agreed to see me anyway. Not while suffering such all-consuming fury.

The hall door unlocked and the bank manager emerged, closely followed by Eleonora and Saker. Mr. Wittol of Hacilith was so gaunt that his black silk coat seemed to flow into the hollow of his abdomen, and almost disappeared from view before resurging over his bony hips. His trousers seemed to hang loose without any legs in them at all. With a reserved and aquiline air he contemplated us before announcing, 'The Manorship of Awndyn is now the property of their Majesties the King and Queen of Awia.' And he gave a bow which set the rose-gold tags on his watch chain jingling.

CHAPTER 3

Mine Twenty, 'Thunder's Salient',
The Lowespass Front, June 2040

The cannons started at dawn. I was circling over the field artillery on the furthest right flank where Capelin Thunder sat on horseback between his teams of gunners. The outermost six-kilo gun fired and recoiled. Men clustered in, white coats like mites, heaved it into position and, while sponge and ramrod flashed, the next one in the line boomed and reared.

I leant against the wind. It rippled my shirt as I turned. This was going to be a hot day – and hard work. The line of cannons stretched along the front of the Paperlands, three kilometres from here to Cyan at the mouth of Valley Twenty in the centre, another three beyond her to Tornado on the left wing where, with six-kilo shot, he too was pounding the fuck out of the Paperlands.

The breeze ripped the smoke from the cannons. By the time Thunder's third had fired, the first had reloaded. Along the ground below me a hundred barrels spat flame and rebounded.

The din was overwhelming. Even fifty metres above them my ears were starting to ring and in a few minutes I'd be deafened. I held my wings straight and chandelled up, faster on the southern turn. Smoke whipped back towards the Wall. And from the vast wilderness of the Paperlands it brought the smell of Insects ... They were massing.

We were ten kilometres into the Paperlands. We'd left our static gun emplacements far behind. I saw them in the distance, on this side of the Wall. Their bunkers gleamed when the sun flashed on the twelve-kilo siege guns lurking inside.

Already Thunder's battery was cracking the walls of the Insects' tunnels. Their pointed pagoda roofs, like whipped-up meringue peaks pink in the morning light, were beginning to shatter. Their tough, fireproof paper walls were breaking with a fibrous texture between papier-mâché, ceramic and bone.

Antennae flicked out of a crack. A triangular head emerged. Two gold-brown legs like blades scrabbled out. An Insect the size of a horse pulled itself through with antlike dexterity. It ran a few steps, feelers swivelling, scented the men of the gun teams, and bolted at them.

Another followed it out of the breach, then another. Then thousands tore down their own cell wall to attack. For an instant I glimpsed them crammed together inside. They struggled to widen the breach, and out they poured!

I swooped low and smoke snatched over my wings. It stung my eyes and blotted my throat. I sucked a breath, flew into the smoke bank. Thick black fumes enclosed me completely, stinking of sulphur. There was Capelin's white horse, glowing as if luminous; he sat like a sack of rice. He couldn't see the Insects. He couldn't see a damn thing. I called to him and he yelled at his aides. They galloped away down the line, bugles trilling. I'd sighted bugs and the cannon must change to canister.

Or they'd be overrun. I cut up through the cloud, out into the blinding sun, bleeding off my speed as I rose until, for an instant, I hung motionless in the air. Tens of thousands of Insects were bristling, erupting out of their broken tunnels.

I tilted forwards into a glide and whooshed down the line with the booming, bucking guns zipping past one by one below me.

Six men to each. There's a loader hefting a red canvas bag of powder. In it goes, shoved down by the ramsman. There's another, loading a tin of canister shot. He's double-shotting it. They all are!

A hundred thousand Insects will run this gauntlet. Here's a gun ready loaded, the ventsman is piercing the touchhole and setting the fuse. Now all the guns ahead were primed and ready, the artillerists in position. Each firer held a linstock with the slow fuse snaked around it, hissing invisible-pale.

I viewed our whole trap, so cleverly designed only Thunder had the chutzpah to try it. We force the Insects to run, and we don't have to move. If all goes well, as he insists it will, we'll funnel them along the face of the Paperlands and into Valley Twenty.

Our fifty thousand men were drawn up in ranks facing the white sea of the Paperlands. I glimpsed Saker's colours, then Cyan's, rippling above the infantry opposite the entrance to the valley, and Eleonora's swan flying in the heavy cavalry some distance to the rear.

All this is land we've reclaimed and cleared of Paper. Along a twenty kilometre front Thunder has wrested a band ten kilometres deep, and on a morning like this I feel it's possible to beat the bugs all the way back to Lazulai.

That's the last cannon, a gap, then archers. *There's* King Saker on his white stallion with an arrow at string. I swooped low, dared lower, making smooth movements with my legs to steer, and my next beat touched the tassel-fringe of the sky-blue flag of Awia, hanging limp on its eagle-topped pole. Saker raised his hand in the air and my feathers whisked over it as I passed above him.

The archers gawped up in wonder. Silver sallets became pale faces, open mouths. They were wishing their wings weren't useless.

'Eyes forward!' he bellowed.

The ground in front of each man stubbled with arrows he'd planted there. They looked to the Wall as I hissed away. On their horizon a pall of smoke was growing and they knew the Insects were coming.

A cannon, a gap, and Cyan's muskets. Cyan Lightning by her sunburst flag in the centre. She'd witnessed my dive over the archers and I could see her grin from here. She gripped her musket by the small of the stock, and brandished it. She was sitting an immense destrier that dwarfed the mounts of the colour ensigns and the lines of the two ranks before her. Her horsehair crest ruffled in the breeze. She tilted up her face as I sailed over, and I looked down into the ammo box on the saddle bow, between her armoured thighs.

Her infantry are deployed in line, one battalion three ranks deep. I felt their grim silence, their muskets loaded and ready, behind the first rank of pikemen in armour – no helmets but full harness.

Next along the line, more six-kilo cannons with their teams waiting, ramrod and linstock in hand, water buckets at the ramsmen's feet. Then the array continues, Awian archers, then line battalions of Tanager musket fyrd; artillery, Eske musket fyrd, all the way to the west wing where Tornado's cannon is blowing breaches in the paper.

Behind us the squares of cavalry waited almost indolently, casual confidence in the attitude of Eleonora's lancers and, behind them, the limber teams waiting to pull the field guns home, when we've funnelled a hundred thousand Insects into one little valley of death.

I sped up the line. Tornado's cannon were booming without pause. I rose to glimpse their pall of smoke.

A six-kilo ball hit the peak of an Insect's tunnel, smashed it, and great shards of the dried saliva spun into the air. The roundshot bounced up, spinning, flew in an arc over the Paperlands and crashed into the roof of the cells again, splintered a hole, bounced, smashed down again further on, bounced a third, and a fourth time, and dropped out of sight in a crevasse crust of Paper. From each strike, a network of cracks spread over the cells and tunnels.

Insects were pouring from the breaches. The batteries were swopping to canister and were blowing bugs apart. I had a second for a breath, plunged into their wall of fumes.

Wreaths of earthy rotten-egg smoke tore away before my eyes. A thinner patch, then another bank – it tumbled from the maw of every cannon. Men closed on one, shoved the wet sponge down its muzzle. The volume of the hiss amazed me, but they're already deaf.

As the ramsman sluiced it out, the ventsman with a glove put his thumb over the vent hole. His teammate was heaving the next bag of powder from the cart. Working intently they didn't see me as I glided in and alighted on the bare ground.

Tornado was standing in the stirrups, bending this way and that in the most incredible shapes as he tried to see through the smoke. He had a telescope closed in his hand.

'Pointless using that!' I shouted.

He jumped and wheeled his horse around. 'Jant! Are Insects out at Thunder's end?'

'Yes! The same as yours!'

'How many?'

'Fifty thousand to run. I saw them. They stretched back, it seemed to Murrelet!'

'Ours are running.'

I coughed uncontrollably. 'You're getting fifty thousand too. For a kilometre into the Paperlands, they're crowding five deep!'

He glanced at his nearest gun, which was shoving in canisters. Bits of fuse and burning wadding littered the ground around us. 'I hope the centre holds.'

'It will,' I shouted. 'I'll be there.'

'If Insects turn at all, they'll turn at Cyan.'

'She'll stand.'

Tornado jabbed his carbine in the direction of the Insects. We could see thin limbs running in the smoke. They became clearer, a cannon boomed, and pieces of carapace flew in the air.

'Watch 'em down the line!' Tornado yelled.

'I will.' I spread my wings.

'Jant!' He bellowed. 'Bring up shot wagons till there's none left. I want lancers here *before* that happens. If they're not here we'll be mincemeat!'

'You'll have the Queen's Own Rachiswater,' I said.

'As long as they *get* here!'

'Sure.'

'And limber teams!' he yelled after me.

Sure. Sure. If we don't drag the field guns out at the same time as we pull back the wing, stray Insects will chew their wheels off. That was the least of my trouble.

15

I flew up, feeling smoke clotting on my skin. The cannon crews' hands and faces were black, their white coats smudged, protection against the sparks but soaked with sweat. Here and there greaves flashed in the oppressive darkness as leg-armoured men plunged their ramrods.

But it was working. I gained height above the spreading pall and saw the Insects charging out of it. The first were lengths ahead, then came a running mass of giant ants, packed so closely they looked fused together. The swarm went on and on, issuing from the smoke, charging at full pelt down the line of guns. Every Insect could smell other spattered Insects. Their fear kept them running, and when they crossed the line of sight of each cannon the firer dipped his taper, lit the fuse, and blew a great hole in the mass.

So a wave of bombardment started down the front of the Paperlands. As Insects ran, the cannon roared, one then the next, then the next, and kept booming as more seethed past. From the left and right wings, to the middle, we were forcing them into the centre and into the valley.

Valley Twenty is a tight u-shaped natural gorge that Insects had filled with their cells and tunnels centuries ago when they took this land. Capelin Thunder and Kay Snow believed it would contain them for twenty hours only, that's all we need, because underneath it we've built the largest bomb ever made.

The Insects' red-brown shells were being blasted apart. Their legs were shattering in the air, heads severed and compound eyes fragmented, lengths of gut ribboning out as the canister raked them.

Six legs jointed above thoraxes the smooth hue of patinated bronze. Each had spines down the back of their tibias. Some were the size of a man, most were the size of a horse – big, full-imago killers.

They scissored their mandibles as they ran. Feet flexed, three-hooked claws spread wide, tore up the naked earth. Not a blade of grass grows here. No animal can survive. The Insects eat everything. The Insects build with everything. They even chew up our wadding and roundshot sabots into paper.

I winged ahead of Tornado's charging Insects, to see the first of the great swarm that Thunder was speeding up the line from the east. Their backs shone in the sunlight filtering through the spreading wreaths of smoke. Globular eyes glinting, throwing off strips of reflection, tails plated, held high – and the smoke dimmed the day to dusk.

I laboured up, till I could clasp the whole battlefront in my arms. The Paperlands lay ahead of me like a pale, petrified sea, and smoke roiling off the cannons had formed a continuous slick towards the Wall.

Directly below me, from the left, down the line, thousands of Insects charged leaving twisted carcasses behind. From the right, also trapped against the front of the Paperlands, more sped on before the line of cannon: thousands of Insects leaving bits of barbed legs and detached abdomens twitching. These two hordes are going to crash together in the middle.

Directly in the middle.

With a bit of luck.

I pulled my wings in and dived. The air whacking up past me cleared a bit of the smoke until I fell so fast it was hard to breathe, fanned out and checked my speed. But in my memory rang Thunder's arrogant voice: 'Luck? It's not luck, it's Natural Philosophy! Ants won't double back onto a scent trail of fear. They lay the trail, we can keep them running.'

I was above Cyan. She was screaming something. I landed heavily behind her. On the ground now I could see wisps of smoke hanging in the air like gauzy curtains, dimming her men in an eerie grey-pink eclipse. They waited, listening to the encroaching cannonade. It was ear-splitting at this distance and getting louder all the time but the swarm wasn't yet in sight.

I ran past the line sergeants to Cyan. She was standing in the stirrups trying to see the bugs.

'Jant. How long do we have?'

'About two minutes.'

Her lips pursed. 'Right. What are you doing?'

'I'm staying here.'

'Until they've run in?'

'Till they've all gone in. It's a pleasure to fight beside you, Lightning.'

'Good. You can bloody well shoot, then.' She plucked my musket from her saddle holster and passed it down to me, then my cartridge box on its strap.

The blasts shook the ground. She swallowed, and forced a ghastly grin, coughed to clear her throat and raised her high voice to the fyrd: '*Hold* fire! *Hold* fire till you hear the signal!'

Up went her hand gripping her rifle.

'Let them come! Wait ...'

I slipped my ramrod down the barrel to check it was still loaded, thumbed back the hammer, clicked on a percussion cap from its dispenser.

Beside us the battalion of archers took a quarter-turn right, showed us their backs and drew their bows high.

'They can see them,' she said.

'Can you?'

17

'No! Oh. Shit, that was the last cannon, I saw the flash.' Her dry mouth clicked. 'It's nearly us. First Hacilith! *Hold* your fire! Let them close … God's holiday, you've all the time in the world!'

'Level muskets,' yelled her sergeant. The two ranks bristled with musket muzzles.

Saker's voice rang out between the cannon fire. 'Loose!'

The archers loosed and a volley of arrows arced up, whistled into the Insects we couldn't yet see. Another volley, and another.

Saker called, 'Level!' and the archers shot straight volleys. My hand was sweating so much the musket twisted in my grasp. I glanced at the percussion cap for the tenth time.

'The fuckers still outshoot us,' Cyan said of her father's archers.

'Yeah.'

'Well … They don't have our stopping power.'

Volley after volley flew in a hard hail of shafts. The archers turned face-forwards as the Insects streamed past. They had twice our range and five times our rate of fire, but Saker can't field as many trained bowmen as Cyan gives muskets to the scum of Hacilith.

We saw the first mandibles hurtle out from before the nearest man. Cyan's horse reared and she leant it down.

'Now show those featherbacks how to shoot! *Hold* till we've range!'

The Insects raged towards us. We can't let them turn. If we buckle, they'll pour after us and leave no-one alive. We had to keep them in the funnel.

Many were horribly mangled: arrows sticking out of them, shells smashed into jagged edges, starred into dents. Some ran on five legs, four legs, even three – dragging their abdomens and unwinding intestines caught on their spines. The dozen balls in each canister had blown some practically apart – here one ran oozing cream fluid from its thorax cracked wide.

Insects were so tightly packed, a hundred deep, that they bowled their dead along the ground. One with only half a head remaining, the ganglia flopping out, fell and was trampled by a thousand claws.

'Wait!'

I couldn't see through the mass to the Insects on the far side. Those didn't seem to be as badly damaged. There are so many, so many, that you never make as much impact as you think.

'Wait!'

I held the gun at arms' length deliberately. Stop the fyrd firing prematurely. One nervous bastard shoots, then they all blaze away and the Insects turn on you as you reload.

Cyan screamed at them to hold.

18

The Insects were closing fast.

That's thirty metres, twenty ...

The archers were glancing at us with incredulity.

'Ready!' yelled Cyan.

Fifteen metres.

'Fire!'

Flame jetted from the muskets. The nearest Insects jerked, midstride – seemed to pause as the balls hit them, holing shell, cracking chitin. Smoke drooled from the barrels and sank to knee level. Company two was already reloading and company three behind them fired over their shoulders.

The sergeants bellowed, 'Load!'

'Fire!'

'Load!'

Cyan watched the rolling volley with delight. She levelled her fabulous rifle and shot into the smoke. What a waste of its performance. Who knows whether she hit? Who knows what effect one shot had? All she cared was that her six thousand men in six battalions were hammering twenty-four to thirty-six thousand lead balls a minute into the Insects and smashing them to bits, turning them into the valley ahead.

I raised my musket to my shoulder and rested my cheek on the sideplate. I looked down the top of the muzzle and sighted on the bayonet notch, but beyond that was just drifting waves of smoke. The endless rush of triangular heads and jointed legs appeared and faded in thinning patches.

Covered by smoke, was gone – revealed in a smaller patch further on.

I pulled the trigger, the hammer flew home, the butt kicked the hollow of my shoulder, and I lowered to reload.

Cyan bawled at her people who obeyed their training like clockwork. Hacilith factory workers know how to make themselves automata. Bite cartridge, pour stinging powder down the muzzle, wad the paper, shove in the ball, ramrod it down, percussion cap. Fire.

Again ... fire.

Again ... fire.

Now my musket was growing so hot I couldn't lay my cheek on the sideplate and gave up all pretence of aiming. My hands were raw.

Cyan glanced down. Sweat beaded her brow, the whites of her eyes were red.

'This is some herding!'

'They're going in.'

'It's working?'

'I need to fly to see ... You *must* stand, *whatever happens*. There are battalions you can't see backing you up. And you're backing up the cannon.'

'Where are you going?'

I slipped my musket back into her saddle holster. Its steel sizzled the leather. 'I have to report to Thunder.'

'Jant, you're conducting an orchestra!'

'Ha! The bastard needs someone to crow at.'

She flashed her teeth in a grin. She'd taken off her helmet and her hair was thick with sweat. 'Tell him we won't drop below four shots a minute.'

'Yes, Lightning.'

'Send me an ammo caisson and a water cart, we can go all day!'

'I'm only asking two hours.' I turned on my heel and jumped into the sky.

I wanted to rise from the smoke, but it was too high. If I flapped up there it would just blot out everything.

I flew smoothly over the fyrd. Their white jackets, gleams of steel, stood out in the gloom, but the Awian archers in blue were scarcely visible. I could hear nothing but the cannons' continuous roar, and the crackle of muskets, jetting tongues of flame rimmed with smoke.

Company by company they fired, again and again as I passed over. They made no effort to aim. Every shot would find a mark now. The skill was only in the speed – and that's why Saker hates it.

I was astonished at how much punishment the Insects were taking, and still they came. Company after company of fyrd passed below me, busy with their ramrods, spitting out cartridge paper. Levelling muskets.

I zipped over six men standing back from their gun. The firer's arm holding the taper dropped, the fuse flared, the barrel boomed and spat a cone of fire – twitched the smoke as the grapeshot tore through it. The pall had taken on the shape and colour of an anvil, and murkily I saw the brass tubes of Thunder's battery shining ahead. In the black smog, the orange splodges of explosions bloomed and vanished a second before each blast. They looked like flowers.

Flowers? I apologise for my floridity. We've all had brandy for breakfast.

A soldier below looked up, musket in hand, and I rowed higher in the air. Chances are one of those buggers will shoot me by accident.

At the end of the line, behind the final cannon, Capelin Thunder was a bizarre eye of calm in the inferno. His Trisian tunic, smutted by the smoke, shone clearly. So did his bald head and shaped white beard.

20

He moved not a muscle as I screamed flat out down the sky. I flared wings abruptly, swung into standing position, hit the ground and ran to a halt in front of him.

'They're pouring in!'

'Of course,' he said, in Trisian.

His horse tried to back from me but I grabbed its guide rein. What a sight we looked! Me, all in black and sweating like a Rhydanne in a steel forge, Thunder in white and a model of cool imperturbability.

'I've never seen anything like this before,' I shouted.

'I grant you,' said Thunder. 'I've never done it before.'

The sluicer nearest me ploshed his sponge in a bucket of filthy water. His teammates scooped up the ropes and heaved the cannon back into place. Its single limber gouged the gritty mud. Sloshed out the barrel. In went the charge, he reversed his sponge and rammed down. In went the shot like two big tin cans. The men stood clear. Into the vent the igniter jammed his sharp quill of powder, down went his hand with the linstock and boom! The cannon flew back and we scythed bugs to bits.

'Fly over the valley,' said Thunder. 'Bring me a description.'

The three kilometres to Valley Twenty were packed with Insects, and second after second yet more arrived. They flowed down the front of the Paperlands into the valley, scrabbling over their cells. Along the front, dead Insects were piling up. More and more crashed into the mounds of dead – spiky limbs bunching, antennae whirling.

Those at the back were still intact and they'd nowhere to run but into the gorge. Hurricane's battery stood west of Cyan's muskets at the valley mouth. His teams hurled buckets of water over their cannons – clouds of steam joined the smoke. They gave the brass wheels under each muzzle a quarter turn, raising them from point blank, and the next charge was roundshot.

It pushed Insects further into the valley. At first they climbed on the roofs of their cells and swarmed away. The gorge kept them in, like spiders in a bathtub – some chewed through the crust of paper and crawled headfirst into the tunnels below. They dropped out of view, and in the valley we'd trapped them.

For an hour and a half Tornado and Thunder sent more Insects down the line. Hurricane and Lightning forced them into the valley. The trickle gradually slowed, until the Paperlands was drained for a radius of thirty kilometres, and their onslaught stopped.

High dunes of dead Insects clogged the valley mouth. Broken ones limped along, some lay pulsing. Lone Insects ran back and forth, and others scaled the piles of dead to enter the gorge.

'That's right, we're dangerous!' Thunder called to them. 'Wall your-selves in! Seal up your tunnels! For beneath you there's a charge that will blow you at the moon!'

I ordered Eleonora's cavalry to support Tornado's artillery as they limbered up, and Hayl's Eske cavalry protected Thunder's cannon. Cyan kept her musketmen in line and, by division, each battalion pulled back and marched to our temporary camp nearby, which Thunder had built beside the entrance to his mine.

Then I gave the field to Eleonora. Her lancers would ride stray Insects down. As all the cannons bounced and jolted over the barren ground behind their six-horse teams, I looked for Thunder. There he was, riding sedately among them. Seeming to glow from within as he did, he looked like a little, bald version of the Emperor.

I sailed down through the smoke and landed beside him. 'Well done,' I said.

'We detonate the charge at first light tomorrow.'

'I'll start moving everyone out. That was masterly.'

He inclined his head. 'Snow insists we've got less than fifteen hours now before I must light the fuse. Here's the order of march,' He thrust a piece of paper at me, and then pointed at Eleonora's lancers. 'I can see many improvements to make. Those barbarians are still strapping on armour and hurling themselves at the Insects.'

'But Leon loves it.'

'I would have thought better of Awia. As I said, there's much work here for one of superior *mind*.'

He pulled his horse's head right and rode around me. I watched him go, before taking off to find everyone on the list, to organise the withdrawal.

CHAPTER 4

Cyan Lightning

Cyan's battalion was to bring up the rear, together with Saker's archers and the lancers. I couldn't find Cyan at her fyrd's tents, so I guessed she'd be with her father and ran across camp to Saker's pavilion.

Saker and Eleonora's is the largest three-peaked tent, though given that we've planned to abandon them all, it wasn't as luxurious as Leon usually makes it, but rather more like Saker's pavilion when he used to be Lightning. The Awian eagle, with Micawater's white mascle, flew outside. The entrance was tied open, and no one visible, although Saker's bow and quiver were on the central rack.

I hollered and heard an answering shout from behind the tent. I walked around the ropes to see Cyan and Saker standing on the rock escarpment above me, watching the lines of troops and wagons leaving far below. Saker was holding his arm extended, looking through the outstretched L of his thumb and closed fingers, the way he does to block out the sun and judge distance. His sunglasses were pushed up on his forehead, with his greying hair tufted over them. Cyan was loading her rifle.

'It's about eight hundred and twenty metres,' he said.

'It's eight hundred and twenty-two.'

'I said "about". So you've gained fifty metres.'

'Fifty four, oh ye of little faith.'

'Guys?' I said.

'Hello, Jant,' said Saker, still gazing into the distance. He reached out for her rifle. 'Give me another go.'

'I haven't reloaded it yet.'

'Well, there's grounds for improvement. At four shots a minute, I can still annihilate you with one hundred from a recurve bow.'

'Yes, dad.'

I sat down on a rock. 'You're leaving tomorrow, after Hurricane but before Tornado. You're leaving at the same time as Leon's cavalry, you're second to last out.'

'Archers always get a raw deal,' said Saker.

'So you've got fifteen hours.'

'Thanks, Jant,' said Cyan. 'We can move any time if there's a change.'

She is Lightning, the Castle's Archer, and the Emperor joined her to the Circle and immortalised her fifteen years ago, at the age of seventeen.

And here I run into a problem. How do I recap without making it heavy going for those of you who've followed me from the start? If I explain, for example, that Cyan Challenged Saker for his position in the Circle and he deliberately lost to her, those of you who remember the tournament will cry, 'old hat!'

On the other hand, if you've just started listening and I press on regardless, I'll make it seem desperately complicated, when really it's not. Our exchanges would be like:

ME: So, after Saker threw his archery tournament he lost his position in the Circle as Lightning, and San dropped him back into the flow of time.

NEW LISTENER: 'Into the flow of time'?

ME: Yes, because the Circle keeps us immortal, the fifty people who are the best in the world at our professions, those best suited to defeat the Insects. The Emperor San instigated this meritocracy – as long as we defend our positions in fair Challenge, he keeps us immortal by sharing his eternal life with us.

NEW LISTENER: Who's the Emperor San?

ME: He *says* he was chosen by god, before god left the world in year zero, to defend it against any threat. When the Insects arrived in four-eleven San changed from being an itinerant wise man and advisor to lead people against them. He set up the Circle in the year six-twenty, with Games to first select the best warriors as Eszai, and Saker had been Lightning from that time.

NEW LISTENER: But not now?

ME: No.

You see? We could go on all day. The only solution I can think of, is to ask you guys who've already heard it to let your mind wander for a bit. There's a lot you can be doing – putting an edge on your sword, polishing your horse – while I place the facts before the newcomers.

Briefly, then, because the memory's painful – Cyan took my good friend Saker's title as the immortal Archer, and his rooms in the Castle. She stayed seventeen – and he began to age ... As an Eszai – 'immortal' in Awian – she abides by the Emperor's command. I took her under my wing and showed her the Castle. She matured into a delightful woman,

24

thoughtful and courteous, but most people still say Saker's the rightful Archer and Cyan an impostor. She'd inherited his steady hand and eye, and tried to supplant his vast experience with her innovation. I think her position's the most tenuous of us all in the Circle, and she thinks so, too. She attracts more Challengers than I've ever seen before. She's hammered by them: she has to hold competitions yearly to shoot against hundreds of men who are convinced they can beat her, and so take her position and her immortality. If she wasn't such an accurate shot, she'd have lost already, so accuracy is the Challenge she sets. The constant anxiety of keeping her immortality spurs the hard graft of her invention.

'You can't hit that with an arrow,' she said.

'No,' said Saker.

'Not even on a good day.'

He laughed. 'Stop rubbing it in.'

'You're beaten on distance. Admit it.'

'All right. For the first time ever, I'm beaten on distance. Not on speed, and not on accuracy under two hundred metres. Give me another go.'

She passed him the rifle and he weighed it in his hand. 'It's coming along.'

'It beats the musket.'

'Ha. Longbows beat muskets. It's my bow you need to beat.' He reached out with a wing and brushed her shoulder. 'I'm proud of you, Cyan.'

'Thanks.'

'I mean it. You're breaking ground. Every time I see this, it's better.' He looked into the telescope mounted on top. 'The sight's off-centre.'

'It compensates.'

'I understand. I wind this? Right. But I don't need it. What if it gets clogged with mud?'

'Flick it down ...'

He sighted along the barrel, pulled the trigger with a sharp crack, and down on the road a big Insect in a cage wagon blasted against the bars. The Insects trapped in the wagons behind it went crazy, ripping at their bars, trying to run from the scent of its blood.

Saker hooted with excitement.

She said, 'I told you! I told you what it does to bugs!'

They hugged each other, transformed by enthusiasm. 'Reload it! Reload it!'

I burst out laughing.

'What are you cackling at, Jant?' Cyan said, reaching for her cartridge box.

'First he coached you, now you're coaching him. Team Micawater.'

Since there can only be one Eszai for each position, my suggesting she was backed by a team, though it's true, was an insult. 'There's no team,' she said, coldly. 'There's just me.'

'There's just Cyan *Lightning*,' said Saker.

'The Castle funds this,' she said.

'Yes, but it's Saker's knowhow,' I said.

'It's all published. Anyone can read my treatises. Anyone can practise. Anyone can apply.'

'Boy, do they ever,' said Cyan.

He did the L-thing with his hand again, and grinned down at the Insect that had collapsed in a tipi of legs. The wagon driver and several other men were peering into the cage trying to figure out why it had imploded.

I said, 'Using a secret weapon that no one else in the Fourlands possesses, *is* against the rules, I'm sure.'

'It's not secret. San doesn't allow us to keep work secret. I've published the design and pretty soon Challengers will catch up.' She pulled the mashed percussion cap off the nipple and flung it down the escarpment. 'Then there'll be a level playing field again. ...I'm sick of looking over my shoulder all the time. I'm sick of Challengers. What's the point of being immortal if you're too stressed to enjoy it?'

'One reason I keep going with the drugs.'

'Jant, you never had a Challenger you couldn't wipe the floor with.'

'I mean, I have to live with a bunch of strung-out Eszai.'

'It's all right for you! You can fly!'

'Cyan,' Saker said warningly.

'Sorry. Sorry, Jant. Sorry, dad.' She bit the end off the cartridge and poured the powder down. 'It's wearing, that's all. San realised a Challenge with muskets is practically random. The ball will fly anywhere, that's no way to decide immortality and San's going to insist on a fair Challenge. Which is a relief, in a way ... When it was fifty/fifty time and again I knew I was only keeping my place by luck.'

'Cy ...'

'Dad,' she said truthfully. 'It's awful.'

'Yes. It is.'

'I stand a better chance of winning with this, than with a musket. Winning *fairly*.'

Saker stooped to the box, slipped out a cartridge and turned it in his hands. 'Jant, the muskets and rifles aren't just for Cyan but for the world. And in the long run, who wins? The Castle wins. We improve at killing Insects. That's the point. We gain ground, we save lives.' He glanced at the dome of Murrelet, a golden stud far into the Paperlands. 'That's our purpose. Your purpose. You Eszai ... My darling, give Jant a go.'

'Ah,' I said. 'It's not really me.'

'That's what *I* thought! But it's kind of addictive.'

'Obsessive, you mean, Saker. Obsessive.'

Cyan ripped the cone-shaped ball from the cartridge and rodded it down. She has a very pleasant voice. 'The bar's being raised higher year after year. I have to keep up with it. I have to do what it takes. Anything it takes to win. I have to use any advantage, the wind, everything ...'

'Of course, Cy.'

'If I don't seize the advantage, someone else will. I know the people coming up behind me. I know the competition closing in.'

'We'll watch them.'

'The margins are too close!'

'It's all right,' Saker assured her. His voice strung with the old obsession. 'We'll keep publishing your scores. If at nine hundred metres they're out by fifty centimetres, the bastards will know there's no point in Challenging you.'

'*Nine* hundred metres?' I said.

'Jant, I can kill Insects at a kilometre,' she said. 'I've been practising. Right here ... here on this crag where potential Challengers can see me. To psych them out.' She glared at me piercingly, and for a second looked just like her mother.

'Your reloading rate really is terrible,' said Saker.

'Well, I'm talking to him!'

She clicked the rod into its clip, thumbed the hammer and offered me the rifle. 'Kill the bug in the last cage.'

I scanned the queue of wagons dubiously.

'That's a big one,' said Saker.

'They all look tiny.' My nails ticked on the metal. I hugged the butt to my shoulder and laid my cheek to the stock. The Insect cages appeared in the sight, jiggling about.

Immediately Cyan switched her attention to her father. 'I shortened the barrel to drop the weight. And I—'

I said, 'Cyan, I don't know what to do.'

'Jant hasn't got *It*,' she said to Saker.

'I've known that for a long time.'

She came to my side and fiddled with the sights. Her blonde hair in a ponytail smelt of soap and the stone of Lowespass. 'Look for the spot.'

'The flaw in the glass?'

'It's not a flaw, it's an etching. Place it over the Insect.'

I let my breath out halfway and squeezed the trigger. The butt slammed into my shoulder, the retort cracked in my ear, and the Insect slammed messily against the rear bars of its cage.

Saker hooted and jumped. In a quick and quite spectacular gesture, he simultaneously slapped me on the shoulder and fanned out his wing to whack Cyan on hers.

I couldn't help hooting too.

She laughed. 'Look at you! The King of Awia and the Emperor's Messenger. Seventeen hundred years between you, and you're like schoolboys!'

'I don't think I killed it. I just ... Wow. That's one unhappy hexapod.'

'Well done!' said Saker.

'Not bad,' said Cyan. 'For someone who grew up with a stone spear.'

'Very cool.'

'It *is* "very cool"!' he said. 'Reload it!'

She shook her head. She tilted the box and you could see there weren't many cartridges left. She slung it on her back and set off down to the tent. Saker laughed at the people fuming around their cage containing the kicking Insect, and followed her.

'There'll be another gale tonight.' I said. 'The wind's gone westerly. See the cloudbank?'

'Oh,' said Saker dismissively. 'It always does that on a June night.'

'June. Gales. Gotcha,' said Cyan.

'No, it's going to rain like Ghallain. Then what will your musket fyrd do?'

'Integrate with my bowmen.' She ducked into the tent.

There was a camp chair outside with a fantastic view of the troops moving away in open order lines below us. The Paperlands filled the whole horizon. Saker spread his wings and seated himself. 'Hacilith men! If you draft them from the same factories, they have some cohesion. But if their powder's wet, they'll run. When they shoot, they move like snails. They drop their percussion caps, they fire out their ramrods. When they catch the Fear, they're off like greyhounds and I have to back them. Jant, it seems to me just another way of getting archers killed. All this unnecessary complication. Her cartridges are too expensive to manufacture and they don't work in the *rain*? In the rain! This is fucking Lowespass, not Tambrine.'

A servant appeared with coffee on a silver tray, and we gazed out at the Paperlands. Its peaks and troughs, like a solidified cloudscape, shone with the dull lustre of eggshell tainted the colour of apricot by the morning light.

On the horizon, like a breaching whale, rose the great ruined dome of Murrelet Palace. It glowed where the gilt still clung to it in patches. The northern half had broken open, fallen sheer and lay in shadow. I'd flown out there once, where nothing moved but Insects.

The dome was buttressed by strands of Paper, as if it was rising from a net, as if it was bulging upwards and stretching them. The surrounding roofs and upper storeys of the ancient city hardly emerged from the mass. Insects had macerated their timbers and they had collapsed, fifteen hundred years ago.

Cyan joined us, sitting cross-legged in her combat trousers, and dunked a biscuit in her coffee. The roseate light played over the Paperlands.

'Beautiful, isn't it?' she said.

'It was, once,' said Saker.

'Do you think we'll ever get there?'

'Not in my lifetime.'

'We will! We will!' she punched his ankle. 'You're going to see it!'

'This is a very exposed position. The sooner we're out of here, the better.'

'Tern says Murrelet's full of jewels!'

'Jant brought her the Filigree Spider.'

'She told me that you flew there,' Cyan said to me.

'I landed on the dome.' I described how gigantic the dome is, and how I'd climbed down through the hole, into the upper room of the palace, but it had been the middle of the night and I hadn't seen much more than the cone of rubble. I'd found the Filigree Spider brooch – two drop-cut emeralds formed the head and abdomen of a spider made of silver filigree – and I'd given it to Tern as a courtship gift. When we married, she bought me the pub in Scree, and I named it the Filigree Spider in honour of the jewel. It was very selfless of Tern to buy me a drinking den at six thousand metres altitude, which she would never see.

'My great-grandmother's family left that city,' Saker told Cyan.

'Who were they?'

'Oh, I don't know. Merchants turned warriors.'

'To fight the Insects?'

'Yes. They had been clever enough to leave first. They retreated to make a stand in east Mica valley. More refugees from Murrelet poured in, and they defended them from the Insects. Everyone turned warrior back then, but they couldn't save Murrelet ... not the manor nor King Murrelet, his family, nor the city ... when it fell San led soldiers to rescue it ...'

'Yes?'

'They're all paper now.'

'And that was five-four-nine?'

'Mm. Yes ... Forty years before I was born.'

'Then what happened?'

He laughed. 'Cy, look! You can see for yourself.'

She helped herself to another biscuit. 'Well,' she said. 'If anyone can clear the Paper, Thunder can!'

'I told you I'm impressed. I never thought I'd set foot on this crag again. I remember being ... down there.' He pointed out, to where Insects' cells folded into the next shallow valley. 'A thousand years ago. We used to call it Mistral's Dip.'

His daughter looked at him in awe. 'Were you shooting?'

'Yes. Of course.'

'But you had to retreat?'

'We lost it in nine-eighty.'

'Wow. Have you seen Thunder's bomb?'

He shook his head.

'Jant?'

'No.' I said, 'Tornado's fighting hard down there. I'm of more use in the sky.' I resist going underground as much as possible, because when I can't spread I feel claustrophobic. Most people involved in planning and digging the mine were human. The Awians were largely of the opinion that they'd shoot or impale any Insects you want, but were buggered if they were descending underground.

'I've seen it,' said Cyan. 'It's going to be great! It'll be the biggest explosion ever. It'll be the biggest sound ever made! San will hear it at the Castle. At the *Castle*!'

So I had told the journalists. The fuse runs ten kilometres south of here, to Capelin's Main Camp. It's packed full of reporters. When he lights the fuse at six a.m. tomorrow, them, and me, Cyan and Saker, will be lying on the ground.

'It's huge!' she enthused. The sun had evenly tanned her skin café au lait, and the hairs of her arms were bleached white over it. Her eyes were bright ocean blue. 'Forty thousand barrels of powder. Two thousand tonnes, Jant! It'll blow the roof off the chamber and *vaporise* the valley.' She thrust her fist at the sky, picturing the solid column of fire that would burst from the ground. 'All the Insects we've chased into the valley will be blown to pieces.'

'To pieces!' said Saker, making it a toast.

'Not to pieces. Into hot gas instantaneously. A hundred thousand at one go!' She bounded to her feet and threw her arms wide at the panorama. 'Feast upon it! This'll be the last time you see it! When we march back tomorrow it'll be a crater!'

Thunder said it will take two days to cool. Valley Twenty and this camp will be gone. Nothing will remain but a crater a kilometre in diameter, and no Insect will survive within an eight k radius. The shockwave will smash their tunnels, the ground will be clear.

'Two hundred kilometres of reclaimed land!' she said.

'Probably more. Other Insects will flee the vibration.'

'Then we set up lines before they run back. They rebuild their Wall further north, and we're thirty kilometres closer to Murrelet and all the jewels!'

Saker smiled at her. 'Cy, only fifteen years ago we thought we could clear the Paperlands by water, and it went wrong. So now we're trying fire.'

'You old cynic. It'll work!' She pointed at him and danced a sidestep. 'I have a present for you!'

She raced into the tent. Saker returned to watching the troops. He wore a dark red shirt, the lacings deliberately loose to be unrestrictive when he draws, the rolled sleeves tight over his biceps. He still had a bracer on his forearm and wore a short, archer's sword on a buckled hanger. The rising wind swept grit across the escarpment and when we squinted against it I noticed the crow's feet at the corners of his eyes.

The land we've reclaimed is utterly unliveable, of course. Insects even chew the soil and suck out the goodness. From the margin of the Paperlands to the stone walls around the camp and mine mouth, Insect-gnawed duckboards zigzagged between great pits from mortar explosions. Sirocco's grenade fire had burnt great black swathes, scattered with wadding and bits of carapace. Along the front of the Paperlands, a huge band of dead arthropods marked where we'd stood this morning.

Cyan came out of the tent, carrying a long box of polished mahogany. She placed it on her father's lap. 'A gift,' she said, with affection. 'From Lightning, to the King of Awia. At Thunder's Salient, while it still exists.'

Saker flipped the clips on the box and opened it. A sincere smile spread over his face, 'Oh, Cyan. Thank you!'

'Because when I was twelve years old, you gave me a recurve bow, I give you the fifteen millimetre calibre Pattern 2040 rifled musket.'

'I'm touched. They're …'

I peered over his shoulder. In the green baize interior of the case lay two exquisite rifles, just like hers. Their walnut stocks were chequered, the steel sideplates extravagantly engraved with his coat of arms.

'They're beautiful!'

'Isn't that your Awian philosophy? If something's worth doing, it's worth doing beautifully? ... When I said they were for you, I couldn't hold the craftsmen back.'

'But why two?'

'Because someone can reload for you while you aim, and then swap them, see?'

'Cyan, I am so proud of you.'

She wiggled her head and whisked her ponytail. 'I'm standing on the shoulders of giants. Though I'd rather you didn't tell my Challengers ... that all I've done is apply everything you've published on archery, to the musket.'

Saker traced the winged hounds that supported his escutcheon.

She said, 'Arrows fly more accurately than musket balls, because they spin in the air. So I took Thunder's idea of rifling from his cannon.'

'But that makes the barrel clog up with burnt powder.'

'Not so much if it's just a quarter-turn. Then, arrows have points, so I thought, what if musket balls had points? I made a conical ball with a hollow base to expand and grip the rifling. You've seen it make a big hole in an Insect. Your arrows cut, this punches. You know a bug can take dozens of arrows ... they cut so cleanly, sometimes they go straight through. This stops them dead. It bounces around inside and churns them to milkshake.'

'They're well balanced,' said Saker.

'I try.'

'They're beautiful.' He kissed her. 'Now, look, Cy. Just because you've made elegant rifles doesn't mean you've finished. Your work's never finished.'

'I know, dad.'

'San wants to kill millions of Insects, not one at a time. You'll still lose a Challenge on rate of fire. You must put as much effort into finding a solution as the centuries I invested in making the perfect bow.'

And they fell to technical discussion again. I left them and flew to Eleonora, then to Thunder who was supervising the withdrawal, then back to camp, where Tern was waiting.

CHAPTER 5

Tern Wrought

The campfires of the fyrd shone brighter as evening drew in. In the western sky, from the direction of Ressond, that ominous bank of cloud rolled closer. It mimicked the jagged horizon of the Paperlands below it, and the sun's red disc sank into it, through the haze.

Tern let me into our blockhouse, one of the few stone-built huts in the camp, constructed by Snow's men while they dug the mine and happily yielded to us by Kay Snow, who'll do anything for my glamorous wife. I wish I could be with Tern all the time, but my work prevents me.

She gave me a kiss. 'Last night I dreamt we were in Wrought together.'

'Oh, kitten. We'll go to your place when this is over.'

'When must I leave?'

'Tomorrow morning at four. I've got you a lancer escort. The next camp is bigger than this, but it's still a bit basic.'

'Basic.' She slid her hands down and unbuttoned my shirt, slipped it off and flung it on the chair. 'I'm used to basic, campaigning with you.'

'I'm sorry.'

'"Basic" will never be a successful trend in Awia.' She put her palms to my cheeks and kissed me. While pressing her tongue between my lips, her hand left my face, and I felt her deftly undo my trouser buckle and buttons.

'Kitten. Kitten. Have you been bored?'

'Not bored. I've been watching you fly.'

She helped me take off my boots and breeches, and naked apart from my briefs I had a quick wash and blew the black soot out of my nose. I knelt in front of the stove, creaked its door open and fed it with the last of the firewood.

The fluting double-whistle of the wind picked up under the corrugated iron roof. Tern shed her riding trousers and joined me on the fur rug. We shared a pot of stew that Tré Cloud had sent, and a little wine. We were so ravenous it tasted fantastic.

'I saw you talking to Cyan,' Tern said.

'She's been with Saker all day.'

'Have you noticed how much she looks like her mother?'

'She's got the blue eyes. She looks like Ata, and sounds like him.'

'If she grows any older, she'll look strikingly like Ata.'

'She won't grow older.'

'She will, one day.'

'I need a bath,' I said. 'I stink of bugs and gunpowder ... and sweat.'

'I like it.'

'Oh, love. What would I do without you?'

She started to massage my shoulders. I sighed, laid on the rug and opened my wings. The wind rose to a scream. Outside, the fyrd would be extinguishing their campfires and battening down their pavilions. In our stove, the timber crackled, the wind drew sparks up the chimney. I opened the vents and the fire jumped high.

Pink and orange flames roved around the seasoned wood, and the curved base of each was blue. Heat like liquid poured from the stove; the smell of hot iron and warm feathers pervaded our windowless little room.

Tern dug her fingers into my hard muscle. 'The bomb makes me nervous,' she said.

'When Thunder lights the fuse we'll be ten kilometres away.'

'But we're nearly on top of it now. If it ignites, we'd be dead.'

'Oh, very.'

'And Tornado's fighting Insects in the main chamber? With his axe? In armour? Without a single spark?'

I looked up at her and shuddered.

The wind rose to a hurricane. It gusted rain in parallel bars across the valley, and outside only the swinging storm lanterns pricked the blackness. A crescendo of spiral whistling shrilled around the end of the building, and moaned under the roof. We listened to gusts beating at an insane speed over the Paperlands, which the Insects had denuded of anything that might stand in its way. The flames cracked and popped, blustering like pennants.

Tern glided her hands over my shoulders and started massaging my wings. The wind crashed, battering the iron door as if desperate to enter. It fluted along the walls. I lay head on arms, feeling my body relax under her expert strokes, and listened to rain prickling, dripping off the overhang.

'Do you always fight in this?'

'Mmm.'

'The weather must have been different when Murrelet was the capital.'

'You told Cyan that Murrelet was full of jewels.'

'I only said jewels are the only things Insects haven't eaten. I said that if people fled in a hurry they might have left treasures behind. Oh, Jant. My beautiful snow leopard ... The front of you looks Rhydanne and the back looks Awian ...'

'Deeper. Ah ... yes ...'

Gusts broke around the building. The wind seethed rain at the door, and the room drew like a chimney. The fire whistled and the smell of wood smoke relaxed Tern. Straddling my backside she leant forward until I could feel her breasts on my naked back, between my wings. She began to kiss the nape of my neck.

The flames, now orange, had already broken the logs down into little squares, and pink light whirled and coruscated within them. Small flames crept and flickered over them. The bottle of wine lay empty beside us.

Tern slipped her hand under my hips and grasped my cock. I was already hard but she pressed and pulled gently and I grew harder. I put my hand behind me, between her legs and she pushed against me.

The storm gathered itself for a manic assault and bashed across the camp, launched torn tents and ropes against the wall. Rain smashed into the side of the house, blew in streaks from the gable end. And the door flew wide.

Capelin Thunder strode in, his beard and bald head streaming.

Tern screamed and jumped up, her blouse unbuttoned and her breasts free.

He raised his lamp and stared at us witheringly.

'You *could* knock!' Tern yelled.

'Comet, my plans are ruined. Follow me!'

'What? The bomb?' I wrapped the rug round my waist.

'Everything is spoilt! Two years' work down the drain!'

Water ran off his oilskin and pattered on the floor. His tabard and leggings were so saturated they stuck to him. He motioned with the lamp. 'I must show you!'

'Fuck you, you can *tell* me!'

Tern padded round him, buttoning her blouse, tried to shut the door and jumped back with a curse. Outside was his bodyguard in full tunnel armour, beaded with rain, reflecting the scudding moonlight. She slammed the door.

In Thunder's other hand he held a long, wooden ladle, which he

35

flourished emphatically. 'The bomb will not work! The explosion will not happen! We have been deceived!'

I got to my feet. He swept the ladle doorwards. 'To the mine! I will elucidate!'

'I don't want to go underground. Insects can scent us better than we can see them.'

Tern brushed past me and whispered, 'Do they *have* sex on Tris?'

'No. It got in the way of declamation.'

Thunder's noble and well-proportioned face has nevertheless a long and narrow nose. It evenly tapers until the tip of it tilts, smoothly diagonal, as if sliced off by a knife. Down this nose he now looked at me with utmost scorn. 'Comet, you must tell everyone I cannot detonate the charge. The bomb has been sabotaged. Oh, you philistines, that my work should be ruined on the cusp of my great success by fools! Fools and their cupidity! You must recount it to the Emperor. You must witness for yourself!'

I picked my breastplate from my kit bag and offered it to Tern, its straps hanging. 'All right. Harness me up.'

CHAPTER 6

Into the tunnels

Waves of rain swept across the path. Water was bouncing off the ground – up to my full height was white-out. Thunder's guards were blurred silver-grey shapes, following behind us as he led the way with his lamp held high. We stepped up onto the slick duckboards.

Rain battered against us, stinging our faces. We strode hastily, heads lowered, seeing the shining slats of the duckboard and the pocked puddles on the pebbles beneath, from which rain was washing all the gritty soil.

Thunder's baggy eyes were rimmed with purple, his head shed water like a boiled egg, his beard was yellow in the lamplight. I could hear nothing but the rage of the rain, and gusts nearly buffeted us off our feet. We struggled against it. Thunder's oilskin flapped like wings, hurling drops into my face.

We passed lines of tents, where fyrdsmen had pulled the guy ropes wringing taut, and were lying on their camp beds clutching the frames. Very occasionally, in the outer rows, a light flickered within, sometimes showing the silhouette of a man whetting his sword, cleaning his musket, or, in one case, smooching a fyrdswoman.

The remaining Select were lean and efficient. What had wrecked our plans? What was Thunder talking about? Why had seeing my wife half-naked passed without comment when any other male would give his right ball for the privilege?

The wall dividing our camp from the entrance to Mine Twenty reared ahead, like a close-packed forest's edge. Lamps glimmered by its picket door within the main gate, and the wind whipped to me the hot, fishy smell of their whale oil. Guards with Insect spears opened the gate, and I followed Capelin through.

The wind cut across the bare ground outside. It forced rain into the joints of my plate, which overlap sleekly, for ease of movement, and I felt it soaking through the padding snap-fastened inside. Water poured off my pauldrons and down my wings I clenched to my back. They're too long to be fully armoured, and I dreaded Insects getting behind me, grabbing my feathers and tearing up under my pauldrons to my skin.

The Paperlands rose black against the sky. The hills to the west were bleak and utterly bare; rain rattled over us, giving us the sense of vast space. From here these hills march unbroken to Ressond, where the gales blow even stronger, and ultimately to Darkling. Under a hunter's moon I saw their profile in shades of grey, as clear as day. Dust-coloured light slipped over their slopes as if groping them, darker and darker into the distance: felt-grey, slate-grey, moonlit patches on the smooth inclines, lying one behind another like the backs of a school of whales.

Thin clouds chased across the sky, whipped to impossible speed. Behind them very bright stars and the full moon shone dazzling. The flapping pennants around the mine mouth were going wild, shredding themselves. And the copper smell of bugs was very strong indeed.

Thunder shouted, 'How fast is this wind?'

The irrelevancies of his questions puzzle me. 'About a hundred and thirty kilometres an hour!'

'Can you fly in it?'

'I'd go a hundred and thirty kilometres an hour in *that* direction!'

'What effect does it have on Insects?'

'None. Why?'

'I just wanted to know.'

Hallooing before him, we reached the pool of light at the mine mouth. Two spotlights roved ahead of us and picked out the path. With every step now, the duckboards bounced up and down, pressing into the eroded ground. Soldiers were clustered around the mine mouth, and their pikes prickled.

'What's happening?'

'You'll see.'

The mouth of Mine Twenty was a desperate outpost. A few big tents, all empty, stood alongside the duckboards, and the mouth of the Insect tunnel gaped ahead, an arched passage of their white saliva mottled with the corpses they'd built in.

Six horses in pairs were miserably labouring on the boards of a huge treadmill. Its windlass turned, winding a thick cable in from the tunnel mouth, where a pair of iron rails on sleepers led into the darkness.

The company of fyrdsmen parted to let us through. I passed between human bodies a little shorter and more thickset than I am, steel plate limbs and the astringent smell of sweat, paraffin from the lamps. Then the point of the arch passed overhead, and we were in the tunnel.

The wind's roar ceased immediately; we stumbled forward and

halted on the tracks. Thunder raised his lantern so it illuminated his bulging brow and eyes reddened by the lashing rain.

'No firearms?'

'I left my pistol at the blockhouse.'

'Good. Drugs?'

'Damn you, it's none of your business.'

'Comet, twenty Insects have broken in so far but the situation is worsening. I planned for them, but ... you will see. Come on.'

The tunnel walls arced up either side of us, until, overhead, their inward curves met in a thick ridge or seam, where Insects once stood on their hind legs to fill in the ceiling of the tunnel. Where the walls were saliva they were smooth, rippled in shell-like curves as the Insects, sometime in the tenth century, had pasted on layer after layer. But, embedded in this matrix, they had used everything they could find. Bones protruded. Skulls, petrified in the spit, randomly studded the walls, some with their eyeholes glassed over, their teeth coalesced. Here was a whole horse's spine, very rusted swords trapped in the white glaze, spear points without shafts. We passed horse shoes sealed behind it, then pieces of what must have been its rider. Then a stone ballista ball, cemented into the central seam, as if still in flight.

Walking down the incline, we passed underground, and safety lamps on poles provided a dim glow. We passed a section where hundreds, no, *thousands* of Awian skeletons glued together formed the entire tunnel. They were articulated, intact; they'd once been people who screamed and struggled as they were dragged here alive and sealed in.

Thunder raised his lantern so it enhanced and shadowed the stacked, crammed skeletons. 'The kourai.'

'They're not the kourai, Capelin. You live too much in books.'

'Well, then. The people of Murrelet.'

'So? So what?'

'The further north we go, the further back in time.'

I couldn't see the point of a history lesson when Insects were digging to kill us this very second. We're five hundred years' too far south for the kourai, and these are too well-armed. I tapped my ice axe on my gauntleted palm and strode ahead. 'Keep quiet, and try not to smell.'

'I don't smell!'

'Oh, great philosopher, if a Rhydanne can smell you, the Insects can.'

We hurried down the tunnel. The debris of ancient battles stopped when we were far enough underground for the Insects not to have dragged them, and the walls became earth, hardened by their saliva. Thunder had reinforced the ceiling with iron props every ten paces. Alongside the wall ran the fuse he'd laid, in its waterproof tube that looked like a ceramic drainpipe, which led from the enormous charge all the way out to Main Camp.

We walked on the sleepers between the rails, where the cable from the windlass was moving all the time until a set of wagons slid towards us out of the darkness. Thunder gestured me back and we stood against the wall. The wagons, hitched together, rattled past us. In each one lay a dead man with his throat and face torn off.

Capelin hastened on, grimly. I killed an Insect for him and we passed a guard of miners. They're pale and battle-stressed-looking men with a handful of words apiece, but they've the courage of polecats. Little Kay Snow the Sapper recruits them from the silver mines of Carniss and the coal pits of Wrought. When I'd wondered why they worked without complaining, Kay had laughed at me. 'Like I used to,' he said. 'It's all they know.'

We eased round deliberate zigzags excavated to contain the blast, and down the last length of tunnel. Water oozed from the ceiling and ran down the walls. The sliding door to the main chamber was in sight, when three Insects scrabbled out of the ceiling and fell on me.

The first reared up – I went underneath, straight into its grasp and rammed the ice axe crossways into its jaws – they closed reflexively and I whipped my katana out of its scabbard and sliced its head off.

The two behind it grabbed me together. Up went my katana single-handed, my hand on the rayskin grip, and swept through both sets of antennae, and stuck in the tunnel wall. My arm out to the right, I had to let it go.

With my ice axe I bashed at one forehead plate, denting the shell. Another blow backed by my weight, cracked it between the Insect's eyes, I got my fingers into the gap and pulled, it widened showing the green-white membrane damp and wrinkled like the flesh of a roast chestnut. I spun the axe round and jammed the point on its shaft into the crack, raked it back and forth pushing it deeper until the Insect spasmed and jerked back.

The third one had hold of my left side, its jaws raking my gorget, seeking purchase, legs razoring off feather fragments, its compound eyes a centimetre from my face. The very tip of its jaw pressed my neck and immediately I felt the hot wetness of blood.

I flapped hard, and its forelegs stretched out as I pulled against them. I chopped through the joints of all four feet, hurtled backwards, dragged my sword out of the wall, and swung it into its neck. The blade bit, and jammed. Sawing it with both hands I cut through, it swept out the other side – and stuck in the fucking wall.

The second one grabbed me again. I freaked out for a second and when I recovered I was smacking it in the maxillae with my ice axe, driving it back against the wall until its head was severed but for one strand, and it collapsed in a copious pool of ichor.

Thunder strode past, swept his oilskin away from the spines and dragged the door open. 'You fight very unconventionally.'

'I'm a Rhydanne.'

'You hurled yourself at them!'

'Only when I'm in harness.'

He stared at me as I pulled the claws off my armour and retrieved my sword. He was assimilating how fast I can move, and seemingly glad to have discovered my gangland fury aimed at bugs rather than himself. 'Come through,' he said soothingly – And an Insect's head burst out of the ceiling above him. I pushed him through the door and thumped it shut.

CHAPTER 7

The main chamber

A tremendous block of barrels atop barrels marched into the darkness of the gigantic chamber. Dim light came from safety lanterns at intervals, set into niches in the stone revetments Snow's men had built along its walls, and the glow of further lamps emanated from the passage leading to the other three mines.

The first bomb was vast. More marvellous than I'd imagined. Ten by ten by a hundred barrels deep. Each barrel was sealed in oilcloth, and from each base sprouted a fuse, twisted together at the end of every row, and at the corner they ran together into a cable twice as thick as my arm, wrapped with cloth tape, that led to the ground and into the earthenware tube.

I looked up: the ceiling was a criss-cross of timbers, and the floor was leather-covered duckboards. No spark must strike in here.

I breathed out in awe and an expression of anger crossed Capelin's face. 'It's all ruined!' He set off towards it. 'Two thousand tonnes of gunpowder. Two years to prepare the greatest explosion ever. Above us, a hundred thousand Insects fill the valley – and now what will I do?'

Tornado, the giant Strongman, was pacing back and forth, swinging his axe. He raised a finger to his forehead in greeting. I nodded and flicked my wings. Soil was pattering off my armour, grinding in its overlaps, but Tornado, with slabs of muscle, eye patch and shaved head, looked as incongruous down here as I did.

'Get many Insects?' he asked.

'Five.'

'We had ten in the last hour. They're digging down from being crowded above us. Like, getting closer. Now, watch him ...'

Capelin Thunder took a copper knife and peeled the cover off a barrel on the lowest row. He levered up its lid and showed me the jet-black grains of double-C blasting powder. He took the ladle from his belt and stirred them. Each grain was the size of a peanut and, slightly rounded from tumbling, they rattled gently against each other. The stuff of death. He pushed the ladle deeper into the barrel and brought it out. It held sand.

He tipped the ladle and let the white sand flow onto his palm. It sifted between his fingers, onto the floor.

'Shit,' I said.

'Every barrel is two thirds gunpowder and one third sand.'

'*Every* barrel?'

'Well, I haven't checked them all. But every one I've tested – yes, it is.'

'How many have you checked?'

'Three hundred.'

'*What*? You've lost a hundred barrels of gunpowder?'

'Maybe thirteen thousand barrels,' said Tawny. 'If they're all the same.'

Thunder glared at him. '*I* didn't lose it! Nobody stole it here! They reached me in that condition!' He brandished the ladle. 'The Castle paid for full kegs! Every single one that arrived from the mills had its seal intact. The selfish, greedy mill owners have sold us short!'

'We haven't time to check more,' said Tawny. 'We *should* check the whole lot.'

'The mills defrauded us! Destroyed my plan! Endangering lives! Mocking my genius! ...Some penny-pinching manager's stuffed his pockets with the Castle's money and sent us – sand!'

I looked up at the ceiling planks. Twenty-five metres above them we'd crushed a hundred thousand Insects into one little valley. We've shaken them up and corked them in, under pressure. 'There's going to be a swarm,' I said. 'We've *made* a swarm!'

'A big one,' said Tornado.

'A swarm that can reach Awia?'

'That can take half of Rachiswater!'

I said, 'Capelin, can't you blow the bomb anyway?'

'I'm going to, but the sand will dull the blast. It'll disperse it.' He waved the ladle to emphasise the volume of the caverns. 'The effect would be many small bombs going off simultaneously in this space, not one big one punching through the ground.'

'I see.'

In the silence I could hear Insects scrabbling. Somewhere, deep in the mine, rainwater was dripping from the roof and placking off a tarpaulin. As I listened, the drips doubled in speed and intensity, and Tornado listlessly began swinging his battle-axe and creaking the duckboards.

'How many will survive the bomb?'

'I cannot possibly estimate,' said Capelin.

'All right. Say half. We withdraw as planned. We blow the bomb as planned. And after us will come fifty thousand Insects!'

'Surely you have the experience to stop them!'

Tornado looked at me. I grimaced. 'Tawny might. Saker might. My experience is telling me I have to report this monumental fuckup to the Emperor.'

'Tell San it isn't my fault!'

I drew a breath and addressed the barrels. 'Capelin Thunder checked the *top* of every *tenth* barrel and therefore caused this slaughter in Rachiswater and wasted two fucking years of taxes drawn from your manors, my lords and lady governors. Or, if the stuff *did* exist, he's lost to the four fucking winds six hundred tonnes of high-grade blasting powder, of which the Castle has always made a strict point of knowing and owning the location of every goddamn gram!'

He went pale, which at least was gratifying. He pulled a piece of paper from the neck of his tunic and unfolded it. 'Here's a list of the mills that supplied us. Visit them. I need to get to the bottom of this. I'll make them pay!'

'Jant isn't going anywhere,' said Tornado.

'You need me here. I'll send a courier.'

'No! I want *you* to do it. I'll bring the thieves to light! I want you to find them and terrify them – as only you can.'

'That many Insects can swarm as far south as Micawater,' I said.

'Tornado will deal with them.'

'Tornado will try,' said Tornado. 'But not on his own.'

Capelin stirred the ladle in the blasting grains. 'It cost a fortune. I thought I was pushing the mills to increase production, and all I get is sand!'

He was too unworldly, too much of an Islander, to know the stresses of the Fourlands I play strains on every day. I was reminded again of Frost's innocence, and how her dam caused her madness. It seems that for every invention there's an equal and opposite reaction – upon ourselves.

But Thunder had no predisposition to madness. 'The manager of Fusain Mill is Spiza,' he said. 'Go there tomorrow after giving the orders.'

I shook my head. 'The Insects we've bottled in the valley are going to burst out. I'll check your stupid list when I'm sure that none of them will stream into Awia.'

He glanced up. 'But we're far behind the Wall. What about all the land we've reclaimed?'

44

'You've lost it.'

I turned to leave the chamber, grateful to put those tonnes of gun-powder behind me, and bracing myself to sprint through the tunnel full of Insects. Tornado caught up with me at the door. He said, 'I'll look after him.'

'Someone has to. Insects won't appreciate his great mind.'

'Oh, they'll find it very tasty.' Tornado rasped his stubble and scratched the ridges at the back of his neck. 'I hate it in here. It's like, claustrophobic.'

'Claustrophobic. Good word.'

'Superlative word, given how knackered I am right now. Here's a tip. Use your ice axe not your Wrought Sword because you can't swing a katana in the tunnel.'

'I know. I've just stuck it in the wall twice.'

He wagged an immense finger at the ceiling. 'We must continue the withdrawal through the dark. Snow says we've got to leave *now*. And put the best fighters last. Insects are going to follow and there're enough to cut straight through us. You know how imperturbable Snow is. Well, you should've just heard him yell at Capelin. He said twenty-five metres of soil and a hundred thousand Insects mean you've got five hours left before they fall on your head.'

'He'll be right. Currently Eske are pulling out.'

'Put me last.'

'All right, Tawny.'

He held out a hand like a slab of beef. We shook hands, his huge fingers enclosing mine completely. Then he rolled open the door for me and whacked me fraternally on the pauldron with a fraction of his strength. I ran, like a ball from a musket, down the bore of the passage and out into the flying night.

CHAPTER 8

How I brought muskets to the Empire

Thunder's superciliousness ruffles my feathers. He's the most recently-admitted to the Circle, but he deems himself the best Eszai, despite the fact we're all equal. And now he's so obviously failed, he wants me to find a Zascai (mortal) to whom he can apportion blame.

As a Trisian he's always held us in scorn. I think he happened to be present twenty years ago when Gio deliberately burnt down their library. An event which, as a scholar studying there at the time, rattled him deeply, and he never ceases to mention it. Moreover, he's never forgiven me for bringing the blueprint of the first musket from the Shift.

When Capelin brought us gunpowder, he designed and built the powder mills in the east of my wife's manor. Wrought became the boom town of the Empire once again. Tern's foundries cast cannon and her charcoal burners trebled production, because charcoal fit for the finest steel was nothing compared to the amount we needed for gunpowder. Mist Fulmer and Captain Wrenn sailed in clipper loads of sulphur from the volcano on Tris, and I flew to Darkling to show Rhydanne how to gather the yellow crystals from the west of the range, which they now trade down through Carniss for industrial quantities of alcohol.

Rayne discovered we had saltpetre by the tonne, because the latrines of the fyrd for a thousand years of fighting in Lowespass had turned into the stuff. Saltpetre, charcoal and sulphur, seventy-five to fifteen to ten. We proofed and improved it, and ran ourselves ragged with joy. A new weapon! This was what the Castle was for!

Not long after, in 2031, I visited Thunder's trial ground to see roundshot fired from a mortar set into the concrete, testing various combinations of powder. The booms and the stench of the smoke clicked my memory, and I realised this was the explosive that powered the muskets which the Equinnes of the Shift land of Osseous had been using for at least two hundred years.

*

I flew to my tower room, unlocked my desk drawers and pulled the topmost open. There was my syringe case and a few ampoules of scolopendium from the Skylark Labs in Brandoch.

'I'm Shifting to Osseous,' I said to Tern. 'Will you look after me?'

She was using the dressing table as a desk to sketch her new capacious coats. 'Jant,' she said, slowly. 'Where did you get those?'

'Rayne gave me a box full ... to stop me contacting the Summerday cartel.'

'You've Shifted twice this year already.'

'That's not enough to get hooked.'

'The last one nearly killed you.'

'I'm San's Messenger to Epsilon. He wants me to go.'

'Oh, *god*, Jant. San has no right! He's ordering you to kill yourself! Last time ... Remember last time? I found you in bed with a rig in your arm. Blood fucking everywhere, it was ghastly! I couldn't tell if you were breathing. I was crying my eyes out! I called a servant to go get Rayne. Lucky I did! You stopped breathing altogether! Your lips went blue.'

'I'm sorry.'

She came to sit beside me and stroked my feathers. 'But you can't wait to do it again ...'

'I have to visit Osseous, kitten.'

'Don't "kitten" me! You don't know what it's like, seeing Rayne whack you! Then Saker tried to take your stash – well, that was a mistake! It took us an hour to talk you out of the corner and get you to put the knife down.'

I said, factually, 'Last time I had to see Dunlin in Epsilon, because he's ahead of the Insect advance at Osseous.'

'I nearly lost you!'

'We're co-ordinating the war. If Dunlin pushes against Insects, they come out here. If we both push, they swarm somewhere else, possibly Dekabrayer.'

'Rayne said if your lips go blue I've got four minutes before you're dead. Four minutes, Jant! She breathed into your mouth.' Tern's voice rose to a sob, her dark eyes tanged with fire. 'I hated seeing it. I don't ever want to see it again. I hate seeing you inject.'

'I'm sorry, kitten. I'm following San's orders ... Um ... It's for the good of the multitude.'

'Stuff the good of the multitude! What about us?'

'Look ... I haven't touched it otherwise, since Saker left.'

'Apart from protecting drug dealers in Summerday?'

'I need it the most at the Front.'

'So you do? They deal it to *soldiers*, Jant. Are you deranged? This will finish you as an Eszai if anyone finds out.'

'You worry too much.'

'No!' she slammed down her sketch pad. 'Shit it!'

'Rayne's got me using Skylarks, I can measure it properly. Don't fret.'

'Of course I'm going to fret!'

'Though I'd do anything right now for a gram of Galt White.'

'Fuck sake! There's no stopping you! You love it more than me.'

'Nothing's as good as you, Tern.'

With my fingernail I broke the seal on two phials and pulled out the stoppers. An overdose that'd kill a mortal or virtually so will belt me into the Shift and – hopefully – the Circle will pull me back.

This medical-grade cat doesn't 'taste' as good as the stuff I distil myself, or the best I've bought from Summerday or Hacilith. They make it to my method from chopped centipede fern leaf, which only grows in the ghylls of Ladygrace. This mass-produced solution doesn't taste as many-layered, or as complex; it's shallower, clinical. I won't drift on the lovely warm waves of bliss and I'll come down dissatisfied. But I've sold my still, I'm officially clean but for the craving, the terrible whisper in the background of my daily life. Having been a full-blown addict, dependent on and off since I was ripped inside out at Slake Cross Battle, I want it so much. The sensation is … ah … there's nothing better. If I didn't keep chipping in and out of the Shift the craving might wear off, eventually, say in fifty years, but San won't give me chance.

I drew clear liquid into the syringe and went to sit on the bed. Tern joined me. 'You should be doing this in the hospital with Rayne.'

'She's at the Front … Will you watch my breathing?'

'I'll watch you. I love you.'

'I think I'll be out for two hours. If you feel me pull on the Circle, don't be afraid.'

She tied her hair back, knelt and supported me. 'Oh, Jant … you're beautiful and unique, and you shouldn't have to do this.'

I held the needle at forty-five degrees to the fattest vein in my wrist, slipped it in. As the sharp tip pierced the skin, a scintilla of heat and pleasure passed over me, that adrenaline kick. I registered a puff of blood in the barrel, paused for a second, and pressed the plunger down against the sweet resistance.

I went limp in her arms.

She lowered me. By then, I didn't care. By then I'd gone.

In Osseous I persuaded Captain Magor the Equinne to disassemble her musket and I committed the parts to memory. I regained consciousness very slowly indeed. The sun had jumped along its arc, beyond the frame of our broken-shuttered window. The sky was just an incandescent empty space; my wings, iridescent with a deep sheen. Wherever the light struck the surfaces in the room they were jewels.

A spasm passed over my body. I felt as if scolopendium was gently lifting me, floating my body a few centimetres above the bed ... occasionally a slight wave of nausea. Tern had tilted my head in the recovery position, I could feel my tongue sagging into my throat but not slipping all the way back to block it. My wings were limp, I could feel their presence, but couldn't move them. Managed a pleasurable twitch and shudder. My eyeballs felt shrunken and as hard as marbles with dehydration – the lids got stuck when I tried to blink. And my arms had been outstretched for so long my hands were screaming pins and needles.

Tern sat beside me, watching me carefully but I don't fucking know ... I passed out and came round hours later.

I crawled off the duvet, down two steps to the dressing table and pulled her sketchpad and pencils on top of me ... leafed through her élan figures until I found a clean page, and began to draw the first musket in the Fourlands.

I'd never give it to Thunder. He was too busy scaling up cannon to monstrous proportions. He'd never thought of giving each man his own gun.

A brisk rat-a-tat sounded at the door. Tern looked at me. I stared at the chandelier of her tears. She went to the door and tried to get rid of our visitor, but I recognised Cyan's voice.

'Let her in,' I murmured.

'Don't be alarmed, my dear,' Tern apologised. 'Our favourite Rhydanne hybrid is tripping his tits off.'

Cyan had seen me in this state before. She'd *been* in this state before, but she still baulked. I was sitting, leaning against the desk drawers and melding into them. The wood grain was sidling off in helical patterns and merging with the carpet. Every surface I touched adhered to my fingertips and stretched long strings of itself when I lifted away. Which made drawing difficult.

Cyan, in snakeskin jacket and jeans, looked utterly amazing. 'I dropped in for coffee and advice,' she said. 'I guess I'll come back later.'

She pulled a handful of letters from the pigeonhole and leafed through them. 'Oh, god. Not Crake *again*. I even recognise his bloody handwriting ...'

She turned to go, but Tern kissed her, motioned her to the

chaise-longue, and she sat gratefully down. Cyan's very lissom. Six hours of archery practice a day is carving her body in celestial ways.

'Tern,' she sighed. 'Is there any limit to the number of times a man can Challenge me? I had ten Challengers last month, here's another batch. This Crake ... he's coming at me for the fifth time. He knows he's good. Last year I only won by a whisker.'

'You still won, my dear. You're still here on merit, still the paragon.'

'A breath of wind in the wrong direction and I'm doomed.'

Tern brought up a chair. 'I'm afraid there's no limit.'

'Oh, god. So I'm going to get the same assholes year after year?'

'Maybe so, until they grow old. But he can only Challenge you once a year.'

'Some are just attention-seekers!'

'Don't let them wear you out, Cyan, darling. Collect them together and convince them to agree to a tournament, in the same week. That's how Saker did it. But you have to shoot against each man personally. You can't arrange heats.'

Cyan rested her head on her hand, elbow on the chaise-longue scroll. 'Dad never had so many Challengers ... Well, maybe at the beginning, before he got established.'

'If any harass you, say you'll tell the Emperor.'

She passed a hand over her forehead and blinked slowly. 'I can deal with the harassment. Dad said that every generation turns up five hundred archers willing to cripple themselves to win at all costs. I think that's an underestimate.'

'It'll improve,' Tern said.

'Between them and the suitors I'm on tenterhooks. I can't settle down. They're distracting me from practising. They're a millstone round my neck ... Jant? What are you doing?'

Watching the three-dimensional structure of gems that was the setting sunlight on her shiny jacket.

Tern gathered up my wings and folded them, placed her palm to my cheek and rolled my head forward. 'Jant? Come on, Jant. We know you're in there. We want to talk to you.'

I offered the pad to Cyan. My hand twitched and rippled the paper. Cyan took it, turned it the right way up and squinted at my tiny, stoned handwriting.

There I'd drawn: eighty-five centimetre barrel, lead ball wrapped in wadding, ignition cap with fulminate of mercury ...

She yelped. 'It's a hand-held cannon!'

'... Equinnes ... ah ... Equinnes call them muskets ...'

'I can use it!'

I was very aware of every shallow breath through my dry mouth. 'It's yours,' I managed. After all, I had enough on my plate with the telegraph.

She said, 'Tern, can your foundries make this?'

Tern shrugged elegantly. 'I think so.'

Cyan examined me with curiosity. Her face was broad and strong, her eyebrows shaped like seagull's wings … My drug made her eyes seem even more intense and piercing, the sane, vivid blue you find in the heart of glaciers. I really couldn't stop staring at her, and she was wondering how to bring me round. I said, 'Make me a small musket, that I can carry in the air. A pistol …'

She nodded. 'Tern,' she said. 'Ring for some powerful coffee. Let's go to the Throne Room and tell San I've got a new project.'

And the rest, you might say, is history, except that it was only nine years ago, and nine years isn't history. Yet.

CHAPTER 9

Capelin Thunder speaks

Comet Jant Shira has asked me to write a few words so you may know who I am and from whence I came, because I am but lately made immortal and my story is an important one.

I was once an artist, the finest painter in tempera, gesso and oils that the Island of Tris has ever produced ... more probably, the best the world has ever seen. I painted the frescos of the Amarot and the debating chamber of the Senate, but my sketch studies and small chiaroscuro portraits are, I think, the most admired.

I was studying in the library of Capharnaum twenty years ago when Gio Ami put the building to the torch. My notebooks I had deposited there were burnt with all the accumulated knowledge of Tris. I witnessed the library rise in flames, and realised what an uncompromising, warlike people had invaded our island and, like all the Capharnai, I was afraid.

The ensuing battle, where many of my fellows were killed, put me in mind of a slim volume I had read in that very library. It was antique, by an anonymous author, entitled 'An Enquiry into the Uses of Saltpetre.' That essay had been destroyed with the rest, but there is a smaller library, at Salmagundi on the east side of the island.

I travelled there, sought out the book and read it. It seemed obvious that, since I had a penchant for invention, my innovations in use from Capharnaum to Galimatias, I could with ease reconstruct this deflagrating substance. The warriors of the Empire would recognise the superiority of Trisian learning and reward me bountifully – more handsomely than the Senate of our ravaged island would ever be able to pay me as an artist. In fact, the greatest patron of all, the Emperor San, would surely give me immortality and initiate me into his Circle so I could bring the fruits of my genius to the Fourlands, forever.

True, I had to give up my calling as a painter and focus purely on machines of war, but the cannon and mortars were themselves an expression of my creative instinct. I have a prodigious curiosity to investigate and comprehend every aspect of the world, whether it be the brushstrokes that replicate my sitter's smile, or the possibility of producing a flying machine based on the kinetics of the Messenger's wings. Some of my fellow Senate say I have sold my soul, sold out to the Empire. They say I have abandoned my artist's spirit and become a creature of the Emperor and an instrument of war. To those critics I reply: an artist must eat. And it affords me greater freedom to seek one generous patron, than to flatter ten who never pay.

I conducted some initial tests of the black powder mixture, adding charcoal to make it burn, and forming pellets so the ingredients do not separate. Then, one evening, as the sun set beyond the ocean in a great blaze of carmine – its light refracting on the ash in the high atmosphere from the burning of so many thousands of books – I took my stylus and wrote to the Messenger. I remember sitting at my table on the flat roof of my house, a bowl of grapes before me. The sea breeze stirred the parchment and I wrote calmly, with great confidence. Soon, I thought, soon I will leave this stifling rock I have outgrown, and sail down the path of scarlet on the ocean to the land where the sun sets. A benighted land, till I set foot on its shore; a land which will embrace me. Before the Emperor of the world in his unimaginable glory I will unveil my contrivance, and the thunder will speak.

CHAPTER 10

Rearguard

My wings rode the wind and bore me up. Fresh air hit their leading edges and roared over the surface of my flight feathers, re-joined behind their tips. The wind caressed me and I flew with smooth strokes, and closed my eyes for a second in its warm roar.

Throughout the night I'd moved the fyrd south, a line of lanterns crinkling as the men kept not quite abreast of each other. The division captains were daunted by my eyes reflecting like bronze mirrors as I'd run from one to the next, through the storm.

By dawn the Eske and Rachiswater fyrds had reached Main Camp and Hurricane's were peeling away. The first sliver of sun showed in the eastern sky dotted with clouds. The wind had dropped, the pressure of the breeze on the stretched skin of my leading edges told me how fast I was flying, and as it increased and ebbed with each gust I tilted my wings and kept myself sailing at the same speed.

Look at Cyan's musketmen reaping the horde! Look what she's achieved! It's fucking fantastic. She's fielded fifty times more musketmen than Saker fielded crack archers. From the streets, pubs and workhouses of Hacilith, she'd thrust into their arms a musket each – trained them till their actions are so automatic they're hard-pressed to describe them. Saker says it takes a lifetime's practice to make an excellent bowman, it moulds their bodies and their minds. Cyan turns out a musketman in a fortnight. And she'd doubled her numbers by fielding women: your musket only weighs four kilos whereas an archer draws over forty. Crossbows were obsolete, she'd relegated them to our safe forts and rear lines.

The cannons had been firing for half an hour. Smoke obscured my view of the troops quick-marching, muskets ready. Their white jackets looked like the foam where the edge of the wave bleeds onto the sand. Flashes gleamed along the line as the sun caught their fixed bayonets.

Between their lines horse teams dragged the field artillery, wheels turning. The captain of each team rode the first horse of the six, pulling the cannon linked to an ammo cart, linked to a wagon with the other five gunners riding high.

Puffs appeared along the line of Cyan's musketmen facing the valley. They poured volleys into the dense swarm of Insects escaping it. Saker's archers beside them were arcing up clouds of arrows, like dashes, reaching their apex below me and hailing vertically down. Insects speeding towards them were festooned in arrows, slowing – the ones that reached the ranks were kebabed, squirming, on the pikes projecting from the front of their line.

More Insects closed on Cyan's lines because the musketmen couldn't load fast enough. They were running onto her pikes four, five at a time as I went over her two battalions. Her lines were each three ranks deep. The first rank was four thousand armoured pikemen, with a flag bearer where they'll turn. Behind them, two ranks of musketmen were firing precisely by company.

Cyan, on her strapping horse, listened to their rhythm. I swooped down and landed beside her. 'Your pikes are filling up.'

'I know,' she said sternly.

'You should form square.'

'It's too slow.' She pressed her lips together. No Eszai can show a sliver of weakness. No Eszai can waver. Six thousand men were relying on her, and if she didn't radiate confidence no way would she keep them in line. And if the line breaks, they're dead. We'll only stay alive if we hold steadfast together to Main Camp. But Cyan had been tempered in the furnace of her Challenges.

'We can take it,' she said.

And the cannon stopped.

It was the gun on our right. The others continued, but from that side was silence. I suddenly heard Saker's shouts it had masked. I looked down the neat line of whitejackets, but all I saw was the stoop of their backs, their arms working as they ramrodded balls down scalding muzzles.

'Now what?' said Cyan.

'I'll go see.' I sprinted to the rear, along the line of men reloading furiously. They didn't notice me in the drifting smoke. I ran past jackets pulled taut between wings and over curved spines. I ran past the rattle and scrape of plunging ramrods, elbows crooking as their fingers, blackened with split nails, dug into the ammo boxes slung on their shoulders. They plucked the cartridge from the criss-cross cardboard, raised it to their mouths; I knew the pleasing weight and tallow taste of the lead ball between my molars.

I ran through a denser patch of smoke, emerged seeing the end of the line and pelted down until I jarred to a halt behind the last man.

The two line-end sergeants with their pennants weren't looking at me. They were gawping at the cannon. The brass six-kilo gun on its spoked wheels was completely unmanned. It stood alone, the lids of the ammo cart open, no sign of the detachment anywhere.

'Where's the cannon team?' I shouted.

'They buggered off!'

Lack of fire had created a gap into which Insects were closing. The archers on the nearest flank of Saker's battalion were desperately trying to kill as many as possible, but Insects were surviving around the edge of their range and racing towards us. In a minute this gap would be full of them. The ends of Cyan's line and Saker's wouldn't have a chance. Then bugs would pour up the gap between their ranks and tear their battalions apart.

I turned to the sergeant. 'Form square! Now, now, now!'

He ripped his bugle from his belt and blew the command. The ends of the lines glanced at him, a nervous ripple went over them, but the musketry crackle drowned the double note and nothing happened.

'Tell Lightning,' I yelled at him. 'Square! Go!'

He raced into the smoke, and at the same time Saker on his white horse plunged out of the ranks of archers. He took it in with a glance. 'The cannon six?'

'Fled.'

'Damn!'

'Saker—'

'*Slow fuse!*' he snapped. 'Look—!'

Something picked me up and smashed me into the ground. A ball of flame blinded me. My eardrums punched agony – a wall of heat and I screamed – grit cut into my cheek – and my whole body began to shiver.

From a far place I heard my own voice in my head. Insects are coming! Get up! I clamped my tongue in my teeth and forced myself to my feet. All around was carnage. Musketmen lay on one side, their clothes blown off, skin raw and the bare ground sprayed with blood. Archers on the other side flayed to the bone. Some were just blackened flesh. Some kicked and flapped – flames sputtering over their melting wings.

The cannon had exploded. We were on the lip of a dish-shaped crater. The end of its barrel lay peeled back in bent strips like orange rind. Its chamber was riven with deep cracks. Saker's horse had been eviscerated by brass shards of the barrel. On the other side shrapnel had gouged through the thighbone of a musketman who lay unconscious, thick blood pumping out.

My hearing tuned back in an agonising whine. I staggered over the matchwood of the block trail, to Saker's stallion. Its ribcage was opened as if with a butcher's cleaver. One side of ribs, with a stiff leg and hoof, projected at the sky. Its guts were blown out, pasted to the ground, and hanging over the raised leg.

Saker, beyond it, lay on his side with a wing in the air. His silk gambeson was scorched black like the crust on beef. His face was speckled with grit blasted into it – blood was welling to the surface.

Then there's a pulse. I drew my sword, stood by him. His eyes were shut. Insects were running towards us, serrated jaws wide, and jerking back as shot raked them. The archers saw him, and faltered.

'Keep shooting!' I yelled. 'Nock!'

Their ranks seemed to surge up as each man stepped towards me and those behind, onto tiptoe, trying to see over their shoulders. A shout rang out – 'The King is down!'

Their faces set hard. The first men ran towards us, their line followed. Their arrowheads raised simultaneously. Immediately I had a rank of archers in front of me shooting straight at the closing Insects, and another behind me, at the back of the crater, shooting over our heads.

Awians are fucking impressive. But there were too many Insects and they were still closing. At my boot toes, Saker stirred. I whacked my heel between his wings. 'Get up!'

The stench of burnt flesh and feather, scorched wool and sundered metal made me vomit into my mouth. I spat. The nearest Insect ran at us, pinned with arrows, then musket fire plucked it off its feet. It collapsed and crawled in circles, gouging the soil into peaks with the edge of its mandible.

I kicked Saker on his thigh armour. 'Get up, you big sod!'

He rubbed his wing over his face, wiping off the blood. Then he scrabbled onto hands and knees, crawled to his bow and grabbed it. His men gave a cheer as he rose to his feet.

Twenty, thirty Insects closed and crossfire from musketmen and archers dropped them, but thousands were speeding towards us. The Awians' wings clamped tight to their backs in terror, all along the line. They knew they were finished but they didn't miss a shot.

'Form square!' rang over Cyan's battalions.

At last! I helped Saker up, thinking he'd lean on me, but he pulled away and ran at Cyan's ranks as the two lines morphed into square before us, like this: the men in the middle of the front rank stayed in place, those on either side of them ran to the rear and turned outwards to form the sides of the square, and Saker stood in the middle of the nearest side with his wings spread, as the ranks behind us ran into the hollow square, and lined it. The outermost division of the armoured pikemen sealed it.

Saker had kept a gap, yelling, 'Get my archers in! Get them in!'

Cyan curvetted her horse in the centre of the square behind him. 'Receive troops!' she shouted at our side. Her musketmen and pikemen shuffled left and right away from Saker, widening the gap. 'First Mica!' he yelled at his archers. 'Shelter in the square!'

They'd drilled this often. They ran towards him – the lines ahead and behind me, and the rest latched on, still flexing their bows and loosing. The whole battalion followed, sprinting across the shallow crater to the gap in the pikes.

Archers shouldered between the pikemen, through the levelled muskets and poured into the square. Saker waved to me and I ran with them – passed through in the middle of the crush. Inside, the men pressing me slowed and turned to each other.

Outside the square, Insects stampeded onto the archers waiting to push through. They slung bows on their shoulders and drew swords. They didn't have a chance. Cyan's pikemen closed ranks – trapped them outside. I saw one man raise his sword, an Insect lunged and cut him in half at the waist. Insects streamed past, rattling down the pike points, and pulled the last of the archers under.

Saker bawled at the ones packed around me, 'First Mica! Are you on holiday? Pathetic! Rank up! These musketai need you!'

The archers complied and lined up behind the musketmen along the inside of the square, making each side of nearly two thousand people now four ranks deep. The musketmen were shooting and reloading as fast as they could, and the square filled with suffocating smoke and the stench of burnt grease.

Saker pointed at the colour ensign. 'You. Off!'

The young man dismounted and Saker wedged his boot into the stirrup and stepped up to the saddle. He looked out over the west side. 'Tornado and Hurricane have formed square too. If we stay here we'll run out of shot. Walk them.'

'All the way to the Wall?' shouted Cyan.

'Yes! Tawny and Hurricane will know we have to. If they don't move, Jant – tell them!'

Cyan sawed her reins and controlled her panicking horse. 'Have we got enough cartridges to make it?'

'Well, that depends how *fast* we go!'

He walked his horse to the far side of the square and looked south.

The Castle's sun flag holstered to the saddle rippled above him, trailed down over the cantle.

Insects were seething around all sides now, seeking a way in, but the pikes fended them off and balls were slamming into them. An Insect reared above the line of pike tips and flailed the air with its four front legs – shots blew its head apart in a spatter of thick cream.

Hundreds of dead bugs were piling up, forming a bulwark on top of which more appeared, running down onto the points. The men were lighting and throwing their grenades now, and explosions blasted in the mass beyond the pike tips.

'Walk!' yelled Saker. 'To me! To the colours! Steady ... keep it steady!'

The men and women of the square uprights took a half-turn towards him and began to walk. The whole square started to crawl, crab-wise, over the ground. Acting as a single organism, keeping up the rhythm of shooting and reloading.

Two dead archers lying in the centre seemed to move across the ground as we progressed. They disappeared out the far edge of the square – the men there, walking backwards, stepped over them and their side reached me: I loped across to join Cyan and Saker.

Her fingers were white on the rifle stock, she was furious. She bawled at her father, 'I'm Lightning, not you! I give the orders!'

'You did. I didn't hear them.'

'Leave it to me!'

'Yes. But ...'

'But *what*?'

'They'll have to go faster than this.'

She shouted, 'Quick march!' and the square began to elongate as the men near her hurried more than the trailing edge.

'Close up! Close up!' bellowed the sergeants.

'One gap and we're dead,' said Cyan.

Saker pressed his grit-blasted cheek and glanced at the blood. Blood and sweat were running down into his collar. I threw him my canteen and he poured water over his face, wiped it off with his sleeve, and flung the bottle back to me.

Musketmen chucked out a layer of packing in their cartridge pouches and started on the next. The shoulders of every man and woman jolted with each shot, but so many Insects hemmed us in that every ball ruptured chitin.

'Keep together!' she yelled.

Saker sniped the bugs climbing down the pikes. Smoke drifted between us – he faded from view, then reappeared. He said, 'When the cannon exploded ...'

'Yes?'

'That wasn't an accident.'

I stared at him. 'Who'd want to destroy a gun?'

He shrugged, three fingers around one strung arrow and four more in the same hand. 'I know what I saw!'

'*What* did you see?'

'Slow fuse leading into the vent. I only noticed when it sparked over the boss. They must have hidden the length underneath – and packed the barrel with charges. *And* sealed it with wadding.' He winced in pain. The whites of his eyes were totally bloodshot. They were running so much they'd washed clear patches on his cheeks.

'Why?' I said.

'Men do weird things when they're scared. It nearly killed us!'

I blinked, uncertain. Had they blocked their cannon to make a bomb, to destroy as many Insects as possible?

'It was the gun *Syrinx*,' I said. 'Thunder will know their names.'

'Fuck these muskets! I can't see! Jant, fly over the other squares. See what shape they're in. Then *come back*. You *have* to guide us!'

I ran diagonally across the square and took off over the jutting bayonets. Smoke rolled beneath me. Our three squares floated like islands washed by the copper waves of bugs. From the camp to the static cannon line, we were pushing through their solid, seething sea, and from the valley yet more were pouring.

Insects broke against the palisade of men. Tried any opportunity to cut in. Chewed the pike poles, writhed on the points, showing pale undersides, and for every one skewered, five more tried to push beneath.

Volley fire jetted from the sides of the squares. Smoke puffed along them – the shots crackled like burning pine branches. Our squares pushed through the horde so slowly, it was only when I glanced from Tornado's to Cyan's that I saw she'd progressed. Tornado's square was the most ragged. Its centre was like a hospital, full of dying and muti-lated bodies being dragged along, on stretchers made from muskets in the sleeves of bloodstained coats.

Tornado waved me on. Over Hurricane's square – their rate of fire had slowed, they were throwing their grenades. They must be low on ammo. Hurricane was pressing them hard – he raised his poleaxe and pointed forward.

To the cavalry. Eleonora was hard-hit and she'd withdrawn to the margin where Insects were more dispersed. She was riding circuits with her men, lancing Insect after Insect with thin spears drawn from the hopper on her saddle. Beyond them, our line of cannon bunkers roared in cover fire.

Cyan's square dropped behind as Hurricane's edged ahead. I flew over her and saw Insects pushing on top of each other. Abruptly, one big ant forced between the shafts and dragged the pikeman to the ground. Sprawling, trying to fend off the claws scrabbling over his armour, he blocked the path of everyone following. The pikeman ahead kept walking, and there grew a gap.

Insects surged into it. More Insects behind, forced them in. Pikemen on either side slowed to kill them – the gap became a dent in the line – the dent became a concavity and, like a dam breaking, the Insects burst through and raced into the middle of the square.

The archers spun round and took the first few. The innermost men started screaming, turned to face the Insects, levelled muskets and shot across the square. Never reloaded. The bugs struck into them and they struggled with bayonets. The lining of the square boiled into knots of fighting men.

The pikes either side dipped in a wave, Insects pulled the pikemen down and the gap widened. Armoured men sprinted away – the giant ants grabbed them and dragged them under the swarm.

I dropped in over the musket butts rising and falling frantically. Men bayoneting the Insects were bitten to pieces. Saker, trapped at the far edge of the square, was bending his bow and shooting with desperate speed. His face glistened like raw meat. I swooped over his arrows and smacked down beside him.

The inner ranks of the square now all faced inward, tangling with Insects. Only a few stretches of line unscathed, their bayonets levelled. One shot each, no time to reload. Sudden silence.

The square collapsed. Insects were grabbing men all around us. Huge gaps appeared, more bugs burst in, then it disintegrated into screaming men battering Insects that cut them limb from limb, sliced into throats and ripped open bellies. Blood spurted, guts uncoiled, and fighting bodies relaxed in the Insects' claws.

Saker kicked his horse and galloped from a standstill at the side of the square. Cyan followed. They hurtled through between slashing Insects, and charged away.

Five Insects closed on me. I crouched, jumped explosively into the air. My first wing beat slapped their compound eyes. The next forced me up. Bugs reared, reached for me. Barbed forelegs scraped my boot toes, jaws sheared closed under my soles. My muscles screamed pain, my sinews strained, but I caught purchase on the air and pulled it down. And climbed.

I rowed higher. Glanced down. A wave of Insects swept over the square and it was obliterated. All that was left was the shape of a square on the ground, made of piled human bodies, on which Insects fed.

Sun glinted on the strewn steel. Rivulets of blood rolled over the dry ground, began to soak in. An armoured pikeman, lying prone, jerked fitfully as Insects, standing on him, forced their smaller, inner jaws into the gaps in his armour.

At the edge of my vision Cyan's horse tore after her father. The flag whipped out behind him. They raced before the front of hordes of Insects chasing, converging on them. Lancers charged to meet them; they passed between the armoured destriers and into Eleonora's cavalry.

Seven thousand men just died in less than ten minutes. I turned in the air and sailed over Hurricane. Insects coming at his square, out of the smoke, were covered with the blood of Cyan's people.

Hurricane howled and bawled blue murder, swearing his square faster. They nudged ahead, and eventually reached the bunkers of our twelve-kilo cannons, which with spherical case were blowing bare patches in the swarm beyond them. His square ran out of grenades, then cartridges. I watched them stop shooting as they passed the cannons, then Tornado's came in, back through the Insect Wall. The squares transformed themselves into line, and the men snaked down the welcome path, into our stone-walled camp.

CHAPTER 11

The Sun Pavilion

I landed and made my way past the field hospital to our headquarters. Shouts and screams cross-cut the air – the hospital was overwhelmed. Men lay on the ground alongside its canvas wall. Some were bleeding from Insect slashes, others were pouring tin mugs of water onto their burns. One man, sitting by the path, was binding a gash in his arm that had split dark red muscle to the bone. At the end, near the palisade gate, a boy with a bucket of antiseptic was sponging down horses raked with claw wounds.

Outside the Sun Pavilion, Tornado was sitting on the crate that covered the end of the Valley Twenty fuse. He was coughing like Fulmer on a cold deck, parched by the smoke. 'I collected all the cannon crews into my square,' he said. 'The ones that survived.'

'I saw them.'

'There are too many bugs.' He pressed his eye patch. 'We should've started in square.'

'Where's Cyan?'

'Inside. Hurricane's giving her hell.'

'Oh, is he?'

'The bastard.'

I pushed the flap and entered. Tern was there, thankfully, holding an oval mirror for Saker, who was sitting at the map table with a bowl of steaming water, picking grit out of his cheek with Tern's tweezers.

I went to her and gave her a kiss. In the depths of the pavilion, Capelin was issuing commands to his static cannon captains, and on this side of the table sat Cyan, in her filthy shirt and breeches with her rifle across her knees. She was staring emptily at Hurricane, the Polearms Master and inventor of the bayonet, who was stomping up and down dragging his poleaxe.

'You lost seven thousand men!' he spat.

'Yes,' said Cyan faintly.

'That's *not* the work of an Eszai.'

63

'No.'

'*You're* not up to it.'

'A breach in a square could happen to any of us,' said Saker.

'Winning is *all* the Castle wants. It's all society cares for. Did you win, Saker? Then what are you? A loser! She doesn't *push* herself to the limit. I don't contemplate *any*thing else. I train *hard*. No Eszai trains as hard as me.'

'I do train hard,' said Cyan.

'You'll lose your next Challenge. And *losing* equals *death*!'

The Castle accrues a particular type of person into the Circle, for it takes an incredible drive to be best in the world at your chosen pursuit, and to dare to level a Challenge, but there's a – thankfully rare – type of character far beyond the class-A personality, something way off the end of the bell curve. Sadly, in our competitive society, people fight and bully their way to the top, who have the cold psychopathology of Arlen Hurricane.

'It's not her fault,' I said. 'A pike got fouled.'

'And where were you? Dicking about in the air?'

'Watching you.'

'You'll *get* more Challenges after this,' he told her.

'Hurricane, bully your Challengers if you must, but not fellow Eszai.'

'Fuck off, Jant Shira.'

'She's a better shot than you'll ever be. Either Challenge her, or leave her alone.' I slipped my arm round Cyan and felt her shaking. I sat down, pulling a pen and notebook from my back pocket. 'Say what you want, but it goes in my next dispatch to the Emperor.'

He reversed his poleaxe and twisted its point in the floorboards. 'Junkie,' he said to me.

'I love you too, Hurricane. Go and do something useful.'

'You're not worth the chair you're sitting on,' he said, and walked out.

'It's all right, Cyan,' I said.

'That man is incapable of any higher feeling,' said Saker from beyond the mirror. He dropped a piece of grit.

'Yeah, well, the Front is the best place for him. One day he'll need us and I won't be running so damn fast.'

We sat in silence for a while, contemplating the carnage.

'That's a lot more tags in the soil of Lowespass,' said Cyan. 'Oh, god …'

'We got out,' said Saker.

'*We* got out. They didn't.'

'Capelin,' I said. 'Come here.'

The Trisian joined us, and for a second stared at the map with a curious absence. Either he needed a moment to ponder this loss of life on a deeply profound level, or there's so much extraneous knowledge floating about in his brain that strands of it occasionally choke the cogs.

'Comet, this fiasco is by no means my fault,' he said.

'Yes, it is. You should have checked the barrels. Now we'll be fighting here for weeks. We lost seven thousand Zascai and almost lost Cyan and the king.'

'But—'

'I wish to god we'd burnt Salmagundi Library down, too!'

'You don't mean that.'

'No. I don't.' I sighed. The map in front of me showed range and graze of our static cannons at various elevations of their barrels, and Saker's bloodstained water drops were puffing up the paper as they soaked in. 'Anybody could have found the recipe. *I* could have found it … You didn't invent gunpowder, you just rediscovered it.'

'I *reinvented* it! I *improved* it, from an inflammable, unstable, unusable compound, into an *explosive*. Nobody ever used it to propel a missile before!'

'Well, light the fuse now.'

'I will, though I fear it'll have little effect.'

Tern poured me a glass of watered wine, but when I raised it to my lips, soot floated off them and formed a scum on the surface. 'I'll send a telegraph to the Emperor. I'll write a full report and send it by rider. I'll visit your fucking powder mills and find out which bastard sold us short. Then I'll have him hung. Thunder, Cyan, stay here and bring up the cannon wagons from the fortress. Their draught horses stand a chance this side of the Wall. Tern, my love, will you go back to Wrought?'

'Yes.'

Saker dipped a sponge and sloshed his face until the water ran clean. He took a towel and dabbed his cheeks as if shaving, though it left blood on the loops of the cotton. Tern lowered the mirror, and he said to me over the sliding reflection of his chin, 'I'll come with you.'

'To the mills?'

'Yes.'

'Why?'

'Fraud shouldn't happen in my kingdom.'

'It's Castle business.'

'A thousand Micawater men just died. This swarm threatens Lakeland. And there was foul play with the cannon exploding.'

'You think.'

'There *has* been foul play,' he insisted. 'It would've killed me if Balzan hadn't taken the blast.' He stripped off his ruined crested jacket and pressed a finger through a burn hole in the fabric, widening its crisp, brown edge.

'And?'

'And ... maybe if I better understand gunpowder, there's some way of making it so it doesn't give off so much smoke.'

Thunder said, 'The names listed for *Syrinx* cannon are Morenzian: Tressel, Lagan ...'

'Find out if they're still in the camp,' I said. 'If they are, arrest them.'

Eleonora entered, in full armour, carrying her helmet with its great sky-blue horsehair crest in the crook of her arm. The plates slid over each other soundlessly as she walked. She passed a glance over Cyan and settled on Saker. 'You're very lucky.'

'I don't feel it,' said Cyan.

'I've never seen a battalion disappear so fast.'

She put the helmet on the table. As well as the nodding crest, which trailed to drape down her back, it bore two splays of iridescent-blued steel feathers which tinted from teal through purple to gold. She reached a hand under her armpits, unclipped her pauldrons, lifted off the curved metal and stretched her sweaty wings.

'What hit you?'

'A cannon exploded,' said Saker, with an edge of adrenaline.

'Well, typical! Us lancers miss all the excitement.' She unclipped her rerebraces, flexed her arms.

'I lost the first Micawater.'

'Careless. Are you getting careless, love? That's your evenings spent writing letters for a week.'

'My whole town will be in mourning.'

'Are you going home? I just heard you say you're riding to Wrought with Jant.'

'I am. What will you do?'

'Stay, of course. Don't make me leave when I'm loving it.'

She unclipped her vambraces and stacked them into the rerebraces, into the pauldrons like shells. Her plates were scallop-edged, embossed entirely with swirling plumes, the spaces between their smooth textures inlaid with gold. The plates on her limbs were fluted for strength. Their edges were tapered so Insect jaws can't find purchase – only the vambrace for her left forearm deliberately has a ridge she lets mandibles close upon so she can swipe the Insect's head off. Recent scratches shining bright on it showed she was adept at this move.

She leant over Saker, put a hand on his shoulder and kissed him, then, as he spread his wings a little for her, she pressed her face to one of their hands, smelling the plumage. She preened her fingers down his flight feathers, zipping the barbs closed, turning the tattered flat bottle brushes back into perfect secondaries.

She started to kiss him and he responded, she reached her wings forward and they caressed them together.

'Come help me unharness.' She picked up the armour from the table, and crooked one finger through an eyehole of her helmet. The buckle straps dangled – they had lines inked on them marking the correct settings.

I said, 'Saker, if you're coming to Wrought, I'm leaving in an hour and you'll have to be incognito.'

Eleonora took his hand and they left the tent with wings interlinked and their arms around each other, unclipping plates of armour. I went to my own pavilion with Tern, washed and dressed in fresh clothes. Feeling light and unbelievably clean, I organised my Carniss mountain horse, bred to be unafraid of Rhydanne, and Saker's spare Balzan, trained like the others. To Balzan's saddle, the royal equerry buckled two quivers of arrows and two holsters behind them, for his new rifles.

Awian monarchs are expected to lead against the Insects. When Saker's wife was crowned, she was given a diadem which never sees the light of day, and a sword she hardly ever sheathes. In Awia, royalty provides a link between us immortals and the fyrd. They need our expertise and experience, but a good king will be closer to his soldiers than we Eszai can ever be.

The equerry brought up our horses. Saker put out his palm, the latest Balzan nuzzled it, and he stroked its neck. His partiality for the best white Eske coursers costs him a fortune. He ran a finger along its breastcollar, letting the six shield-shaped pendants on each side hang loose.

'I'm sure I said you should be incognito.'

'Jant, how can I, riding beside a winged Rhydanne?'

'You look very distinguished these days,' Tern said to him. 'I like it.'

'Thank you.'

'It's swarming out there,' Cyan said. 'Have you got enough arrows?'

'Yes, love.' He embraced Eleonora and Cyan, while I spoke to Tern and kissed her. All this time Tornado had been bellowing, ordering the fyrd into parade to witness Thunder lighting the fuse.

I stepped up to Favel's saddle, pressed the rein, and she lowered her head and turned tight left. Saker and I threaded our way round the rear of the assembled troops, and twisted in our saddles to watch.

Capelin raised the box and revealed the fuse end lying like a rope in the ceramic pipe. He set his taper to it – a brilliant white flare jumped and raced into the duct. Quickmatch burns at ten metres per second, a rate which as a Rhydanne I can see, but humans and Awians don't have such fast flicker-fusion in their vision, so to everyone else the flash would have vanished instantly.

Saker pulled an elegant watch out of his inside pocket and looped its chain on the pommel. We passed between tents, the gates opened, and we spurred through onto the supply road. A fuse ten kilometres long, burning at ten metres a second, will take sixteen minutes to reach the charge.

We galloped, me with sword drawn, him with an arrow at string, past Insects surrounding the camp, trying to chew the gates through their iron grids. Behind us the original Wall towered, gleaming white; the various breaches we'd made in it spilled down into chunks and rubble. We rode, dwarfed by its height and strength, and all the time Saker was checking his stopwatch.

'Here we go. Five, four, three, two, one …'

The ground shook. Four blasts melded into a clap of thunder, and rolled over the moorland. From far behind the Wall, a thick stalk of soil and black smoke burst up – and began to mushroom out as if blooming. We gasped at the force of the tremor. Saker's horse shied sideways. He swore, but it was drowned in a massive hooray from the camp. The soldiers acclaimed Capelin, whistling, blowing bugles, chanting his name louder than the explosion.

'He gave them a spectacle,' said Saker.

'And killed some Insects.'

'Not enough. They'll be fighting hard for weeks. Eleonora's bringing up the Tanager fifth to twelfth.' He shortened Balzan's rein. 'Ah, listen, Jant! Listen to them! The applause of the audience feels good, doesn't it?'

'There's nothing like it,' I said.

'Yes! Yes! To hear your name hailed. To hear the crowded stands cheer you till the air vibrates! Until it deafens you! Don't you feel you can do anything? Shout back at them like god! I remember it well! I loved it! … Once.'

CHAPTER 12

Saker Micawater

Saker had aged fifteen years since he left the Circle and it was difficult to accept. Having been the only Archer, unbeaten since the Circle began; having held the position – no, *lived* it – for fourteen hundred years, losing him was a shock to us all, but it struck me the worst. He'd been my closest friend for two centuries. Now, he's mortal, he's aging … and he's going to die.

When San dropped him, the Circle felt so different I sensed it for the first time. I became conscious of the Circle as a real entity and, since then, if I concentrate, I can feel my fellow Eszai.

A star had blinked out of a well-known constellation, and it no longer gave me my bearings. I missed him in the Castle. With his departure, and the new Eszai who joined us, filling spaces left by the deaths at Frost's Dam, it took years to find some semblance of balance.

The papers had been harsh. They'd said Saker was guilty of dereliction of duty, that he'd harmed the Empire by giving his position to a semi-pro, that Cyan was just an average archer. He married Eleonora a few weeks after leaving, and these days lived mainly at Tanager Palace. Every time I visited on business I made a point of seeing him, and every time he looked a little different. Time's changes were accruing. Then I was caught up in the preparations for Mine Twenty, and a year passed. I met him next, on the beach as Swallow's pyre was being lit, and it took me a second to recognise him. He wasn't as I'd remembered.

He was now forty-seven and, since we were so used to him being frozen at thirty-two for ever – I mean, he'd been thirty-two for fourteen hundred and fifty-three years – the changes in his appearance frightened us. Saker was supposed to be thirty-two! We didn't want him to grow any older! We didn't want him to die. We were afraid of the visual reminder of time's passing, the time we were cheating; the effects time was having on him, it would be having on us, if the Emperor didn't constantly hold us above its flow.

Saker was thirty-two in the year 620 when he won his immortality at the Games. He was thirty-two when I joined the Circle 1198 years later. He was thirty-two in the year 885 when Tornado joined the Circle, and damn well thirty-two in 2008 when Ata Dei gave him a night of lust on her ship. He was thirty-two in 622 when he was nearly killed in the Great Battle for Bitterdale, and thirty-two in 1993 holding the Front at Alula over the exact same ground.

He was thirty-two in 1485 when Shearwater took advantage of the famine to force him into a deal for his manor of Peregrine, and he waited five hundred and thirty years for Shearwater to die, so he could buy it back. He was thirty-two in 1414 when Ata built caravels, thirty-two in 2020 when we sailed a pair to Tris, and thirty-*seven* when Mist Fulmer scrapped them all in favour of clippers.

Now there were grey hairs throughout the blond, especially over his forehead. Grey among his stubble, grey feathers speckled his golden wings, but none yet in the array of long flight feathers of which he's proud. Year by year he was changing. The lines delineating his cheeks to his mouth were deepening, his cheeks sagging down. So was the crease at the edge of his mouth where he often pulls one side of it taut in a half-smile. But they're lines of wry humour, because someone who's been alive for fourteen hundred years sees the droll side to our antics.

The fan of wrinkles at the corners of his eyes, once only visible after a night's council of war, were now plain to see. He's caused them by squinting into the bright distance, because when Saker isn't slaying Insects in Lowespass he's shooting deer on his estates – or targets with phenomenal accuracy, or very small birds a great distance away, because archery is still his passion.

But if age has made him look more fearsome, it's misleading. Really, I think he's mellowed; relaxes, smiles, and laughs more readily, because he has the wife he always wanted. Most Awians find intoxicating the blend of still-unbeaten marksman, music connoisseur, rock hard soldier and loving father, so Saker's sarcasm is less acerbic these days, they jump to attention at his slightest word.

Some changes were subtle and I only noticed them after an interval of years. In the summers of Lakeland Awia you'd first notice that his skin tans darker and a little more shiny, but his eyes are brighter from laughing at the world slipping by. There were more hairs to his eyebrows and nostrils, nowadays, and the skin wasn't tight on his forearms. His biceps showed starkly with hollows at elbow and shoulder, as if his strength was surfacing. There were wrinkles at the side of his neck, hollows, too, around his collarbones. The ends of his fingers don't heal so fast when gunpowder dries and splits them along the fingerprint whorls.

He's always had grace for such a big man, which is partly his noble background, mostly his martial pursuits. He hadn't lost the deliberation in his posture, a great understanding of the presence of his body through having lived in it for so damn long. Nor had he lost his economy of movement, his incredible patience, nor his surety and nerve that allows him to stand stock still while Insects close in range.

He still uses the same bows, and packs the same strength at an eighty kilo draw, but is he slower to span them? Yes. He still has that freakish depth perception, but I fear there's less perfect copperplate in his handwritten letters to me.

One thing he no longer does, is compulsively touch the scar on his palm from his marriage to Savory. The scar's fading, and perhaps his memory of Savory is fading, too. Instead, he always makes a point of writing to his children, neat blocks of text around little sketches of the Front: peel towers, bastides and fortress. Remarkably lifelike Insects prowl the margins.

Age shouldn't encroach on Saker, who's escaped it for the longest time, but it is, and he feels it. He doesn't seem to care that he's going to die so soon. Aging will seem very fast to him. Life's going to be brief. We were too afraid to breach a conversation on the issue. Nobody understood it but Eleonora, and, since he has her, he's no longer lonely.

I hope Eleonora has resilient four-poster beds in Tanager to tie him to, because when Saker is getting more – and definitely more adventurous – sex than I am, something has really bloody changed.

'Tern wrote to me about your drug use,' he said.

'The Emperor keeps sending me to the Shift.'

'Yes. Hmm. Well, there must be an easier way in.'

'There isn't. Trust me.'

He looked at the barbed wire fences either side. 'What are you doing in the Shift?'

'Co-ordinating the war with Dunlin.'

'Dunlin. Dunlin Rachiswater was my friend.'

'I know.'

'I wish I could see him.'

'There's no way.'

'Come on, Jant, there has to be *some* way,' he said ebulliently.

'What did Tern say in her letter?'

'It upsets her, seeing you unconscious … She runs to me, and I can't bear to see her distressed.'

'San needs to know where we are in relation to other worlds.'

'It's going to kill you.'

This was uncomfortable coming from Saker, who might only

have twenty years left. I'm not sure about the fraternal attitude he's adopted. I've never had a brother, so I'm not in practice. The best I can do is 'fellow gang member', and that doesn't really fit. I said, 'There's a swarm building at Dekabrayer. Insects could burst through into the Paperlands or anywhere in the Empire. I can't tell where they'll emerge. We've got to be ready.'

'Where's Dekabrayer?'

'It's a Shift from Epsilon.'

'Have you been there?'

'No. I'd die.'

'The Equinnes with their muskets ...' he said vaguely.

'I've already told the Equinnes all about Cyan's innovations. They'll start to make rifles now. Or, they would, if Dunlin hadn't introduced flying bombs and Sentient Drones.'

'Tell them, a bullet with ridges round it will—'

'No, Saker. We're as backwards as Rhydanne in comparison. After Frost's Battle the Vermiform told us she could taste saltpetre in the soil, okay, but also uranium. That's what Dunlin's looking for.'

'Why?'

'I haven't the faintest idea.'

Once you're past the last line of trenches, the road becomes paved. We passed through the checkpoint at Calamus Bastion and into Awia. Saker hung his bow on the saddlerack. 'God, it's good to see greenery after all these weeks.'

'It's just Oscen. We've seen it a thousand times before.'

'Yes, but will I see it *again*?' He looked at the gorse bushes, grassy hillocks and white tails of fleeing rabbits. On Oscen Hill, my semaphore tower was flexing out the symbols of a message. Saker watched it. 'What's it saying?'

'That's Eleonora's call for reinforcements going down the Rachis line.'

'Amazing.'

'I'm pretty hooked on my telegraph.'

'It's the best thing since the Black Coach!'

The semaphore telegraph was another discovery I'd brought back from Tris. The Trisians have just one line, from Capharnaum to Salma-gundi. Once I'd understood the principle, I networked it out across the Empire, and now I have fifteen lines, five hundred stations, and counting.

He was drunk on the scenery. Where I saw a gorse bush, he saw vibrant yellow blooms, an intricate maze of prickles in which duellist birds hopped and strutted. When we passed the troops I'd sent south he saw fathers and brothers glowing with relief. They'd be even more glad to have escaped when the news of the slaughter reached them, as it soon would. They joked as they passed wine flasks down the line; they couldn't wait to slap the dust off their jackets and go home to their families.

Their crowd thickened at Oscen Bridge. We trotted off the road and splashed through the water, up the bank and across fields of ripening wheat. It whispered around our horses' chests and brushed our boots as we pushed through, leaving two tracks in the grass-gold field. We rode along the verge speckled with poppies and small sunflowers, and onto the baking highway. In the distance, Rachiswater River shimmered in the rising heat.

Saker threw open his arms. 'Home!'

Since leaving the Circle he seemed so much more alive. He'd woken up. Becoming mortal shattered everyone's expectations and allowed him the possibility of change. He was free from the trammels of our beliefs of what Lightning Saker should be like. The expectations had clamped down on Cyan instead. And he had the freedom he'd always wanted. The freedom to recreate himself.

It's a shame he only has a finite number of seconds left to do so. But time's only valuable when it's running out. He doesn't take minutes for granted any more. He's determined to live every one.

With boundless joy we galloped downhill and swam our horses across the river. That night, we stayed in Rachiswater Palace, which he had largely refitted. The following day we continued down Barb Street and stayed overnight at the reeve's house, then next morning we set off, before dawn, to Wrought.

CHAPTER 13

The Powder Mills of Wrought

Familiar landmarks in the pale dawn revived the level fields. As we passed through my wife's manor, our horses' hooves ground on the heavy, gravelled road, and the breeze cooled my damp hair. The tall chimneys of the steelworks poked up from the horizon in the direction of Wrought town. We turned at the Colliery Crossroads, out towards the coast, on a road running between beet fields with dark green hedges. They counterpaned into the distance, seguing into marshland, and there, among the fringes of the saltings, glittered the sea.

Fusain Gunpowder Works stood on its own in this flat farmland, surrounded by canals that convey the finished powder to hulking magazine ships anchored in the middle of the River Wrought. A few gunpowder barges with red triangular sails were already gliding out to meet the current – as they passed behind hedges and trees, they looked like they were sailing on the land.

We passed the sign to Fusain, and rode between alder and willow coppices, where the wood for charcoal was being grown. Ahead of us, seagulls cried over the tawny reedbeds, around the myriad stagnant inlets of the sea. The gunpowder works was hidden by a pine plantation, and a single, stark birch tree stood among them, bone-white, as if it had been washed.

'Can you hear that?' asked Saker.

'What?'

'The grinding sound?'

'It's the incorporating mill. It mixes the powder, day and night.'

'Constantly?'

'We get through a lot of powder.'

Pleasant, lilac-grey smoke was rising from the charcoal furnace and, as all the gunpowder buildings were in their own parkland, it was peaceful and tranquil. Away from the Front, I'd had a good night's sleep for once and felt refreshed.

The drying houses were setting up a thermal already, trailing clouds from their chimneys. High in the dawn sky, layers of cirrostratus were inked pink with the growing light, and the sun rose behind mist above the reedbeds.

We clopped across a stone bridge over one of the small canals that connected the complex. Two punts were passing under the arch; the puntmen in flat caps and braces paused with their poles and stared up at us. Their boats were loaded with barrels wrapped in oilcloth – they were taking unfinished powder to the next stage of processing. Their square sterns flew red warning pennants. Between them, the still water reflected the peach and powder-blue curdled sky.

We reached a high perimeter wall and reined in. I dismounted and walked to the wire link gate and had a few words with the guard. As he opened the gates I returned to Saker. 'We have to walk.'

'Why?'

'No horses in the complex. A spark from the hooves could set it off.'

He swung his leg over and stepped down.

'No metal,' I unbuckled my sword belt. 'No weapons, and no boots.'

'Does he know who I am?' said Saker.

'He hasn't a clue.'

'Good.'

'But he knows me, and word's already gone to Spiza.'

The guard approached, offering pairs of leather shoes. He looked with extreme consternation at the two packed quivers on Saker's saddle and the new rifles' beautifully-tooled holsters.

'Look after Balzan,' Saker smiled.

We walked through the complex of small buildings, each behind grassy earthworks designed to buffer any blast, and thick double walls filled with soil and covered in ivy. Behind the lake, with its fleet of swans and screen of chestnut trees, stood the saltpetre refinery, a long, low building issuing steam.

This was nothing like Hacilith. Only the Awian eye for aesthetics could design something this functional to be so idyllic. The lake supplied the solvent water and the woods had been planted for blast protection. Wagons on rails were carrying flaky salt crystals out of the refinery to the drying sheds.

'Where do they mix it?' said Saker.

'Way over there.' I pointed to the river. 'In the little buildings with the waterwheels. You heard the millstones grinding.'

'Yes. Right then, that's where I'll start.' He set off to the plantation.

I followed the earth track to the manager's office, which was neat Avern stone with white-rimmed windows. As I scraped mud off my shoes on the step, a small boy opened the door. I walked straight in past him to the office where a paunchy man with feather dandruff resided behind an immense desk covered in ledgers.

'Are you Spiza?' I said.

'Yes ... Comet.'

'The manager?'

'Yes. To what do I owe—?'

'All the barrels you supplied were short of powder. By as much as a third. Sand was packed in them instead. We lacked six hundred tonnes, Mr. Spiza. Sand sadly does not explode as readily, so Thunder's charge at Mine Twenty failed. We had to call off the advance and seven thousand men got killed.'

All the colour drained from his face.

'Seven thousand men sacrificed themselves, Mr. Spiza. A thousand Awians and nearly Lightning and your king. If it wasn't for a few Eszai holding the Front a swarm of Insects would be closing on Rachiswater this very moment.'

He sagged, like a deflating tyre.

I said, 'The Emperor relies on you to supply the powder he paid you for.'

'But we did!' He leapt to his feet. 'Every barrel leaving here is full to the brim! We weighed them ... fifty kilos weight per barrel! The quality is checked five times and proofed. I check it myself!'

Sweat was spreading through the armholes of his fat waistcoat. He pulled out a handkerchief and padded his brow. I motioned he should keep talking.

'Sand ...? We don't have any sand. Please, tour our facility. See the magazine, it's all checked to your standard ... Comet ... oh, please do sit down, won't you?'

'No. These full barrels, are they sealed when they leave?'

'Of course. A waxed cover and a tamperproof seal. They're perfect when we ship them. Maybe it's Grough Mill—'

'They had your stamp.'

He stuffed the outsized kerchief back in his pocket, fanned out his wings and composed himself. 'Comet, the ten thousand barrels you commissioned from us were perfect. We know the Castle's work depends on it. I'm loyal to the Emperor and to Thunder ... and to the King and Queen, and my Lady Governor Tern. The war is our business.'

'So where has six hundred tonnes of blasting powder gone?'

He left the chair and went to the window, looked out at punts sliding past each other on the narrow canal. Then he returned to the desk and pushed a pile of ledgers towards me. 'You accuse me of fraud? Here. See, we bought sulphur and nitrate. So having bought it, we need our returns. Why wouldn't we mix it? Every gram is accounted for ... All up to date and above board. I employ a hundred honest men. Why would I risk our livelihood?'

'Has anyone ever stolen powder?'

'Not a pinch. When they leave they change clothes. They carry no bags. Every mill is secure.'

In the end I had to agree that the accounts looked sound. On paper at least, Spiza had not lost a grain of powder. Neither had he lost his indignation, nor fear. He puffed up and down, repeating variations of: 'We work for the Empire, against the Insects.'

I closed the last tome. 'When you have a full shipment, who takes it?'

'The Wrought Wagon Company took yours to the Front. The powder we're making at the moment will be stored in the floating magazine.' He opened yet another account book, turned the page and ran his finger down the names for each shipment. The same few names appeared again and again in random order.

'What's this one? It's hard to read.'

'Nell.'

'A lady?'

'A lady of sorts. She has tattoos. Roses like cauliflowers everywhere.' He made a gesture as if block printing his arms. 'And all these little pictures between them.'

Roses on her arms. 'So she must be a Litanee?'

'Oh yes. The Litanee gypsies. They're incredibly good. They work very hard ... it's humbling to see.' Out came the handkerchief again and he wiped his hands on it. 'To be honest it's difficult to find anyone in Awia who'll work that hard, with such a good attitude ... for such a low wage.'

'Ah.'

There was a knock on the door. 'Coffee, coffee! ...To be honest, nothing's rolling on the highway these days that isn't in some way dependent on Litanee. They're so incredibly efficient. You may have noticed.'

'They carry a lot of the Castle's supplies.'

'Well, really I think Awia would grind to a halt without them. And Lowespass – begging your pardon.'

'These other names: Fullam ... Allen ...'

'Are in Nell's company.'

'It's all the same company?'

'Yes, well, she bid lowest.'

'I see. And they shipped the ten thousand barrels of gunpowder?'

Spiza raised round shoulders in agreement. 'They took the last shipment of triple-F musket powder north yesterday. They'll be on the Broad Road by now.'

'Well, I'll catch them up and ask them.' I shook his hand: his palm was moist to the touch. He bowed like an ex-fyrdsman and gratefully showed me the door. 'And please, Comet, remember to check Brolga's mill in Grough. If anyone sold you short I do believe he—'

'Thanks, Spiza.'

Outside, Saker was standing by the porch column watching the swans. Spiza's expression melted into a blend of astonishment and apprehension as he recognised who it was. Saker smiled mildly at him and we walked to the guardhouse.

'Did you find anything out?' he asked.

'Six hundred tonnes of blasting powder really is missing. It's serious. I'll telegraph to the Emperor. I need to know who has it, why, what the fuck they want with it. The Litanee are my next port of call.'

'*All* the Litanee?'

'Just one troupe. One of the names, Tressel, was the same as the cannon team.'

'Really?'

'But it isn't a rare name.'

We collected our horses and thanked the guard, and the gate swung closed behind us. 'What about you?' I said. 'Enjoy the tour?'

'Oh. Musket powder smokes appallingly because of the black charcoal. That's what we need to change. I urged them to think about it.' He stepped up into Balzan's saddle and slipped his foot into the far stirrup.

'I'll fly. Here.' I passed him Favel's guide rein. 'Take her back to Wrought. I'll do the nearest three mills and meet you at the manor house. Wait there, enjoy yourself, shake Raggy up a bit. Raid the cellars.'

'All right.'

Saker cantered off with my thick-coated mountain horse lurching behind Balzan. I ran, leaned into the wind, and with strong wing beats pulled myself high into the air. Wrought unfolded below me. There, the dark green fields gave way to buff-coloured sedge fringing the salt marsh, where acres of reedbeds prickled and chuckled as the sea fingered between them. The breeze cut up the smell of brackish brine, dried and rotting bladderwrack. It carried the sound of a factory bell from the direction of the steelworks. I leant on the salt-and-iodine wind and turned towards the washy scent of saltpetre. A pine plantation bristled below me, riven by ditches in the poor, soggy soil, and the tiled roofs of Brolga's Mill showed beyond it, with a glimmer of its own canal and low ships sliding out to the great tarred hulks chained motionless in the river.

Brolga's Mill and Kingfisher Mill protested their innocence and their records seemed above board. Blasting powder had been carried out of each one by a different company, on wagons or by barge, but *always* by a person with Rose tattoos. What would the Litanee want with six hundred tonnes of blasting powder?

I'd no idea, but I was going to find out.

CHAPTER 14

Wrought Manor: Sacrament

The breeze blowing from the saltings broke into unpredictable, peculiar eddies around the elaborate roofscape of Wrought. I landed lightly on the main hall ridge, surrounded by thin, black stone chimneys, glided down to the grass and bounded with sheer energy through the door of the North Tower.

I could hear Saker pouring his heart out via the grand piano, and when I entered the hall he stopped playing. It was about nine p.m. I threw my leather jacket onto the back of a chair. 'Go on.'

'Yes, well the damp has affected it.'

I sat down at the table and Raggiana, Tern's Steward, brought me beer, steak and potatoes, and took away Saker's used plate of the same. More basic fare than he's used to, I suppose. Tern's fashion house makes most of her money these days. All the weapons her factories produce go straight to the Front. Wrought never sees any profit from them, but at least it doesn't have to send fyrd.

'The powder mills look sound,' I said.

'If you believe them.'

'If we believe them. But Litanee gypsies carried the powder from all three.'

'Litanee carry everything,' Saker said, and paused in his playing to make a note on a manuscript.

'I know.'

'Are you going to look for them?'

'Yes.'

His saddle bag sat on the chair, flopped open and full of manuscript books; a sheaf of handwritten score lay on the table, its edges curled by use. I realised it was the same one he'd taken from Swallow's desk in her manor house last year.

'The Litanee do our dirty work,' I said.

'Well, god knows what they gain from it.'

'A living.' I selected an apple and took a bite. 'They don't have much choice. They go from one short-term job to another.'

'Oh, does that appeal to the Rhydanne in you?'

'*You* don't have to work at all.'

He glanced at the window without taking his fingers from the keys. 'When does a king stop working? When he's dead … There's a certain kind of bliss in going unnoticed,' he added dreamily. 'Like in the powder mill this morning. It'd be worth doing the gypsies' rootless jobs to have their freedom.'

'Don't romanticise.'

'Come on, Jant. How many times have you drafted them?'

I shrugged. You do see gypsies in the fyrd, but not often. They usually have a harder life than soldiers, who at least know the Castle will feed them.

Saker started playing again, consulting the manuscript in one hand and repeating very deliberately a sequence of notes.

'What are you doing, anyway?'

'Reconstructing Swallow's symphony.'

'Her unfinished symphony?'

'Yes.'

The sheaf of paper in front of me had been carefully tagged with placeholders. He was holding some pages from it, and copying down Swallow's furiously-fermenting scrawl into a foolscap notebook. 'She liked big noise and high drama, that's for sure,' he said. 'It whirls along. There are more tympani in this than I can right well get a grip on.' He put the manuscript down and looked at me directly. 'It'll take years. She was better than me … of course. She was so damn good.'

'I'm sorry, Saker.'

He reached out. 'Pass me the rest of it. There's a pattern here somewhere.'

I picked up the dog-eared papers, uncovering a green diary beneath, and took them to him. Tern's grand piano stood in the window bay and, through the quatrefoil stone-mullioned windows, you could see the servants' children playing on the lawn outside. They were running down a slope with their wings spread, and gliding the last few metres before they hit the grass. Waiting in the queue to glide, a girl beat her wings vigorously and drew herself up onto the tips of her toes. In a year or so she wouldn't be able to do that.

You could hear their giggles faintly behind Saker's broken music. The clear, late daylight fell across the piano, and left arched shadows on the walls, coloured circles from the roundels of armorial glass with Tern's family's martlet device. A split staircase at the far end rose to the rosewood and wrought iron balcony, which with its torchières and brass jardine stands with dark-leaved plants, led to Tern's master bedroom.

Beside me, on the long wall below the balcony, and half in its shade, hung a long tapestry in maroon and gold of the Castle's amphitheatre, with Saker in the foreground teaching me to fight Insects. Beyond it, the shadows of the staircase fell on an older, threadbare tapestry depicting Tern's father, Francolin, leaving on exile to Lowespass Fortress. He had stirred a rebellion against the king, back in 1891, causing me to chase Shira Dellin all over Carniss, and the king exiled him. Tern never saw her father again. Francolin's treason bankrupted his manor, which is why, after haunting Wrought alone for a year, Tern decided to marry. She put herself up for marriage, and soon money and gifts flooded in from her suitors. Tern gradually unwrapped Wrought from its winding sheets, and set the spiky-roofed pad on firm foundations again. She tested my dedication as a suitor so much she drove me to drugs for the first time, but I won her, with my gift of the gab, my prowess in bed and my link to the Circle.

I finished the beer, and picked up the book that had lain under Swallow's symphony. It was calfskin-bound, with gold-edged pages and secured by a clasp. I opened it and immediately recognised Swallow's frenetic, cuspate handwriting. This was her diary. Saker was carrying her diary. But it wasn't this year's; it was printed for ten years ago and half the pages were blank.

20 March 2030
C filled my dressing room with wildflowers and came to see me after the show. Me in front of the mirror, taking off pan stick!
Collect tuxedo
Brent is sadly lacking, bassoons fall behind time.

1 April 2030
I will join the Castle! I will, I will, I will! The Castle owes it to me. Pretend to *be* hard enough and you *become*!
Don't be tired. Never be tired! Push yourself! The Emperor will see!

2 April 2030
All I've achieved, all I do, and they still see me as a little girl! Either they want to sleep with me, or they assume a fatherly attitude. Some don't even believe a woman could have composed all this music. They try to discover which man had written my symphonies!

Swallow's self-urging and orchestral notes were all brief apart from the last entry, which flowed over so many pages she'd scribbled out the dates. I poured another beer and read on:

Sunday 27 June 2030
Today the Trisian arrived. Crowds packed north quay since Jant had advertised the arrival of Thunder's Challenger for weeks. Everyone was curious to see him.

It was drizzling and drops splattered the ensemble every time the wind flicked the pennants. They stuck like ropes around the flagpoles.

Jant flew in, a cross-shape against the clouds. He made an exhibitionist (but slippery) landing on the quay, to a little tentative applause, and ran to meet me. I was supervising Brent's band.

The music in my mind has been growing bolder. I am nearly ready to birth my symphony. At first I heard single notes which, like echoing bells, rang with mysterious meaning. I also heard long runs of quavers chasing up and down an invisible keyboard in my head. I always have music in my mind. I can't get rid of it, I have to channel it, exorcise it by writing it down, trapping it on paper. The five bars of the manuscript become a five-barred gate or wire fence to snare the notes. Sometimes I sing to release them, quivering like cage birds. I strolled the quay, composing in my head, since I needed a symphony as somewhere to record all those sounds, and clear them from taking over my mind.

The basso continuo was tumultuous because the smash of the waves was being incorporated in it. The recitativo was peculiar because the babble of the crowd resounded in my ears. Then, while I conducted the ninth and tenth recitals of Brent's band, I began to improvise an aria to be sung by a girl Challenger, who deserved immortality but was pushed into the background, as other men won it ahead of her, with the eyes of the crowd upon them.

Chorus of sobbing, reverberation of note in mid-scale. I paused and the sobbing continued. It was the slap of the wind on the topsails of a massive clipper.

Captain Wrenn sailed his ship *Cormorant* into harbour. Being the ex-Swordsman, he makes a great deal of money teaching men and boys swordplay, 'Enough to Challenge the Swordsman'. But he makes a greater fortune from this clipper Mist gave him.

The Trisian philosopher stood at the prow, taking it all in. He didn't let Wrenn fly any flag. He disembarked and Jant welcomed him at the gangway.

This man Capelin, is nearly bald, with a trimmed beard. He wore an odd robe gathered with a rope belt, and has a self-assured tenor voice – he could play the Lord of Lazulai in 'The First Insect'.

Jant said Capelin used to be a serious artist, who depicted people with great realism on the walls of the Amarot. And he's thrown it over to Challenge the Artillerist! Do you see how the Castle warps people from their calling and destroys art? This man is a painter! Well, then, he should be a painter, not an engineer of war!

At first I pitied Capelin, that he'd chosen to shun his true vocation in a bid for immortality. Then rage took over. A man of such talent and intelligence shouldn't lay himself at the Emperor's feet. Shouldn't bare his throat to San! It should be the other way round! I wished I could see the Emperor begging Capelin to paint for the Castle. He should be desperate to grant him immortality for a mural of 'Philosophers in the Capharnaum Marketplace'. Instead, Capelin seeks to be the Artillerist, of all things! The world has mangonels enough!

The band played 'Welcome' and Jant showed Capelin to the coach. He seemed both superior and withdrawn, as if he didn't want to touch anything. Maybe he was awed by our clipper (Tris has no trees or ships). Or maybe he was seasick.

He sat in the carriage as if in a poisonous bubble, and his only accompaniments were one small boy and a very heavy crate. Jant went with him, I followed in mine; we made our way through the crowd. Capelin found the throng distasteful, our pennants gaudy and the coach uncomfortable.

I wanted to work on my symphony, but I had to offer them hospitality. Jant was brought down to a strange state of composure, and hadn't dried out from flying in the clouds. I think he dopes himself to take the pain out of flying. His distance flights are beyond the limits of human – not Rhydanne – endurance and he still keeps going. I wonder if it's possible for immortals to die of exhaustion?

During the meal Jant tried to draw him on the nature of his Challenge, but Capelin kept it secret. He's like any man. I can't get to grips with them – they always seem overly loud and self-important, but they have no depth at all.

Jant stirred a drop of cat into his wine, not caring that I noticed. And became even more relaxed. If I could keep him here a month, I could get him off that stuff permanently. That'd show I'm worth a place in the Circle. If Tern is too indifferent and self-centred to help him, I will. She said I should leave him alone. Well, I can cure him, when she hasn't tried.

They embarked on the coach, the Trisian so superior he floated above everything. Jant an arabesque of long legs, folded into the coach like a spider, and drew away for the Challenge. I will follow tomorrow.

Monday 28 June 2030
I rehearsed what I'll say to the Emperor. Very important to be word perfect. Set off to the Castle. I am nervous but I must try. I *must*!
The rain a forte pizzicato on the roof of the coach.

Tuesday 29 June 2030

Wednesday 30 June 2030

Thursday 1 July 2030
Bunting has me in some coach-house, for I am ill.

Friday 2 July 2030
So angry I can't hold the pen! Fainting – Dizzy! – Delirious! What San did to me no one's had to suffer in the history of the world!

Saturday 3 July 2030
I shrink from setting this down. But I must record what happened and tell the true story. I must face it head on, as it whips up my anger, and that fury will inspire my symphony. I shall pace myself … I shall pace myself. I have the whole of the return ride to write it, and I'm writing on the coach.

Wednesday was that bastard Capelin's Challenge. I'd been staying at the Castle, in Jant's Myrtle Room, and I joined him and Tern in the Eszai's seats tiered below the Emperor's box. Opposite were stands overflowing with rabble who'd poured in to watch, because, as Jant said, Thunder always puts on a show.

The Trisian's odd appearance, lofty attitude and heavy crate had set tongues wagging. Spectators had come from the four corners of the Empire. There, on the grass, a single tarpaulin covered his siege engine – no bigger than a bass drum.

Beside it, Thunder's huge trebuchet stood like a ship aground. I listened to the hubbub of the crowd, for I was taking notes. They were in a tense, jeering mood, a burbling of deep woodwind and light percussion. Beside me, Tern's luscious, cantabile voice said, 'Do you know what it is?'

'Capelin won't tell me.'

'It's so small!'

'Don't judge it till you've seen him use it,' said Jant. Which was the sort of thing men always say.

Thunder had chosen to shoot first. He led his team onto the field and messed about with the treb. Jant pointed out its latest perfections but

I wasn't really listening. This was the perfect scene for my symphony. I thought it might become a Challenge Symphony. Listen, there's Tornado's bass tone and Jant's string section. There's the Emperor watching in his majesty. Here's Thunder whirring the windlass, creaking down the great arm and thudding a slingshot into the cup. There's a windsock streaming. While he messed around with it we looked down the field to where, two hundred metres away, referees had fixed a huge white section of Insect Wall. How many people had died cutting it out and bringing it here?

Thunder pulled a lever and the ball whooshed into the air. A *thwack* sounded like a snare drum and a crack appeared in the Wall. A referee climbed from his dugout and waved a red flag. Then for some reason, he ran away.

'He hit it precisely in the middle,' said Tern.

'He always does,' said Jant.

All the time I was steeling my nerves for my address to the Emperor. Pretty soon the Artillerist's position would be settled one way or another, and I could speak with San. Moreover, the music that constantly plays in my head was beginning to align with the scene on the field, assimilating the applause. I knew I could write this symphony. Instantly I heard the entire opus, every note, saw the three dimensional shape of the whole piece. I couldn't wait to write it down!

On the field, the Trisian emerged from his pavilion. Beside Thunder's magnificent tent, Capelin's was no bigger than a booth. His small boy followed, carrying a twisted taper of the sort you use to light lanterns. It was sparking.

Jeers and cat calls fluted over the benches. 'Baldy! Baldy!' the mortals laughed. Capelin took it with disdain. He was a good performer. He stood by his diminutive machine, bowed to the Emperor and to the Zascai. He didn't bow to us.

Everyone stood, with a rattle like castanets. Capelin held aloft a pocket watch then, like a magician whisked the cloth from his machine. The Zascai laughed uproariously. His siege engine was a shining brass tube like a stout post horn. It rested on a trolley. He piccolo'd with screws beneath it, then took the taper from his boy, who ran off and watched from a distance. Why so far? I thought, and I began to dread.

Capelin set the taper to the cylinder. Boom! Fortissimo!

Everyone recoiled onto the benches – this terrible sound, this *new* sound knocked us flat. It was thunder, manmade thunder! It untuned the air! It was louder than all the tympani in the world.

Jant clutched Tern to him, though patently she didn't need it.

Tornado took a step back, then he squared his shoulders and his expression. Hurricane looked furious, Cyan looked curious, and Mist dove for his cigarette case. Absolutely everybody looked at San, who was impassive. The mortals were picking themselves up, all fear and horror.

But Capelin was intent on his watch. He raised one arm in the air, brought it down, and a boom more sfortzando than before! Every orchestra together couldn't be so fortississimo! A ball of fire erupted from the Wall. Huge chunks flew into the air, more furioso than any force of Nature could fling them. Then smoke covered all, and people were shrieking.

As the smoke cleared we saw the Wall reduced to rubble, on the grass. Some Zascai huddled in groups. Others watched with wild surmise. Smoke was issuing from his stage device.

'Bravo!!' I sang out. 'Encore!!' I turned to Jant. 'It throws sound!'

'It throws fire,' he said. He was still squashing Tern's breasts against his stupid little pecs. 'It must be some kind of chemical.'

'Which?'

'Some kind ...'

Capelin swept the stalls with a gaze of scorn and beneficence. I hated him. He stuck his taper in the soil and bowed, looking up at the Emperor. He announced in a voice a pitch too low, 'I place my cannon and many other inventions at your service, Eternal Emperor, and I claim the title Thunder.'

San stood and extended his hand. Capelin strode up the steps and passed so close I smelt the acrid smoke on his robe. It was pungent and acidic, like match heads and men's urinals, and I realised that from now on, everything would smell like that.

He kissed the Emperor's hand.

'You are Thunder, the Artillerist,' said San. He took Capelin into the Circle and made him immortal. Down on the grass, the former Artillerist became just a mortal man again. He felt the Circle dropping him, and cried out in rage. He leapt up and charged at Capelin. I didn't see, because I was dreaming how, soon, it will be my turn to kiss San's hand, and what the instant of immortalisation will feel like. But Jant swore. He jumped down the benches, spread his wings and glided the last few stands, sprinted towards the beaten Artillerist and reached him before he'd run half the distance. Jant drew his sword and held him back.

'It's a trick!' yelled the former Artillerist. 'A set up! He's a stage magician! The wall was on a fire pit! He blew up coal dust! Fuck you, Messenger, let me get him!'

This was my chance. I picked up my guitar and walked to the Emperor's box.

I looked up at San's thin form, his white fyrd general's clothes, though not at his face. Behind me, Tern called me, but I ignored her. I summoned my voice *enfatico* that can stun an auditorium. 'My lord Emperor, I state my petition to join the Circle, for I am the world's greatest musician. At your service I place my music and my life – they're one and the same.'

He raked me with a gaze that searched my mind, and a depth of unwelcome that made me squirm. 'Governor Awndyn. This is the seventh time you have appeared before me with the same request, and the answer is no.'

I bowed. 'My lord, I've finished my Symphony for a Thousand, and if you were present at its première, you would approve my talent.'

Now everyone was listening to me! The stands fell hushed.

'I know your talent,' San said. 'I've heard your ten symphonies. You *are* the best musician in the world; perhaps the best in history. But the purpose of my Circle is to fight the Insects. You cannot help.'

'I can inspire men to fight.'

'If that was the sole use of your music, you would wither away. In fact, to put your music to any *use* whatsoever would mar it. Pressure to *produce* would destroy your ability to create.'

'It's proved its use in making me money and I still create,' I said.

'Money is a very crude measure of success.'

'I can inspire men to love.'

'Oh. Are they not capable of that on their own accord?'

Laughter burst from the terraces. I ground my teeth. I was shaking with fear and now everyone was laughing at me. Thousands of people, the laughter like sawing violins bearing down on me. All the Eszai, I hated them all! Jant, Cyan, Tornado, this new Thunder! I was as good as them! Why wouldn't San see that?

'Swallow,' he said firmly. 'These men and women you claim to inspire to love or fight are mortals. Their fashions change and they will produce another musician with a different style. If such a one Challenges you there could be no fair competition. It would be a matter of taste.'

'I can command any style. Immortality would give me a chance to explore the genres within me and bring them to birth. As for those who Challenge me, well! Quality shines out no matter what we're playing.'

'Musicians are not soldiers. They resent leaders.'

'They recognise my gift.'

San sighed. 'Ah … Do they? Thunder has just destroyed that wall.

A demonstration of power no man can deny. Yet many people cannot recognise good music. They would question your place in the Circle. And what petitions would flood in! Writers, painters, poets and dancers would seek immortality. These are men's crafts, their arts, but no reason to live forever when Insects are consuming the Empire. After Thunder has brought us cannon, you offer us concertos!'

I was trembling but I rallied: 'You're condemning all artists to death and only allowing warriors to gain eternal life.'

'They are only immortal for a while. But without them, the hordes will overrun us.'

'I've proved myself as a warrior.'

'Swallow, don't try to be something you aren't, in order to gain a prize whose criteria you do not meet. You make your own prizes every day. Why do you lust after the one I offer?'

'I want to live forever.'

'The Circle protects the world from the Insects. The Castle still works for you, Swallow. If it weren't for their skill and leadership you'd be struggling to survive instead of composing. Take the chance to compose while your music can thrive, and we'll ensure it lives forever.'

'But I will not?'

'No.'

The hope drained from me. I felt people's amusement, loathing and schadenfreude radiating from the stands like heat. I gasped, but the Emperor continued, 'Do not come here again, Swallow Awndyn. Petition me no longer! You are a peerless musician. Go, be a musician! You will never be an immortal.'

The crowd was delighted I was cut to the quick. They started laughing, with a horrible vindictive edge. Some of them called 'Oooh!', some shouted, 'Never be an immortal!' – and it spread until the whole stand was bellowing spiteful laughter at me. At me alone.

Boiling in embarrassment I was stranded before the Emperor. I couldn't go forward and I couldn't go back. I don't know how, but as the laughter swelled, somehow I made my way down onto the grass.

Hurricane called, 'Loser! You don't belong with the Eszai!'

His thuggish followers in the opposite stand started chanting, 'Loser! Loser! Loser!'

Deafening slow clapping.

'Loser! Loser! Loser!'

I halted right before him and began to sing. I recalled the first canto Act III of *The Mayor of Diw* and gave him Ata's defiant aria at full blast.

How unfair he was, how I must be given room to fly: the words rose unbidden from my memory and I sang like I've never sung before.

The savage chant of the crowd battled with my soprano.

Loser! Loser! Loser!

Tern watched from under her parasol, with her poker face. Jant and Tornado had gathered beside Thunder's brass cannon. They didn't know what it was, but they liked it. They were waiting impatiently for him to explain it and I was just an entr'acte.

I doubled my intensity, used gestures *drammatico*, but the crowd's din surged and drowned me. Hatred knotted within me. I hated them all! I loathed the Emperor! I detested the Eszai!

Loser! Loser! Loser!

All I could do was go, and die. I was an inferno of hatred in a woman's shell. I left the field with my head high, still singing, and the laughter rang in my ears louder than the cannon.

5 July 2030

The coach draws in to Awndyn. My hatred burns white hot and I'll wreak havoc on the place. I am a vessel of hatred for everything and everyone. Everything and everyone! Except dear C. I will write to her ... she will understand. She will hear me scream. Dear, dear, C ...

All the following pages were blank. I put the diary down.

'D,' Saker was muttering. 'D, D, D, D. Not F.' He looked up from the concert grand. 'What were you reading? Oh. Swallow's diary ... I found it in her desk drawer. I couldn't bring myself to burn it.'

'It just stops.'

'After Thunder's Challenge? Yes. She never wrote another word after that. Not another word. Just music. This ... thing.' He riffled the Unfinished Symphony. 'This tangle of a masterpiece with all the cannon. Poor Swallow.'

I looked at her name on the diary's fly leaf. The block of its gilded pages caught the sunset light.

'I should've burnt it,' said Saker. 'It says things about me that I don't want to become common knowledge. She never understood why I'd give my life for Cyan.'

'And about me.'

'Ha, yes. She thought she could stop you taking cat.'

'Poor Swallow,' I echoed. I pushed the book away, an artefact of a great composer. 'The truly ambitious recognise the impossible.'

'Getting you off cat?'

'No. Joining the Circle. Only an insane person keeps levelling the same petition and expecting a different answer.'

'She wasn't insane. She was trying to break through.'

'But San told her it was impossible. To keep trying *was* insane. Maybe she *was* mad.'

'Maybe she was Eszai material.' He played trills distractedly, changed them to tremolos, and then into a savage up-and-down glissando that echoed off the balcony. 'Where a bit of madness helps. Cyan's refined your musket to five times the range and accuracy. Possibly therefore she's five times madder.'

The sunset was blazing, flat and golden through the windows, and the hall seemed cast in red shadows. Saker's half-shaded face was burnished bronze. 'San killed her,' he said. 'San's rejection killed Swallow. Oh, our Emperor has much to answer for!'

'But ...'

'Did you hear the Symphony of a Thousand?'

'No. I—'

'It opened soon after that diary entry. August. August ... that would be ten years ago. Shit ... The concert hall in Hacilith was only just large enough to hold it. She scored it for a thousand instruments, three choirs of men, women and children. It raised the roof. Jant, you were too busy building the telegraph. Swallow herself didn't attend. She didn't conduct it; she never even heard it. She stayed in Awndyn all that time. San killed her, all right. Just like he's killing you.'

'What?'

'Making you inject all that scolopendium and going to the Shift.'

I pushed my sleeve back and looked at my arm. Surely it didn't show quite so much. 'He isn't killing me. He's keeping me alive.'

'One day, Jant, you won't make it home ... It was the repeated shocks that wore her out,' he said. 'She was strong, but changes and changes and changes exhaust our energy and sap our resilience. Eszai who focus on just one thing stay firm to their mark and keep their strength. Swallow had focus in spades, but she was naive to think that San would change his mind. Of course, after the Challenge, she wouldn't want to live the rest of her life fluctuating idly with sick fatigue and languid doubt, like a Zascai. She couldn't stand living with broken hopes. Death was purer ... She was so very naive.'

'Naivety leads to misanthropism.'

'Oh, for sure.'

He performed a most ideal arpeggio, and another, running into sharps and flats until he couldn't think of any more and switched to scales in double thirds. It reminded me of the time they tapered me off cat, that rainy late summer after Cyan's Challenge, in Micawater Palace, with Saker downstairs standing by the window, playing the violin, and the Lake Gate open to the muddy public. The trompe d'oeil figures stepped out of the frescos, falling, tumbling, gesticulating, onto the coral patterned carpet.

'Swallow suffered from a great fear of dying,' he said. 'She experienced the world so richly and loved her sensations so much, she didn't want it to stop. She was extremely scared of no longer existing. That's what drove her to petition San seven times. But then ... after that Challenge she knew she'd blown her chance to get into the Circle ... Maybe the world didn't seem so bright and vibrant to her afterwards.'

'Rich sensations ...' I said.

'Yes. A rich internal dialogue. She had a wealth of wonder in the simplest things. Blackthorn blossom in the May sunlight made her cry out in joy.'

'Like the Shift. The world must have seemed like the Shift to her.'

'That's how she composed so well,' he said. 'It was her Shift. I never liked to see you addicted. I always tried to take scolopendium away from you. I tried to make you stop, Jant. And yet ... I've wanted to see the Shift myself. The beauty of Dunlin's court. The crazy places you describe.'

'I thought you didn't believe me.'

'After Frost's Battle, when the worm-thing appeared. The worm-thing I couldn't shoot ...'

'The Vermiform.'

'... Then I had to accept there was a worm-thing. Do you see?'

'Yes.'

'When I left the Circle the Emperor invited me to dinner with him. Just him and me, remember? San told me all manner of wonderful things. He told me Dunlin leads many nations against the Insects. Your Equinnes. The blue ones ...'

'The Tine.'

'And the fishy women.'

'Naiads? Stinguish? Thula?'

'Oh, god, I don't know. Why didn't you tell me?'

'I *did* tell you. I've been telling you for years.'

Saker shook out his hands, drained a glass of brandy from the piano top, and began playing a sensitive melody that was very compelling. 'San told me cat wasn't the only way to Shift. Someone at the limits of endurance may Shift, like ... oh, like a badly-wounded soldier. Or you can reach Epsilon through meditation.'

'It'd have to be very profound,' I said. 'A shark told me once.'

'Well, have you tried?'

'I can't keep still long enough. But I bet the Emperor could.'

Saker looped the piece again. 'He didn't give me the impression that he visits the Shift. Rather, that he's wary of it. Frightened, even. I don't know why.'

'He's old enough to have perfected meditation.'

'Fighting Insects, I'd want to.'

He started again with a smooth transition, and the music blended a many-layered harmony. 'Rayne has visited the Shift. Even my daughter admitted she's seen this Gabbleratchet. So I want to see it.'

'No, you don't!'

'I'm not frightened. What could it possibly do?'

'Oh, you wouldn't believe!'

'I *do* believe ...' Neat key change, little flurry, the tune started again. I felt all the tension flowing out of me.

'Peaceful, isn't it?'

'Yes.'

'Do you think I can play myself into the Shift?'

'With that?'

'I didn't write it. Swallow wrote it for me. Before anger wrecked her music. Before hatred destroyed it. Back when I thought there was a chance she could love me.'

'It's relaxing.'

'It's a musical joke ... At the end there's a *da capo* and it refers you to the start. So you start again and play it through, and you reach the *da capo* again and return to the beginning and play it through, and you reach the *da capo* and you just go seamlessly round and round. There is no *coda*. It's a palindrome, beautifully done, a ring, a circle ... a never-ending circle. That's what she called the piece: "The Circle".'

He smiled wistfully. 'The joke being, of course, that as an immortal I could play it forever ...'

Key change, grace notes, the intertwined melody washed over us. 'Thank god for the brandy. My fingers never used to hurt before, but I'm older now ... I've always wanted to. And now I can. Let's do it.'

'Saker—'

'Listen ...'

I laid my head on my folded arms and let the pellucid notes flow over me. I was more relaxed than I've been ... ever in my life before. The constant churn of thoughts in my head ceased and I was surprised at their absence. No language ... just nothing ...

Swallow had accessed the calm at the heart of immortality, the calm we should all feel but never do. She had torn aside our anxieties, reached through the depths of being to the peace that lies beneath. It lies beneath everything, this sea of nothingness – and how stupid we are to cover it up with our daily worries. Swallow could not only see it, she could express it, and now I was feeling the stillness underlying reality; the serenity of space beyond all the planets; the tranquil release of giving up in the face of immeasurable distance, immeasurable time; vastnesses and possibilities we cannot conceive. We are so tiny at the brink of infinity that in grateful thanks we yield, let go, and relinquish ourselves. It is the act of death.

I saw the room as just a thin picture stretched over the motionless presence, printed on tissue through which I could easily push my fingers and tear it. There's an empty space beyond. So, since nothingness underlies everything we know and grasp and wish to do, of course there's only calmness left.

The sunset faded into pink, then grey, and the hall became a patchwork of dappled shades. We were both still drained from the battle and I dozed as wax drops fell silently on the candelabra base beside me. The light from its candles didn't reach the window bay, where Saker played the melody with his eyes closed, being the instrument through which it plays, it plays itself.

The flurry happened twice each cycle, the end sealed to the beginning with no audible join, it looped the same refrain ... Flurry, key change and lost, it played him.

I suddenly had an image of my mountain. A pointed peak rosy with the light that comes before dawn in high Darkling. It was so solid, so weighty. But even the mountain was unreal and I scratched it, eased my fingers through, peeled down a strip and opened a portal. Nothingness lay behind it, it lies behind everything.

Saker nodded over the keys. The pointed panes backed by darkness behind him were mirrors barely reflecting the length of the piano. The muscles in his forearms flickered as he played. The key change, the grace notes, the ring began again ... and every few minutes it looped time round ... one, two, three in the morning ...

He was hypnotised, caught up in the cycle and unaware of anything else. He nodded, played on, his head drooping. Your instinct is to wake with a start, shake yourself, but he forced himself through, held himself to it, and kept going. Played, and sank deeper.

And played. The candles guttered out. Round and round the music flowed until the notes lost all meaning. As when you look too long at a printed word, it becomes simply a shape on the page. Then you realise nothing is real and you're a step towards the Shift. The notes seemed to sound together, one chord, the time between them was collapsing.

And round
and round
and round

I opened my eyes and saw with jolting clarity the hall a flat unreal picture. The floor was slick with moonlight. Saker played in a trance, his cheek resting on the piano top. Reality wore paper-thin like melting snow while it seemed unchanged. Suddenly in patches here and there, transparent – and I saw through to the infinite . . .

He was completely under. I was hypnotised, but not as deeply. Music has a greater effect on him. He sagged forward – onto the piano and his hands slipped off the keys with a horrible discord that echoed round Wrought.

He's gone. Was he Shifted? I couldn't tell. Moving slowly, I fumbled for my tin containing my syringe, uncorked a phial and pulled a dose into the barrel. I paused when the plunger reached my normal measure, then sucked in more. A dose and a half will send me there. Through my trance I felt the weight of terror that grips me when shooting an overdose. But the chord still rang a faint chime and Saker lay on the piano.

Don't move, my friend. I'll be right there.

I sank it in the crook of my arm and slumped on the chair.

and then it was as simple as leaving a room, to walk through.

'But we're not walking,' said Saker.

'Don't overthink it.'

'How can I hear you?'

'You can't. We're following the same train of thought.'

'Just nothingness . . .'

'The Emperor must know it well.'

'No wonder he's scared.'

Saker sounded decisive: 'Where am I going? I'm going to Epsilon.'

The brightness was so piercing I threw my arm over my eyes. Lowered it, we were standing high on the upper tier of an amphitheatre, on a promontory, with the ocean sparkling blue on either side. The marble tiers were packed with creatures, and people, every kind I knew and most kinds I didn't, shouting and cheering and watching the combat in the ring.

A huge spider, the size of a coach and bright red, with black fangs the length of scimitars, was chasing down an Insect – a big one! – scurrying across the pitch as fast as it could. The spider jumped with all eight legs, covered an almighty distance and landed squarely on the Insect, plunged its fangs into its carapace – we heard the crack and the creatures cheered.

Saker stared at it, beside himself with elation. 'This is it! This is what I thought it'd look like!'

'You're lucky. I see the city—' I pointed to the horizon where Epsilon, thirty carat gold, blue glass shards and concrete, tumbled towards the sea. '—And Cyan saw a blasted heath.'

'Why should it be any different?' He gazed at the shining seats, trying to take it all in. Huge arches behind us, standing high around the rim of the amphitheatre, framed the sea, and a variety of ships, some with brocade sails, some giving off smoke from steel chimneys, some that change the very action of the waves into power, slipped peacefully between spouting whales and glistening shoals.

'Where's Dunlin?'

I pointed at the box, some rows below us on the long side of the oval, and Saker set off towards it. He was gleaming in sun-gold scale mail on a scarlet leather arming shirt, with a crimson scarf tucked into the neck and the tassels hanging between his wings. On his legs, he'd imagined into being fluted gold plate armour with gothic edges and riding boots with sunburst rowel spurs. At his waist manifested a red leather quiver full of spaced arrows with striped flights. Over his shoulder appeared a sinuous bow on a strap zigzag-embroidered citrine and carmine. His hair and wings without any grey, honey-coloured in the sunlight.

I said, 'You're just a projection, here. You can look like anything you want.'

'This is what I look like.'

As we walked down the steps I gave myself a snakeskin jacket like Cyan's and skinny blue jeans. Inland we could see the vibrant grassland, with herds of epochs timelessly grazing, and further off woolly mammons with their golden calves, shining necklaces and designer label baseball caps. Their jewellery flashed in the sun as they lumbered nose to tail across the plain. There were groups of flummoxen with shaggy coats, huge horns and a head at both ends, standing quite immobile, permanently puzzled as to which end should lead.

A pair of aerial cuttlefish rose from the crowd, floated over and inspected us, changing colours constantly, then zoomed off, tentacles trailing, to tell Dunlin.

Saker watched them go, spotted Dunlin in the spectators' box draped with silk, tried to make his way there but distracted by the creatures on the way. He stared at the voluminous jaws of a great group of Social Morays, standing tall and wriggly on their tails, chatting happily amongst themselves.

We passed a couple of Spriggans, dark green ivy people with thievish grins, whispering about us behind leafy hands, giggling and twitching their tendrils round our feet. Then a pensive group of thick-furred Stalos, ogres each with his hunting dog, sat watching the scarlet spider devour more Insects. The Spriggans' living ivy bumbled up their hairy legs.

We descended to the level of Dunlin's box, and picked our way through the crowd, apologising all the way for treading on toes, paws and twigs. Tine on the steps were selling refreshments, calling, 'Ladies' fingers! All organic! Made out of organs!'

Marsoupials with furry ears were lading broth from their open pouches. A friendly Nomble was handing out water bottles, and the big blue Tine were selling buckets of blood.

'Those are the Tine,' I said.

'My god! And what are those?'

'Igigi.'

'Can they fly?'

'Oh, yes. On their days off.'

The crowd of three hundred Igigi took up two whole rows, laughing and chucking stuff into the ring, all tanked-up and unruly, opening beer bottles with their hooked beaks. These Igigi have the head and wings of an eagle, human arms and body, and body odour too. They get lumbered with all the heavy lifting and manual jobs, digging ditches and baking bricks.

'Damn,' said Saker. 'Those stinking things can fly?'

Some entertainment at the far side of the ring, a formation flight of the shining steel Sentient Drones and a Tine Choir of Ejaculating Cocks, which was a thing to behold, but we hardly glimpsed it – so much was going on. It was hard to thread through the packed crowd, pushing thieving hands off our swordbelts, and thanking the people who moved. Saker headed to a gap but it turned out not to be – a space where the Elephant of Conscience was sitting, quite invisible but you can feel when it's in the room.

There was the Great Lavra, a huge, hulking being with slow-flowing skin of bright orange molten rock, steaming and cooling on the surface to black cinders. We steered clear of it and climbed the next set of steps – now we could see out of the far arches across Osseous plain to the mountains under the turmeric sky, where nothing lives except crabby hermits in their shell-like little caves.

And up we came to Dunlin's box, but before we reached the railings a great cloud of elegant women arose as one from the benches and crowded round us. They were tall, thin and very comely, with four arms, eyes faceted like diamonds and thin cranefly wings like leaded glass blurring faster than even I could see.

They pressed themselves around Saker, spanning his broad chest with their hands. 'Mate and die. Mate and die.' Whickering around us with seductive smiles, licking thin butterfly-tongues against his neck. One was trying to undress me. 'Mate and die. Mate and die.'

'You or me?' he asked them.

'They're Ephemera.' I waved them away. 'They only live a few days.'

'Like midges,' he said, exhilarated. 'Get off my backside!'

'Dunlin likes them.'

'*Does* he?'

'They fight Insects too. Because they know they'll die, they lead Forlorn Hopes. Buzz off!' I told them. 'We're not Epher-males ... It'll never work.'

'What are those white monsters ...? People? Candle white with flames for heads?'

'Something horrible out of Dekabrayer.'

'Does Dunlin use them too?'

'Yes. These are all Dunlin's peoples.'

We passed two Beetles sucking reflex-blood lovingly and fetishistic-ally from each other's shoulder joints, past the High and Beautiful Beachcombers of Vista Marchan, past a single proud Nereid, clothed in a drape of constantly-moving water. She can command any marine animal when her feet are in the sea. Then there were a couple of small Porkles, and before we could reach the gate into the private box we had to pass a gigantic glass aquarium.

Thula swimming inside it immediately swept over to examine us. Beautiful women and muscular, scale-perfect men, they pressed up against the pane in curiosity. The women began to kiss the inside of the glass, their incredible hair swirling out around them.

Saker said, 'Mermaids!'

'Ah, no, don't—'

He'd already gone to gaze at the breathtaking, high-cheekboned girls forcing themselves against the pane, their fish tails flicking to keep them upright. 'Mermaids! Jant, like in the stories! You never said they were real!'

'They're not mermaids. They prey on mermaids. They're Thula, escort to the Nereid.'

'Thula ...'

'Don't look at them!'

A Thula girl tilted her head to give him the most lascivious gaze I've ever seen. She flattened her fish-cold nipples on the glass. Her silver skin was iridescent – dark scales on her shoulders and the tops of her arms, grading to paler silver below, and her rib cage ended in curved slits under which pink gills tiered where lungs were supposed to be.

From the hips she tapered into a sumptuous platinum tail, with rays of cartilage keeping the fins open.

Saker pressed his hands to the glass, matching her unnerving claws. Enchanted, he said, 'She wants me to swim with her.'

'She certainly does. They'll drown you.'

'But … she's magnificent!'

'Believe me, they'll seize you and hold you under. It's how they get their meat.'

The Thula beheld him longingly with large eyes of sapphire blue. Behind her plump silver lips, her teeth were short and sharp, and water washed into her mouth and out of her gill slits.

'She's breathing water.'

'Yes, but she can't breathe air. She can haul herself out of the sea but she slips back in when her gills start to dry.'

'She's curious … about me.'

'She's wondering what you are.'

He spread his wings and she widened her eyes. 'She wants to kiss me.'

'She *wants* your warm, beating heart.'

'Jant, I can fly underwater.'

'There'll be a swirl of blood, and you're gone!'

Also in the tank were a mirth of Stinguish and a few Maidmers, which have the heads of codfish but human lower bodies, legs and genitals. Saker studied the Thula as if he didn't know whether to fuck her or fry her. I pulled him away.

'Let go! I want to watch.'

'You haven't time!'

'Where are the mermaids? Can I swim with actual mermaids?'

'Not here, or she would've eaten them.'

The tank became shallow at one end, and basking with the warm water washing over him was a naked man, brawny, his kelp-brown hair tangled with shells. Mournfully he watched us pass, with sloe-black, doleful eyes.

'Is that a merman?'

'He's The Great Silkie. On land, he's a seal. At sea, he's a man. Got cursed the wrong way round.'

We came to Dunlin's box. Dunlin had been watching us since the tank. He was on his feet with a shocked expression. '*Lightning*?'

Saker stared. 'Dunlin …?'

'Lightning, why are you here? Are you …?'

'He's not dead,' I said. 'It's a Shift. Not with drugs, no! With music! Can you believe it?'

Dunlin scrutinised Saker, who stood astonished, overwhelmed at seeing his old comrade-in-arms. Whatever he'd planned to say had evaporated. Then he bowed. 'Dunlin Rachiswater! I've waited so long to speak with you.'

Dunlin opened his arms. 'Then come here.'

They embraced like brothers. Dunlin was shorter, barrel-chested, in a pleat-backed coat, breeches and boots. Nothing here looked regal at all – what I'd thought was a canopy was simply a sunshade. Also in the box was Dunlin's Map of All Worlds, a large black newt with no distinguishing features and a white goose.

The goose was a goose. Let me describe the map. It was my original chart of Epsilon, on a plain trestle table, but now with ten or more layers above and below it. Dunlin had cut pockets into the table at specific places and pasted maps below to signify portals into other worlds. Layers of maps were suspended on struts above, interconnected at angles, illustrating further worlds tangling into gnarly nexuses. At places one or two maps hovered alone, and near the middle he'd constructed an origami tower, representing god knows what. The whole thing was a fabulous sculpture – chaotic in its hopeless, fanatical attempt to show reality. Diagonally, in red pencil, in a menacing arc across all the worlds, he'd marked the front of the Insect expansion.

I found the Fourlands between Epsilon and Plennish, something called Sidney above Plennish and, below Epsilon, the horror of Dekabrayer with the Front creeping onwards.

'Really, you're not dead, are you?' Dunlin pressed Saker's shoulder. 'Don't say you're staying?'

'No ... So much has happened! I'm married now, to Eleonora Tanager, and—'

Dunlin frowned.

'His Shift won't last long,' I said.

Saker tried to figure out what to say. 'Dunlin ... I came to thank you for saving Cyan from the Gabbleratchet. And to make a few requests ...'

'The Vermiform saved Cyan.'

'But didn't you ask it to?'

'We agreed to rescue her, on condition she doesn't come here again.'

'What's that?'

'It's a goose,' I said.

'Look!' Dunlin gestured at the pitch, where the spider was sucking the last bug dry. 'This is our confederation against the Insects. I'm not a king, any more; there are no titles here. All these people struggle with the Insects. We're testing new inventions.'

'That spider's very effective,' I said.

'It's a Cell Spider.'

'Do you have any spare?'

'No. Not really ... I could do with more, myself.' Dunlin ran a hand over his grey hair and stretched out his long, cinnabar-red wings. 'I can only find one Cell Spider per world. They're solitary, so they must be able to Shift. They're the only natural predators of Insects I've found as yet, but those fangs will drive through plate armour, too.'

Saker was still dazed, so I kept going. 'What else are you testing?'

'The Sentient Drones ... which are invaluable, although their satellite's in orbit around an entirely different world. And I've discovered some Insect parasites. Insects from Plennish have yellow ticks clinging to their shells – you won't have seen them. We're trying to infect more.'

'Any success?'

'I think it's slowing them down at Sauria.'

I said, 'We've been filling Insect passages with gas from lime kilns. It suffocates them. And we're blowing them up with gunpowder charges. I know you're looking for uranium.'

'Yes?'

'San says you can mine it in Lowespass if you help us clear the Paperlands.'

Dunlin laughed. 'Ah, Jant. Always asking for assistance. You don't know what you're offering. That weapon's so powerful you can't occupy the land afterwards. The Plennishers only use it *in extremis*. They don't half destroy the Insects, though!'

'Then glowing bugs attacked us. They tunnelled to Osseous and spread the contamination to my country.' A chiselled woman, Magor, who captained the Equinnes clopped in, and sat on the bench, watching the Cell Spider perforate a new batch of Insects.

Saker stared at her. He said to Dunlin, 'The need for these innovations is proof we're overwhelmed.'

'Oh, Mica! Just what I'd expect you to say! We're progress. There's no stopping us. But it's good ... very good ... to see you again.'

'I'm grateful for the chance. I'm glad you're still ... in existence. Still fighting.'

'I'll never stop.'

Saker nodded hesitantly and swallowed. 'I've been wanting to visit since I left the Circle ... I have a request.'

'Yes?'

'I'm mortal now, and at some point I'm going to die. Before my death, however it happens, I will ask Jant to give me a dose of scolopendium and lead me here, as he did for you. Then we can fight side by side, Dunlin, the way we used to. As we did for twenty years. Rachiswater and Micawater – just think what we could achieve!'

Dunlin looked uncertain. 'And you'd live here forever?'

'My second chance at immortality.'

He broke into laughter. 'Of course! You'd love it! And we need you. We'll show you Epsilon! Osseous. The Aureate. The Airfield!'

'Hey!' I said. 'Do I have a say in this?'

'Comet,' said Saker. 'I know you brought Cotinga through.'

'Ah. Well—'

'And Exhellanie from Shivel, when the Insects got him.'

'We kept it secret!'

'Tern told me how much they paid you. I know San forbade you to bring men here, because he doesn't want a drugs epidemic, but you're saving dying people, aren't you? In my will you'll be remembered ... generously.'

I shook my head. I didn't want to think about it, but Dunlin and Saker, one silver-grey, one scarlet-gold, shook hands and laughed.

'And what do you want from us?' said the goose.

Saker almost jumped out of his skin. 'It spoke!'

The goose regarded him disdainfully.

'This,' said Dunlin. 'Is *The* Monogoose. One of the most powerful beings of all time.'

'There's always One Monogoose,' said Magor.

It padded on webbed feet to Saker and pecked experimentally at its reflection in his highly-polished leg armour.

'I'm delighted to meet you,' he told it.

The goose tipped its head and observed him beadily. 'Well, you haven't answered my question.'

'I want a more efficient and frequent means of communication between the Empire and the Shift, so Jant doesn't have to keep pumping that vile drug into his veins.'

'Chance would be a fine thing,' I said.

'Tern hates it,' he said. 'And so do I. San should realise it's improvident and I think you'll thank me, because it causes you no end of grief.'

Dunlin glanced at the goose. The goose returned to nibbling Saker's cuisses, and said, 'Dunlin, give them some Verms.'

The old king of Awia beckoned us to his map and we gathered around the three-dimensional edifice. I stood near part of the Epsilon badlands where the Igigi originate, and some Musussu – sinuous dragons with long legs, single horns and a bad case of religion. All the names on the map were in different handwriting, various alphabets, bizarre symbols. Thousands of hands (claws and paws) had contributed to it. And beside every label, sat a Vermiform worm.

Dunlin hovered his finger over the thin, pink worm on the dot representing Epsilon. It stretched, hooked itself over his knuckle, and inched energetically onto his palm.

He said, 'Saker, the Vermiform has worms in all these worlds, observing constantly. They bring me news, help me organise. It has some in your world too, right now – in Micawater, in Tanager, in the Castle's Berm Lawns. It's my messenger.'

'I thought I was your messenger,' I said.

'Jant, you can't be everywhere. The Vermiform *is* everywhere. If you can communicate with it, you can speak to me.'

Saker said, 'Can they tell us where the primary Insect tunnels are? The ones leading from here? So I can block them and we don't get re-infested?'

'If it can survive Insects long enough, you might convince it to explore Lowespass.'

'I want to reach Murrelet. We were practically at Mistral's Dip when Thunder botched our advance. If I can prevent bugs Shifting in, Eleonora and I, and Cyan, can reach the ruined city!'

'Are you closing on Murrelet?' said Dunlin.

'Yes. We were just south of Quartforche.'

Dunlin raised his eyebrows. 'Then you have advanced.'

'I want Murrelet back. I want to run the road through Quartforche the way it used to be. Think what it means for the Castle to reclaim it … and, besides, my family originated there. I want to walk in that ruined palace, with Eleonora. I want to dance with her in its hall. Wouldn't you? Dunlin, the more you help us, the more we'll add vital detail to your map. Do other worlds adjoin us? Can we chart Insect passages themselves?'

Dunlin indicated the Fourlands on the edge of their nest. The north of our continent disappeared into it, surrounded by Epsilon and Osseous through which marched the front of their unstoppable advance. Sure enough, there was a worm coiled on the symbol for the Castle. Dunlin addressed the one in his palm: 'Vermiform, can we have some more?'

A pause. Then, behind us, the pitch erupted. Soil and sawdust surged up – a trunk of intertwined worms cannoned out of the ground, flinging earth, stones and bits of Insect all over the spectators, who started bawling. It rocketed to the height of our box, tapered to a point and bent towards us, its fleshy surface bulging in ridges. It sculpted itself – a seething woman's face emerged. Its eyes flicked open, its floating hair snaked.

The column filled the whole pitch, swelled to breasts, waist and hips, widened and flattened to the shape of a dress fishtailing out to a mass of worms.

She leant towards us – her face blocked the audience, who were in screaming disarray.

'Kiss me,' she said.

Dunlin laughed. Saker was staring with a half-smile, forcing himself to feel entertained, rather than backing off in horror. She threw a tentacle between them and wrapped it twice round my waist. I pulled against it, but she wrenched me forward and her face flowed into the box.

The worms of her face moved against each other. Her mouth yawned wide and I saw her tongue made of woven worms. She stank of damp soil, carrion so old it's merging into pungent humus.

Thousands of tendrils wound me in a total caress, stroking my body – thighs, bottom, wings, throat – lifted me off my feet. Terrified, I struggled. I snatched a breath, then her face poured forward onto mine – her hair whipped over and tangled – I felt her forehead flowing around my temples, hooding me.

My skin swarmed with worms. Her tongue forced into my mouth – forked and wound around my tongue. She tasted of earth and skin.

I tried to spit. I tried to claw them. She pinned my wrists – kept my jaw open. And she was entwining my tongue, dividing into many tentacles and caressing the roof of my mouth, pulsing against my teeth, twisting down my throat.

I fought, suffocating. Worms flowed into my shirt and trousers, pressing my belly button, my nipples, my feather tracts. They squeezed tense with incredible pressure, working themselves tighter and tighter, suddenly clenched unbearably rigid then gave a shudder and sigh, and relaxed. They fell away from me into a loose pool on the floor.

Worms made their way down my chest and between my feathers, out of my bum crack and over my balls, down my thigh and dropped out of my trouser leg. Her disconnected tongue was still crawling around inside my mouth. I spat it onto my palm – breathed in the thankful air!

'Rapist!' I panted.

A satiated ripple passed over the surface of her pool. She cackled. Then she gathered herself, sucked all her worms together into a tendril as thick as a tree trunk. It rose up, and she said, 'Care for them, won't you?' The tentacle whipped out of the box, spiralled down into the soil and disappeared.

Saker was watching me, both shaken and hopeful, and he was growing transparent. I could see the edge of the box through him. I looked down, and glimpsed the floor through my boots. I was fading out, too, but not as fast.

'You're getting all hazy!' he said.

'No, you're the one who's going – back to Wrought. Look!' I pointed to his hand; he held it up and we saw the bones and blood vessels within.

'You're going home,' said Dunlin.

'Remember our deal! On your honour as Rachiswater?'

'Not Rachiswater. As the leader of the worlds against the Insects.'

Saker addressed the Equinne with desperate urgency. 'Are you Magor? Jant said you use rifles? If you make the bullet with ridges they grip the rifling. Did you know that? Do you know ladder sights?'

'No! Do you know breech loading?'

They started shouting all sorts of ballistics tips urgently at each other, but his voice grew fainter and now he was fading. He smacked his hands down in frustration, realised it was futile, gave a smile of capitulation, bowed to Dunlin – and was gone.

'That wasn't a long trip,' Dunlin said.

'He was only playing the Circle Sonata. He didn't shoot an overdose.'

'Never, ever let him touch cat, Jant.'

'No, of course.'

'Not until he's at death's door, and then you can lead him through.'

The worms that been the Vermiform's tongue had curled up in my palm. My hand was so translucent they seemed to be hovering in mid-air. Dunlin's kindly face, Magor's surprised, vexed expression, the mystery goose and the silent newt were greying out.

'What is that Monogoose?' I said.

'It's an immortal being. It's been alive for longer than any of us. It's even older than San ... and the Vermiform. If it gets killed – if someone kills it – then somewhere in the universe a new Monogoose hatches instantly, possessing all its memories and personality intact.'

'There's only ever one Monogoose,' said Magor.

'You wouldn't believe its wisdom. It's the most sagacious, experienced person ...'

'But still a goose?'

'Don't be too enlightened all at once,' said the goose.

Down on the pitch Tine were bringing refreshments onto the piles of soil – whole Fajita Trees, marzipandas, and tea dragons on silver chains, steaming aromatically.

I reached out a finger and stirred the air, and the whole arena started to spiral round and round, into a whirlpool around my finger and creased up, pulling away at the edges into long folds revealing, behind it, the dark hall of Wrought.

I wound it onto my finger ... and in Wrought I woke.

CHAPTER 15

It begins

I jolted awake. I was lolling backwards, the half-back of the chair pressing my spine. In one hand, my curl of fingers still grasped the syringe. My other palm was cupped and held the Vermiform worms. Vermiform worms. Oh, shit. They crawled up my arm and into my top pocket.

I pulled myself upright. As I did so a mighty yellow glow lit up the windows and I suddenly saw all the night trees bordering the lawn.

What was that? I tottered to the window, past Saker who was slumped unconscious on the piano. A roar rolled against the window-panes. An explosion! A tremendous explosion, out towards the coast.

I stared. Another fireball bloomed, some distance to the west. It uplit the bases of the clouds, lit the gardens for an instant in sickly amber bright as day. Several small flashes followed, and a few seconds later the thunder of them all combined rumbled the length of the gardens and crashed against the house.

Above, in the Steward's room, hasty voices. Raggiana slammed his bedroom door.

A third explosion, nearer, burst like a gigantic sun behind Wrought wood, and all the panes in the window cracked simultaneously.

'Out!' I yelled. 'Raggy! Get everyone out! Saker?' I shook him.

He groaned and stirred.

'Wake up!'

He swatted me.

'We've got to get out!' I tried to drag him. Instinctively he reached for Swallow's manuscript, staggered to his feet and followed me. As we passed the table he grabbed his bow and quiver, and shoved in the manuscript. I pulled him after me out of the great hall and down the steps to the chill night air.

Raggiana took up the shout. 'Out! Everybody out!' Tern's staff were spilling, half-dressed, out of the North and kitchen wings, and stopping to stare at the three infernos blazing on the horizon.

'Keep going! Further!' I yelled at them. 'Down to the woods!'

I launched myself past them, hauling Saker, and they followed, pouring behind me down the lawns, when at once there was a colossal explosion, and glass blew out of all the windows in the hall.

It picked me up and threw me through the air. I slammed into the grassy slope head first and lay dazed. My neck was screaming pain. I couldn't hear anything. I couldn't believe ...

My hearing was just a blank. No buzz, nothing. I rolled over, down the bank, and with tunnel vision found myself looking at a maid whose face ran with blood. No. No. It was just a head with no hair, and a torso, nothing else. It looked like a horrible seamstress' model. All around me were bodies and bits of bodies, skinned like steak. People were struggling to pick themselves up, crying, screaming, and looking to each other.

The middle of Wrought Manor had been blown out completely. The wings on both sides were intact, but the Great Hall was an empty shell with a few flames burning on the smashed balcony – clouds of acrid smoke were pouring out. The bay window, where I'd been standing, was just a hole. The roof was gone. The parquet floor had been raked up and hurled out. All around me, shreds of clothes and skin scattered the grass.

I stood up, clutching the back of my neck.

Between me and the house, Saker was levering himself onto his knees. His wings dangled. Arrows and pages of manuscript splayed around him. He hadn't been thrown as far as me. Most of the bodies around me were women. Many of the whole ones were moving now. Oh, god. Oh, god.

I walked among them, back to Saker. He said something I couldn't hear. I shook my head, in agony, and gagged at the smell: thick black smoke, with the salty stench of blasting powder. Cooked flesh, burnt hair and feathers, and a smell like black pudding from someone's blood.

There was Raggiana, lying in the midst of bits of pulverised stone and glittering glass. I took his hand and he gripped mine tightly. As I stared at him my hearing recovered.

'Raggy, can you hear me?'

The slight young man nodded, and cried out.

I spoke slowly: 'Raggy, help me get the people up. Find the gardeners to help ... Bring our carts round. At least one for the hospital and an-other for the ... morgue. Can you do that?'

He swallowed. He was too stunned.

'Then we start a bucket chain to put the fires out.'

He shook his head, trying to understand.

I paused for a minute. 'Are you with me, Raggy? Come on ...'

'Yes ...' He retched. His lips were bleeding and his face was scarlet in the flickering balcony fire-light.

Behind me, Saker cried, 'Hist!'

I spun round to see him pointing to the tall hedge, past the gardener's storehouse and shattered glasshouse. I caught a slight movement in the darkness.

Saker raised five fingers. He picked up his bow and half-empty quiver, and ran over the black lawn towards the bushes. The flames from the house were throwing crazy shadows, and among them I made out people fleeing ahead of him, through a gap in the laurel hedge.

Without breaking pace, he slipped through it. I left Raggiana and followed. When I caught up with him the intruders were some distance away, at the garden wall, beside the huge, locked, Wrought iron gates, and the first figure was halfway up a ladder, climbing over.

Saker halted and stared at them dreamily. Abruptly he picked five arrows, nocked the first to string, flexed his bow and loosed. The intruder on the ladder gave a scream and fell to the ground.

It was a woman. The other four stepped in front of her and levelled their muskets. We had no cover! I dropped flat on the wet grass, but Saker stood still. 'Get up, Jant,' he murmured. 'Their effective range is two hundred metres. Mine is over three hundred. Let them shoot.'

The four men aimed at us and pulled their triggers. Smoke bloomed from three of the guns. The balls spat gravel from the avenue, ahead.

'Now,' said Saker. '*You* don't have time to reload.' Loosed and dropped the first man with an arrow through the heart. '*You* don't have time to run.' Loosed and dropped the second. '*You* misfired.' Loosed and dropped the third. 'And *you* need to gauge your range.' Loosed and dropped the fourth.

'Shit ...' I said.

'Jant,' he said. 'Epsilon gives me a hell of a hangover.'

The woman who had fallen off the ladder sprinted into the topiary.

'She has an arrow in her left forearm,' said Saker. 'Go catch her.'

I brought her down on the grass some distance beyond the bushes. She fought me for a second – I felt her strength – then she realised it was pointless and lay panting. Saker's arrow transfixed her arm, between the two bones, and blood and the dew were rubbing off the soot-paste that coated her completely, for camouflage, and revealing the story of her Rose tattoos beneath.

I let her kneel up. She was about thirty, with long, curly dark hair, a heart-shaped face and a proud, wild expression gashed by pain. She wore a black vest and threadbare work trousers, and the muscles of her tattooed arms spoke of a labouring life. A Litanee gypsy, and by the size of the rose on her right shoulder, the leader of a troupe.

Saker approached, looking pale. With one hand keeping an arrow at string he effortlessly picked her up and slammed her against the wall. 'Who are you?'

She spat at him.

He released her, took a step back and drew his bow. *'Who are you?'*

'Connell!'

'Why did you try to kill me? Me and Comet?'

'I'll say nothing,' she said in Litanee.

'Jant, speak their fucking lingo!'

'She's not talking,' I said.

Saker bent his bow till the tips arched, but she stood defiantly, pierced arm held out straight, face caked in soot.

'You killed all those people. *Why?'*

Nothing.

'Do you know who I am?'

Nothing.

'I'm the *King*! This is the second time, isn't it? The first time was the cannon. It was no accident! Was it you?'

Nothing.

He yelled in rage, seized her, snapped the flights off the arrow in her arm and pulled the shaft through. She screamed, horribly.

Saker held the point in front of her eyes. 'I should have used a broadhead!'

'Connell,' I said in Litanee Morenzian. 'Come quietly, for you're dealing with the Castle and the crown.' I switched back to Awian. 'Let's deal with her later. Tern's staff are dying.'

He nodded, and picked her up in a fireman's lift, with her head under his bow arm. Other than squeezing her wounded arm, she made no motion and not a sound as he carried her past her dead comrades, who also had Rose tattoos, back to the burning mansion. People were stumbling about on the lawn, couples helping each other, some kneeling next to dead bodies, screaming and pleading, some wandering in confusion. Two hysterical women were rushing into the North Tower to rescue something, and Raggiana was hopelessly struggling to urge people into filling water buckets, to form some sort of chain.

When Connell saw where we were going, she started kicking and screeching, 'No! No! No!'

Why doesn't she want to go back? I wondered, then I figured it. I grabbed Saker's wing. 'Stop!'

Looking down the lawns we saw a sharp jet of flame erupt from the pumphouse and the explosion knocked everyone in the bucket chain flat like cards. We shrank from the bang, squeezed our eyes shut, and a wave of heat gushed around us. When I next looked, smoke filled the walled garden and I couldn't see anyone standing. Not Raggiana. No one at all. And then the screams of the dying began.

'Another one!' said Saker.

'Another explosion to catch the rescue team,' I said.

'What ...?'

'Because they knew we'd go to help.'

He couldn't believe it. He tried to think it through and still couldn't comprehend it. He hauled Connell in front of him and shook her. 'Is it true?'

She looked at the sky.

'They planned it,' I said. 'And it's our powder. The missing blasting powder. Come on.' I set off towards the carnage, but Saker didn't move.

'There might be another ...'

'Oh, for San's sake, who knows!'

I couldn't tell why the Roses should suddenly want to kill us, but I had to help the survivors. We made our way down the lawn and into the smoke. Bits of bodies lay around, in the dust blown out on the shockwave. Feathers with gristle attached caught on the grass. Beside them were three vertebrae, still articulated, pale pink. Raggiana lay on his front, balled-up, his arms over his head, thankfully alive but as tense as rigor mortis, with his long ginger hair full of ash, and a fire began to roar in the North Tower.

I knelt beside Raggy and tried to coax him out but he fended me off. So I left him and held one of the buckets under the broken water pipe until it was full. I motioned Saker to drop Connell and move aside, and I hurled the cold water over her.

It washed off all the soot. I flicked my knife, slashed her vest into halves and ripped it open, revealing her tattoos. In the firelight I read them.

'Lock her inside,' I said to Saker.

She was spitting and dripping, glaring at me. She cried, 'Did you hear the earlier explosions?'

'Three beyond the woods. What were they?'

She laughed. 'The powder mills of course. The ones you visited.'

I was stunned. Why? Many, many people must be dead or dying out there.

'Fuck ...' said Saker.

'Did *you* do it?' I yelled at her.

She forked wet locks of hair from her face. 'So you need to find the other bombs.'

'*What?* What other bombs?'

'In the market place ...' she glanced at the sun rising behind the coppice. 'And in the steelworks.'

'*Where* in the market?'

She shrugged strong shoulders. She'd say no more.

Saker pushed her into the windowless brick potting shed and turned the key. 'The market and foundries,' he said. 'People will be—'

'Going to work now. All right ... You ride to Plume Forge. Take Balzan, go as fast as you can. Stop people entering. I'll fly to the market; it's further. If I can't find the bomb at least I can clear the place.'

He nodded, and ran off towards the stables.

I returned to the steward, who was gradually uncurling and shaking like a waif. 'Raggy, I know your friends have been murdered – but keep it together, okay? Okay? Take the stable hands and get the wounded to hospital. I'll send the fire engines.'

He gazed at the gore on the lawns and nodded mutely at a dis-embodied wing that had been blown against the potting shed wall.

'I'll be back as soon as I can. Keep a close eye on Connell – there in the shed. Litanee gypsies help each other. They're sworn to – it's their only code of honour. It's the only law she cares for. Any other Rose or Oak will let her free. So set a guard.'

'... Yes, Comet ... Leave it with me.'

I ran, and took off. I turned through the smoke of my house and spiralled up on the rising heat. The hall was a splay of rubble and broken glass extending onto the lawn. If you think of the great hall as the horizontal between the two wings of Wrought's H-shape, then the North wing is the first vertical and now it was a formless glow beneath the clouds of smoke. Its roof was failing and falling in. The fire was beyond control inside, and its tower was now hollow. A blood-red flickering leapt from its open top: it was drawing like a kiln.

Higher, in the plain of arable and marshland, I saw the remains of Fusain, Grough and Kingfisher Mills burning fiercely in the dawn-grey light. A bell was clamouring.

It must look horrific down there. The bombs would have hit both the day and night shifts, as they changed at sunrise. And it's wiped out half of our powder production. I envisaged the soldiers at the Front running out of gunpowder, and the Insects cutting into them, as I flew over town.

I dropped into the market square. Around a hundred stall holders

111

who had been setting up had heard the blasts and were standing among their half-erected stalls, gaping skywards at the plume of smoke.

They switched their attention to me as I landed. I ran up onto the plinth of the Butterstone and gathered them round – their faces full of fear, shock and amazement. I told them the mills and manor had been attacked. Plenty of men and women started wailing and cursing because they had family in the mills. I sent some to harness fire engines and drive them to the manor. Then I divided the crowd into three and sent them all to the mills, and I didn't mention the bomb in the square.

When the market was empty, apart from its manager, I gazed over the stalls – barrels, boxes of vegetables, rolls of cloth, crates, bales, bags of fodder. Carts were parked nose to tail around the edge of the square. Fuck, fuck, fuck. Blasting powder could be hidden in anything! Where to start searching? Had I time? This was a nightmare!

The market manager and I ran between the half-filled stalls, looking for gunpowder barrels, any trace of a fuse. The clock in the crenellated Bank Tower showed quarter to six.

No fuses led out of the surrounding buildings. Every single cart seemed suspicious, but the market manager knew them. I had them towed away.

We watched the hands move to the hour. We held our breath as the clock began to strike six … and nothing happened. The town emptied – everyone headed out en masse to the mills, wary of further bombs, with ambulance carriages and carts.

I stood on the steps of the Butterstone, and was discussing with the manager how best to search the cafés, bars and shops around the square, when a clatter of hooves on Chirk Street made us jump.

Raggiana Vitrix, his coat flying from his shoulders like another pair of wings, galloped round the side of the bank into the square, the hooves of his frothing stallion striking sparks from the cobbles.

'Comet! Comet!'

He curbed the horse steeply in front of us. 'She's gone!'

'Connell?'

'Connell! Gone!'

His long waxed coat settled on his thighs, his red hair tangled with soot, and he was pallid with terror. 'I had to take the maids to the hospital!'

'Damn it! I told you not to leave her!'

'I only left her for ten minutes!'

'I told you to put a guard on the door!'

His horse skittered away from my scent and he pulled it straight angrily. 'Comet – the guard was killed.'

The manager jumped down the steps and grabbed the stallion's rein. Raggiana wiped sweat off his face, smearing dirt all over it. He looked at me in despair.

'There isn't a bomb,' I said. 'Is there? She fucking tricked me.'

Raggiana bowed his shoulders somewhere in his coat cape. 'When I returned from the hospital I found Parula with his throat slit. The door was unlocked. Someone let her out.'

'I *told* you Roses help each other!'

'Yes, Comet. I'm sorry.'

Well, what do we do now? There was no point searching the grounds. Connell would be long gone. I swore. Behind me, the clock in the Bank Tower whirred into the introduction of its half-hour chime, and we all involuntarily braced ourselves for an explosion. There was no explosion. Raggiana, utterly downcast, hugged his arms to his concave stomach, and his black horse rolled its eyes and slathered foam all over the market manager's hand.

'Raggy,' I said.

'Yes, Comet?'

'Ride to the steelworks and find the king. He'll have shut down the whole place. Tell him there's no bomb. Probably. Tell him Connell hoaxed us and she's escaped. Ride back with him and I'll meet you at the house.'

'Yes, Comet.'

'What's left of my wife's fucking house.'

He nodded, lips pursed. The manager let go the Pelham bit and Raggy sawed the rein, gave his horse a kick and hurtled off in a shower of sparks. He galloped past the line of stalls, drew his sword and neatly skewered a loaf from the last stall. Sword up, with loaf on it, he slewed round the corner of the bank and was gone.

The market manager surveyed the deserted shop fronts, restaurants and cafés, their stacked round tables and upset chairs, the trodden leaves under the vegetable stalls. 'I'm going to search every shop anyway, just to be sure.'

'To be safe.'

He watched me shake out my wings. 'Raggiana will send you word,' I said. 'And Lady Tern will be in touch. Whatever happens, keep each other informed.'

I ran down the Butterstone steps, broke into a sprint. By the time I reached the pastry stalls I had the right speed. I swept down my wings and jumped, hauled myself into the air at the level of the shop fronts, past the bank and out along the street where Raggiana had gone.

I prefer feeling the air under my feathers to the cobbles under my feet. I strained, beating down the air with the long forearms of my wings. All the time I could see the smoke filling the sky ahead – the morning sun shone dully through it.

Tern rebuilt this end of town after the firestorm of '15. It all matched the manor house; she'd insisted on the buildings coordinating in the same style like a fashion collection, and I flapped past arcades of blind gothic arches above the row of shops. Now the town survived, but her home was burning.

I alighted on the lawn. The bodies had been cleared ... mostly ... but patches of blood remained. God, people had been blown apart! Maids, servants and their children had horrible burns ... Blasting powder designed to kill Insects had been deliberately used on *people* – now I had chance to think, my mind reeled with the enormity.

Ten fire engines were drawn up on the forecourt, pumping their tanks and spraying the flames. The fire was diminishing, but more from having burnt itself out than from their efforts. The blast had vaporised everything in the hall from the cellars to the sky above. Only the very ends of the hammerbeam roof remained. The North Wing's entrance tower was a smoking shell, its servants' quarters completely drenched. Water was running off the paving and pooling on the grass.

I sat on a bench by the smashed glasshouse. I could track Connell from the potting shed to the estate wall, then who knows? We'd left the goddamn ladder in place, and riders must have been waiting on the road.

My Fusain reeve arrived and related the horrendous details of the gunpowder works. A hospital representative brought me a report of the wounded. So far, nearly a hundred people had been killed in the five explosions, and the women of Fusain were still bringing in pieces from as far away as Thorne Hill. The injuries from burns, debris and shrapnel were the same again, and more victims were likely to die.

I half-sat, half-lay, against the scroll iron arm of the bench, while the sky behind the smoke grew a more assertive blue. I watched smoke billow into the South Wing, destroying our carpets, our double four-poster bed, tapestries, Tern's clothes, her haute couture wardrobe and the office of her designer label.

The head fireman came to explain whatever the fuck it was they'd been doing. 'The North Wing won't burn much longer,' he said.

'Oh ... right.'

'It's damped down, but our tanks are empty.'

'Ah ... Okay.'

'And it's all gone, inside. It's unsafe. It'll have to be dismantled.'

'Gosh ... Really ...?'

I think I thanked him. At any rate, they left and I sat and stared blankly at wisps of smoke rising from the black façade of the palace until Saker and Raggiana returned.

Saker dismounted by the blown-out windows, glanced inside and left Raggy to lead away his sweating horse. He approached, down the ornamental steps, between the monkey puzzle trees. I got up and walked away, the length of the lawn with my back to him, but he followed anyway. 'Poor Tern,' he said.

'She'd only just finished rebuilding it!'

He glanced at the smoke issuing from behind broken mullions, rising past the blackened beams. 'How could Connell dare?'

'Well, I don't know, because Raggy fucking let her go!'

'Don't be hard on him. He doesn't know about Litanee.'

'Everyone will have to learn!'

'Jant. You're shaking.'

'No shit I'm shaking. Look at my fucking house!'

The shards of the great bay window drew our gaze. Smaller bays in the north and south wings were shattered but their frames were intact. I set off abruptly, up the slope towards it, and Saker joined me. 'Why would Connell want to blow us to pieces?' he said.

'How am I going to tell Tern?'

'Does she have a grievance against Wrought?'

'People ... actual people. You and me ...'

'Or Awia, or the Castle?'

I snapped out of it and tried to follow his conversation, 'It could be to do with money. The powder mills paid Connell just enough to keep working. The Castle doesn't pay them well, either.'

'Simoon never digs into the treasury if he can avoid it.'

'Damn him! Does he think Litanee *want* to live in wagons?'

'They don't?'

'Saker, who the fuck would live in a caravan if they had a bloody choice?'

We crunched over the rubble and bits of wainscoting, fragments of beams, and pieces of piano. The firemen had trodden the tulips flat into muddy water under the bay window. I put a leg into the window frame and eased myself into the hall. 'I read Connell's tattoos. I know a bit about her.'

'I only saw roses.'

'Roses. Right.'

You don't look at the roses entwining her arm. You look at the pictures between them, framed by the briars. All the gypsies from Litanee

115

tell their life story in their tattoos. They are either in the Rose or Oak tribes. They start at the right wrist, inscribe tattoos up their arm as time progresses, to their right shoulder, then across their chest and neck, and down their left arm. When that's full, by about age forty, they tattoo their back, and then – if they live that long – their face. They record their life events, their most proud moments, their relationships, achievements, adventures or abilities, and there's a symbol for each one you can read if you know the code. It obviates the need for introductions when they can scan each others' life stories at a glance. They often need to team up quickly and knuckle down to work, for example when wagons gather for the harvest, so they display their strengths and preferences, and all the subtleties of their life history because, as I keep telling everybody, a Litanee will always help another one, regardless of law. It's an intelligent rule, given their lifestyle: if your fellow Rose saves you from starving, another day he might call on you for help. And it's just rescued Connell from the noose.

'They put blasting powder in the cellar ...'

'Early this morning,' said Saker. 'Or Raggy would have found it. Watch where you're walking. The joists have gone.'

There was just enough space to stand before the floor opened into an enormous hole. It had been splintered upward by the force of the blast. Peering into the cellar, I saw nothing but the pitted wall. It stank of wet, burnt timber. Tern's wine cellar, together with any evidence of barrels or fuses, had been blown to atoms. So had the hall's oak panelling, the table where I'd been sitting, and the piano.

I walked gingerly round the hole, through the scorched doorway and back to Saker. He said, 'Tell me what you read on her arms.'

We wandered around the house and peered in the other windows while I spoke. 'Connell's about thirty, because she has one sleeve and half her chest completed. Her right wrist was first; it has the date she left Litanee, back in '25 when she must have been roughly fifteen. Obviously, she joined the Rose tribe. Her parents weren't gypsies but stayed in Vertigo. They died soon after: inside her arm there's two graves with an anchor and distaff drawn on them – a sailor and a spinner.

'She worked on the harvest in the Plainslands and Awia, you can see from a haysheaf, a sickle and some grapes. Probably your grapes, Saker. Our assassin has sailed twice to Tris; over her elbow there's a clipper with two tallies. She worked with the Ghallain gauchos herding cattle: there's a lasso and a steer skull. She's exceptionally good with horses and loves them. There's a big piebald cob rearing inside her biceps and a horseshoe, too. So, she can do farrier work. Above is a bowtop wagon – she has her own and probably built it herself. The huge rose on her shoulder says she leads a troupe. I guess you shot four of them. The heart on her breast says she's married. Quite recently.'

'You read all that at a glance?'

'Yes.'

'And the bodies of the other Roses? Who were they?'

'I don't know. They were covered in soot.'

Saker picked up a fragment of martlet glass. 'Our Connell is very accomplished.'

'Most gypsies are. They have to be.'

We walked towards the stables, and I think he was contemplating the great chasm between them. A gypsy girl might gather brushwood to sell, and it becomes the fire that roasts his venison. Between her roses she might depict an olive branch, when it's his Donaise olives they pick, or a twisted sheet, when it's the linen of Tanager Palace they come to wash. The great strength in these humans' precarious existences suddenly seemed threatening. 'God!' he said. 'Could it be an uprising of Litanee?'

'Maybe,' I said.

'Can you find them? Can you find Connell?'

'I can find anybody.'

We were entering the stable courtyard towards the gable end of the main coach building, across the cobbled yard. Raggiana came out of the gap in the sliding barn door, wiping his hands.

Without any warning, the Circle broke.

I felt as if I'd been torn apart. Ripped across the middle. A feeling of vertigo, dislocation – I lost sense of myself – and felt the vast freezing space of infinity. An immortal died.

I dropped to my knees and my field of vision blacked down to just one cobble. I'm fainting. Oh, god, not now!

The Emperor relinked the Circle and suddenly I felt my lifeline again, but I couldn't shake the feeling of a body ripped apart. I felt the hard cobbles pressing my knees and a drag upwards on both shoulders from Saker and Raggiana trying to stop me falling. They leant forward into my widening field of vision.

'Comet?' said Raggiana, terrified.

I fought to drag my mind up through layers of consciousness. I saw an image of an eel shaped like a large intestine swimming away to my left. Then my mind presented a clear memory of Connell's tattoos. And then my sight cleared. I was in Wrought stable yard, and I struggled to speak.

Saker helped me to a mounting block and sat me on top. 'Steward,' he told Raggiana, 'Go give some reassurance to your staff.'

Raggy dashed away.

'Now, Jant. What happened? The Circle broke, didn't it?'

I nodded.

'You got that distant look.'

He dropped on one knee, the better to see me, for my head was bowed and wings winnowed out. My long hair caught on the surface of my feathers. I felt weak all over.

'Who was it?' said Saker.

'Not Tern ...'

Anger and fear broke through his patience. 'Of course you can feel Tern! Who else? Feel for them ... You said you could! Who's missing?'

Doing this isn't second nature to me, the way it used to be for him. I closed my eyes and concentrated. I could feel thin, gold threads, shimmering and tenuous, radiating from my chest to all the other members of the Circle. I nebulously sensed them, as when someone's close beside you, you have an impression of their personality. Mostly I was loved and warmed by the earthy dark red of Tern, and it was difficult to penetrate her succulent colour to detect the others. There was the formless but intense white light of Capelin Thunder, the stolid tan of Tornado, the optimism and pragmatism of Ella Rayne, which I rendered as the brown of her pinafore dress; the brilliant glacial blue of Hurricane, and Mist Fulmer's flippant gin pink. By now I should have traced Cyan. Cyan is pale jade. I tried a little harder and located everyone else, but I couldn't feel her.

'It's Cyan, isn't it?' said Saker, his voice breaking.

'Yes.'

He let out a tremendous sob. 'My girl!'

He collapsed onto his knees, face buried in his hands, and cried loudly.

I put a hand on his shoulder. What else could I do?

I thought of Cyan at eight years old, when I smuggled her from Ata's Tower on Grass Isle to the rowing boat at night, and lifted her on my shoulders over the wet sand to the darkened coach. Or when I found her bound to the mast of the *Honeybuzzard*, as the ice-cased flagship stove and groaned.

Saker wailed in earnest and it was ugly to see him cry. His shoulders heaved, he covered his face. But I was too numb to speak and, even if I could, I didn't know what to say. I remembered Cyan running out onto the lawn at Awndyn, her honest face turned up, begging me to fly carrying her. I lay in the warm sun while she climbed all over me, and made daisy chains, and I braided my feathers in her hair. She loved my juggling. I taught her how to read a map. And Saker taught her riding and whisked her off on a purebred hunting with the bow.

And she grew up. Brought up by Swallow, and neglected in favour of sonatas, she missed her mother who never returned from Tris. She believed her step-sisters' propaganda, and despised Saker through her teenage years. Tern showed her how to play poker and bezique and I taught her how to drink tequila slammers – one, two, three! – on her sixteenth birthday at the Caterwaul Club. Then, later, defiant at the Front ... I could remember her taste, and scent on my fingers like the faintest tang of the sea.

I pressed Saker's shoulder but nothing could stop him weeping. Cyan wrote to me when she fought with him, and disappeared to Hacilith for weeks on end.

Everyone had a hand in saving her from herself. I saved her in the city when she overdosed on cat as if it was a brand new drug. And I nearly lost her then. Cyan Dei, Cyan Peregrine, then Cyan Lightning: Saker gave up everything for her, and now she was gone.

'First Swallow, now Cyan,' he managed, and dissolved into sobbing.

At length, he tried to stand but his legs were too unsteady. He sat, leaning against the mounting step, staring unseeing at the cobbles. His fingers were white on the block's edge and his wings unfolded like a cloak. 'Cyan ... dead?'

'I'm sorry ... I know it's inadequate but ...'

'I put her in the front line ...'

'She wanted to be Lightning. She knew what it meant.'

'I didn't mean to kill her!'

'It's not your fault.'

He wasn't listening. He was fighting for breath, his face contorted and puffy. Eventually he wiped his nose. 'I'm supposed to die. Not my girl ... She's seventeen.'

'Thirty-two.'

'Seventeen! I love her. I love my little girl ... She's clever. Smart ... Oh, Jant – everyone I ever love *dies*. Swallow. Sav'ry. Linnet. I try to save them but they won't. They won't ...'

He disappeared into his hands, screwed up his handkerchief and pulled his wings about him, dragging the feather tips on the cobbles.

I rubbed his shoulder. 'Saker.'

'Not Cyan ... I thanked Dunlin for her. Just ... why?'

'I'll fly to the Front.'

'Yes. I need to know!' he gasped, trying to be businesslike but unable to breathe. 'I ... I'm riding to Micawater. Whatever killed ... my girl. My ... *lovely* girl. *Must not* kill Leon.'

'Don't worry.'

'Don't let her die! I can't live without her! Come back and tell me ... was it Insects?'

'All right.'

'Was it Roses? If they killed ... her ... I'll hound every bastard human from Gilt to Tanager. That's what I'll do! I'll round up every gypsy in Awia and hang them in the Grand Place.'

'No!'

'They're humans covered in flowers. They're easy to find.'

'Not easy to understand!'

'Is the Sturge big enough?'

'Think what San would say!'

'San ...? Did he see this coming?'

'It's probably only Connell's troupe.'

'Could San have stopped this?' He jumped up and raced into the stable, into the tack room, and tore Balzan's saddle and his rifle holsters from the peg.

'Wait till I return before you do anything,' I said, but I might as well have been talking to the hayrack.

He settled the saddle on Balzan's back, crouched down to buckle the girth and suddenly spoke quietly. It sounded like composure, but it was shock. 'Listen, Jant. This is most important. Bring her to me ...'

'Cyan?'

'Her ... The body of my little girl, my precious girl, you must bring to the palace ... to the Lake Mausoleum.'

'I see. Yes, if you wish.'

'Forget the rubbish about the Starglass. I want her in Micawater. She was my daughter. She always was ... really ... no matter what she called herself.'

His broad, powerful body wilted. He kept his head lowered, wouldn't look at me. Trying to find a purpose, any purpose, he took out a brush and worked on the horse's withers, then its back in long sweeps from the cantle to the tail. Then he folded an arm on the saddle and rested his face in the crook of it, his hand still through the brush strap. His voice came from a great distance. 'I try to prize them, but they won't ... Tell Eleonora to join me at Micawater. If she's still alive ... she must be ...'

'Of course. But will you stop this nonsense about humans?'

'I liked wingless. I married one, once.'

He fixed Balzan's headstall and clipped the rifles and quivers on the saddle. Then he clicked his tongue and Balzan followed him from the straw-sweet air, into the courtyard. He mounted, looked down. 'There might be a gunpowder charge hidden in my house. I'll have it searched. Connell won't kill Lory and Ortolan!'

'Please stay calm.'

'Everyone knows we move the children there in June. They know Leon calls it the summer palace.' He sobbed and glanced at the ruined house. 'Hurry and tell me what happened. By then, I'll have all the roads blocked. All the woods combed. I'll have every gypsy wagon searched. If Connell's in my kingdom I'll catch the bitch.'

'Saker, no.'

His eyes were bleak, just intense pain. 'Eske owes me a favour, too. Connell won't escape ...'

'We should tell Aver-Falconet.'

'Fuck the Governor of Hacilith. Fuck the fucking Morenzians.'

'This isn't the battlefield. This is a new kind of problem.'

'It's my country, Jant. We do what I say, now.'

He walked Balzan slowly under the stable arch, and the clop of hooves became a flinty squelch as they reached the gravel avenue pooled with firemen's water. They quickened into a trot, then a canter, and broke into a gallop, which faded fast away.

Oh, for fuck sake. Damn it, damn it, damn it, Saker. If all you have is arrows, everything looks like a target.

I soothed Raggiana, instructed him to telegraph the Castle, and left him in control of our injured staff and our mourning families. It was an unenviable task. When I jogged out to the avenue Balzan's hoof prints were still there, filling with water. Before, boys with rakes would have smoothed the gravel immediately. Where were the gardeners' sons now? I hoped they'd survived.

The elaborate curlicued gates stood open, black paint peeling off the sinuous metal. I ran at them, took off halfway down the driveway, and my wings whacked the topmost swirls as I passed above.

It was going to be an arduous flight. Cyan Lightning was dead. My best friend was cast so deeply in grief that he didn't know what to do – and he wasn't in control. Fortunately his rare and brief storms of violence wear off quickly, in my experience, leaving him desolate and morose, which is unpleasant but a good deal safer as far as the humans are concerned. In one night Connell had destroyed half the gunpowder presses in Wrought and my wife's mansion. How could I describe this to the Emperor? Fuck it, how would I explain it to *Tern*?

CHAPTER 16

Flying to the Front

I'd always thought that Litanee were fine people. I admired the way you find them everywhere – if you're broad-minded or lowly enough to glimpse the invisible human being behind the menial task. Whether rolling up in time for the harvest, carting arrows to the Front or olive oil, figs and dates out of Tambrine, they know where seasonal work is found. They wash pots for the Quartermaster at the Front, or dishes in the restaurants of Fiennafor. They lock barges through the Awndyn-Moren canal. When work dries up they roll away and live off their pennies till the next news of labour trickles down their grapevine.

Hardship made them leave home in the first place, and I can relate to that. Litanee is a rocky, storm-cleft coast. Their towns are either built into the wave-torn gullies, like Vertigo, or between the sparse oat fields of the cliff top, to the edge of Cathee forest. The youth growing up find there's no employment, no money, and precious little space. They're stuck, as they say, 'between the cliff and the Cathee', and nobody really wants to tangle with the Cathee. So the Litanee teens move out, either to Diw and join the coastal trade or build a wagon for the road and follow family footsteps into the Rose or Oak tribes. And start their tattoos.

The Litanee who stay at home don't celebrate their life story on their skin, but they've always decorated themselves with knotwork tattoos. The rovers in their wagons ink their hearts on their sleeves – indelibly Litanee. And why not?

Sometimes they congregate in troupes, sometimes they travel alone. Their roses or oak leaves carry them invisible, in a world of their own. They answer to no one – which I liked. But why attack us? And was it just Connell, or were all Litanee rising? The thought chilled me. Their little bands pervaded the world, a hidden brotherhood I couldn't see; I couldn't stop.

Depressed enough by this, as I crossed into Lowespass it began to rain. The sky was zinc. I flew through suffocating curtains of water slanting down into the Paperlands, where it streamed off into the river. In Lowespass all the seasons seem to melt into the same monotony. There's no differentiation between summer and crisp winter; this cold rain permeates everything. In fact, the tents only dry out when the mean wind blows the water off.

I lost height as my feathers sogged, and glided down past a bastle farm with a few clots of dejected sheep, over the army road, to the great stone walls of the camp. Every feature stood out, forelit vividly by the sun against a gunmetal sky.

The camp was awash with mud. Most of the fyrd tents had been dismantled and a great collection of packing crates stood around the Sun Pavilion.

I landed outside it. My boots slipped on the sludge, then caught on the grit. Rain beaded the pavilion's brass sun bosses and muddy water was rising up the cream canvas. Tern hurtled out and embraced me. She clung to my wet shirt, which was sticking to my skin. She seemed tiny in her riding coat and I felt a pang of guilt that she was still stranded here, then a welter of despair because, confronted with her warm body in my arms and her dark hair against my cheek, the smell of her perfume, all her exquisite quirks and wonders, I couldn't bring myself to tell her the news.

'I felt Cyan die,' I said.

'Oh, Jant, it was awful!'

She pulled me into the pavilion. Tornado, Capelin Thunder and Eleonora were inside, sitting round an empty table. 'What happened?' I said.

'It nearly got Tern,' said Tornado.

'*What* did?'

She waved him silent. 'It wasn't meant for me.'

'Saker knows,' I said. 'He's devastated. He plunged off trying to be revenged on something.'

'I don't think it's going to be that easy,' said Tern. 'Let me show you.' She pulled me outside into the rain and we sploshed onto the path towards the watchtowers, with Tornado and Eleonora following. There was a ragged hole in the gate, through which you could see the road outside, and one of the towers was charred to half its height.

Tern pointed to a shallow depression in the road, burnt black. There were small fragments of wood and metal everywhere. She picked one up and gave it to me; I turned it over to see the blistered remains of a red lacquered surface. It had been the chassis of a coach. So the torn bits of brass were coach fittings and – oh god – it was strewn over a huge area!

'The coach exploded,' said Tern. I didn't reply. I was thinking of the carnage at her house. 'Cyan was going to the fortress to fetch the cannon wagons. She climbed into the coach. It started, and ...'

'It blew up,' said Eleonora.

Tern surveyed the crater, silently. 'Jant,' she said. 'It was the most appalling blast ...' She extended her hands and mimicked a dome of flame. 'It killed her immediately.'

'I was standing here,' said Tornado. 'And it blew me over ... there.'

'Shit.'

Tern rubbed her nose. 'The coachman ... it blew his body through the gate to the other side. And there wasn't a stitch on him.'

'There wasn't any skin on him,' said Eleonora.

'Leon!'

'It made me puke. I thought I'd seen everything.'

Tornado pointed at the piece of panel I held. 'That's the running board. The roof went up – there. Like a grenade burst or something. Like a whole box of shells!'

'What about Cyan?'

'Nothing survived,' Tern said, in the mid-unctuous caramel tone she usually reserved for criticising the catwalk.

'Oh, tell him, Tern!'

'No.'

'We found a hand,' said Eleonora.

'A ... *hand*?'

'And the sun off her brooch ... It was bent ...'

'Is that all?'

'Jant, it was gruesome! There was blood and bodies everywhere. A horse's skull got embedded in that tower ... As for the outriders – I had to send fyrdsmen out with bags and a shovel.'

I stroked Tern's hair and my hand settled on the nape of her neck. She was vulnerable, delicate, yet strong. She looked up, 'I was in the coach behind. Yes, yes, I'm all right ... I think but ... oh, fuck, only by a fluke. The burst flipped my coach over. I fell onto the ceiling and I was so numb, I didn't move. I just lay like this.' She curled her fingers. 'I felt as if my whole body'd been hit by a hammer. The blast felt solid. I was ...'

'Stunned,' I said, remembering lying on the lawn.

'Stunned. Yes. Tawny ripped the door off and pulled me out. The horses were still in the traces but ... all their bones were broken. They were mangled.'

'They were paste,' said Eleonora.

'Shut up, Leon!'

'Cooked paste.'

Out of the corner of my eye I saw something pink-white speared into the watchtower at above head height. It was a shard of bone. I dropped the fragment of carriage ply; I didn't want to stay here any more. I enfolded Tern with a wing and walked with her back to the pavilion.

We sat down at the table. In her riding overtrousers with flat silver buttons up the sides, smeared with mud, Tern was more beautiful than in any ballgown. I was filled with tenderness; she'd always been a survivor. She was graceful but unbreakable. Her aura of strength made me kiss her. 'I won't let them hurt you.'

'Who? Who killed Cyan?'

'I'll find them.'

'Jant, what are you not telling us?'

I explained about Connell and the gunpowder, but *still* I omitted the pressing news of Wrought. Was I going to wait till she read it in the papers?

Capelin Thunder hadn't moved from the table all this time. At first I thought his silence was remorse, but I began to suspect his mind was engaged on a new project. I said, 'Wake up, shit head! This was the powder you ordered!'

'I am not responsible for the carters appropriating it.'

'They haven't just targeted Cyan!'

'What?' said Tern.

Capelin said, 'How should I know your conflicts? I designed gunpowder to kill Insects. True, any Trisian might surmise you riven barbarians would soon employ it to murder each other, but how you use it is your concern. I simply invent, and what happens to it afterwards is not my responsibility.'

I went for him. I pounced halfway across the table, was arrested in mid-air and yanked back. Tornado had grabbed my shirt. Capelin had risen to flee, but once he realised Tornado had me in an inescapable grip, he settled down and spread himself in a thin, supercilious voice: 'You Eszai destroyed my island. I *used* to be an artist. I could have been an artist now. The Emperor made me the Artillerist, so I can ship blasting powder where I damn well like. How was I to know you're infested with thieves? I don't follow your grievances! I'm not surprised mortals have scores to settle!'

'Shall I let him go?' said Tawny.

'Yes!' said Eleonora.

'Jant, cool it,' said Tern.

'Just let me kill him a little bit!'

Tornado dropped me onto the bench beside Tern. She caught a handful of my feathers and I put my head in my hands. If Connell had hit Wrought and Cyan simultaneously she was a superb strategist. I feared these were the first points of a scheme beginning to emerge from her Litanee network spread throughout the world and thoroughly supplied with our powder.

'You know more,' said Tern.

'I love you, kitten …'

She leant back, the better to view me. 'Has this happened to you, too? I can smell it on your feathers!'

'It wasn't a coach …'

'Then what?'

I steeled myself and told her everything. She paused, then leapt up. She clenched her fists, shouted, 'Oh, god! No!'

She whirled round, shook her fists at the ceiling, stamped down the length of the pavilion and returned in a fury.

'Tern …' I said.

'This Connell!' She drew her knife and flourished it. 'I will have her liver! I'll have her hung! I re*built* that hall. It's my grandmother's palace! Francolin's palace! The black stone paradise! It cost me—! Oh, god! This will bankrupt me *again*!'

She put a hand over her mouth and tears welled up. I tried to take her hand but she resisted.

'The South Wing's unburnt,' I said quickly. 'Our bedroom, your office, they're fine.'

'That's *all*? What about my *friends*? Raggy?'

'Raggiana's all right. Well … he's a bit burnt and very scared.'

'Parula?'

'Was killed. I'm sorry.'

'Becard?'

'Tern, I don't know him.'

'Using blasting powder to destroy buildings is very interesting,' Capelin murmured. 'One could—'

She rounded on him. 'It's not a *building*, you fucking freak! It's *my home*! My friends! *And they've suffered enough!*'

Capelin blenched at the force of her anger. She pulled a fistful of her hair, 'I need to be there! I need to visit the people in hospital, see the families … oh, shit, it must've been horrific!'

I thought of the torn-off wings with shreds of muscle adhering, chunks of flesh like cuts from a butcher's counter.

'How many died?'

'Over a hundred. Don't ask to see them.'

'I know what they look like! I was nearly one myself! And I need to see the house ... My poor goddamn house ... Capelin? How much blasting powder do you think was in Cyan's coach?'

'About a third of a barrel.'

I yelped. 'You've lost enough powder to blow up *four thousand* coaches?'

'At a conservative estimate. Or two hundred and forty halls the size of Wrought.'

'All right,' said Tornado. 'Kill him a little bit.'

I snatched the front of Capelin's tunic and hauled him over the table. Back went my fist.

'Jant!' Tern snapped. 'How will that help?'

'Let you know when I've done it.'

'He's a worm. Drop him! ...I *said*, drop him!'

'I've dropped him, kitten.'

'Don't punch him: make him *work*. Connell could be hiding bombs everywhere. Maybe she's targeting women. You have to warn all the Eszai, especially those with houses, tell them to search top to bottom. And telegraph all the manors, the city ...'

'Of course.'

'And San.'

Eleonora picked her overcoat from the table. 'I'm returning to the capital.'

'No,' I said. 'Not Tanager. Saker asked you to join him at Micawater first.'

She grimaced, then laughed. 'What? Add six days to my journey in the middle of a crisis? I'm handling this from my stateroom, he can pick up the kids and join *me*.'

'He asked you to bring Cyan to the Lake Mausoleum.'

'Always with the sentiment.' She swept the coat over her wings, thrust one arm, then the other, through the wide sleeves. 'I'm the Queen. Awia's my kingdom. Saker's my consort. Otherwise we'll stumble over sentiment, and get blown up. I've already sent Cyan's right hand by rider to the Castle, where, I believe, it's the tradition to bury you Eszai under tombstones in the Starglass Quadrangle. Not in Micawater.'

'Damn it,' I said. 'He won't like that.'

Tornado said, 'Cyan would've wanted to be buried in Valley Twenty ... like, at the furthest reach of our advance.'

'For such a big boy, you're an awful sap, too. If you want to hack your way through the swarm, go ahead.'

I said, 'Burial at the Castle allows Cyan her honour as an Eszai.'

'Exactly, Jant. Tell Saker to join me at Tanager.'

I said, 'Your Majesty, please be equitable and consider the Litanee. Don't tar them all with the same brush. Saker's threatening to imprison them.'

'Excellent idea.'

'Leon!'

'So the sentiment doesn't always stall him!' She towelled off her hair, shoved on a broad-brimmed hat, headed for the tent flap and almost walked into Hurricane.

He shouldered in, letting the canvas slip closed behind him. He dripped with rain. 'Your horses are *ready*.'

I said, 'Arlen, am I glad to see you!'

As nobody's ever said this before, it threw him on guard. '*Are* you?'

'Yes. Who better to hold the Front?'

He stuck his poleaxe in the floor and gestured with his other hand, holding a covered tumbler. He drinks a faddish brew of blueberries, ram's testicles and crushed sea krait fangs, in the belief it'll further his fitness, though he's as fit as it's possible to be. He calls it 'winning by the accumulation of marginal gains'. I live in hope that one day 'the accumulation of marginal gains' will make him sick.

He said, 'If there were any gypsies in the camp, they've gone. I heard you so I searched for tattoos, I didn't *find* any.'

'Will you stay here?'

'Yes! Me, Capelin, Sirocco. I'll defend the Front like I defend my *title*. I'm not leaving it to the fucking *bugs*. I can defend best from the *fort*ress, the magazine is full.'

'Good.' I said, 'Tornado, will you ride to the Castle to receive San's orders? Capelin, you go to Frass and secure this end of the valley.'

Hurricane considered this. 'Not a bad plan, for a dope fiend.'

'Gosh, thanks. I was thinking as much last night, when I i.v.'d twice the dose that would kill you.'

He didn't know whether to be impressed by this or not. He hesitated, then shrugged and sneered. 'All right, Shira.'

'Do me a favour and don't use my caste name.'

'Sorry ... Shira.' He laughed silently out of the corner of his mouth. It was half a grin and half a grimace; it showed all his brown back teeth on one side like a dog with apoplexy. He went out, chuckling. Leon followed, and toggled the flap open so Tern and I could see their escort waiting patiently in the rain – the Queen's Own Tanager Lancers and a varied panoply of Awian gentlemen starrily devoted to my wife.

I kissed Tern and she placed the tip of her finger on my nose. 'Jant, find Connell. Don't let her set another charge.'

'I'll try, but please be careful.'

'I'll be fine.'

'Maybe not, when you see what's happened to the North Tower, the Martlet Window and the Boiserie Bedroom.'

'That's just stuff. It's the people I'm concerned about.'

'What about the Filigree Spider?'

'It's safe in my jewellery box, in your room at the Castle.'

'I'd love to see you wear it.'

She spread a wing from the box-pleated slit in her coat and brushed my face. I kissed its hand, taking in the biscuity scent of the rounded feathers, which overlapped like soft tiles. Paler down grew in the crook of her wing. She smelt like a small bird cupped in your hand, crumbly, warm, delicate but independent. I always feel a surge of love when I recall how my queen of green baize, seemingly petite, plays her hand in life as wily as her card games; she's tougher than a gangland lass.

Her feathers tickled my throat, sliding up and down as she breathed. 'You said you took cat last night. Why?'

'Because Saker found a way into the Shift.'

'*Saker* did?'

'He's a virtuoso pianist.'

'I know. So?'

'So ... So I think I'd better explain all that later.'

She folded her delicious wing back inside her coat, walked out into the rain and mounted her palfrey. 'Please don't do any more cat.'

'I won't.'

'Not on your own. Not with all hell breaking loose! You must catch this absolute bitch for me. Oh – whoa! ...Caprice always reckons you're going to eat her.'

'I never eat them without horseradish sauce.'

She leant and pressed her lips to my forehead. Some locks of hair trailed from her diamond pin. They were the same dark chocolate as her wings, and their shade changes throughout the year: they're almost black in winter, and I fancy then she looks slightly Rhydanne, muffled in furs when we walk in the snow.

'I'll telegraph you,' I said.

'If I'm not at Wrought, I'll be at the Castle.' She tapped Caprice's side, started forward and with Eleonora and her escort rode out of camp. I ran and took off, bound for Micawater.

CHAPTER 17

Micawater

I flew non-stop through the evening, all night and damp dawn. Some-time around ten a.m. next morning the ground assumed the familiar lush rolls of the Mica River valley, which was excellent progress. Nimbus clouds piled high over the Foin Hills tinted woodpigeon grey and pink. The rumbustious river caught their colours, churned them up and reflected them skywards like the iridescence of ancient glass. I turned and followed it down the valley.

It glitters, does Saker's river, with countless tiny mica flecks carried down the Gilt tributary, from up where the gold rush grounds used to be. Kilometres passed and the river matured and calmed but, even here, anyone who swims in the pure, clear water emerges shimmering with flat crystals, head to foot.

I passed over the town. There was his palace. I pulled in my wings and dropped into it like a wasp into a very ornate flower. I knifed smoothly down the sky; the roofs of the palace passed under me – the colonnaded portico, the main building, out over the double staircase, dropped to the fountain parterre – the striped lawns beyond tilted into view.

I spotted Saker, a little figure on the archery field alongside the lake. A sort of impromptu bridge – a walkway floating on punts – had been constructed from the lakeshore to the tree-covered island. It was un-dulating on wavelets in a sudden breeze. I skimmed the lawn with my wingtips, flared and landed next to him. In shirt sleeves and quiver at his hip, he was whacking arrows into a butt at just one hundred paces. The bereaved father: he drew the bow regularly, automatically; he was in a kind of trance. His red-fledged arrows bristled in the target.

Swish-thunk. Swish-thunk. There was something soothing in the sound of the shafts hitting. When I approached him I realised he was writing her name with arrows across the target. He stopped when the quiver was empty, hurled it on the ground and bent down to pick up a new one. 'How did she die?'

I explained the coach bomb. He listened intently, not looking at me, and I looked down the field at the arrows in the N of CYAN.

'Eleonora has sent Cyan to the Castle.'

'What, in a saddlebag?'

'... No, Saker, she—'

'Don't cosset me! I know there won't be much left.'

'Just the right hand,' I admitted.

'Is that all they could be bothered picking up?'

'It's all they could find ... It was fast. She didn't suffer ...'

'Ha!' He snarled. 'They set a bomb here, too. For me. Here! Here on my own grounds! The most evil, cowardly act I've ever seen!'

'Was there an explosion?'

'No. The lakeman found it.' He shouldered his bow and nodded at the island. 'In the mausoleum.'

I followed his gaze. The roof of the tomb, among the island's oak trees, shone as coral-coloured marble, wet from the last shower. Tall hollies and flowering rhododendrons clustered thickly around it, hiding its sparkling aventurine columns, the statues among the bushes and the pediment filled with figures, but the undergrowth had been trampled where the floating walkway joined the shore.

'I rolled out the bridge so Harrier's men could carry the barrels away,' he said bitterly. 'What is this Connell? How did she know I'd lay Cyan to rest there? How did she fucking get in? ...I'm going to lock the Lake Gate permanently! ...I mean, who ...'

'Be calm.'

'What I'm trying to say is: what sort of tattooed monster coldly sets a bomb waiting for me to lay my own daughter's body in the grave?'

The bomb wouldn't have only caught him. Me and Tern, Eleonora, Lory and Ortolan at least would row across the lake in formal mourning to carry Cyan to her vault.

'It would've killed me, too.'

'Oh, yes, it was very professionally done! Fuses ran to the back of the island. A canoe was hidden on the lakeshore. The *fucking* gypsies had stowed barrels of blasting powder behind *Martyn's* tomb. And *Teale's*, and my brothers', and all behind the bushes. So when we set foot in there, that bitch would light the fuse and blow us to bits!' He slipped into disgust. 'I can't believe it. How can she conceive such a thing? To murder a family in mourning, while they buried their daughter? To turn my mausoleum into a fireball!'

We fell silent, regarding its walls. They would have contained the blast and smashed Saker, Eleonora, Tern and myself to hot ash in an instant, against the tombs of three generations of his family.

'*Why?*' he yelled, and stormed off across the lawn.

I followed.

'*Why, why, why?*'

Because with the flick of a match Connell could obliterate the royal family and several Eszai.

'And stop!' he yelled at the sky. 'Fucking drizzling on me!'

'Saker ...' I said.

'She was Cyan Micawater. Eleonora denies me the right of burying her, and Connell tries to fucking kill me!'

'But—'

'And my other babies!'

Hastening towards the rear of the palace, we approached the rose beds of the knot garden. Saker flexed his bow and shot at the first rose bush – the arrow zipped through and half-buried itself in the soil behind.

As we reached it, I saw he had neatly severed one of the blooms; it lay on the ground with a length of stalk. He snatched it up without breaking pace and shook it at me.

'If you did that with a rifle, you'd burn the stem!'

I stared at him.

He ripped the rose to shreds as he strode up the Melowne Steps, along the terrace, and in through the French windows to the Mosaic Gallery. Inside, he halted, pulling off his archery glove and staring down the gallery to his children.

The glove was stained pink from the rose petals. I came in, startling Lory and his sister, who were playing with blocks before one of the lamp-bearing statues.

'No, no, let them stay,' he said to someone through the doorway. His voice echoed slightly off the agate of the Cornflower Landing. 'And search all the carriages for bombs. We're going to Tanager in the burgundy. Please set a meal for Jant – hall at twelve?' He shoved the glove in his quiver, cast Lory and Ortolan a strained smile, and set off down the long mosaic, reflected in the mirrors covering the wall.

'What are you doing to the gypsies?' I said.

'My Select Fyrd are rounding them up.'

'Not putting them in jail?'

'No. I can't. I shouldn't. Anyway, there's too many. My Select are picking them up with gusto – I didn't know there were hundreds. If I cram them in the Sturge, the conditions will be terrible. In two days it would ... Well, anyway, one gypsy's been slain already.'

'How?'

'An officer's brother was blown up at Spiza's Mill. So he stabbed a

Rose in return. Just like a sodding Cathee thing to do. I'm ashamed. Now, look, there'll be more repercussions. That's one reason I can't throw gypsies in jail. The jailers might kill them.'

'Really?'

'Half of Wrought's raring to lynch any Rose now.'

'Oh, god.'

'Your steward said so. Once they read the flaming rant the *Standard* printed this morning. Everyone's frightened. My staff, your towns-people. These powder charges are terrifying because nobody can see them. We don't know where they're hidden. But they need Roses to light them.'

'So you're getting rid of Roses?'

'None of those Sula's questioned so far admits to knowing anything. But they'd say that, wouldn't they?' He paused, and glanced at his reflection oddly, as if not really recognising it, or allowing himself to, and pulled at a strand of grey hair.

'So, what are you doing?'

'Throwing anyone with tattoos instead of wings, out of the country.'

'Please—'

'I know San won't agree. I'm trying to do the right thing, but, Jant – what is it? This is for their own good. If they stay, my people will turn on them. Connell *murdered* my lovely daughter. She dares to kill an Eszai! She tried to kill me three times. She killed a hundred and eleven people in Wrought.'

'A hundred and eleven ...'

'Raggiana said the toll's still climbing, because the burnt victims are dying, and he hasn't finished counting the ones missing from Kingfisher Mill. He said some will never be found.'

'Shit.'

'Yes. Shit. Do you see?'

He started again, towards the triple archway at the end of the gal-lery, over a mosaic of spearmen holding a leopard at bay, then a hind fleeing from hounds in full cry. 'Will you explain my position to the Emperor? I know Litanee can make their way back across the border. So my guards are telling them, that if they do, we'll impound their wagons. That'll stop them. Isn't a Litanee without his caravan two days away from ending up in a Hacilith workhouse?'

This was dire.

We reached the last slender gold statue holding a spherical oil lamp, turned on a mosaic of nestling quail, and returned up the gallery, over a bear raiding a beehive, and a stag having an exceptionally hard time with a snake.

'They could creep in on foot,' he said. 'Maybe more bombs are already set. But I've stopped them moving the stolen powder. I have Awian guards now on every magazine, every new shipment to the Front and they require papers, and I've allocated a hundred men to each mill.'

'Litanee help with your harvest.'

'The townspeople will volunteer instead.'

We reached the other end of the gallery, turned on a mosaic of a shepherd with lambs, and walked up and down the long room twice.

'Lory and Ortolan will be safer in Tanager, and Leon has more resources than I do.'

'She's too heavy-handed.'

'Isn't she? But if Connell's targeting me, I won't draw her fire onto my family. I'm going to hunt her down, and ask her, face to face, *why* she murdered my darling.'

The last thing I wanted was the king on a revenge trip. He pointedly left me standing on a mosaic of Morenzian wolves running from Awian fire-breathing eagles, that dated back to the 415 civil war. He went to speak to his children.

The mirrors covering the inside wall reflected the stunning view of the landscaped grounds and lake, because the outside wall was simply glass between its columns: centuries ago Saker had glassed-in the mosaic that used to be part of the terrace. But the mirrors and elegant torchière statues were new – the Mosaic Gallery used to have vine-painted walls and fluttering oil sconces, given that it was fourteen hundred years old.

We used to take off our boots to avoid damaging the mosaics, and the hypocaust floor beneath. But Micawater no longer had the pickled-in-aspic appearance it used to. Since leaving the Circle, Saker had transformed the Mosaic Gallery from an antiquity into a ballroom and the mirrors reflected nights of dancing and laughing masks. Now the guest rooms had running water and you could have a hot shower without having to trudge to the bath house. When Saker's brother had given him the place, 'to preserve for all time', he had really rolled up his sleeves about it, but now as a Zascai he'd ceased to care for a promise made so long ago. He'd dragged palace and town into the twenty first century in a mere fifteen years.

He crouched by his two kids. 'Lory, Ortolan. This is Jant. Remember Jant?'

They looked up brightly. They were sitting on a mosaic of a tortoise eating a bowl of cherries, and between them they'd constructed a rickety tower of blocks. 'They're building a little chateau.'

'Great,' I said.

'Jant's good at building little chateaux. Which is fortunate, con-
sidering—'

'Saker, stop it!'

'Go find the mosaic of the henhouse with the tiny chicks. That was
my favourite when I was your age.'

Lory and Ortolan jumped up and raced down the gallery. 'Jant,' said
Saker. 'Will you bring me the Emperor's advice?'

'Of course.'

'God knows I need it.'

'It's here! It's here!' called Lory, standing halfway down the gallery.
His sister was stuffing the end of her sash in her mouth. Lory Tanager
had a confident and open bearing, because Saker began his training
with sword and bow when he was aged three. Awians are born armed.

'Well done!'

The eleven year old and four year old ran to him. He crouched and
picked them up, one on each arm. 'Say goodbye to Jant. When you
next see him, he'll look just the same. It's the still hub of a world that
turns too quickly. Now, listen. We're going to see mother. You mustn't
go outside, and you mustn't hide from Hoopoe. Will you be good?'

They nodded, wide-eyed. He blew gently on their wings and his
breath parted the feathers to the down. They giggled and hugged him.
He gave them each a kiss and lowered them to the floor.

We went out to the terrace and closed the glass panelled doors
behind us.

'Wonderful, aren't they?'

'Gorgeous. So—'

'Lory can already ... Oh, fuck it. Jant, I can't eat, I haven't slept. I'm
exhausted.' He leant on the balustrade and looked down into the first
limpid pool of the parterre, which reflected the rear of the house. 'I just
keep wondering what's the last thing she thought ... and now you've
told me about the bomb, I'll be wondering what it felt like.'

'She never felt it.'

He put his hand over his eyes. Tiny, at the margin of the pool, the
water reflected us above the balustrade. The fountains had all been
switched off and there was no-one in sight. He'd sent them all home.

He cried a little. The loss hits like a physical blow. 'What have we
done to deserve this?' he said. 'How could we have hurt a gypsy?'

'I'll find Connell.'

'She won't touch Lory and Ortolan. They're all I've got left ... Cyan
– see, I can say her name. I'm not ashamed of crying. Cyan was only
seventeen. That's too young to die. She had all infinity ahead of her.'

'Yes.'

'A girl so brave doesn't deserve to die like that. To turn our own Insect weapon on us is … It's despicable! And she'd been coping with immortality well. Hadn't she, Jant?'

'Yes.'

'That makes it all the more painful.' He whacked the balustrade and didn't say anything else, but stared down the slight slope of the lawn to the lake with the mausoleum and oaks around it stretching for the sky. I walked the length of the terrace and back. Through the glass I saw Harrier's wife scooping up the children to prepare them for the ride to Tanager.

A brief shower of rain fell, and a gust of wind behind it splattered the drops against the stone. Then, as if the day's quota of rain had been fulfilled, the sun re-emerged and the whole place began to steam.

Saker took something out of his pocket and began measuring it between his hands. It was a roll of quick match. His eyes were shadowed and his brow furrowed.

'She was brave, wasn't she?'

'Cyan was, yes.'

'Not even Hurricane could daunt her. Jant, when I threw my Challenge and let her be Lightning, people said I'd made a mockery of San's whole system. They said it meant the Castle wasn't a meritocracy at all. Remember what the newspapers said? How they misread me? I was burnt by the hatred. They said I'd skewed the Circle. They said I'd let Cyan *inherit* my position. If Eszai's places can be passed from father to daughter the Circle's no better than this fucking pile. The *Standard* and the *Intelligencer* called for Challengers to come, and beat Cyan as soon as possible. Turf her out. But she held her own. Didn't she?'

'Yes, Saker.'

'So she was worth it.'

'Yes.'

'She died unbeaten, too.' He wound the quick match into a roll. 'During the Challenge I thought perhaps San wouldn't let her in. Maybe he'd refuse her, and open the position to general competition. But he did make her Lightning because he knew the system would right itself. He knew she'd be inundated with Challengers and she'd either square up to them, or fail.'

'She stood on her own two feet.'

He squeezed his eyes shut.

'She deserved the position,' I said.

'Ah … good.'

'What is that stuff?'

'Um … it's … the fuse from the mausoleum. Look. They laid it in haste. They didn't tape it properly.'

He showed me a link where lengths had been joined, tugged it, and the ends came apart. The bomber had simply slit the brown paper coating and shoved the new end inside. Quick match is string soaked in glue and covered with black powder. It would have raced to the charge. 'Connell didn't give herself much time to run,' he said. 'She cares little for her own safety. That's something else I don't understand.'

He dropped the fuse and it fell five metres into the terrace pool, shattering the calm reflection. Then, startled, he put a hand to his mouth and brought away a smear of blood. 'It … gunpowder always cracks my lips.'

'It cracks my fingers, too.'

'Caustic stuff. We're wrong to turn away from bows, Jant. I feel it here …' he tapped his chest. 'Bows are pleasing to handle … smooth wood and wax …'

'And gunpowder?'

'Is poisonous.'

'It was Cyan's life.'

'They live by it, they die by it! Fuck the Trisians for bringing us this scourge.'

'To the Trisians, we're the land where the sun sets,' I said, quoting Capelin.

Saker rubbed his lips, red raw from the drying effect of the powder. 'Well, I don't fear inventions old or new that crawl out of their damn library. But dangerous *philosophies* will go … boom.' He spread his hands in the shape of a fireball.

Then he sagged against the balustrade, shoulders hunched, and stared at the lake. Beyond its far bank, rising into the distance, landscaped stands of beech and walnut convened to direct the eye down a vista with a few fallow deer grazing, to a statue with its wings spread, on a column on the horizon. The sky changed constantly, with subtle-shaded pearl-white clouds, lemon-yellow and a stormy blue, which I couldn't tell if it was the colour of the clouds themselves or the naked sky behind them.

Saker didn't give a flap about it. He was folded into his grief. The Donaise sun hammered the surface of the water. The infinitesimal crystal flecks that hadn't settled out in the lake cast it back and glistened. On the far shore in a pool of trees, a columned pavilion mirrored the house, and from it a carriage driveway curved uphill to his telegraph tower, cunningly hidden out of the house's line of sight.

'I rode in at four a.m. The tears in my eyes turned the lamps to stars. Thankfully Balzan …'

I waited, but he didn't finish his sentence. I walked to the end of the terrace, where the panes of the hall's lightly-ornamented windows looked black against the shortbread-coloured stone. That hall used to be the stateroom of Awia.

Saker had one thing in common with Cyan. They were born at the right time. She was born at the perfect instant to make the most of the gunpowder revolution, and immortalised at a good age to innovate. He grew up in the Insect swarm of the seventh century.

Watching the clouds flock shadows across the lawn, I thought, it's hard to believe he knew this as the Insect Front. In 619 the Front ran behind that hill, the lake must have been a trodden swamp, and the Mosaic Gallery a field hospital. In his mother's reign, San and his army almost lost Awia. In the bitter fighting, day and night, Saker dedicated himself to stopping the Insects slaughtering his people. Insects had killed his father, his grandfather, and three of his younger brothers. He fought constantly, and the army called with hindsight the 'First Circle' collapsed around him. The archers who survived must have been tough as bugs and practised to perfection by the time the Games threw them against each other.

I sat on the balustrade and stretched my wings. His mother, Teale, was beside herself in despair that Awians were streaming to Hacilith as refugees once more. She was striding around that stateroom and yelling at his older brothers, inciting them to fight in the grounds teeming with Insects. 'If you want it so much!' she shouted, 'Go and get it!' and she hurled the jade sceptre through the window. That pane, there, the one at the end.

Saker was coming back from the battlefront and he saw it smash the glass and fall with the shards two storeys into the flowerbed. He picked it up and returned it to her, though the claw had broken off the eagle and it's missing to this day. He said, 'Mother, our family will never lose Awia, because I'll stand there with the archers. There' – where the statue is now – 'and I won't move. We'll shoot until we either push the vermin back, or the world runs out of arrows.'

It was the most desperate time, but he did it, and they forced the Insects into Bitterdale and held the Games on that very spot. And Saker had made Cyan's life just as desperate, but the desperation was the making of both of them.

Now, under the warmth of the sun and refreshing breeze, Saker gazed at nothing, down at the pool with the basking bronze mermaids. The surface of the water had restored the reflection of the rear of his house.

'Don't start that fidgeting with your scar again.'

'What ...? Oh. That. Forget that! It's not important ... At least I'll soon be with Leon.' He shuffled his wings and sighed. 'I know Cyan didn't like me to begin with. I'm glad we were reconciled at ... the end. I'm glad I got to know her ... how she really was. The rifle brought us together.'

He rubbed the raised tramlines of his Savory scar. 'She was only seventeen. Why do we destroy the youth of every generation? Cut her dead when she could have achieved so much more?'

'It's an achievement to have been Eszai.'

'She should be in Peregrine, alive ... and she would be, too, if I hadn't landed her with being Lightning.'

He turned from the vista, leant his backside on the balustrade, and looked up at the great rectangular windows of the second floor. 'I feel like it's my house for the first time ...'

Abruptly he slammed back into the Mosaic Gallery and darted down it. I followed, through the Green Drawing Room, Trisian Library, Reception Hall, to the Dining Room where a cold meal had been laid out for me.

'Food!' he said. 'They think of everything, these people!'

'Thanks, Saker.'

He went to the window and looked out. You could see the rotunda boathouse with its spiral rack. A few groundsmen were dismantling the impromptu bridge and loading the punts into it. One hand rustling the fletchings of the arrows in his quiver, the other with fingertips dug into his scar, he said, 'Insects didn't kill Cyan. Humans did.'

'Yes.'

'Hmm. Is that enough food to get you to the Castle? Is that all right?'

'I'll be fine.'

'Telegraph me at Tanager. I'll be waiting. I need the Emperor's advice ... You'll have to go soon, I'm afraid. It's one o'clock already.'

'How do you know?'

'I can see the sundial by the lilacs.'

'A sundial?'

'Yes.' He forced a smile. 'You never have to wind them.'

CHAPTER 18

Flight to the Castle

I flew over Micawater town, which Saker had kept much as it was in the year 687, the same as the palace, and any modernisation was invisible from the air. In all my life I'd never seen it so deserted.

No one sitting on the fountain's basin. No one on the green, or in the adjoining marketplace. No one loafing by the plinth of the Quadriga Statue of Gyr, Saker's brother the charioteer, galloping four copper horses in hand, the most famous sportsman of his day. Everyone must be terrified. They were all indoors and the streets were empty.

I've always thought Saker mustn't appreciate being constantly re-minded of his deadly brother but, because the citizens raised the statue in 625, he couldn't get rid of it. His manor must be cloyed with memories he won't allow himself to remove – maybe his cellar's packed with Gyr's statues – like living with other people's skeletons in your cupboard.

I flew over the idyllic rows of shops, Town Hall and muster office with its Insect siren, over the Alula Road. The town meandered, streets of the same biscuit-coloured stone with roofs of pale grey tile. Here, people's houses are spread out between almond trees and carefully-tended kitchen gardens. Awians like a great deal of personal space, it comes from having wings. Their sense of aesthetics, personal expres-sion, dignity and display; they'd never allow themselves to be crammed together in the noise and filth, exploited to death like the humans in the back-to-backs of Hacilith.

The houses dwindled into immaculate olive groves and vineyards through which the Austringer Road wound up over Donaise Magna. All the gates of the estate were painted the same sky blue.

If Saker hadn't preserved it in its chocolate box perfection, it could have been as big as Rachis or Tanager, with their beautiful skylines. To think, it was the largest town in the world once, before Hacilith over-took it thirteen centuries ago. Nervous people clipping the vines waved thankfully as my bird-of-prey shadow flicked over them. I recognise a nationwide clampdown when I see it. It's ugly and hate-filled and takes a hell of a long time to reverse. If Micawater had grown to a big town, these guys might have wider horizons, broader minds, and not be so damn scared.

I crested the belvedere on the summit, with the kourai statue on its tower: an idealised young man with his wings spread. Awians stick these statues here, there and everywhere to commemorate the brave sacrifice of the youth.

When Insects first appeared in 411, in the distant north at Lazulai, they made a small enclave of their Wall, and ate everything inside it. The Awians watched them, fascinated, and even dropped in food. When the news reached the Pentadrica, Queen Alyss came to see what was happening. At that point the Insects, which had stripped their enclave bare, burst out and slaughtered Alyss, her retinue and hundreds of Awians. The Insects ranged around, eating cattle and crops, expanding towards Lazulai. The young men and women of the city, the kourai, took up arms for the first time – bill hooks and boar spears – and ventured to round up the Insects and kill them all. The Insects massacred every last youth. But they made the original offensive, which Awians hold dear to this day.

Eventually Lazulai fell, and the families of those brave people fled south to Murrelet. A hundred and forty years later, their descendants fled south again, from Murrelet to Micawater. It's been a steep learning curve.

So, the Pentadrican elite having been devoured, their country collapsed in chaos. The Plainslands and Morenzia began to seize borderlands, while desperate Awian refugees surged in. All three nations fought over Pentadrican land for four years, the only civil war we've ever had, until, in 415, San brought them to a settlement. Humans and Awians signed the peace treaty at Dace, and San led them against the Insects instead. His campaign successfully slowed the Insects' advance, and the kings of Awia and Morenzia proclaimed him Emperor that same year. They gave him Alyss' palace, and he made it his Throne Room. He built a curtain wall around it, and it became the Castle.

You see kourai statues so often you hardly notice them, but Saker had infected me with his melancholy mood. It was hard to believe I'd never see Cyan again.

As he says, she was only seventeen, but there's been one younger Eszai. The youngest was sixteen, she was one of my precursors as Messenger, who got cemented into the Wall somewhere east of Col Oriole, and starved there beyond rescue, until the Emperor couldn't hold her any more.

I could have been the youngest Eszai ever. I was fifteen when the landslide forced me to leave Darkling. I'd taught myself to fly by then. In fact, if I hadn't been spiralling over the sheer arêtes, a wolf pack wouldn't have eaten the goats I was supposed to be tending, Eilean wouldn't have thrown me out of the shieling, and the avalanche would have crushed me, too.

I'd taken to the air and left Scree Plateau. If I'd known about the Castle then, I'd have flown straight to the Emperor. I wouldn't have had to live in the city. What a waste of time my seven years in Hacilith had been, like a loop snagged from a tapestry. But I came from nowhere and I knew no better, so it's pointless mourning those years of strife. I had to suffer them, to learn about the world and the Castle. But still, I glided, wistfully, contemplating how I could have snipped off the loop of Hacilith and been immortalised at fifteen. How bizarre. What would it feel like to live in my fifteen year old's body forever?

Exciting! Sexy! Confusing for all the Zascai who often don't take me seriously enough at twenty-three.

I reached the Castle early evening, and landed in the Starglass Quad. The Throne Room's South Façade loomed, pierced with the great Rose Window high above, and step-topped with pinnacles. Riant sunlight lit the elaborate wall, deepening the shadows of the stonework and almost vivifying the fifty statues in niches, from the great Tympanum Portal to the height of the rose.

I ran towards the entrance. The statues represent the immortals, they carry weapons or tools to signify their positions, and they'd been carved from life, from the original fifty who'd won through the heats of the Games. I passed Rayne's statue, which stands as a cornerpiece to the portal, and others line up, leading into the doorway itself.

I passed into the shadow of the carved lintel. The two guards uncrossed their halberds; I entered the dim, green marble narthex, with frankincense lamps burning on ledges. The fan-vaulted ceiling was lower here, so when you pass through the carved amber doorway, you're hit by the full effect.

I stepped through the threshold. The dazzling Throne Room soared around me. There was San, on the Sunburst Throne at the end of the aisle, its long, gold flames radiating at his back. Harlequin light from the rose window fell upon the ebony benches and the scarlet carpet.

I walked down the aisle, past the carved bench ends. Beams from the high, pointed windows shone across the immense vaulted space, slanting lancet-arched panels of light on the glittering mosaic of the opposite wall, ascending to the gallery where guards with longbows watched, and highlighting the huge onyx columns of the arches striding the hundred metre length of the hall, their tops drooping with acanthus leaves and dripping with carving. Above me, the ceiling bosses of ships, trophies of arms, beasts and Insects seemed alive.

The walls above the arches coruscated with an Insect battle in polychrome mosaic on a gold background, soldiers and cavalry filling the walls, in ancient lamellar armour and each man an individual lovingly rendered, perhaps from life, from the men of the first army.

The Emperor watched me all the way. I felt the strength of his scrutiny. His face was shadowed by the top two straight spines of the sunburst and the wavy rays either side of them. The glorious light behind him shone from four pointed windows in the apse behind the throne. All I could see of the Emperor's face were his pinched cheeks and shoulder-length white hair, but I felt pierced to the core by the strength of his insight: the pale grey eyes you can never meet.

I reached the space before the four dais steps, stopped in one of the shadows of the rays, and bowed, feeling my katana hilt press my back.

'Comet,' said the Emperor. 'Tell me.'

I related the bombing of Wrought, Cyan's death and Saker's reaction, standing quite still. A step to either side would flare the sunlight in my eyes. 'The King of Awia requests your advice,' I said.

'Tell him this. He must not persecute the Litanee. All the peoples of my Empire have always been free to travel throughout the world.'

'He said the newspapers are stirring up hatred.'

'Will you write to counteract them?'

'Yes, my lord.'

'Extend a hand to the Litanee. Encourage the Awians to overcome their fear. Litanee people should remain in Awia if they wish. Tell Queen Eleonora and King Saker the Castle will help them find Connell Rose, and she must be brought to me.'

'Yes.'

'Not to Eleonora. Do you understand?'

'Yes, my lord.'

'We must stop the hatred festering. I will protect the royal family. Where might Connell be?'

'She could be anywhere. She could have reached Litanee by now.'

'Then ask Governor Aver-Falconet if he will tactfully search Litanee.'

'Yes, my lord. Tornado's on his way here.'

'Then I will have him scour the Plainslands, as Eleonora is combing Awia, and Hurricane searches Lowespass. We will design a net to catch Connell. She will not remain at large for long. As she is not forthcoming about her reasons for murdering Lightning, I am interested in speaking with her face to face.'

I shivered. 'Yes, my lord.'

'Co-ordinate them and keep me informed. I also want you to pub-licise a contest for the position of Lightning to be held here as soon as possible. We are not daunted by the threat of black powder charges. Speak to the musketmen and archers, so they may devise a competi-tion and set a date.'

I bowed, met his fathomless eyes, and glanced for relief at the stained glass windows behind him. Each had a design of the people and bounty of each of the four lands. To my left, on the mosaic around the windows, the tumultuous vanguard of the cavalry crashed into a serrate swarm of Insects, filling the space above the gallery with bronze carapaces and silver blades. They're a comfort. The standard bearer with the moustache, I like him best.

San said, 'Be sure Queen Eleonora has no doubt that Litanee must not be expelled from Awia, nor imprisoned, nor harmed in any way.'

'I will, my lord. Thank you.' I bowed, and left.

I ran past Breckan; Kay's and Sirocco's rooms, under the Breckan Bridge and along the front of Carillon, the Treasurer's apartment, then Gayle's on the ground floor. Mare's Run on my left was a cliff of elegant pilasters and sash windows, curved to fit in the gap between Carillon and the curtain wall. I passed the Master of Horse's rooms, then the Sailor's, then the raised pond reflecting water lilies like porcelain bowls.

On my right, behind the two rococo red and white storeys of Carillon, behind its louvred bell tower, the Throne Room's walls stretched to the sky. The great spire of the Throne Room dwarfs the northwest bridge and the theatre's cupola; it draws your gaze to its sunburst apex, shining in the sky.

I threw open the door of my tower in the curtain wall and ran up the three hundred and thirty steps to my apartment. I booted the pile of newspapers away from the entrance and went in. There was the usual stack of letters on my desk. I grabbed them, sat on the split-level steps between my study and bedroom, and glanced through them.

One letter was remarkable in the quality of its cream-wove paper, my address inscribed in a sophisticated hand – the Sailor's:

> The Flagship *Gerygone*
> Cobalt Bay
> 21 June '40

What ho, Jant!

Having received your – perplexing, I might add – semaphore ask-ing for the gen on missing gunpowder, I thought you might fancy a head's-up of the latest from our beloved Grass Isle.

I uncovered a cache in a smugglers' cave. It's a dry, man-made affair in the cliff, which I've known about since the blessed days of Ata, and in it yesterday, lo and behold, ten kegs of blasting powder appeared. Though there's space for a hundred more. While the Grass Isle customs were recovering them, some Litanee attacked. They seized a policeman, Cargeen, and carried him off. Bally cheek. If I'd been present it'd never have happened. They escaped scot-free and resumed their activities, blithe as larks.

So I sail my old tub to Cobalt and lie in wait, and last night I pop out the telescope and what do I spot? A nippy little schooner rounding Cobalt Point. The dapper thing scoots by out of view to everyone but yours truly, and anchors off Cullion Cove where she disgorges a rowing boat that lands them ashore.

They aren't real smugglers, because it's full moon. Smugglers only sail under a blank moon. The stolen powder is their cargo, right enough. Now, Jant, as this schooner is new to me and dashed efficient, I thought I'd let you know before blowing her clear of the water. Give you a chance to come and look, what?

And while we're on the subject of explosions, what the blazes do you mean by trying to keep the five inland at Wrought secret? You cannot keep the damn things under cover, Jant, because they are *explosions*, and *id est* I can hear them. Give a chap some credit. So maybe you should flutter over and tell me what the bally hell is going on.

Ecanath tuam cai sanhizerai and all that. Oh, by the way, tell your wife I play four-of-a-kind in spades.

Yours,

Mist Fulmer Harandis

Admiral of the Fleet for the Eternal Emperor San

The curlicues on his signature took up half the page. The other letters weren't so hot a lead. I wrote statements for the *Wrought Standard* and *Moren Intelligencer* and sent them by courier. Then I went up to my telegraph on the roof of Lisade and rattled off messages to Aver-Falconet, Saker and Tern. I love being in my telegraph hut with a cold beer and a fine commanding view of the Castle, all the way out to the semaphore at Binnard. I like to imagine the guys in Binnard One thinking, 'Oh, shit,' when I flex my callsign. Wake up, suckers! This is genuine Rhydanne Speed!

Saker bunged a reply down the line while I was coding Tern's. I replied, he answered and we kept going all night. Look what I've saddled myself with – the addictive love of talking to my friends, but also the vacuum attraction into the always-eager lugholes of four nations ... god knows how many millions of people.

Before, I hadn't been so aware of their constant greedy listening. Newspapers don't suck me dry the same way, their timelag gives me breathing space. But with the telegraph I feel the weight of people listening, an attendant hush from the extremities of the continent, a void I ache to fill with sound. I sit watching, like a spider with my fingers on the web, and read the chatter of four lands pouring information like colour into my black-and-white, rounding out my worldview.

I didn't move a muscle but for my arms sweeping the levers across the console, until the sky began to wake. The darkness diluted to pale powder blue and the Throne Room's spire and roof seemed cut-outs against it. The moon's silver disk, consumed by verdegris, hung directly beside the spire that bisected the air through my right windowpane, springing at the sky like a frozen fountain.

I reluctantly scraped my soul off the semaphore line, poured it back in, signed off, relinquished the console to Jackdaw and tore myself away to the kitchens. 'Tré! Tré! Rustle me up a cooked breakfast.'

Tré Cloud the Quartermaster looked up from the cast-iron range that ran the length of one wall. 'Jant! Bit early for you, isn't it?'

'I've been awake all night.'

'How very Eszai. Don't start pulling on the Circle, because I for one can't stand it.'

'I was driving the telegraph.'

'Your telegraph. You're swopping one drug for another. Here, have a coffee. Wedge open the crack of dawn.'

'Thanks.'

'Hall serves at five. Can't you wait?'

'No.'

'What do you want in this cooked breakfast?'

'Everything.'

Tré sighed and beckoned a couple of maids. I sat down at the massive, bare wood table, which was frayed with knife scars and smelt of pastry. Tré organises all the supplies for the Castle and for thousands of fyrd at the battlefront, and only rarely does cooking himself. He's friendly and usually flays me for news. This time he noticed my bloodshot eyes and cut me a bit of slack.

I feel like I'm two men. One is slick, formal, public-facing, strumming the semaphore to send out San's orders, letting its two-thousand-kilometre serpent suckle at his chest. The other wants to crawl into a quiet room to think about Cyan. Maybe shoot some scolopendium.

Definitely get drunk. I won't even have chance to mourn her, will I? Because the Castle's split me between being Jant and Comet, and now I must be Comet.

'Here. One Tré special, done to a turn.' He slipped a platter of rashers and eggs in front of me and presented me with a fork. 'Bacon is not well-known to cure battle stress, but I'll try.'

'Do you think I've got battle stress?'

'The kitchen is eighty metres long, Jant. You were doing the thousand metre stare.'

'It's Cyan,' I said. 'She was killed.'

'I know, I felt it. I dropped all the goddamn orders.'

I related everything while I pushed bacon around my plate with the fork. I didn't feel like eating after all. There's no swift cure for battle stress. We move men who've become terrified of Insects off the front line and put them in support roles, because if you send them home they suffer more long-term trauma, thinking Insects are invincible and seeing them everywhere. Those men you can never re-enlist, because they think they've failed.

'I haven't failed,' I said aloud.

'Jant, nobody's saying—'

'The gypsy bitch killed Cyan! Then I let her escape. Of course I've failed!'

The windows above the row of sinks looked out onto Carillon court, and down the length of the room ran scrubbed cupboard doors. Beside us, a fire-blackened hearth gaped in a brickwork chimney arch, fettered by the clockwork mechanism that turns spit roasts for the Castle's feasts. Its iron spikes and bars were spotlessly clean, but the aroma of browned meat-jelly, gravy and suet flour permeated the very fabric of the room. At the end, where the storerooms began, a small army of cooks were washing potatoes in the sinks. At the draining boards girls were clinking stacks of dishes.

Behind them, a very fat little boy sitting on an upturned pail was fishing into the floor. He wore dungarees, and held his rod straight, and his line led directly into the tiles, a hallucination that made my eyes water.

'What,' I said slowly, 'Is that?'

Tré followed my gaze. 'Oh,' he said apologetically. 'He's my son.'

'You can see it?'

'Of course I can see him. He's my son!'

I couldn't spot a resemblance. Tré was sinewy, crew-cut, with sunken cheeks and a square jaw. He works flat out – arguably he toils the longest hours of any Eszai, which is saying something. The chubby boy was greasy-haired, his forehead knotted with habitual disobedience. I trailed down the kitchen to him and knelt where his line ran into the floor. A tile had been prised up, and through the hole I could only see a deep, black space. 'What are you doing?' I asked.

'Fishing,' said the boy.

I accepted that as a fair response for having asked a stupid question.

'He's fishing,' said Tré, appearing beside me like a stork. 'It's a long way down.'

'A very long way,' said the boy.

'How far?'

The boy said nothing.

'Gabby,' Tré addressed him. 'Talk to the Messenger.'

'How much line have you reeled out?'

No answer.

'Gabby,' said Tré. 'Talk to Jant and I'll make you a plate of chips.'

'About twenty metres,' said the boy.

'What!'

'I catch custard fish.'

I looked up. 'He catches carp,' Tré rectified. 'Blind white carp. About this big': he held his hands half a metre apart.

I peered into the hole but saw not a glimmer of light. 'What's down there?'

'The old cisterns of the Pentadrica. All this place is built on Pentadrica palace, you know. The Throne Room was originally Alyss' stateroom, before San extended it. Down there are the palace cisterns – the kitchen was built on top.'

'Wow.'

'And the Dining Hall, and this end of Carillon.'

I began to envisage the floor as just a thin, tiled crust that could crumble at any time, tipping me into a limitless void. I backed from the hole lest my weight should break it open, and the boy chuckled.

'They left cisterns?' I said. 'I thought we just had wells.'

'Oh, all the wells drop down into it.'

'How did you find out?'

Tré shrugged. 'I've always known.'

'Well, I had no idea!'

He shook a thin finger at the prised-up quarry tile. 'Jant, you don't haunt the kitchens much. I've defended my place in the Circle for three centuries and I know every millimetre of the Castle and demesne.'

'Give me that.' I reached out to one of the maids who was drying a spoon. She tossed it to me and I held it above the hole. Dropped it. The spoon turned over and over, falling into the void.

We waited.

We waited.

'Did you hear anything?' said Tré.

'Sh …'

Nothing.

'You're ruining my fishing,' said the boy.

We never heard a splash. 'How deep is it?' I asked him. 'How deep is the water?'

'Dunno.'

'And how often do you catch these custard fish?'

''Bout once a day.'

Carp, so long-bereft of light they'd lost their colour and their sight. Reduced to ghosts but for the bulk of their pale muscle, had they been swimming in the pitch darkness beneath our feet for two thousand years? I sat back on my haunches. The Vermiform gave me a sharp jab in the chest, then swayed out of my pocket, observing everything, but fortunately Tré was too involved with his intractable son to notice.

The worms had been so quiet I'd forgotten they were there. I supposed they'd been spying on everything. I took a handful of coffee and sugar sachets from the pot on the table, poured some sugar in my pocket for the Vermiform and stuffed the rest in my pack. These sachets of concentrated coffee match the stuff Tré brews for caffeine content and almost for taste. You're supposed to squeeze them into a cup of hot water, though recently I've taken to ripping them open in-flight and sucking them down, it's more convenient.

I said goodbye to him and the boy who had resumed ignoring me. I don't know where the child had come from because Tré Cloud has always stayed single but occasionally has a fling with a cook. Maybe also once with Ata because, for reasons never disclosed, a hundred years ago Shearwater Mist called him out for a duel. Mist beat him all the way around Carillon, and would have skewered him conclusively if Gio hadn't run in and disarmed them both.

I went out and took off, rejoicing in my strength. The cool air had no lift whatsoever. I flapped over Monument Courtyard, up past the cliff of the Throne Room's North Façade, over the white limestone lantern that's the base of the great spire, directly above the Emperor's Throne, the place where the prime meridians cross, the centre of the world.

The tower ascends, more slender as it rises seventy metres, through stages of complicated openwork, a stone lace of quatrefoils. Gargoyles lean from its four corners up to the last stanza of false arches, beloved roost of my good self and a host of small white doves, from which pinnacles ascend like a marble arpeggio to the final smooth spire, long and tapering-thin. It ends in a spike, like a lance, bearing the huge gold sunburst boss – which shines like a second sun by day, and reflects the stars after nightfall. You can see it for a hundred kilometres across the Plainslands, and you know the Emperor holds our existence firm in his hands beneath.

It's breathtaking. It dwarfs you. I've lived here two hundred years and every time I fly over I see new details. It never ceases to uplift you and flatten you into insignificance at one and the same time.

I flapped over three more steps of delicate buttresses, flying higher, over the Throne Room's roof and away over the Plainslands.

And here I must ask you old hands to let your attention wander, again, while I bring the newcomers up to speed. I can fly because I'm half Awian, and so have wings like another, longer, pair of arms jointed from my back just below my shoulderblades. Awian bodies – some say, their minds as well – preserve the accoutrements of flight, but they can no longer fly. But I'm from the high cordillera, and my mother was a Rhydanne huntress, a lithe mountain people adapted for running to hunt and to mate, and for survival at high altitude among the granite and ice. My father was an Awian trader who caught her one day – I'll never know how – but probably it was nasty, because it was the only time my grandmother ever witnessed Awians, and she spoke of them in the plural.

My wings are lengthier than normal, influenced by my leggy Rhydanne build, and with my Rhydanne fitness I can use them to fly. I have the fortune of being a freak. None of us really reach the Castle without a jolt of the wheel of fortune, and how can you separate fortune and brilliance? Our stories are varying combinations of the staple of hard, hard work with various degrees of the garnish of natural talent, and luck ... and sometimes privilege, too.

I'm grateful to the Emperor for providing a sanctuary for us, and such a nonpareil Castle, a community where we can give the world our knowhow. The Castle rescued me from my drug turf wars and the murder scene of Felicitia. It rescued Sirocco Tassy, who was trapped as an apprentice blacksmith to a very hard master. Otherwise no one would have heard of us. Our talent would've been wasted. San allows us to fulfil our potential, he gives us the scope to work, the freedom to stretch our wings.

We glory at the fact we come from every kind of background and every goddamn era, and San helps us work together, keeps us in check but gives us chance, so the world benefits from our service. Otherwise,

Ella Rayne would have died a servant in the mid-six hundreds, Kay Snow would have died a labourer in the eighteenth-century tin mines, and Tornado would have fought as a mercenary in Lowespass until the end of his days.

So the Castle raised us from our terrible lives. Because to hate where your life's heading but just wait patiently until it's over, is the philosophy of the whore. You can hide your face in your wing and wait till the world's finished shafting you, taking its pleasure on your body, soul and time – or you can go looking for the Castle.

The Emperor tries to keep the paths to the Circle clear for all, but even he can't remove the hand of chance. I used to think he was the only man who could halt the wheel of fortune and turn it as he wills, but I'm older now and I know better.

After five hours slogging across the Plainslands I picked up the onshore breeze and smelt the fresh, salt sea. North of Cobalt Head, the wind had flattened the clouds to a thick bank on the horizon, poison blue and broiling like spit in lamp oil, in which inkblot birds fought for movement.

I glided over the seacliff and it dropped away beneath me, a hundred metres to the white-topped waves curling in on a full tide. Ahead, the gunship *Gerygone* rested at anchor with the potential of a panther.

Over the next half hour I battled against the wind, closed the distance and began to recall her gigantic size. *Gerygone*'s ochre-striped hull was longer than three *Stormy Petrels* moored nose-to-tail, the biggest ship ever built. She packed the firepower of Lowespass keep, and her four naked masts pinned the sky. Mist Fulmer the Sailor must have seen me because a line of flags tugged up to the foremast: *At last! What kept you?*

Closer, and I saw him at the bow rail. He hailed me with his soigné cigarette. I settled into a glide, brought the hull below me, opened flat the decks, let all the staring faces pass under me, then the mast heads like the tallest trees of the forest. The lookout ducked, the ship dropped behind; I turned with the wind and let it speed me back over the topmasts. Against the repoussé water, traced the fine line of Fulmer's smoke.

Very few Awians smoke because it fucks their bodies up so much. But those who do, really go for it. Having twice the air capacity and exchange of a human, it gives us quite a kick. The idea is to keep fresh air in your airsacs while using your lungs to smoke, but Fulmer isn't into harm reduction and more often uses both. Smoking is a sea trader's habit, given that tobacco's grown in Peregrine and shipped to Hacilith, but Fulmer hates to display his origins. Given that – and the fact that it's not a welcome vice in the court of Awia – he'd have stopped by now if he wasn't hopelessly addicted.

Fulmer very much wants to be part of Eleonora's court, the playboy of the eastern ocean, but his background makes him an outsider. He's assumed the chipper brand-new slang of her closest set, and sounds like the louchest of the in-crowd swells on a club night, which I find a bit much. I curled down the leeward side of *Gerygone* and balanced in the air at the level of his face. Vast as the ship was, she fitted him as if tailored.

'What ho! What ho! Jant, it is a rare pleasure! Well, maybe not so rare but still very much a pleasure. Hop aboard!'

I stepped onto the deck. Fulmer drew on his cigarette in an amber holder and exhaled a cloud of smoke. 'Now,' he said. 'How's your thalassophobia?'

'I'm not afraid of *Gerygone* – but we have to search her.'

'Why? I felt the Circle break … It took me flat aback. Tell me all: who died? What's happening?' He ushered me towards his cabin. 'After you, please, consider yourself my guest. The sun is over the yard arm, is it not?'

CHAPTER 19

Rich and Strange

Mist Fulmer, immaculately coiffured and spotlessly dressed, poured me a gin and tonic in his cabin. He passed me the glass, then seated himself in great style in a gimballed chair at his navigation desk and surveyed me critically: my ten-year-old t-shirt and leather jacket.

'Bally hell,' he breathed. 'It must be serious.'

I recounted everything. On hearing of the Litanee he jumped up and ordered his first mate to search the ship for bombs and the crew for tattoos. On hearing of the destruction of Wrought he whipped out another cocktail cigarette and lit it with a handsome silver lighter. 'I'm very sorry for Tern. She must be suffering. We want to know *why* these terror-mongers ... Terror*ists*, want to kill you. We need to catch one in flagrante ... I'm glad I can help.' He glanced at a pocket watch. 'If the smugglers follow the same routine tonight as for the last three, they're due in two hours. Time for some chow?'

'Yes!'

'On *Gerygone*, there's no such thing as a ship's biscuit.' He leant back, snapped his fingers, and a valet began bringing in sea bass *en croute* sauce *mireille*, and the best fruit of Lakeland Awia.

'Fulmer, are you sure they're smuggling gunpowder?'

'Bless you. They're too far away to be sure.'

'I can fly over them and drop a grenade.'

'No. I want that schooner. She's new to me. I don't know who paid for her but she's a goer. I fancy adding her to the fleet.' He adjusted the cigarette in its holder. 'They'll surrender when they see *Gerygone*. Smugglers always do ... Now jolly well pin back your lugs, you big seagull. I placed a company of marines at the harbour in Cullion. They're ready to pounce tonight, when the smugglers land. Their captain wants you to join the fun – if you apprehend them, you can discover their contact ashore. I will tack after their schooner in *Gerygone* and catch her simultaneous. Very good?'

'Very good,' I said.

'Peachy. I'll repay any heartbreak they caused my Lady Tern ... a woman of sublime taste and a minx at cards. The loss of her house ... all her treasures ... her dresses. It beggars belief. Are you finished? Pray join me on deck.'

He stood up and swept out his coat-tails. I followed his aromatic smoke the length of the deck and up the fo'c'sle steps to the bow. Looking down, you could see the anchor rope issuing from its brass-rimmed eye in the hull, and the ivory-white figurehead, her arms and wings thrown back. She trailed a banner on which was carved *Gerygone* in raised gold script.

'They round yonder headland.' Fulmer conjured a telescope and scanned the horizon. 'This is a clement evening, is it not?'

'It is.'

'I do hate to break the silence with cannon fire.'

'Actually, you love it.'

'Pardon me, but I don't. One should be content to exist beautifully without causing such mayhem, but the smugglers will sail. Have a gander.' He passed me the telescope.

Fulmer, like the rarest liquor, is best taken in small doses. He complements his bird-boned face with a cravat of water-grey silk tied four-in-hand. It suits his brown hair short at the back and sides, longer and curly on top. His swallowtail cut-away coat has intricate box-braiding in trefoils on the forearm. A millimetre to the left or right, and it wouldn't be perfect. As were high-waisted suit trousers, front-pleated, and his sword hanger which boasted eight flawless buckles and a stirrup hilt sabre with acorn tassels (as now worn).

Beginning as a clerk in the harbourmaster's office at Tanager, Fulmer used to be very much Eleonora's man, and her courtier, when she came to power. Well, if you have a wit that quick and moonraking ambition, it's no good sitting in an office sketching sail plans and dreaming at the oceaned window. Eleonora made him captain of our sister ship when we sailed to Tris and, working to a large degree as her informant, he returned with our caravels packed to bursting with gold and spices. When the last Sailor was killed San opened a contest to find the next, and Fulmer breezed into the Castle and beat his competitors hands down at every trial. He raced to Tris, he knew the route, and brought back yet more wealth for Eleonora. He circumnavigated the Fourlands in the fastest ever time, and loved to say he was the first to set a spatted shoe on the north coast of Awia for fifteen centuries since it fell to the Paperlands.

So San joined him to the Circle. Fulmer set up the clipper trade to Tris and became a rich man. An incorrigible dandy and a dashed efficient dancer, he is all bonhomie ninety-nine percent of the time, but he hasn't got used to being Mist. If a sailor disobeys a direct command his grand sense of theatre may well flip, revealing a streak that varies from the waspish to the downright severe.

The sun sank behind Cobalt cliff top and the sky darkened from pink streaks, through all the shades of purple and the stars began to prickle. The *Gerygone* ran like clockwork and Fulmer listened to the small sounds of change of tide and watch.

'She tells me if anything's wrong,' he smiled. 'Jant, many Roses are embroiled in smuggling. They know how to move in secret. That schooner is swifter than anything on land. If they're using her, they've already taken your blasting powder anywhere.'

'Everywhere?'

'Potentially. I'm very impressed that you've beaten your fear. But perhaps a little fear gives us the zip?' He aligned his cufflinks and looked at the waves. 'Do you remember Shearwater Mist?'

'Of course.'

'I met him, once. When I was a boy. And, of course, I was trying to impress him. I said: "I'm not afraid of cold water." And he said: "I am." ... And that ... is the moral of this story.'

Sails at varying distances were brigantines running coffee, silk cocoons and tobacco to the mills of Hacilith, leaning on the wind fore and aft. The night breeze blew over us. Fulmer stood facing into it and ruffled not a hair. On an unseen cue the sailors extinguished the lamps and we were plunged into darkness. The susurration of the sea came more clearly. It licked and lapped and clicked at our cutwater, but *Gerygone* gave not a creak.

Fulmer peered at the horizon. 'Dead on time!'

He pointed with his cigarette and handed me the telescope. I looked through it but only saw the black water and the greyer half of the sky above.

'See the star ...? A lantern.'

'How can you see a lantern at this distance?'

'Practice.'

I searched the horizon but couldn't glimpse anything. 'They're miles away!'

'They don't fancy the sporting odds in buzzing past a man-o-war. They think we're out of sight.' He fastened the 'scope to his eye. 'Ah ... the schooner dropped her landing craft! Away she goes! Jant, go catch the rowboat, we'll run down the schooner.' He whirled round. 'Anchors aboard! Sail fore and main – and the boom main – I want her on the *star*board tack nor' nor' east ... Dee? What are you *wait*ing for?'

'Aye ayes' resounded all over the ship and men swarmed out of the hatches like Insects. They set arms like iron bars to the capstan, their broad backs billowed, and the thing began to turn.

Fulmer was so clean and snappily-dressed he seemed to stand out in sharp focus, as if suddenly transported from a ballroom to the deck. His intelligent eyes laughed. 'Now, Jant. Lay aloft, and to Cullion. You'll find your fifty marines and their captain at the Red Lion on the harbour front. There'll be no more than four smugglers in that rowboat. You'll have them. Cullion has a lockup, so you can fling them in custody … *Eva! Dee!* Tacks and sheets or I'll *haze* you!'

Fulmer was obviously going to spend the next hour shouting his head off – without losing one ruche of his cravat or scuffing his two-tone boots.

I took off as the *Gerygone* began to move, angled up into the air, found my pace and flapped higher, out of sight of the ship and her prey. The wind bent the sensitive quills of my flight feathers and brought the memory of Tern running her fingers through them like a harp. Oh, Tern; she's lost everything and maybe more bombs are being planted at this very moment to kill her.

I reached the apex of my flight and sailed down with fixed wings towards Cullion Cove. The sea cliff's black wedge hid it for a second, then opened out and revealed a handful of houses. They looked as if they'd been cast like dice all down the narrow, rocky gorge and out onto the quayside. Their tiled roofs stepped down at varying levels; gritstone wall corners stuck out at angles. The hunter's moonlight glossed each roof dark red, but the road and stream that cut together through the centre of the town were invisible between them.

The last of the road's hairpin bends emerged onto the quay. The stream ran out towards me, and past the humpbacked bridge was the pier. The Red Lion pub stood square and whitewashed beside it. Not a lamp showed there. Few ships dock at Cullion, which lies between the big ports of Awndyn and Peregrine. The clippers sail out of Awndyn to Tris, the coal freighters come in from Wrought, and Peregrine brigantines take luxuries to every part of the Empire.

I zipped over the cliff top, descended before the dark cliffs with their needle stacks, flew low and fast over the cobble beach, flared my wings and landed in front of the pub.

A single lantern on the open ocean showed where the smugglers were rowing in. I slipped into the beery barroom.

CHAPTER 20

Connell speaks – in the landing craft

The fat policeman was all in disarray. Lagan poked a knife through his shirt and tilted the blade till it pinched his skin. 'Not a peep!' Lagan was stressed and the porky policeman was squirming in the bilges, so I slapped Lagan's knee and he desisted, sat back on the bench.

'And put the knife away,' I hissed. Any fool could see it shine. Our boat bucked, rode the crest of a wave and slid down, wallowing, into the trough. Tressel and his boy stepped over the benches, settled down, and figured the oars into the rowlocks.

One oar each, we set to rowing. The boy was in the stern with the dark lantern and the policeman, trussed hand and foot and gagged, lay in the bilges between our feet. I'm sure all he could see was the sky, and that only out of one eye, because Lagan had closed the other for him. I huffed and strained, my arrow wound burning. Tressel rowed silently. Our oars touched the water, lifted, leaving dots either side of our wake. The mass of the land loomed closer and soon we were in its shadow, which seemed to mute our sound.

There was no movement, no figures. Cullion was as shuttered and silent as it had been these last three nights. I clicked the telescope closed and dropped it back in my pocket. 'Eleven o'clock and all's clear.'

Lagan grinned. He'd set his foot on the policeman's cheek. I shrugged, then with a hand on Tressel's shoulder and the other on the mast base, push-jumped my way between them and into the stern where I took the tiller from the boy and steered into the quay.

Tressel and Lagan's oars dipped, breaking the black water almost without sound. Lifted, dipped again, moved us on – I turned the tiller and the pier approached. After such a gradual journey it seemed to grow quickly and came alongside all at once. I tapped Lagan's broad back and Tressel's skinny one, they drew in their oars and we were among the bladderwrack. I grabbed one of the pier's legs and pushed past it scraping the sharp barnacles. The rusty mooring post loomed above. I stood and threw a loop of rope over it, grasped the rickety pier planks, jumped up and looked around. The quay was deserted.

Tressel joined me, soundlessly. Lagan and the boy rocked the first barrel free and heaved it up to us. With Tressel I grabbed its rim and hauled it onto the pier. Another barrel, and another. Four in all. By the moonlight I caught a glimpse of MICAWATER BRANDY stencilled on the side. Each had a canvas cover and its timbers were smooth. We lined them up and took a breather while Lagan tightened nooses around the policeman's wrists and ankles. He made a cradle of his hands and his boy stepped up to beside us. Then he planted his foot on the gunwale, scrambled up, and gave us the other ends of the rope. We hoisted the policeman bodily – up through the seaweed, over the edge of the pier. Lagan crouched and wiped his knife on the porker's stubble.

He cut his bonds, prodded him to stand, and shot me a glance to say 'ready'. I laid a barrel down and started pushing it. The others followed, one barrel each.

It took all my strength to get my barrel going. Pain flared in my forearm from the bound arrow wound where the king had shot me. I pushed my weight against it, my feet out behind, grasped its rim and shoved it on. My peacoat strained across my back. Its hem brushed the barrel as it rolled on its copper band. MICAWATER BRANDY came and went every time the damn thing turned.

Everyone knows me in this town. The good people here are bonded as close together in spirit as their houses are attached. They're all in cahoots, the policeman had said. Well, now I wish they could see him stumbling on his lead.

You see, the houses in the town are connected together. With secret passages, false floors, fake cupboards without backs, hidden rooms. Your contraband can be handled from house to house, from family to family and escape the excise men till they sob in despair. Your bolt of fine silk, your bootlegged whisky or 'Micawater brandy' can be handed into a house at the quayside and, passed from home to home, it can make it up to the top of the cliff without ever going outside.

We reached the end of the pier, lugged our barrels onto the quayside cobbles. I paused for breath and looked to the town.

A figure detached from the shadow at the side of the pub, ran over and stopped in front of me. A tall silhouette. *Jant*. So he's caught up with us! More men clattered out of the darkness, jumped out from behind boat hulls, piles of nets, running down off the bridge parapet and out of the alley. They joined Jant, and our way was blocked.

Soldiers! Too many! I twitched my hand and my dagger slid into my palm. The action wasn't lost on Jant. He raised his arm and pointed his pistol at me. Every soldier readied his musket – those on the outskirts dropped to one knee to aim.

'Let Cargeen go,' Jant said to Lagan. Lagan just screwed the point of his knife through the policeman's scarf till he yelled. We waited. Jant waited. And I couldn't see his damn face.

'Let him go.'

I yelled, '*You fucking idiot!* We'll never give in! Not while there's breath in us!'

Jant slipped his wings out from the back of his coat and slowly opened them. Wider and wider he spread them, longer than you would have thought possible. They splayed behind the kneeling troops, the limbs strung with muscle, the feathers like blades tapered a metre above his head.

Lagan spat. *Slash* went his knife across the policeman's throat. A gout of blood sprayed out. Black drops hung as if in slow motion, and spattered on the boards. Bang! Flame jetted from Jant's pistol. Lagan fell straight back stiff.

The soldiers cocked their muskets. 'All of them,' said Jant. Flame spat from their muzzles and the air around me sang. Beside me, the boy fell. Tressel spun into the water. I stabbed my knife into the canvas cover of the barrel, slit it open and yanked out the fuse.

I flicked my lighter and lit it – it started fizzing. Sharp gunpowder smoke leapt into the air. In the sudden flare I saw the Messenger's eyes open wide. His great wings curled like shields. He turned on his heel and sprang away – I gasped and dived.

Freezing salt water filled my nose. I hit the water so steeply I somersaulted completely around, opened my eyes through sheets of bubbles streaming past me. All was black. Above me, the wavering underside of the surface. Above that, a distorted point of light shone surrounded by a halo. Then the water, the sky, lit up bright yellow, brighter than day. I saw all the colours in an instant – every detail of the sea bed – my own shadow cast on it. The green water lit into the distance with my hanging shadow as a long streak. Then a tremendous force pressed me down and I coughed out all my air in a big silver bubble. Stunned, I sank, arms, legs outstretched.

Everything went pitch dark. My body cried out for air. My lungs screamed to expand. I shook myself and beat for the surface, broke the waves and panted in air. A heavy rain was pattering down and all around me things were falling. I couldn't see anything, couldn't hear anything but the pounding ringing of my ears, but I sensed great chunks of stuff hitting the water.

Pieces of the pier, I thought. The barrels. The soldiers. My friends. Spouts jetted up, chopping the waves into rafts of foam. I snatched a painful breath and duck-dived. Underwater, I shook off my coat and struggled out of my boots. Another breath, then I struck away from the quay. Every time I thrust my arms forward I saw their skin dead white between my tattoos like the arms of a corpse. My head was thumping, my ears were singing, and it was further to the shore than I'd guessed. I kicked out again, rose to the surface, but I was giddy. I swam on, trying to keep straight, the headland ahead, directly to the beach, but it seemed miles. At length I was only kicking. Trailing my arms. Then I floated, kicked, and floated. Eventually I could do no more than float, and my arms and legs were numb. My sinuses and eyes stung raw. Then, I became aware of a gentle back and forth movement. When I next kicked, my toes hit the shingle. Gratefully I sank underwater and crawled out.

I lay where the waves were breaking, feeling each one wash over me and lift me a little. The sea itself was trying to push me out. My cheek pressed on a big, wet pebble and I was oddly pleased at its smoothness. Every time I breathed out ripples ran around it, and all the while the waves played with the lace on my blouse, inflating it and trying to ease it over my head. I felt happy to stay here, growing colder but comfortable because the pebbles were so round and, after all, if I moved I'd be colder still, but I found myself watching a little point of light in the distance. It bounced on the shingle by the pier, backlit by the fire's red glow that was casting awful shadows down the beach. The point of light zigzagged, pausing here and there but it slowly grew and I realised it was coming towards me. I got onto hands and knees and began to crawl. That just brought the light hastening faster, and it resolved into a lantern held by a marine. Tall Jant Shira the Messenger was striding beside him hurrying him on.

'—Dead,' he was saying. 'Actually fucking killed him!'

'The Emperor will—' said the marine.

'Will what?' spat Jant. 'Have my hide?'

I flopped down, but they approached until all I could see were the toes of their boots. Jant took the lantern, crouched down carefully and I saw his face. He had wrapped his t-shirt around his head like a turban and it was blood-stained over his ears. His jacket hung off his naked shoulders. On one side it was burned to a cinder and the sleeve was missing. He smelt of scorched wool and melted feathers. He rocked back on his heels and coughed horribly, while the marine raised the lantern above my face.

'It *is* Connell,' he said. 'We've got her!'

'Is she still alive?' said the marine.

'Well ... for now.'

Jant reached out a sooty hand and pushed the strands of hair away from my face. 'It's the bitch all right. I'd know that rose anywhere.'

And the rose knows you, I thought. Then I fainted.

CHAPTER 21

Jant again – Back to the ship

The marine called two other survivors and carried Connell away. I hobbled to the edge of the waves, fell hands and knees in the water and soaked my face and neck. I swished my head from side to side and the chill fucking sea drew some of the heat from my burns.

These terrorists are prepared to die rather than be captured! I wrestled with disbelief and the agony made it impossible to think. I raised my head and flicked my hair back.

There, on the horizon, beamed the searchlights of *Gerygone* closing on the schooner. The schooner that's carrying gunpowder barrels. If the smugglers light them, she'd go up like a bomb!

I have to warn Fulmer. I drenched my t-shirt, tied it around my neck, dumped my frazzled jacket and shook out my wings. I ran along the beach, reached the speed of take-off, swept my wings down and nothing happened. Air whistled through the feathers as if through a sieve. I forced a burst of speed, and more, tried again, twisted both ankles on the pebbles and painedly climbed into the air.

I turned out to sea, but my right wing wasn't pulling like it should. I couldn't gain height. I just touched the waves! My wingtips flicked an arc of drops. I stretched on each flap, trying to grab the air, having to reach higher above me on the up-beat and pull down further, till the single long finger of each wing met below my body. Shit! If I scrape the water, I'm dead.

I beat harder, desperately, and rose ten metres. I was flapping the stink of brine and my own burnt feathers, and a great exhaustion weighed me from the shock. I was coughing – my throat seared – lungs aflame – wouldn't expand – the roof of my mouth was all blisters. Terrified, I focussed on the *Gerygone*, willing her closer, larger. But she was moving away over a huge distance. I flew and flew but seemingly got no nearer. Whining with agony I put on a burst and gained on the striped hull. Her bow wave was cascading as she heeled at full speed to the open ocean, sail on two masts. A fine twist of smoke was rising from the fore artillery hatch. *Gerygone* was going like a rocket, leaning on the mid-tack, and completely eclipsed the schooner which I couldn't see at all.

I flew into her light, keening through clenched teeth. My shadow skeeted over the waves. Mist's lookout yelled. I flapped strongly, rose and grazed over the railing. Crashed onto the deck, shredding my jeans and stripping the skin off my shins.

Mist ran to me, horrified. 'What happened?'

I opened my mouth to speak and it filled with thick sea water, coming from nowhere. It poured down my naked chest, and I saw it was blood.

'Get the doctor!' he shouted.

'No!' I spat. 'The smugglers will blow the powder ... They won't be taken alive.'

He grabbed my shoulders. 'Jant? You were in that blast?'

'Connell lit her barrels. The schooner will do the same.'

'You're burnt!'

'Had to warn you!'

'Can you walk?' He pulled me up with surprising strength, and supported me between the mainmasts and coils of rope to the far rail which he propped me against – I clung on instinctively – and gazed at the shape of the schooner, its high stern, two masts, no lights at all but every stitch of canvas bellied out and moon-silvered, running rapidly into the darkness.

'I have half her wind,' said Fulmer. 'I'll be on her back in five minutes.'

'Then you'll both blow up!'

He unhooked a megaphone from the rail and hailed the schooner. 'Heave to, in the name of the Castle! Schooner, you cannot escape! Reef your sail and surrender ... Or be destroyed!'

If anything she seemed to gain speed. She heeled even further, bowsprit pointing skyward between deck and sail, graceful as a marlin. The water wet the dry wood along her flank, up to her railing.

'Be destroyed, then!' Fulmer yelled. He gestured, and the pair of searchlights at our bow and stern converged on the schooner and slickly illuminated her. Barrels packed her deck and we saw swift movement as the crew crouched behind them.

'Oh, serendipity. If you want something done properly, Fulmer Harandis has to do it himself! Dee? Is the roundshot cooking?'

'It's ready, sir.'

'Then let's have an aiming shot. Fire!'

A blast below our feet shook the deck. Fragments of the schooner's railing flew into the air, bits of gunwale and hull. Flame raced up the edge of her foresail.

'Well aimed!' Fulmer called. 'Dee, you hit her midships! Excellent shot – we'll have you Challenging the Artillerist next year.'

'Thank you, sir!'

'She responds to our advances, now give her a warm embrace.'

'Aye, sir ... Ready, sir.'

'Fire!'

The same blast jarred the deck. A tiny light sped away towards the schooner and brightened as it flew. Then we all recoiled from the flash and boom. The ship blew into a fireball. A glare of orange light, fizzing particles arced out, it gathered itself and mushroomed up – and darkness clutched back. Shards of timber pattered down onto the surface of the water. Nothing was left. Nothing at all. The ship had gone. A wave rolled over the single long timber of the keelson, and then it sank below the surface and vanished.

'Olé!' cried Fulmer.

Smoke was flowing up the side of our hull from the cannon below our feet. I was shaking, suddenly chilled to the core. The agony of my burns raised me into a separate, floating sensation. I swallowed against the spines in my throat, a horrible catchy dryness like carbonised hessian. 'Fulmer ... you killed ... how many people?'

'Usually ten on a brandy runner. But, Jant, you're feverish and you're making a mistake. They're not people, they're terrorists.'

I shrugged, too hoarse to reply, and stumbled to his cabin. That, too, stank of fag fumes; it aggravated me into coughing and I retched, but my throat had swollen shut and blocked the vomit from passing, so it sunk back down and stung. Will I never be free of this smell? I'm a Rhydanne, for god's sake, not a stoker. I'm built for the mountain top, the thin air club, not this vile smoke. My head swam. Why was I freezing cold and shivering violently, when my lungs are on fire?

I sat down at the table, unbuckled my pack and slipped out my syringe and a phial of cat. I carefully measured a dose that would kill the pain without putting me under. I held up the syringe, tapped out a bubble until liquid flowed from the fine, hard tip. Steady, Shira. I wiped an alcohol pad over the crook of my arm, pressed the needle against the outside vein and watched it sink into the soft skin, registered a puff of blood and pushed the plunger down past the graduations.

My eyelids flickered. The rush. Ah ... I sat there for a minute, feeling it hit, listening down into my body. Then swallowed hard, pulled the needle out and stowed it, and was soothing my burns in the washstand when Fulmer walked in. He placed some folded clothes on the table and gave me a carafe of water.

Scolopendium was bursting in pleasure in my brain. What pain? What pain? I could tell it hurt – I felt the tightness – but I didn't care. Water was dripping off my arms. I croaked, 'I put Connell in jail.'

'What about the others?'

'Other Roses? I don't think any survived.'

'What about my marines?'

'Twenty died.'

'The deuce! …Jant, that is dashed extravagant.'

I drank all the water and it helped me speak, though, in over-compensating for the slur of cat, my voice sounded taut. 'Do you have any more? I need a decent guard.'

'No. I don't.' He slipped off his coat, revealing a satin-backed waist-coat, and studied his reflection. 'My marines are ashore at Tanager and Diw. I haven't trained more than a hundred since I wiped out the pirates.'

'You've none in Awndyn?'

'Even if I had, I wouldn't give you them!'

I made my way round the table to the mirror which, given its size and splendid frame, should have been out of place, but was the natural focal point of Fulmer's cabin. Under the film of water, my skin was vivid red down my right side. My jaw and right ear were worst, the back of my hand. My lips were bleeding, seared and split. My hair was crisped, I'd lost an eyebrow, and my shoulder was so incandescently scarlet that my Wheel scar showed pallid white. Fulmer was goggling at it.

This time, she got me. All her previous attempts paled into insignificance. I was very lucky to be alive, and *very* pissed off. I ran my hand over my right wing, and the black, carbonised lumps of the covert feathers crumbled into powder. Patches of feathers were missing – I could see to the reddened skin – and the patagium membrane across the elbow was blistered. I'd lost the width of most of my flight feathers; they'd shrunk back halfway to the quill and smelt matted and sulphurous, like burnt hair. I looked like a dead pine tree. I looked like a plucked crow.

'Oh, *shit* …'

'I'm sorry,' said Fulmer.

The drug had touched my features, too: face relaxed, pupils pinned to fine lines, and the irises too high because my eyes were slightly rolling up. Fulmer recognised the signs from Tris, but he didn't say anything. I returned to the basin and bathed my burns. He sat down at the table, carrying his ten-centimetre cigarette holder as if it was lit. 'At least you're safe. This won't happen again now you've caught Connell.'

I leant over, running with water. 'Yes. I instructed the marines to guard her. But to take her to the Castle, I need more. I need outriders and a prison carriage.'

'Well, send on the flicker to Cobalt.'

'You'd better hightail us back to Cullion so I can read it.'

Fulmer appraised me. 'I'll bring *Gerygone* about, into the bay. While I do that, here—' he pushed the clothes towards me. 'A shirt and trousers. The shirt's one of my Dartes, though it'll be too tight. The trousers are slops. Nobody on *Gerygone* has your height.'

'Thank you.'

'And the doctor's waiting outside. Though, seriously, he's freaking out over treating an Eszai and he's never seen a Rhydanne before.'

'Then let's show him what a fried one looks like.'

Fulmer curvetted out, and the instant he left the cabin, crooked up a wing as a windbreak to light his cigarette, and simultaneously scratched the back of his neck with the wrist of his other wing. His wings' patagia were pierced with fine gold bands, and wide rings, too, around their wrists and fingers.

The ship's quack wrapped my neck and shoulder in wet gauze. Nothing more could be done. I soaked Fulmer's cream paduasoy silk shirt, and the bottle green flannel trousers in the basin and put them on. I lopped off my hair to above my shoulders and pulled out all Tern's feathers that I tie in it, and the malachite beads, Rhydanne style. The beads went in my pack, the scorched hair and laddered jeans I jettisoned out the stern window. Then I drenched my wings in water, and staggered out to stand at the bow, clinging to consciousness in the cool breeze, as *Gerygone* raced before the wind to Cullion.

The bow wave broke in black and yellow streaks from the lantern light. Above the long extremity of Cobalt headland, the sky was almost clear. Only a slight mist of cloud covered the pale, full moon. Thin clouds like streaks of ink lay horizontally around it. They tiger-striped the sky in grey bands, apart from their ends around the moon, where its light showed them lilac.

I used to suffer from a phobia of ships. Understandable, with a wingspan like mine: waterlogged feathers would drag me to the depths. But over the last ten years Fulmer had helped me overcome my fear. Aboard *Gerygone* I'd felt relatively safe, first at dock and then on the open ocean. Little by little I set myself the challenge of smaller and smaller vessels until I could sit in a rowing boat without fear of drowning. Which wouldn't, I hasten to add, ever prevent me drowning if I touched the water. I won't go so far as to say I can surf Cape Brattice in an open kayak, but I was proud of my achievement, which had taken me years. As an immortal, I've come to realise that's what years are for.

However, seeing Fulmer comprehensively annihilate the schooner had shaken me. The blisters in my mouth had popped, leaving flaps of skin, and I kept coughing blood. If it wasn't for the scolopendium chiming in my veins I'd be phobic again.

At Cullion we anchored in the deep channel. Fulmer joined me, in the glow from his open cabin door and, through the telescope with a tremulous hand, I examined the place where the pier had been. The explosion had obliterated it, and the boats we'd used for cover were scattered as matchwood. All the windows of the Red Lion had blown out, and in the darkness nothing moved but bunches of bladderwrack hanging from the harbour wall, drifting up and down mopping the top of the wavelets.

The signaller at our morse lantern looked to me, but Fulmer motioned me to save my voice and told him, 'Ask them to telegraph to Cobalt for cavalry and a prison wagon. And to Tanager: tell King Saker that we've caught Connell.'

The flicker at the excise office responded, and I imagined the telegraph towers bathed in their floodlights, gathering themselves to dance. With a glow of satisfaction that I'd caught Connell Rose, I returned to Fulmer's cabin and fell asleep on the floor, against the curve of the hull wall. And next morning my burns really, really seared.

It took two days for the Governor of Cobalt to find us troops.

Telegraph
To: Jant at Cullion Cove / From: Saker, Tanager Grand Place
Do you still have Connell under lock and key?

To: Saker / From: Jant
Yes

To: Jant / From: Saker
It hasn't stopped the bombings

To: Saker / From: Jant
News?

To: Jant / From: Saker
Last night Fulmer's house in Tanager, blown up completely.

To: Saker / From: Fulmer
My house *what*?

To: Fulmer / From: Saker
Not so much as a collar stud left.

To: Saker / From: Fulmer
With respect, I can do without the sarcasm. My house is packed with
treasures, my one and only halidom, and you're saying it's ruined? Did
you catch them?

To: Saker / From: Jant
Ten symbols only, you're clogging the line.

To: Fulmer / From: Saker
Bombers notcaught. Whole Grand Place is rubble, twelve dead. Stay
there, I'm coming to see Connell. Unofficially.

Next morning, from the deck, I saw six horsemen riding along the
cliff top, outlined against the sky. They decanted down the steep road
through Cullion, which is so precipitous that its cobbles are laid on
edge, a stepped surface for hooves to find purchase. Their clattering
reached me, as muted and fractured as a fall of dominos.

'They're too few to be our escort,' I said.

'It's King Saker,' said Fulmer, with his eye to the telescope. 'The glib
bastard.'

I flew unsteadily to shore and landed just as Saker and his en-
tourage were walking their horses to a halt, and peering around at the
unfamiliar buildings. 'Welcome to Cullion,' I said.

Saker looked down from the saddle, alarmed, 'What happened to
you?'

'I was in the fireball.'

'You should consult Rayne.'

'I'm sending Connell to the Castle first.'

'Well, you said you were waiting for an escort,' he said exuberantly.
The breeze was blowing his horse's mane. 'Here we are, at the Castle's
service. Jant, this is Sula. Sula: Comet.'

'Call me Jant. I thought you said you're officially not here.'

'I'm not. I'm in Tanager. We didn't find any bombs in the palace ...
but the Grand Place is devastated. They did it at night. Fulmer's house
and the two adjoining, fronting the square, are just piles of wreckage
... They killed all his servants and his housekeeper. Yes. I know ...

We got dogs to sniff out a powder charge in Serein Fioré's house in Rachiswater, too. We defused it. Lucky for him.'

'Did you find the Roses?'

'No. Three were lynched in Wrought. Someone hung them from a low branch ... Jant, I tried to discover who, but everyone's struck dumb. Then a bunch of Spiza's mill workers overtook five or six Roses leaving on the Broad Road and butchered them. Turned the wagons over and burnt them with the bodies inside. So, in response, hundreds of gypsies are massing outside our palace day and night in a goddamned protest, singing and slamming on the gates. Yes. We've increased the guard, but of course they won't go. Connell's ignited a wildfire. It's gaining pace and spreading. Leon's trying to control it, but the rage is intense. Where is the fucking bitch?'

'In there.'

'I want to see her.'

'If you insist. But—'

'I'm a witness and a victim. I'm taking her to trial.' He stepped down from Balzan and kicked his spurs folded. Then he looked out to sea, shading his eyes. 'Ah, *Gerygone* ...'

'Yes.' I glanced at the flagship, and noticed she was lowering a landing vessel. Mist must be on his way.

'I toured her at her launch. Big, isn't she?'

'Twenty guns.'

'I wonder about Fulmer sometimes.'

'I wonder about him all the time.'

Saker took his coat off and threw it on the saddle. 'The *Mallard* painting shows her destroying the last pirate caravel. She was firing a broadside.'

'She can fire a broadside every three minutes.'

'He is, you know. He's compensating for something. Jant, we haven't staged down from Tanager, we've ridden hard and our horses are blown. Show me Connell.'

CHAPTER 22

Connell speaks – in jail

Daylight shining in my face had woken me hours ago. Through the barred window, Allen had whispered that today my rescue would come. But I didn't know how.

I lay on the bench. My clothes had dried on me, but they were stiff with salty tidemarks – kerchief, breeches, and the sorry remnants of my blouse – itchy and uncomfortable. Having come so far, you've probably formed the opinion that I'm some sort of criminal. Well, I'm not. I've never been in jail before and I didn't know what to do. They've trapped me in here for two days, a tactic to make me frightened and depressed. They know I'm a Litanee and I need my freedom. They can hang me if they want, it's not like I've anything to live for, but being locked up I can't stand. The Castle deals in infinity, and I'm afraid they might leave me here for years – maybe centuries. She assured me that won't happen. She also said they'll never beat me, so I can give them backchat.

A wall of iron bars sectioned off this alcove from the rest of the excise office. A policeman sat at his desk, with his back to me. There's nothing in my cell but the bench and a tin bucket in the corner.

'Hey!' I called. 'Hey, it's breakfast time.'

'No breakfast.'

'Coffee? Water?'

He lumbered off to a side room and returned with a mug. He thrust it between the bars so roughly that half the water slopped down my front, and he started leering at my breasts. I guzzled the water, then went and pissed noisily in the bucket. When I'd finished the policeman was leering more than ever. He had no tattoos. He was a governor's lackey.

'They've come for you, petal,' he said.

'Stop calling me "petal".'

'But you're covered in 'em. I like 'em. And your red, red lips.'

I wiped a hand across my chapped mouth. Then some door crashed open. The policeman started, gave a bow and disappeared into the side room. Two soldiers entered, walking a barrel round on its rim between them. One of my barrels – from the sea cave, not the wagons. Good. I watched, very on-edge, but with a strange tinge of triumph. They've taken away my freedom like she said they would. They're probably going to hang me. But we hit them, we did! The Castle tasted our sting!

Jant followed the barrel in and placed his weird-looking hand on it. Hatred roiled my guts immediately I saw him. Then in came King Saker, the fucker who'd shot me and ruthlessly murdered four of my troupe. Are these two joined at the hip?

The soldiers stopped. One of them produced a jemmy and levered up the lid. Jant nodded at them, and they removed the planks and left. He gazed at me and settled back until he perched on the edge of the barrel.

He'd lost one eyebrow, his flat, slanty cheek was tomato red and his neck was bandaged. Satisfied, I dwelt on this while he smoothed the surface of the gunpowder and examined me. So I had the chance to examine him. He looked wiry and tired but you can't fool me. He's two hundred years old! And Saker's over a thousand! Jant's a 'danne who started off a shopkeeper, like one of us, and now look at that silk shirt! He fucks on piles of banknotes and swigs champagne all day with his posh wife.

He coughed into his hand. 'Connell, why are you killing us?'

I said nothing.

'Why did you steal powder?'

I said not a word.

'Did the blast jar your wits?'

'Did it blow yours clean away?'

'It nearly burnt my fucking lungs out, thank you so very much.'

'You shot Lagan.'

'We destroyed your schooner.'

'Oh. Murderers!'

'That's a bit rich. Mist wants to know how you could afford such a ship, and who built it.'

'It fell from the sky.'

'I ask again ...'

'It fell off a really big wagon!'

Then Saker growled, 'Why did you kill my daughter?'

I didn't say anything. His immense age made me queasy. In comparison, I felt as if my end was very close. Which, of course, it is.

'Why did you kill her?' he said.

I gulped. 'I want to kill all the immortals, until the Circle falls apart.'

'Immortals? Not me?'

'Just Eszai.'

'Not the Queen? Not my little chicks?'

'I hate the wankers who call themselves the Best In The World!'

'Why? Without them, you're Insect paper.' He came to the bars. I backed until I pressed against the whitewashed wall. That put more than an arms' length between us. I couldn't get over the fact he was from the deep past but looked like any well-built soldier.

I rallied. 'I'll kill because we've nowhere else to go. No matter what I do, I can't get anywhere. No matter how hard I work, I'll always be your fucking slave. You've got it all sewn up ... you rich pricks! You have all the money and the rest of us have nothing. I hate you! And I'll destroy you, because the world has changed.'

'Damn straight the world has changed!' snapped Jant. 'I changed it!'

'Did I kill Tern?' I asked.

He had another coughing fit over his sleeve. 'You tried! *Why?* Do you understand what you're doing?' He dipped one hand into the blasting powder and brought it up, letting the shiny grains trickle between his fingers. 'Tell me, where are the other barrels? ...Tell me, Connell Rose. Make the rest of your life slightly easier.'

'You found them in the cave.'

He dug both hands in it and flung it in the air. 'Ten! There were ten in the cave! Where are the others?'

I smiled. So Rax had managed to get them onto the wagons.

Jant yelled and hurled a handful of pellets at me. 'The court will wipe that off your face!' He slid off the barrel and paced up and down, pushing grains of double-C powder out of the way with his toe.

'How many more of you?' said the king. He didn't show his wealth overtly but it's there. His understated shirt was a quality weave, full-grain leather formed the seat and inside leg of his riding breeches, his spurs were shaped like talons, and his sword was very swish. But his hair was flattened at the front, spread about like a tussock where a rabbit's been sitting.

'How many bombers?' he repeated, so threateningly that Jant looked up.

'Hundreds.'

'All Roses?'

'Not even all Litanee, but everyone the Emperor crushes beneath his heel.'

'San has never crushed anybody! You're insane.'

'Our lives are so quashed by you, so stifled, so frustrating, we won't stop until we've killed every last Eszai.'

Jant slipped the keys in his pocket.

'Just like Cyan Lightning.' I said. 'I hid half a barrel on her coach suspension. I wonder if she smelt the slow fuse?'

He swept on Jant in sudden rage. 'Get her out!'

'No.'

'Unlock the cell!'

'No!'

He kicked the bars. 'Give me the fucking keys!'

'What would you do?'

'I won't leave a mark.'

'No!'

He paced across the room and kicked the opposite wall. Then he drew his sword, pushed it between the bars, and would have plunged it into my chest, but I screamed.

'Saker!' said Jant. 'Do you want your guards to hear?'

'She *murdered* my *daughter*!'

I screamed most heartily until he withdrew his sword.

'Cyan was worth a thousand of you!' he said.

'We're all the same!'

'Oh, bullshit! Did you invent rifles?'

'Can you shoe a horse?'

'She's insane,' he said to Jant, who was regarding me wryly, with sparkling eyes. He can't be amused, surely? It must be the reflection on the Rhydanne tapetum lucidum. I peered closely – yes, just like she told me, he's got green eyes with vertical pupils. They close narrower than human pupils, to cut out snow glare, and the membrane reflects light, so he has integral sunglasses. He doesn't need to wear sunglasses at all, but she said he does to hide the effect of drugs. I can't use the sun glare trick on him, and he might try it on me. He was agile, with a smooth, fast flow to his movements, a distance racer.

I told him, 'You still think you're a Hacilith worker, but you're not. You're one of *them*.'

He shrugged.

'What are you doing to my people?' I asked Saker. 'Expelling them from Awia? Depriving us of the few pence we earn a year?'

'It isn't your right to cut corn.' He sank onto a chair and half-spread heavy wings, like an eagle's, but that didn't daunt me. They're going to hang me, so what else can he do? I no longer cared for my safety, for anything. He glanced at Jant. 'I hate speaking Morenzian when I'm rusty,' he said, a lot faster in Awian.

'You're doing fine.'

'I haven't spoken it so much since Savory.'

'Or since my first week in the Castle,' said Jant.

'It was the only way I could communicate with you.'

'Ah! She *is* fluent in Avian. She's listening.' Jant came to the bars. 'Connell, is your life really so awful that you're willing to die, for the chance of taking an immortal with you?'

'Yes.'

'You don't fear death?'

'No. As I've never loved life. When the Castle hangs me a hundred more will rise, howling with indignation, to start where I left off.'

'Which Eszai's next? Who are you bombing? Give me a name.'

'No.'

'Tell me which place. Whose house?'

'No.'

'You must have the most incredible mind to co-ordinate your groups. You have the prowess of an Eszai.'

'She …'

'Doesn't she?'

'Yes, she – oh. Shit.'

He stared at me. 'Who is "she"? Another woman? Your friend? Your leader?' He grasped the bars. 'I thought *you* were the leader.'

I've said too much. I shut up completely.

Saker pointed at Jant's pocket. 'Let me in the cell and we'll soon find out.'

'Don't be an idiot!'

'I won't break any bones.'

'I'm not letting you be escort if you're going to hurt her.' Jant pressed his face to the bars so hard their pressure turned his red cheek white. 'Connell, it doesn't matter if you've stopped feeling conversationally inclined. When you stand in front of the Emperor, you'll find yourself telling him everything. Silver tongue, silver ears; he's got the silver fucking lot. You can't even prepare yourself for the terror.'

He returned to the barrel and leant on it. He produced a bloodstained handkerchief and coughed into it, closed his eyes and swallowed – I thought he was about to faint.

'Watch her all the way,' he said to Saker. 'I've seen plenty of Rose around, and a fool could break her out of here.'

'Not that they are fools,' I said in Awian.

'Not that they are.'

He looked me up and down, reading my tattoos like a book. He could have been from Litanee, the expert way he read me, and I hated that I couldn't read him so easily. Northerners don't wear their heart in pictures on their skin. Awians are aloof, Rhydanne are enigmatic, and immortals are as adept at hiding their chequered pasts as they are their feelings. We Litanee, by contrast, are wide open.

'We can't scare her,' he said eventually.

'No. Do we "bombers" scare you?'

'Try me, Connell.'

'I did. Did it burn, much?'

He folded his handkerchief carefully. 'Be grateful that it's me who caught you and not the Queen,' he added.

'We should throw her to Leon,' said Saker. He stretched a wing and scratched between the feathers with a hand that seemed stronger every minute. I felt pliant and vulnerable, like a hare in the hunter's grip. He could twist me apart.

There was a rap on the door and a fyrd captain entered. He stood on the threshold, anxiously regarding the grains scattered all over the floor like waxed black rabbit droppings. Jant motioned him impatiently into the room.

'The prison carriage is ready,' he said.

Jant nodded. 'And outriders?'

'Thirty.'

'Only thirty? This is suspicious,' he said to Saker. 'They've taken too long and not brought enough.'

'I scoured the ranks to find the best,' said the captain.

I called, 'Thank you for your diligence!'

Jant scowled at me. 'Stop wasting time.' He threw the keys to the captain. The unshaven lackey wore a brigandine steel plate jacket. He opened my cell door and held his hands for me to imitate, so he could put cuffs on them, but instead of raising my wrists I clicked imaginary shackles on him!

Next thing I knew, I was in a headlock. He grabbed my arms and cuffed them. Then he twisted a fistful of hair and would have dragged me to the coach but Jant said, 'No! Be civilised!'

Saker said something laconic in a language I've never heard before, and Jant snapped, 'What's up with you? You've turned savage!'

The captain flung the keys onto the desk, grasped my handcuff chain and yanked me out of the cell.

Outside, a handful of dust-stained featherback horsemen accompanied us up to the cliff top and the waiting coach. Allen and my thirty gypsies, disguised as Cobalt guards, were on horseback behind it, with muskets. The coach was grey steel, thick enough to stop a ball. Its windows were barred, like an Insect cage wagon, and the jail's own coachman was climbing up onto the driver's seat.

I noticed immediately that its four horses were Turvy Horses. Then glanced away lest I reveal it. I knew my love wouldn't leave me! I was alert – every muscle!

Behind us, Saker, on an Eske courser with his archers, was distracted into watching a chap in a seaman's coat running towards us past
the last houses of the town. Ahead of us, the grass of the cliff top, then
Maple Wood where Allen had fused my wagons.

The captain opened the prison carriage door revealing two benches.
I stepped up inside – not easy with my hands cuffed – and sat down.
Jant swept onto the other and slammed the door.

'Forward!' the coachman cried. We didn't move.

Jant was preoccupied with trimming his pistol, but this roused him
and he glanced to the window.

'Hey!' yelled the coachman. 'Walk on!' But the horses remained
stock still.

'For god's sake!' Jant spat.

We heard the coachman crack the reins, then he plied the whip. The
four mares, however, didn't budge. Jant poked the muzzle of his pistol
against my ribs and yelled out the window. 'Whatever you're trying,
I'll blow her away!'

Then he cried out. The captain had shoved his musket against Jant's
forehead. Jant gingerly drew his head back from the window and the
captain, astride his horse, extended his arm so the barrel followed him
in, pressed so firmly to his forehead it puckered the skin. As the captain
reached out his arm, his cuff rode up and I saw around his wrist, his
Rose tattoos.

'Drop that thing,' he said to Jant. 'Or I'll blast your Eszai brains all
over the inside of this coach.'

Jant screwed his barrel more painfully into my ribs. 'In the name of
the Castle—' he said.

'Fuck the Castle. In the name of the Muse,' the captain said steadily.

I felt a surge of hope, but he was trying to stare Jant down, and
realising that the owner of those Rhydanne eyes wouldn't submit. 'I'll
kill you,' he snarled.

'You won't,' said Jant.

The captain cocked the hammer. 'Let her out.'

I followed Jant's rapid logic: If I die, I lose all eternity. A gypsy lass
isn't worth it. She can't escape, anyway. He pulled the muzzle from my
ribs and opened the door.

I stepped out, relieved. The captain was still looking into Jant's
bizarre eyes. ' "In the name of the Castle" won't work any more.'

'It never fucking did.'

'This is the end of your immortality.'

The captain's finger bent to the trigger and his head exploded. It flew into three parts in a burst of slime. His musket fell, and his body slopped forward onto the stallion's neck.

I stared in the direction of the shot. Saker was lowering his gun from his shoulder. I grabbed the horse's rein and glanced down to where a piece of the captain's nose and cheeks lay on the ground like a mask. Whatever that shot had been, it wasn't a musket.

My gypsies raised their muskets and let Saker and the Awians have it. The noise was deafening. Bangs and balls pinging off shields. Two Awians slid to the ground – then one Rose exploded horribly. Now they'd have to reload. I feared the Awians' arrows.

The stallion shied sideways, yanked my arm. It was going to bolt. I jumped onto its shoulders, pushing the corpse upright, saddle pommel behind me. We train these Turvy Horses to obey the opposite commands.

'Whoa!' I yelled, and he lurched as if spurred, then went like the wind.

The corpse was flopping behind me, its lower jaw still attached by the skin. Galloping at full pelt, with the stallion's hooves bashing the ground, throwing turf in my face, I gripped with my thighs, twisted, and searched its trouser pocket for the handcuff key. Found it, wrestled it out of the pocket and stuffed it in my mouth.

The Awians in a cloud of smoke zipped arrows at my Roses. Three fell, the others galloped away. Arrows flew after them and another four Roses reeled from the saddles.

The coachman bellowed and shot at me but god knows where his ball went. I rived my horse into the line of the coach and heard Saker yell as the steel chassis blotted him from view.

The corpse was bashing its slimy chin on my shoulder. There was a tongue in there, too. Its boots were in the stirrups and my bare feet hung loose, bouncing with the striking hooves. I unlocked my shackles and dropped them. With one hand I leant for the reins, with the other I grabbed the corpse's arm and pulled it round me in a hug.

The stallion was neck out, charging in panic. I let him have his head, the wood was in front and nearer every second. My friends in their fyrd uniforms were belting away on the cliff road, out of range of the archers, but where was Allen?

I glanced back and saw him on my tail, galloping his hardest, fyrd jacket flapping. Jant was out of the coach and levelling his pistol. I saw a puff of smoke and heard the crack, and Allen rolled forward and blood burst from him all down his horse's neck. Miraculously, he didn't fall. But neither did he straighten up. He slumped over its neck and bumped with every hoof beat.

Jant started running – and actually closed the gap! I screamed. The stallion pounding under me couldn't run faster no matter how hard I kicked it. I forced it at the closest part of the wood. Rhydanne are sprint hunters. If I can outride Jant he'll give up and take to the air.

A thwack, and I felt a point stab my back. I glanced behind. Saker was gaining on me at a gallop, past Jant, bending his bow. His arrow had gone clean through the corpse's coat of plates, chest, and was raking my back.

I pulled the corpse's arm over my head and a second later three arrows dropped vertically into it, wedged in the plates.

Its slack jaw and horrible chin were spattering blood and muck into my hair, down my front. I thought it'd be my shield but Saker's shooting straight through it!

Here's the wood. Can I make it? Gusts of air battered me. Jant was beating his wings, hovering above me. I can't shake the Messenger *and* the ex-Archer!

Another arrow jutted through the corpse, gashed my shoulder. I looked back and it ripped my cheek. Jant was whacking the air down, his great wings blustering my head, balancing to drop on me.

Pain stabbed my shoulderblade. Saker had pinned the corpse to me! I yanked apart from it, leant left to see him very close, bow at full draw.

'Sorry,' I said to the stallion. I dropped the right rein and hauled the left one left and up with all my might. The stallion's head jerked left, his shoulders collapsed under me, and I hurtled off his back and smacked into the ground. I was up and running into the wood. Behind me I heard the thud and a horse's scream as Saker's horse ran into my fallen, kicking stallion. I sped between the trees, and heard a whoosh like sail and a thwack of boots. Jant had landed.

CHAPTER 23

Jant – Maple Wood

I landed and sprinted into the wood through nettles and brambles, chasing Connell. She was some distance ahead but I gained easily. Shallow wounds were bleeding down her face and back.

Ahead, the trees thinned into a clearing. Connell raced into it and jumped up inside a huge, wilted bush. It wasn't a bush. A solid, rectangular shape lurked beneath the haphazard branches. The neighbouring ones were the same – eight gypsy wagons, painted green and brown for camouflage and piled with boughs.

Is this Connell's headquarters? Were the wagons full of gypsies, priming their muskets? I jogged forward between the trees. I didn't like it. This reminded me of when we ran into Gio's ambush in the woods, decades ago, and Saker got stabbed. I'm not going into the clearing on my own.

I called for the others but they didn't respond. I called again, waited, then I turned and dashed back. Ahead of me, a gunshot sounded – one of the Awian soldiers putting the injured stallion out of its misery.

Saker had extracted Balzan from its tangle, though his white horse now bore a clear hoofmark in red on its chest. He was standing beside it, stroking its neck and calming it. His three surviving archers had followed. Fulmer was riding up on one dead archer's horse, and was leading the other one with the two dead men laid side by side over its saddle, their wings tucked into their belts.

I tore over wet ground and weeds. 'There're wagons in there!'

'Where is she?'

'In a wagon. I can't go in!'

Saker called to his friends, 'Circle the wood! Hurry!'

'*How* could you have lost her?' called Fulmer.

I pulled out my handkerchief and coughed into it until blood bloomed on the cotton.

'I thought a fucking Rhydanne could catch a fucking racehorse! Let alone a girl with bare feet!'

'He's burnt,' said Saker. 'Let's go in.'

I said, 'Are you *listening*? It could be an ambush! The gypsies have muskets.'

'Muskets! You should have run in anyway!'

'And get shot? Saker! Last time we tried something like this, Gio stabbed you in the kidney!'

'He missed my kidney by a centimetre.'

'Or he wouldn't be here now,' said Fulmer.

'That's not the point!'

'Yes, it is!'

'You nearly died!'

'That was the Swordsman! Connell's just a gypsy!'

'Try this,' said Fulmer. He tilted his cigarette lighter so it glinted, then threw it to Saker who looked at it, puzzled.

'What's this for?'

'Red hot roundshot.'

'I understand,' I said. 'But it could be a trap.'

Saker said, 'They'll be very unfortunate to spring a trap with me in it!'

'I'll stay here,' said Fulmer.

'No crossfire!' Saker called. 'Wait for the Roses to come out! Take prisoners if possible – Actually, fuck it. Kill them!'

It was like flushing Insects out of a wood where they've gone to bay. We strode through the brambles and onto the clear leaf litter. I motioned Saker into the cover of a dense holly bush and stopped him. 'Eight wagons.'

He peered between the branches. 'The door of the nearest is ajar.'

'Do you have fire arrows?'

'A couple. Why?'

'To trigger the powder inside.'

'Oh. I see.' He selected from his quiver an arrow with a head like a pointed metal cage, stuffed with tinder cotton. He opened Fulmer's lighter, dropped fluid onto the cotton and lit it – a long, bright flame flared high.

He set the arrow to string, bent his bow and took aim through the bush at the nearest wagon. The flame trailed up like a pennant. He held his breath halfway and loosed. The arrow zipped through the gap in the wagon door. Instantly the roar of an explosion curled me up. Above the bush, the wagon roof hurtled skywards on a spout of flame. I wrapped my arms around my head. Another bang as the next caravan exploded, blowing planks above the trees.

Fragments of wood clattered around us through the canopy. When the last had landed and leaves were fluttering down I lowered my arms and stared through the bush. Smoke blotted the clearing completely from view.

Saker had turned aside and shielded his face with his outstretched wing. He lowered it and shuddered. We could hear his friends' horses protesting beyond the margin of the trees.

'God!'

'Sh!'

We approached the remaining wagons gingerly. It was like walking into smog. As the smoke thinned we saw that the clearing was strewn with objects blown out of them. Pieces of intricately-carved wooden frame. Shards of window glass. Tattered shreds of the canvas covers and padded brocade interiors. Here was a bunk bed ladder, there pieces of a stove chimney. Of the first wagon only the base and its four wheels remained. The carriage ply roof of the second one hung free, and we saw how camouflage paint had been slapped over the vibrant red and gold carvings. Some papers had blown out of it and lay scattered on the grass.

'Nobody here,' said Saker.

'I bet the others still have powder in. Don't touch them.'

'I won't.'

I was trembling. The bangs had shredded my nerves. My burns stung, my ears were throbbing. That gung-ho idiot seemed to have forgotten the feeling of being dashed at the ground as the searing shockwave punches you.

But he was clenching his jaw so hard it dimpled both cheeks. He walked along the front of the caravans. Then he bent and picked something up. 'Here it is!' He held out a fuse, which ran from all eight wagons and draped away into the woods.

We followed it, out of the clearing to an oak tree. There, propped between its raised roots but quite dead, was the man I had hit with my pistol shot. His sightless eyes fixed on the clearing; he held a taper that was still steadily smouldering. The fuse ended just a hand's width from it.

'If he'd lived a few minutes longer he could have lit it,' said Saker. 'I must be more careful!'

'Try being less stupid!'

The corpse's tattoos were lurid against his pale skin. Around his mouth and bearded onto his neck, blood froth was drying into tiny circles. 'You hit him in the lungs. Good shot.'

'Damn it, Saker. He was a man, not a target! He was called Allen, married, three children, liked fishing.'

'How do you know? Oh. You read his tattoos.'

'Yes! And he was my age!'

'Nobody's your age.'

I slipped the taper from his fingers and stamped it out. Saker rested the horn tip of his longbow on his boot and looked across the clearing, to where the dead man's gaze was fixed. 'He knew he was finished, so he stayed and Connell escaped out of the spinney in that direction. Good trap. Nice try, girl, nice try ...'

He returned to the wagons and started poking about the articles scattered on the grass. I knelt next to the dead gypsy. Clots were forming in the folds of his kerchief and shirt. He could have been any man. He could have been me, if I'd never joined the Circle but stayed a frustrated mortal in gangland Hacilith.

There was no exit wound, so I supposed my ball must still be inside him. I glanced over his tattoos and his chest bore a fresh one, newly-scabbed, an exploding barrel encircled with flames.

'You were so proud of being a bomber that you record it for all to see? Well, look how much good it's done you! I write my life events on my arms, too, but I do it differently.' I shoved my sleeve back for the corpse to have a good look at my old track marks.

'Jant!' said Saker. 'Look at this!'

He was crouching in the tussocks with a piece of paper in each hand.

'What?'

'It's music!'

'So?'

'It's Swallow's handwriting!'

He brandished the sheets, which were charred round the edges. I darted to him, took one and scanned it. Sure enough, it was a manuscript and in the five bars danced black notes written with the confident sketchiness of a musical genius going very fast indeed.

'Are you sure?'

He fixed me with a glance. 'The handwriting of the woman I loved? Of course I'm sure! It's the same piece. It's the piece I've been *reconstructing*! This is it. I recognise ... It goes: da da damm. Pause. And here ... this one follows on ...' He placed the pages beside each other and started scooping up more. 'This one – is the same. And this ... all from the symphony! But the sheets aren't numbered. I can't tell the order.'

He paused, and for a second his eyes filled with tears. 'She never numbered the damn sheets.'

'But—'

'I used to tell her to, but she wouldn't.'

'Why?'

'It put her off her stride.'

He eased the quiver on his hip and knelt down. 'Jant, why was one of Swallow's manuscripts in a caravan?'

'She was their friend, remember. And benefactor. She studied their tunes.'

'*Tunes!* Listen to what I'm telling you! This isn't gypsy gambols. It's her *unfinished symphony!*'

He bounded to his feet, grabbed my shirt front with his free hand and jerked me closer so I was looking up into his face. 'It's *priceless!* Swallow's last score! The world will go wild! And ... and ...' He glanced at the manuscript he was clutching. 'It continues! So she's not dead!' He let go of my shirt and enveloped me in a gigantic embrace that I thought would crush my ribs. I simply waited until he stopped.

'She *must* be dead,' I said. 'She died writing it. You remember seeing how the notes faded out.'

He scooped up the sheets and tried to figure whether they were part of the same manuscript. 'But here they are strong again,' he said, seized by romance. 'We thought she was dead, but she'd gone with the gypsies! We can find her. We can save her!'

'Saker, she *is* dead. We saw her body on the pyre.'

'... Saw *someone* on the pyre ...'

'Come on, Fulmer's waiting.'

But he was eagerly reading the symphony and losing himself in it. Here, on the grass before six wagons reeking of smoke and stuffed with blasting powder. He ran his finger down the pages in an attempt to order them, set aside the first sheet of passionate quavers and hummed down the second. I picked it up. There were no words but the musical direction was inscribed between the staves in what was undoubtedly Swallow's hand: *with hatred.*

'Swallow did go with the gypsies.' I said. 'She's behind all this. She's their leader. She's the bomber.'

CHAPTER 24

'No,' he said.

'Let's get out of here,' I said. 'Connell's gone.'

I couldn't shake a creeping sensation that the corpse might re-animate, and jerkily set his stomped-out taper to the damp fuse and blow us all to jelly. We made our way back to Fulmer.

'You've lost Connell, haven't you?' he said.

'Yes.'

'They killed Auk and Merganser.'

Saker climbed into his saddle and sat there, lost in thought.

Fulmer said severely, 'I thought a Rhydanne could—'

'I was in a fireball!' I rubbed the surface of my wing, and held up a palm covered in fragments of the scorched, wet feathers. 'And the Cobalt captain was a Rose!'

'They were all Roses. Couldn't you tell?'

'He put his musket to my head. Right here!' I relived the cold metal dinting my skin. Fulmer pointed at the dead Awians, which sparked my fear to rage. I plucked my pistol from my belt and, arm out, pointed it straight at his face. 'Ever had a gun set to your head? You fucking fop?'

He went pale.

'*See what it feels like!*' I cocked the hammer.

'Jant ...' said Saker calmly.

'Your life flashes before you! You review your past in a second! *And I have a lot of past!*' I grabbed Fulmer's stirrup leather, raised my gun barrel and shoved it against his chest. There was a pleasing firmness. 'Tell me, why's this scarier than a crossbow?'

'Arp—!'

'It's a messier death. It's more certain! A fucking *Zascai* did this to me!'

'Jant,' said Saker. 'If you don't put that damn thing down, I swear I'll throw it off the cliff.'

Reluctantly, I lowered the pistol and eased the hammer closed.

Fulmer rubbed his chest, shuddered to settle his feathers and adjusted his shirt cuffs. Satisfied that being held at gunpoint had not affected him sartorially, he recovered his customary poise: 'Well, that's a world first.'

'Firearms are unreliable,' said Saker. 'You could have killed him.'

'It's not loaded.'

Saker made an infuriated sound and cantered away to round up his men. I yelled after him, 'I haven't gone through two hundred years of hell for some mortal to blow my head off!'

Mist Fulmer, with slow deliberation, pulled his silver case from his inside pocket, clicked it open, selected a viridian green one from a rainbow spectrum of cigarettes, and tapped it on the case cover. 'First, I'm not a fop, I'm a gentleman. Second, how did the Roses know we had requested outriders?'

'I sent a message to Cobalt on the telegraph ...' I looked at Mist and found him looking at me. My hot skin prickled. Dread suddenly pressed so heavily upon me I sat down on the grass. 'They're breaking my codes ...'

'Jant, nobody breaks your codes.'

'They're reading my telegraph!'

'Only governors and Eszai know how to!'

'Swallow was a governor! She has the code book!'

Mist screwed the cigarette into his holder and found he had nothing to light it with. 'Swallow Awndyn ...?'

'I think she's still alive. Shit! If she deciphered my message, she can read everything I send down the line!' I pummelled my fist in the grass. 'If they're reading it, I'll have to hand-deliver everything. They're slowing me down. She's closing me down! Who knows which of us is next? Tern's in Wrought, and—'

He stopped me, sympathetically. 'You're in a tizz about Tern. Saker's in a lather about Eleonora, and I admit I'm not terribly bucked about losing my house, with all its corking treasures that made me *me*. But we'll catch Connell, and Swallow, if you say so. Poor Captain Merganser and Reeve Auk Lemma were both Tanager courtiers. Eleonora was fond of them. She'll pull no punches when she finds out.'

'She'll make it worse!'

'Why?'

'Treating Roses badly will turn more against us.'

'Huh. Skip it.'

'Then more Litanee, then maybe other Morenzians. Everything we've done so far has fucked this up! Shit! ...How can I telegraph San if Swallow can read it?'

Saker trotted back with his guards, declaring, 'Come on! Let's track Connell!'

'She's had quite a start,' said Fulmer.

'She's on foot. Jant, you're a good tracker and I'm the best hunter in the world. Let's go!'

'It's Swallow we need to find.'

'Chances are,' said Fulmer, 'If Swallow is alive, she's sitting in Litanee. That's where these terrorists are coming from, after all.'

'I can't ride into Litanee without asking the governor's permission,' said Saker.

He leant and flicked the lighter for Fulmer, who drew on his cigarette so hard that, with lungs and eight airsacs, he demolished half of it in one inhalation.

'I agree that killing Rose bombers before they leave their country would make Awia safer,' he said.

'It'd start a war.'

'Well, try to think like Swallow. You know how she thinks better than anyone.'

'How can I think like a woman who's gone mad?'

'If she was mad, you'd already have caught her.'

Saker pulled the manuscript sheets from his quiver and brandished them. '*This* was her hiding place.'

'How long ago did she abandon that wagon and that ditty if she was ever here at all?'

'. . . I don't know.'

Fulmer exhaled an Awian amount of smoke and narrowed his eyes through it, looking out to the *Gerygone* lying at anchor on the hammered silver sea. Then he flicked ash at the dead horse and decapitated gypsy, who still had his feet in the stirrups. 'Thirty of them. They were only wearing partial uniform, see, it's way too big for him. If you hadn't been in such a dashed rush, you'd have noticed . . . Connell rides as well as the Master of Horse. Tell her so, if you catch her again. Tell her she's as good as Hayl, and see if she won't spill all Swallow's plans for a chance of immortality.'

'Awia presses charges.'

'Oh, Saker. Didn't you lead the peaceful side when the Castle solved the Eske Rebellion that way? I can sail these two unfortunate courtiers back to Tanager on *Gerygone*. That way I can take the news to the Queen. You can leave the dead gypsies, the wagons and the carriage to me, too. It's got Turvy Horses, hasn't it?'

'Yes,' I said.

He continued to fill his bones with tar and nicotine. 'I'll stay on my ship. I'll watch the flickers. Let me know if you need me, or my twenty cannon ...'

'Here's the lighter,' said Saker.

'No, Your Majesty, please do me the honour of keeping it, as a parting gift. Marcel himself made it; from *the* Brooke Street tobacconists. It's the bee's knees, the ant's antennae; one cannot buy finer. Human-designed, and infallible ... It's stylish and effective. Like me.'

'Thank you.'

He turned his horse. 'Jant, this affair gives me the pip. Catch Swallow, what?'

'I'll try.'

'Good. Oh, and remember, red *never* matches bottle green, so try not to get shot.'

'Goodbye, Mist.'

'A hearty pip pip to the both of you. Fair winds and following seas.' He described an elegant arc with the cigarette, then walked the horses away towards Cullion and, as he did so, we saw his flamboyance desert him, and a hard expression crossed his face.

CHAPTER 25

Fulmer

I think Fulmer, being new to the Circle, struggles with the scope of immortality. When he was mortal, and an inveterate social climber, he reached a false summit from which the Awian aristocracy blocked his further ascent. I've suffered their slights myself, when I was courting Tern, so I know how they scar a man. But Fulmer wanted so desperately to mix and dazzle in Eleonora's court, that he dressed more and more perfectly and memorized the *Etiquette*. Every barbed comment hooks and plays him, to shape himself to fit in with those bastards, though it's easier to become immortal than to join them.

Some things aren't written in the *Etiquette*. As Saker said, you simply know them because you've always known them, and if you don't, you might as well be carrying a billboard saying 'I used to be a harbour-master's clerk'. Fulmer makes faux pas so slight that only Eleonora's crowd notice. And they laugh at him trying so hard to be a healthy pack member. They love his trepidation that they'll hound him out.

Fulmer hasn't realised that, being Mist, he doesn't have to be part of their vain and shallow world. He could slob around in an old Tanager Bay t-shirt, as long as he's the Sailor, and *they'll* emulate *him*, until he sets a fashion for old t-shirts. He could tell the lords and ladies, 'History will remember you badly, because I'll write it!' – and they'd eat out of his hand.

That's what's so great about the Circle. It lifts you from the mortal's rat race. Admittedly it puts you into a more competitive one, but at least the Castle's fair. Fulmer's desire to run in the wheel of the upper class pains him badly. And they know it, and they love being able to taunt an Eszai.

When he was Zascai, Eleonora's patronage made him captain of the *Melowne*, which gave him the practice he needed to become Mist. She was his stepping stone – by all the ladies' accounts he's very giving in bed, but he'd rather have a word from her. His big projects are fantastic, but Society drags him down. So, as Mist he uses his gunships to bombard the Insects. He communicates with the gigantic Sea Kraits to destroy the coastal Paperlands. But as Fulmer he serves Steinasri Fleuve Nicholl brandy 1960 (not 1961), coffee with the dinner (also 'not done'!).

Why not?

Because it just isn't.

And fish on a Wednesday in December, not knowing what 'everyone knows', that it wasn't so many decades since Queen Jardine choked on a bone. I wish I could tell him he doesn't have to care. I'd like to see his hardness, which cracks to severity, melt to a nature more congenial and sweet. I know it's in there. I wish I could make him understand. I need to watch him. And then I realised, that's how Saker used to feel, about me.

CHAPTER 26

Awndyn

Saker rode circuits of Maple Wood until he was forced to admit he couldn't see any sign of Connell. Hooves had churned up the ground and, though he sent riders to search the hedges, coppices, farmhouse and defused wagons, Connell had vanished without trace.

He rode back to me. The gibbous moon was low and large, almost transparent to the blue sky, over the stand of poplars that surrounded Drussiter farmhouse on the low hill. 'Without track dogs, what can I do? I'll check the beach, Drussiter ... Awndyn. I'll search the border. She'll probably try to nip into Morenzia by the canal bridge ... that way.'

'That's where I'm going, to Awndyn. I'll send a message to warn all Eszai, and I'll meet you there tonight.'

'At the manor house ...'

'Yes. At *your* manor house.'

'Very well. But god knows I don't want to go back there, now. It'll be like holding a séance.'

'Saker, have you ever held a séance?'

'Yes ...'

'They don't work.'

'Actually—'

'*They don't work.*'

Awndyn is a hub for my Black Coach and the terminal of the coastal telegraph line. I landed by the white weatherboarded turret of my semaphore tower. Every tower has two masts, that is, two sets of arms, so they can send and receive at the same time. I entered and climbed upstairs to the chief operator, seated at a slope-top desk before the great viewing pane.

I wrote a message warning all the Eszai and recalling those who weren't at the Front, to the Castle. The risk of Connell or Swallow reading the code outweighed the fact my friends were going to be blown up if they stayed where they were. The operator began to sweep the levers across the console. They controlled cantilevers that moved the arms above us, and we watched the station on Awndyn Hill spread and fold in my wings' callsign, and begin to repeat the first moves of my message.

And away it went at the speed of sight, spelling itself laboriously over the Downs: Awndyn Three to Five, Dace River Six, Clobest, to the Eske Hub, and out to all the outposts of the Empire. Swooping at a rate of two words per minute, my message being ten words long, that is five minutes through thirty-five stations, over a distance of two hundred and eighty kilometres; it will reach the Castle in an hour.

The Awndyn Hill tower mirrored us. Like an exotic dancer in a floor-length dress, she sinuously scissored her black and white arms to our melody. I watched her zip through her symbols, then lower her arms in readiness, and I fell in love.

Then I gave sealed letters to fast riders at the Black Coach mail office, which never closes, and watched them gallop away, each to a different Eszai, to the Governor of Hacilith and to the Emperor. Across the world, the telegraph paddles will fold in silence. I'd warned my friends not to broadcast their movements, now Swallow's code book lies in terrorist hands.

I had Awndyn Manor house searched before I dared enter. My burns were agonising and my whole body was shaking, so after dinner I went to the annexe and shot up a phial of scolopendium into my unburnt arm.

I lay on the Awian chaise longue and watched the streaky sky darken, flickering whenever a sparrow flew past the intricate leaded windows. Although they gave onto a sea view, I preferred the annexe to Swallow's study or the hall, because they were still pervaded by that weird musty smell. I preened my wings with a sinking feeling of grief for them, feeling the stricture of my burnt skin. It'll take a year for my flight feathers to moult through. They'd grow back faster if I pulled them out, but I can't afford to ground myself.

Branches of wisteria crawled and spiralled around the window. They tapped on the glass, but they couldn't get in. Night fell, and dew beaded into grey canopies the spiders' webs covering the lawn. Glow worms flickered in the flowerbeds. The constellation called the Lawyer was tilting south from her zenith, as if dipping her starry scales into the sea. Two of Awndyn's three lighthouses winked beyond the north wing of the sleeping mansion, and the pier lighthouse gilded a path across the ocean. Beyond the south wing the sea was just a black expanse, no waves, no movement at all.

I could see across the lawn to the conjoined chimneys of the main house. They stood tall above the low roofs and cast striped moon-shadows over the grass. A single lamp burned in an iron cage by the porch, and glittered the panes in the bay windows. It cast a tongue of light, moths curled around it, and the rest of the house lay dark and almost blue in the chirruping summer night.

Saker must have come in while I was unconscious, because he was suddenly sitting on the backless chair unlacing his boots. 'Jant,' he said, 'When you fall off the wagon you land with a crash.'

'I'm fine.'

'Don't relapse. Please. Not now.'

I pulled my wings in, sat up and recounted everything I'd done. He listened carefully. '...Well, I'm grateful. I couldn't find Connell. I'll return to Tanager tomorrow; Eleonora will be relieved to hear we're not the target ... This sepulchre is making my skin crawl. I can't decide whether Swallow's dead or not.'

'Resurrected to wreak vengeance.'

'She had a temper enough to raise the dead.' He pulled off his boot and stared at the sole of it. 'Breaking vases ... and harpsichords.'

'She wants to break the Circle.'

'Yes.' He levered off the other boot. 'Swallow knew I loved her ... and part of me still does ... I mean, love her music. But she didn't care about me, so I'm safe, I think. After I lost my Challenge I might as well have stopped existing.'

'She should've listened to you.'

'She wanted to be immortal on her own terms. Well, nobody can. It's impossible. You can only be immortal on other people's terms.'

'San's rules.'

'Oh, and those of the admirers and musicians who choose to listen to her music ... I would have married her, Jant.'

'I know.'

'Because of her music, her spirit. No wonder she attacked Cyan first. She ... hated Cyan. Absolutely hated her, because I asked her to look after my girl, when she was growing up.'

'And because Cyan was a recent Eszai.'

He looked down to hide the pain. 'She mistreated Cyan when they lived together. It was my fault. I regret it ... I thought the two could be my family. But she wanted to be the Musician, not my wife. It's her folly ... She'd be immortal now, instead of ... pushed to this extremity.'

'Bunting witnessed her dead body.'

'Bunting? Call him. We must revisit his account.'

Saker lit a candle with Fulmer's lighter, and the flame yellowed his face. He put the candle aside, flicked the lighter and gazed at it in melancholy fascination. Flicked it again, and again, and each time it provided a perfect flame. 'Did you see what the rifle did to that man's head?'

'I was next to him.'

He said nothing for a while, but flicked the lighter and watched the flame. 'I taught myself archery, you know,' he said quietly. 'When I was eleven, I walked out of the palace ... though they'd forbidden me to, 'cause of Insects. I went to San's bowmen.' He flicked the lighter. 'Do you know, your eyes reflect every time the beacon beam passes the window?'

'I only see a glimmer.'

'Ah ... right ... I made my way to San's infantry and asked them to teach me. I had this notion I could stop the Insects, and I'd used to spend every day practising with my child's bow. I never let go of it. What else does a boy do, who can extinguish a candle with an arrow? Who can hit the spokes of a galloping chariot? Who can put twelve shafts in the air before the first hits the ground? I was a better hunter with my recurve than they were with theirs. When I trained with the longbow men my brothers found out and jeered ... relentlessly. A prince should lead the cavalry, they said ... But the cavalry weren't holding back the swarm.'

He closed it, flicked it. 'Winning the Games made my brothers' taunts worse. For ten years ... then they stopped ...' He snapped it shut, flicked it. I think he was trying to break it. 'It takes tens of thousands of hours practice to become perfect enough at your skill to be Eszai ... and, when you are, that's only the beginning of hundreds of thousands of hours more ... Jant, look at this thing ...'

The lighter was a weighty silver disk with a salamander coiled around it. The creature's eyes were first water rubies.

'Fulmer likes to savour the wealth he's made,' I said.

'What? No, I mean ...' Flick: another almond flame.

'You'll wear it out,' I said.

'Yes. This will wear out. This—' he brought his tinder box from his coat pocket '—never will. This lighter is convenient and powerful. This tinder box takes skill and practice to use. But anybody can use a lighter. So people stopped using tinder boxes oh ... back in the eighteenth century I believe they invented matches. Now everyone uses lighters, because lazy always wins. Do you understand?'

'It's the difference between bows and guns.'

'Exactly. Bows need training and strength. Guns are lazy.' He weighed the salamander lighter and his ancient fyrd-issue tinder box, one in each hand. 'Jant, who can hold back this tide? Even if I give every man a rifle my archers have ten times their efficiency at two hundred metres. But men will adopt guns because they're too lazy to train and, you know, I think they like the bang. Today you saw how messy it's going to be.' He held them out. 'The effect of the rifle shocked me. But you'd choose it, wouldn't you? You'd choose the lighter?'

'Yes.'

'Oh, Jant. You don't get it. You don't get it, at all. What happens to those millions of hours of perfection?'

'They're in the past.'

'No. They're not. They're here.' He tapped his chest.

'Why not keep both?'

He looked at me uncertainly.

'The lighter might be more convenient, but when it runs out of fuel it's worthless. Remember your sundial and your watch? They both have benefits, so you kept them both.'

He sighed, and smiled. 'I'm glad to hear you say that.' He placed them on the table.

At this point Bunting came in with a cafetière the size of a binnacle, and put his tray down. 'Bunting,' Saker said. 'From the bow to the rifle, do I have to start again?'

Bunting regarded him, perplexed. 'Why did you stop?'

We questioned Bunting about his discovery of Swallow's corpse, and his story remained the same. He became distressed at the memory, and more so that we seemed to be doubting him – and when we showed him the manuscript he recognised Swallow's writing but couldn't explain it, and grew even more upset. Eventually we let him go to bed. Under the influence of coffee as strong as bitumen my high had long gone, and I was tired, too.

'Mist's right,' I said. 'Swallow's probably in Litanee.'

'Well, Dunlin said the Vermiform is everywhere,' said Saker. 'Why don't we ask it? Maybe it can see her.'

I dug in my pack for the worms, which I'd put in a jar, and tipped them onto the table. They lay in a soggy lump. I stirred them with my finger and they pulsated feebly.

Saker tipped a spoonful of sugar beside them. The worms disentangled themselves, crawled over and devoured it, and started dancing in energetic loops.

'It eats sugar.'

'It eats anything.'

He asked it, 'Do you know who Swallow Awndyn is? Can any of you see her?'

The worms started crawling in a circle. He stirred them, and they spiralled up and down his finger in a precise network. 'Does that mean it doesn't know?'

'I don't know. Maybe.'

He sighed. 'If Swallow is masterminding this!'

'It would certainly explain where her money went.'

'Oh, god. After all I did for her.'

I glanced around the annexe room. The tiny, elaborately tessellated panes of the oriel window were asleep with the night behind them. We heard the sighing of the wind over the marram grass and the susurration of the ocean beyond.

'I remember her father.'

He gave his ironic smile. 'I remember the previous families.'

'Of course.'

'And this place being built. And the town. And Swallow ... sitting next to me at the piano there, playing duets. When I was recuperating from my wound ... hands over each others' on the keys. We could clasp hands in a quaver rest without missing the beat ... And now I know it will outlast me.'

The Vermiform crawled onto his arm and made bracelets. He plucked at the worms but, braided together, they were incredibly strong. 'It doesn't know, does it?'

'It's not telling.'

'Then we must think about this logically. Swallow and Connell may ride anywhere, but their barrels are difficult to transport. They sailed them by schooner to Cullion, then what?'

'They must have loaded them onto carts.'

'Connell will be prepared for road blocks, so what would she do?'

The Vermiform swarmed off his arm onto the table and crawled in a big, thin ring, came together into a point and suddenly spread out. There, as if I had drawn it, was a map of the familiar twists and turns of the Moren River and the straight line of the Awndyn-Moren canal.

'By barge!' I said. 'Look, it's the canal.'

He leant closer.

'The canal ends just the other side of town,' I said. 'Connell can load powder on the barges and take it straight to Hacilith.'

'Then let's go to the canal basin.'

'What, in the middle of the night?'

He glanced at the window, exasperated. 'Very well. At first light, then.'

'Thank you,' I said to the Vermiform. It swarmed over the spilt sugar and seethed there for a few seconds, then it drew back. It had arranged individual sugar grains into 'YOU'RE WELCOME' written on the table.

'Give me half of them,' said Saker. 'So I can speak to Dunlin.'

Some worms crawled to him, and the rest climbed back in my pocket, and I went to bed.

CHAPTER 27

Heavier measures

The sound of boots on the path woke me. I lay in the oak poster bed, listening to them scrunching below my window, then grappled for my watch. It was four in the morning. I'd only had three hours' sleep.

I sank back with a groan, and then peeled myself out of bed and threw open the shutters. On the manor house forecourt Saker had assembled his three Tanager heavies and a company of Awndyn Select infantry. He sat attentive on his horse before their ranks, with his rifles in the saddle holsters. A pink line of dawn was showing along the sea's horizon and the faintest colours were seeping into the grey.

He glanced up to see me half-naked at the window. 'Jant! What time do you call this?'

'I call it four a.m.'

'It's five past. Come down!'

The Vermiform was sitting on the shoulder of my shirt on the chair back. It crawled into the pocket as I picked up the shirt and flung it on. I rolled my eyes at the mirror as I passed and ran down the zigzag staircase with its linenfold panelling and creaking treads, swung round the newel post at the bottom and out to the forecourt. Saker nodded at me, turned his horse and walked off. Apparently I was supposed to walk beside him, and the fyrdsmen fell into line behind us, marching two abreast.

'It's this direction,' said Saker. 'Isn't it?'

'To the canal basin?'

'Of course.'

With lips cracked from gunpowder and bags under his eyes, he looked shattered. Being in Swallow's house had haunted him all night. He'd never bargained for such close proximity to her, to the music they'd enjoyed together, to her grand bedroom he'd never got anywhere near. I don't believe he'd slept at all, nor even gone to bed, just spent all night in the annexe listening to the sound of the sea.

And now he'd adroitly assumed the role of Governor of Awndyn.

'Jant, I want you to fly ahead and spy out the wharf. Caution is the watchword. Come back and tell me if you see any gypsies.'

I nodded. I ran, flung open my wings and sped into the gaunt dawn. Having trouble steering, and expending twice the effort with so much vane missing from my feathers, I flew unevenly above the road, with the sand dunes to my left, towards the canal like a lead strip between the cornfields.

The basin was hidden by a row of houses, all red herring-bone brick bellying out between black half-timbers. I swept up and smacked into the roof of one, crawled to its ridge, concealed from the dockside by a chimney stack. I pressed against the chimney, and strips of eroded mortar cascaded out and went skittering down the tiles, dropped off the roof and crashed onto the wharf cobbles. I shrank back for a second, then peered round. Nobody seemed to have noticed.

Five big barges were moored at the dockside, loading. Stevedores swarmed all over them. Each barge had a crane attached to its stern; the nearest was hoisting a crate. Two bargemen raised their arms as it lifted between them. A stack of similar green crates obscured my view to the end of the wharf. The second barge was loading wool bales for the mills of the capital. The third one was swinging aboard bundles of firewood.

The fourth barge sat low in the water. It was a boat I'd seen before, being one of the flotilla that provisioned the Castle. Its bargeman in oilskins leant on the cabin doorjamb, smoking a pipe.

Then there was a pyramid of barrels, then wheelbarrows of amphorae of that terrible wine Awndyn produces. The last barge was painted black, with its deck planks removed, loading barrels from the pyramid. The wharfinger's shouts were muted in the early morning air.

A man with Rose tattoos walked straight beneath me. I glimpsed his shoulders and shaved head; he disappeared under the roof's overhang, then emerged from the gable end, strolling down the quay. Grey vest and fyrd trousers: he sported a big, naturally-inked Rose on his shoulder, with a ribboned tiller and a barge horse with SH for the Shivel Horsefair.

He passed the pyramid of barrels with care – they were gunpowder kegs. God, there must be a hundred! He joined the group at the black barge and looked up to its crane, which was holding one keg aloft. It turned slowly above him, swung aboard; two stevedores lowered it into the well deck and back swung the crane. His big hands caught the hook and fixed it to the strap of the next barrel. The barge bore neither name nor insignia. I studied it until my eyes stung – the arms of all its bargemen looked clothed because they were netted with tattoos.

They must have a lookout. I eased around on the roof. There, by the warehouse wall.

I hopped off and flitted back to Saker. He reined in his horse, halted his fifty men and watched me land. 'Roses are loading a barge with powder barrels,' I said. 'It's the black one, furthest on the quay.'

'Is there a guard?'

'They have a lookout.' I pointed up the road. 'On the right, there's a warehouse with a weathervane. The man in the dark fatigues, standing in its shadow, against the wall – he has a crossbow.'

'Stay here.' Saker dismounted and took his bow and quiver. He walked up the road and was back a few minutes later. 'They don't have a lookout … This barge, would it be first on the wharf if we round that side of the houses?' He pointed left, to a maize field extending to the reeds on the brink of the canal.

'Yes.'

'How many Roses?'

'Twenty. It's not Connell.'

He looked distant for a second, as if seeing through the field. 'Troupes everywhere. Did you spot their leader?'

'A man, shaved head, similar build to Sula. Um … He has the biggest Rose *here*. He's been a bargeman for years, married, two kids, they live aboard, plays the guitar. Trades at Shivel Horse Fair.'

Saker laughed. 'Their tattoos are invaluable. If I take him alive will the rest surrender? Given that they're sworn to help each other?'

'I can't say.'

'We'll try it. Sula?'

'Yes, my lord?'

'Take everyone up the road and wait behind the warehouse. Listen for my whistle. When you hear me, come in and arrest them. Don't shoot unless I say.'

'Yes, my lord.'

'Beware of crossbows. Cyan flooded the market with cheap outmoded crossbows for any criminal to buy. Jay, stay here and bring our horses up last, or they'll hear the hooves.'

We stood on the verge and watched the fifty men, led by his two courtiers, begin to creep quietly up the road. He grunted approval, turned and descended the verge into the maize field like a man wading into the sea. He seemed a lot happier now he was master of the hunt. We moved through the maize field slowly, pushing the stalks aside, smelling the cool, silky grass scent of the unripe corn and listening to the bustle of the wharf – geese on the river and the barge cranes clacking.

Saker stopped before the last maize stalks and dropped to one knee. With a click he fitted the bowstring into an arrow's nock, and I heard the faint clack of its shaft on the bow riser. By his boots, a ladybird that had fallen off one of the green stems was crawling over the dry soil.

I came to his side and looked out between the stalks. There was the end of the wharf, fifty metres distant, the barge bow-on with gypsies working to and fro on the deck. Their leader was looking up under the next rising barrel.

'The one who looks like someone chopped sticks on his face?'

'Yes.'

'His left calf will heal easiest.'

'I'm ready.'

He bent his bow and the bodkin point protruded from the edge of the corn. Loosed, and I was away after the arrow. The man screamed, crumpled to the ground, and a moment later I had my knife to his throat.

Recognising me, the gypsies backed off. The muscular man was puffing, his shin folded under him, bleeding freely with the shaft through it. I smelt his fear and pain, the heavy bulk of his sweating body, and the fact I'd caught prey thrilled me.

His bristly jowl hung over my blade. I pricked him with the point. 'No one shoots! Tell them!'

'You heard him, don't shoot!' he called to his troupe, who stood like statues, wide-eyed, mouths open here and there. I motioned for them to lower the barrel and they duly cranked it down.

Saker strolled onto the wharf with an arrow at string and passed an investigative glance over the Roses. 'You're under arrest,' he said loudly. He stood by the barrel and studied the men on deck. 'I'm the Governor of Awndyn, and if anyone makes a move he'll join your leader on the ground.'

He held the arrow shaft on the mark of the bow, stuck two fingers of his other hand in his mouth and whistled. His soldiers ran onto the quay, past the gabled fronts of the houses, past the pub with the sign of the Frog and Pepper, to the side of every gypsy. They were two to each Rose, who made neither move nor sound till the soldiers walked them away.

I was still crouched beside the boatman; he was sprawled on the cobbles with my knife under his chin, drip-white and panting.

Saker waved me away, seized his shirt and dragged him to the edge of the cut. The water rippled smoothly from the bank. He dropped him so his top half was over the edge, stomped him between the shoulder-blades, ducking his head underwater, and kept his foot on the guy's back, holding his head under while he struggled and kicked.

'Can you?' He stomped him under again. 'Breathe like a mermaid?'

'Ark—!' The man arched his back, strained away from the surface, thrashing his head, flicking off drops. Saker pressed the instep of his boot against the arrow shaft sticking out of his calf. He shrieked.

'Is Swallow alive?' Saker demanded.

I yelled, 'Let him go!'

He put more pressure on the arrow. '*Is she?*'

'I'm not – argh! Yes!'

'She's alive?'

'Yes!'

'She's alive, where is she?'

'I don't know!' yelled the man.

'What's your name?'

'Rax!'

'Where's Swallow?'

Rax was rigid, trying to keep his face off the water.

'*Where is she?*'

'Nobody knows!' he gasped. 'We just get orders.'

'Who gives you orders?'

'Connell!'

Saker kicked the arrow so hard it tilted and Rax gulped a sob of air like a scream backwards. 'Someone must know where the bitch is hiding!'

'Only Connell! She rides to us!'

'How many groups are there?'

'I don't know!'

'He's just a little cog,' I said.

Saker took his foot from the arrow and stamped Rax once more between the shoulder blades, splashing his face in the water, then hauled him off the bank and dumped him on the cobbles. 'Where were you taking the powder?'

'Hacilith.'

'Where in Hacilith?'

'Connell wouldn't say.'

Saker slipped his bow from his shoulder and rubbed his fingertips on the string. 'Jant, fly to Hacilith and warn them. Rayne first. Go on.'

'I'm not leaving you to torture Rax!'

He shook himself. 'Torture? No, I'm interr—'

'You were!'

'I had to find out! Otherwise she'll kill more people, she might kill Rayne!'

'There are better ways – we'll take him to San.'

'There's no time!' He examined Rax, who was sallow and fainting, and then glanced at Jay, waiting beside the tavern with the horses. Saker was holding his wings splayed low, in threatening body language, and Jay hadn't dared approach.

He folded his wings and beckoned Jay to bring Balzan. Together, they bumped Rax up into the saddle. He screeched with pain and then stoically sat motionless, his leg locked out straight, fletchings in his calf like a badge and the point projecting a clothyard from his shin. Blood was running into his boot. His soaked grey vest was skewed, showing the tattoos around his neck.

Saker took the reins. 'What does the drum on your chest mean?'

Rax glared at him, sucked a breath. 'Awndyn music festival.'

'Is that where you met Swallow?'

'Yes.'

'Is this her retaliation? Because San refused her?'

Rax drooped forward onto Balzan's neck. Saker prodded him with his bow.

'I'll tell the Emperor you're on a revenge rampage,' I said.

'You may tell the Emperor anything you please, Comet. Because I'm not his damn hawk any more! Rax, why is she bombing Eszai?'

'She hates them ... Can't you feel how much she despises you, too?'

'... But why?'

'Because the Emperor not only thwarted her, but humiliated her.'

Saker stepped back and stared at me. 'She's turned into a monster.'

'And you're on the way!'

'I'm doing this for the Castle! She's killed hundreds! Remember Wrought!'

Rax fastened his hand over the arrow shaft and moaned. 'I don't know anything else ... The troupes work independently. That's all, that's all I know. Swallow gave me orders in advance. Everyone got instructions at her festival ... She only wanted me to load the stuff ... because it's my boat.'

Saker said to him conversationally, 'Not many people enjoy an audience with the Emperor.'

'Please let me go.'

'I have two children as well. Lory and Ortolan. The Awndyn doctor will fix your leg. As long as you don't try to escape, you'll see your kids again.' He gave the reins to Jay and watched him lead the horse and Rax off the quay, towards town. He sent Sula for more fyrd to reclaim the barrels. Then he sighed, looking down the quayside, and said, 'Jant, I'll find horses for all the Roses and take them to the Castle.'

'All right, Saker,' I said, 'But be careful. There'll be dozens of troupes. Stay clear of inns and coach houses ... stables ... Shivel manor.'

'Oh, I've learnt my lesson. No gypsies will get past Warden Sula and a hundred Awndyn Select.'

All the other stevedores had fled the wharf and left the barges deserted. We stood looking at the stack of barrels, as the double-windows in the houses' steep gables rouged with the rising sun. A seagull flew across its red disc, momentarily vanishing in the glare.

'Swallow's clever,' I said. 'No one troupe knows another.'

'The sections of an orchestra don't communicate with each other, Jant. They just play.'

'An orchestra, ha ...'

'Yes!' he shouted. 'An orchestra! They rest until she cues them in, to play at the right time. She conducts them – and she has the timing of a genius! We can't cover the whole Empire as she starts the crescendo.'

If the troupes were communicating at all, I couldn't see their means because they were too damn simple. Any traveller could be carrying orders – who was in cahoots and who wasn't? What could I do, damn it? I couldn't stop every man on the road!

I said, 'Out of Rax's troupe, beware the one with the skull on his chest. He's a knife fighter. The one with the stirrups is a crack rider.'

'And *I* am tempted to shoot the fucking lot.' Saker paused in counting the barrels and extended his hand to shake mine. 'Jant, look after the Doctor ... for me.'

I nodded, then turned on the ball of my foot and sprinted down the quay. I opened my wings, elbows first, then whisked out the splay of my flight feathers, pushed my feet harder against the cobbles to overcome their drag, jumped and took off.

I beat up, into the rose-flecked sky, and turned south for the city. At about a hundred metres altitude I glanced down to see Saker standing alone at the quayside, waiting for his reinforcements. The column of soldiers with their gypsy prisoners, respectively olive and black, were making their way along the road between cream-green maize fields, towards the jail in the ramshackle rust-red cluster of Awndyn town.

High tide pared the white sand beach to the thinnest crescent, almost glowing, where waves that seemed as smooth and hard as enamel, broke from lilac to foam.

CHAPTER 28

The city

I flew to Hacilith, following the canal. The airflow soothed my burns, and I tipped water from my canteen over my bandages, but with every wingbeat they smarted and chafed. I tried to glide but I dropped height quickly – I'd lost too much feather, so I had to keep flapping on laboriously.

Saker was acting weird. He would have stabbed Connell, and he had no qualms about twisting his arrow in Rax's wound. Had he been like this all the time he was Eszai, and hidden it?

Well, Saker's always become furious when people whom he feels are under his protection are threatened. It piques his self-imposed duty of care for the vulnerable – children, people who are close to him, his soldiers, cottars, or women. Especially any women, the romantic old fool. As long as he thinks he's trying to save them, he feels justified in any action, and I don't know how far he'll take it.

The gypsies are catching innocent people in every blast. It's the thing most guaranteed to rile Saker. Only the self-consciously moral feel the need to protect the rest of us poor bastards, and they'll fail their own morals, when they do.

Below me, the clouds thickened into a lumpy white sheet that looked solid. My shadow flickered over its surface and a headland of cloud stretched out ahead. The country of cumulus is always peaceful no matter what's breaking loose below. I wish I could land there and walk about; meet the people who live there and, if possible, live there myself.

The hot air given off by the city ramped the clouds into great piles and shaggy-stalked mushrooms, as if the mills and smokestacks were replicated in the sky above them – as if they were pushing up the cloud. I flew between puffy columns like suspended Insect architecture. They hung as weightless as the pillars of kelp underwater, between which the diver soars.

The headland ended like a bay, in a clear stretch of air, and suddenly ten thousand streets were spread out beneath me.

So it's sunny in Hacilith. I glided down the sheer face of the cliffs of cloud. Their bay arced out either side – then I was below it – and black factory chimneys bristled at me like cannons. Acrid air caught my throat. Below me, lines and lines of terraces in Piteem. The shine of the canal split into a network of parallel wharfs in Galt, with warehouses, cranes, millfronts and metalworks around them, barges moving like beetles.

Ahead, the estuary – looping, branching, braiding rivers with boats in the centres of the main channels, mudbanks between them, and piers like black lollipop sticks planted further out in a sandy-coloured expanse of sea.

There's the Brandoch coast; there's the hip of Morenzia, looking just like the map. It was mid-afternoon and the ocean sparkled. I wheeled above the city. That green rhombus is Fiennafor Park. That heliograph flash is sunlight on the Bronze Palace, with the plaza and the candy-pink and white Bullion Palace beyond. That spire with the four bartizans is the university main building. I bit my lip, pulled my wings in and dropped, eyes half-closed against the rush of air.

Over Old Town, the blocks of the university like a sliding puzzle. A flock of pigeons beat up from the surrounding rooftops and sped round and round. The university's spire like a lance passed below me. I leant right and turned, bleeding off my speed, over lecture hall, labs, the refectory, and brought the spire in front of me again. Then, wings flexing, adjusting constantly, I balanced against the buffeting breeze and brought myself vertical. I grabbed the thick iron spike, stepped onto its narrow base and stood atop the tower.

The tapering spike was cold and rough and smelt of weather-beaten metal. Its base just wide enough for the arch of one foot. I hung onto it and looked down the precipitous drop of the university's tower and all its windows, to the roofs of the Medical Faculty.

The Vermiform hung from my pocket, waving wildly.

'Do you like flying?' I asked it.

It threshed its worms in great excitement.

'Well, have a good look. That pointed roof is Rayne's house. It's the oldest building in the city. It's wood and the rest is stone. That oval roof is the lecture theatre. Bit different from the Front, isn't it?'

The flow of Old Town murmured below us. The city carried on as normal, which seemed so strange. I'd expected the bombs to have stopped everything. I expected the streets to be empty and everyone inside, like Micawater. But I could see yellow melons on the first market stall beyond the corner, students sitting with their bikes flat on the grass. I don't wonder the gypsies have forgotten what Eszai are for. May the Insects break through here, swarm the whole city, chew it to buttresses of paper anchored to the tower. Then they'd remember why they need us.

We need Rayne. I tucked the Vermiform back in my pocket and jumped off the tower. Spiralled down. Landed in a crouch. I climbed the steps to the lecture hall and paused outside its double doors. The Doctor's voice was in full flow inside '—Will attack the soft parts of one's abdomen but these will be covered in armour so you find—'

I crashed the doors open and walked in. Benches tiered down to the lecture floor, where Rayne stood next to a dissecting table with an Insect on it.

'Comet!' she said.

The students in the benches strained round. I descended the steep stairs past them, to her side. 'You're burnt,' she said.

I stretched out a wing and spoke to her behind it. 'We must evacuate the building now. Everyone.'

She saw my expression, dropped her ichor-covered hacksaw and raised her arms. 'Year Three, the lecture is over. File out quietly, *quickly*, and in order.'

A clatter as they swept away their notebooks and picked up their bags.

'Tell them to go as far from campus as possible.'

Rayne raised her eyebrows but complied. 'Leave Goldthread!'

'Go into town! Tell everyone you meet to do the same!'

They looked at each other, deathly quiet, and left speedily, glancing back at me. The door banged behind the last of them.

Rayne said, 'Jant, this had better be good!'

'Bombs could be planted here.'

'*Here?*'

'Very likely.'

She smeared her hands down the front of her apron and looked about. Beside us, she'd neatly cut in half the giant Insect on its metal table and dissected it to show its mangle of ganglia. The rest of its tangled white nervous system unravelled like string onto the floor and into the hollow cores of its severed limbs. At the back, beside the blackboard, Insects were piled ready for dissection; the air was thick with their coppery, acidic smell and that of formaldehyde.

'Why would anyone want to bomb a Year Three lecture?'

'Swallow wants to kill every Eszai.'

'Swallow? The *singer*? She's dead.'

'She faked it!'

'Dead is dead, Jant. I—'

I took the old woman's hand and pulled her to the side door that I knew led into her house. She didn't resist but trotted after me. By the door I trod something underfoot that compressed with a crackle. It was a brown paper fuse. It ran from the corner of the door, half a metre, into the pile of Insects. 'Look!'

I knelt down, grasped the fuse and yanked it hard. It came free and the top Insect slid off the pile and thumped to the ground. I dashed to it: lying on its side, it was spilling black powder out of its thick, hollow thorax. I rocked it over and powder poured out onto the floorboards. Large blasting grains had been packed tightly inside the exoskeleton, and a hole drilled into the shell to take the fuse.

'It's full of powder,' I said.

'This one is, too,' said Rayne. 'And this!'

'Swallow turned Insects into bombs.'

'To kill me?'

'Yes, Ella.'

She pulled herself up to her full height. 'While I stood lecturing?'

'Yes!'

I rubbed the paper fuse-covering between my thumb and forefinger, and felt the hard string inside. Black powder grains flaked from the glue-covered twine and sprinkled out of the end of the sheathing, like pepper.

'Ten Insects for the students to dissect. In fifteen minutes I'd have given them out ...'

'Come on!'

I hastened her ahead, through the door, and suddenly we were in the most incredible museum, the passage to her house. I followed the fuse from the Insects – it ran, in rough-and-ready fashion, down the first dimly-lit side-aisle, at the base of the shelves, and looped up through an open sash window.

I ran to it. The fuse hung out, onto Goldthread Street, and dangled behind a privet bush, behind the black iron railings. The normal passers-by strolled up and down the wide pavement outside – and any one of them could be a bomber in disguise.

Rayne joined me. 'The usual suppliers delivered the Insects this morning.'

I turned to her wrinkled face. 'Did delivery men cart them in?'

'And carried them into the lecture hall, yes.'

'Were they gypsies?'

'All carters are, round here.'

I stared past her, at the shelves packed with specimen jars, preserved in alcohol and formalin, the chests and cabinets and boxes.

The crammed chaos surrounded us. Jars of organs white with age, floating within their crimped ducts and lace-snaked membranes. Glassware stored in crates with straw. This bloody museum of Rayne's and her seventh-century house were tinder and neat alcohol. One grenade through one of these windows, and the whole lot would go up.

I pulled her through the museum, past jars containing every anatomical peculiarity collected over a thousand years. A hand with six fingers, a curled-up foetus, the skeleton of a man whose skull bulged bone, dust caught in its shrubby growths.

We emerged into her house. Her study, where sunlight from the little side-street beamed through the slatted shutters. A tome lay open on her desk, covered with Insect dissection diagrams, and her lecture notes.

I dragged her to the door but she pulled free. She ran from display case to sideboard. 'What to take? What to take?'

'We haven't time!'

'It's irreplaceable!'

She ran to the bookshelves beside her bed in the corner. Wildly scanned the titles. 'Some dead singer can't—!'

'She doesn't care!'

Rayne stepped up onto the crochet cover of her bed, reached high and grabbed an old book from the end of the shelf above it, then barged out into the street.

With my next breath I caught an oddly familiar smell, and it stopped me dead. I turned, and traced it to Rayne's desk. I stood there, still, like a Rhydanne hunter, and inhaled long through my nose. An image formed in my mind – the dregs in Swallow's coffee mug. The same musty odour. I followed the scent among the formalin, camphor, turpentine and old plaster, to an envelope on her desk. It was open, full of dried leaves.

I picked it up and sniffed it. As I did so, behind me was a *crash*! of window glass, the *chink* of a bottle breaking, and kerosene blue with flame slooshed out of the window aisle, across the bare museum floor. The flames seized onto the lowest shelves, crackled up the edge of the first display case.

I stuffed the envelope in my pocket and darted out, to Rayne on the far pavement. I grabbed her with both hands, hugged her and bent over her, my cheek on her hard bun.

Rayne on the lecture floor would have been thrown against the pews by the shockwave, speared with fragments of shell.

She battered the inside of my wing. 'Jant! Let me see!'

I unwrapped her, revealing her face staring up. 'It won't blow! You took the fuse from the bugs!'

'It's *burning*!'

She tried to push my wing down, but wasn't strong enough, and simply crushed the feathers on my forearm. I lowered it, while keeping the other folded tight around her, and let her see.

The front of her half-timbered house looked completely normal. My feathers bent against her stained linen dress and apron. She glared like a gladiator's grandmother, the book under her arm. A cart went past.

Then, through the window, the daffodil light flared.

'Someone threw a lit bottle of kerosene through the window. Did you see who?'

She pointed up the alley, to the junction with Goldthread Street, the main road faced with the museum's windows, and the high walls of other faculty buildings. 'How could I? It's round the corner!'

Flame filled the bow-windows of her little house. Smoke was pouring from under the eaves. The bull's-eye panes began to crack – and then smoke, stinking of boiling formaldehyde, began flowing out of an open window, high in the lecture theatre behind the museum.

Rayne watched in horror, her mouth agape, a black slit, her hands hooked over my wing.

'My collection! My books! ...Fifteen hundred years!'

She sagged. I shuffled my wings under her armpits and pulled her back from the junction, away from the heat.

A crowd was gathering, people running out of the university buildings along Goldthread. I yelled at them, 'Go *that way*! Go to Godwit Street! Go to Southgate!'

Then clanging of bells, hooves and wheel-rims on the cobbles. Two fire engines galloped past the junction, and drew up their horses by the museum main entrance. They stopped, stared at the flames, realised there was bugger all anyone could do, and started moving the people back.

I shouted to a fireman. 'Evacuate everyone! There's gunpowder inside!'

'Yes, Comet!'

Rayne squirmed. 'Jant ... Oh, Jant. I would have been in that ...'

'Yes.'

'You have ... been in one?'

'The explosion on Cullion Pier, four days ago.'

'Your voice is hoarse.'

'The air was fire. I breathed it in. I've been coughing blood.'

She stared at her house. '…Who patched you up like that?'

'Some quack on the flagship.'

Her house had become a furnace. Tiles were falling off the burning rafters, leaving black fingers within the leaping flames. Then, with a sudden thunder, the roof caved in, and a huge mass of alcohol-yellow fire stretched to the sky.

Flames were roaring out of the windows and licking up the outside wall of the lecture theatre, and starting to catch. You could hear retorts from inside as the last of the jars burst. Flames streaked up, then a triple detonation as the heat reached the Insect bombs and set them off.

I had to get her out of this ancient little side-street. I started to lead her down to the junction with Sinter, so we could turn back onto Godwit Street – and a gigantic explosion boomed beyond the lecture theatre. We flinched together, against the wall. It shattered all the windows, and blasted the glass against the History Faculty opposite. Men and women still pouring out of the building were caught in the flying shards, and started screaming.

'The library!' yelled Rayne.

Another explosion behind it smashed a column of flame into the air, the height of the University's spire. Black smoke braided up, and in the hot air just kept climbing. We could hear screams and cries coming from behind her burning house.

'The dispensary!' Rayne tore at my wing to be free, but I held her.

A double explosion, louder still. Crump-crump! Fragments of tile and brick flew into the sky, and two trunks of solid fire thrust up above the roof of the lecture hall. They twisted, vanished, but the smoke continued to an extraordinary height. A weird, complete silence. Long enough for Rayne to look at me, perplexed. Then began more screaming, shrieking in a voice ripped with agony. And the ineffectual firebells rang again.

Rayne screamed. 'The patients! It was the hospital! The hospital!'

And she fainted in my arms.

I carried the Doctor to a hotel I knew nearby, because it was the nearest place I could think of that might be safe. I lay her on the bed and drew up the blankets. Then I reported to Governor Aver-Falconet, and helped the Zascai as much as I could. By the time I returned to the hotel, dusk was gathering but you wouldn't know it – the Faculty of Medicine was still blazing. It filled the air with haze. From my window high over Old Town I watched fire engines from every part of Hacilith clustering around it. They seemed tiny, pointless. It was worse than Wrought. The firemen gave up on it immediately and started soaking down the buildings of the Science Department, Insect testing labs, Graduate School and the surrounding houses.

I pushed up the sash window and a breeze buffeted in, carrying shouts and bustle, the stench of smoke, burning creosote, the sulphur trace of blasting powder. I sat on the sill and watched.

I usually feel safe by open windows. They afford a chance of escape into the high air. They offer me a chance to fly and see what's happening. But now my friend, the air, was tainted with the scent of cooked flesh, and I didn't want to see what was happening because it was too horrible. How could Swallow bomb the hospital? How could she murder hundreds of innocent mortals simply for the chance to kill Rayne?

Rayne was the most valuable human being in the Fourlands. Rayne had never hurt Swallow; damn it, she'd saved Swallow's life once by instructing me how to treat her Insect injuries. Had Swallow forgotten that? Had she totally lost her mind?

Behind me, Rayne stirred and murmured. She was an indistinct shape in the dark room.

'Hush, Ella,' I said.

'The patients!'

'I've got you a coach and—'

She sat bolt upright. 'Jant, is that you?'

'It's me.'

'Have you been to see the hospital?'

'Yes. And the dispensary. There weren't many survivors. I'm sorry.'

'Where are they?'

'I had them moved to Fiennafor.'

'Ward Twelve?'

'Yes.'

She sighed and sank down again. 'Good,' she murmured, and flaked out. An hour passed. I sat with my legs drawn up and my long, pale bare arms on my knees, wondering where Swallow was and what bombs I couldn't hear were triggering now. The firemen relinquished the glowing embers of the science complex and I saw the red light reflecting on their helmets as they moved back and forth, sealing off the streets leading to Galt.

It must have been nine p.m. when Rayne woke. This time she burst out of bed and stood facing me, a short silhouette. 'Where in San's name am I?' she demanded.

'"The Exile" in Little Awia.'

'A hotel?'

'Yes, and I want you to—'

'I need to see my hospital!'

'It's gone, Rayne. It's still burning. Look.' I beckoned her to the window and she propped her hands on the sill and leant out, drinking the estuary air with its morbid stench. The lines on her forehead deepened.

'Oh ... I can smell it.'

'It burnt down the Department of Future Studies as well. Godwit Street. Half of Goldthread Street, the accommodation block. They stopped it before it lit up the rest of Old Town.'

'And my house?'

'Burnt to the ground. I'm sorry ...'

'Pshaw!' She prodded me in the chest with a withered finger. 'I was bound to lose it at some point. It was just a matter of when and how! All my books are copied in the Castle's library ... And ... and ... Fifteen hundred years of samples! ...I'll just have to start collecting them again!' She drew back from the window and looked at me directly. 'How could a musician turn out the Lights of Reason?'

'San refused her entry to the Circle, so she's set bombs everywhere. Cyan—'

'Yes. I felt that ... I was right in the middle of a chest operation, pretty bad time to feel the Circle break. I spent the whole night crying ... She was my friend.'

'Wrought, Cullion. Now here.'

'Then there'll be more?'

'Yes. She recruited gypsies to do it. At the Awndyn Music Festival.'

'A festival!'

'Rayne, these gypsies are alienated. They don't fit into the world – they were looking for a place – but the world won't accommodate them ... They weren't dishonest people, to begin with ...'

'No ...'

'No, damn it, I think it's the world that's dishonest. They start with honest expectations and the world just tramples them. So the Roses have turned to Swallow. She gave them friendship. They're musical people, and her music's enthralling. I expect the festivals have given her chance to feed them her nonsense, her spiel about how much San wronged her – and they've lapped it up. They agree with her. They think immortality's her due.'

'I see.'

'Didn't you receive my telegraph?'

'I did, but ...'

'Then why didn't you return to the Castle?'

She shrugged. 'Jant, I've so much work to do. I must put my patients first, even now. I'm going to Fiennafor to treat them.'

She turned and staggered, which alarmed me off the windowsill. She has the resolve of an Eszai, but unfortunately with the body of a seventy-eight year old. 'You're in shock,' I said.

'Don't you dare tell *me* what state I'm in! Have you explained this to Aver-Falconet?'

'Yes.'

'Because other Eszai have houses in town.'

'I've checked them. I don't think they're at home.'

'Are you sure? Simoon brought his carriage by, yesterday. I don't want to lose Simoon – he's holding half the world together.'

'He'll have left for the Castle. I've a coach waiting to take you there.'

'All right,' she said, reluctantly. 'But I'm going via Fiennafor Hospital, Ward Twelve.'

'You're putting your life at risk.'

'That's what I do.'

I sighed. I couldn't dissuade the Doctor from her duty. 'Come on then ... No, hang on a minute. Tell me what these are.' I brought the envelope of dry leaves from my pocket, opened it with a squeeze, and gave it to her.

'You took these from my desk?'

'Yes.'

'Quick thinking.'

'None better.'

She pursed her lips. She tapped the leaves onto her smooth palm and the fusty smell rose from them. '...Well, they aren't inherently valuable. Not like the book I saved ... which is the only surviving copy of a Trisian treatise on medicine.' She fetched it from the bedside table and sat down on the duvet. 'In fact, ah ... here we are ... it mentions this leaf.'

She found the correct page and passed the book to me. It illustrated a plant like a bay tree, whose small, stiff leaves, dried dark brown, were indisputably the leaves she now held. 'Atheudos,' I read.

'Atheudos. Yes, Capelin brought them for me. He knew I'd be interested and over the last few years we've been researching it together. This stuff has fascinating potential.'

I came to sit beside her. 'Really? What?'

'It can cool people down. I don't know a better way of describing it. Jant, we think it might be applicable for the treatment of severely wounded soldiers. An infusion of the leaves lowers the patient's metabolic rate to the point where he enters a deep hibernation. Breathing becomes depressed, bradycardia ensues and body temperature falls. He—'

'Goes cold,' I said.

Rayne stared at me.

'As if she was dead.'

'Who?'

'Swallow!' I jumped up and bounded around the room. 'Swallow faked her death, and this is the drug she used! It's the same smell!'

'It only comes from Tris.'

'Rayne, the clippers leave monthly.'

She looked concerned. 'Who would use …? No, Jant. No. It's very difficult to bring the patient round again. In rats we've had mixed success. The dosage is extremely tricky.'

'To Swallow that wouldn't matter.'

'She'd have to be desperate.'

'She's *always* been desperate. For recognition, for eternal life, and now for revenge! It matters nothing to her if she has to die to achieve it.'

'That would be insane.'

'She's just blown your hospital up. What more proof do you need?'

Rayne dropped the leaves into the envelope.

'She must have drunk them like tea,' I said, and described what I'd seen in her study.

'Then she *is* insane. The properties and dosages are unresearched. She could have died … I'm surprised she hasn't.'

I took the envelope and sniffed it. 'Oh, Rayne. A new drug. Why didn't you tell me?'

'You! You have enough problems with *Scolopendium intricans*.'

I felt a twist of envy at the fact she didn't trust me, but related so well to Capelin. Theirs was a meeting of very great minds, to which I wasn't invited. 'You know I'm interested. I used to be a pharmacist.'

'No. You used to be a drug pusher. It was a long time ago. Now we need you sober.'

'Ella, I wouldn't …'

'Are you taking cat at the moment?'

'I'm drinking it.'

'I thought you must be. Or you wouldn't be flying with your wings scorched to bits.'

'I'm in control.'

'Jant, you can't control it. You know that.'

'I'm high-functioning. I—'

'Ha. Sometimes you don't function at all.' She sighed. 'All right. Stay on a low dose. Pause a minute before each one, and realise you don't have to pick up the needle. You'll get enough pain relief and the

214

sensation you crave from drinking it. Remember your tolerance has dropped. I'll help you kick it again ... if we get through this.'

'Thanks, Ella.'

'Your burns are superficial.' She walked to the window and stared out. 'Atheudos is not an abuseable drug. If Swallow used it, someone would've had to keep her warm until the effect wore off. She would have to be resuscitated with very great care.'

'Connell. Connell must have done it. Taken her body away in the gypsy wagon. Shit! I wonder whose body they put on the pyre?'

Bang! sounded down in the street, and in at the window. Dust puffed on the frame. I grabbed Rayne and pulled her back into the room.

She flailed, off balance in my wings. 'What was *that*?'

'Musket shot.'

A chunk of stone had been blown from the edge of the frame. Its chipped surface showed white.

Rayne narrowed her crinkled eyes. 'Did someone just shoot at me? *Did* they? Why *me*?' She flared into anger and yelled at the window: 'I've been saving your lives! Since the year six twenty! I run the field hospitals! I cured the Fescue Plague! And your stupid cholera! And your stupid-stupid smallpox! ... Jant! Stop it with the fucking feathers!'

I released her and approached the window. The glimmering city extended before me. Taking care not to show myself I leant on the wall beside it and peered out obliquely. Below were the grey mansard roofs on the other side of the street, their chimney stacks and balconies. Not a soul to be seen; the street was deserted and, of the upper storey windows I could see, most had their curtains drawn and only a few were backlit. The angle of the shot showed that it had come from the roof of one of the merchants' houses.

'I can't see anyone.'

Rayne was standing in the darkness. 'I saved hundreds of thousands of lives and they shot at me ...'

'You're an Eszai.'

'But I work for them.'

'Being immortal is a death sentence now. See? I don't want you to go to Fiennafor. I want you to gallop for the Castle with the coach blinds drawn.'

'No. My patients need me.'

'But—'

'Even if those bastards shoot me. I care for my patients till the end of my life. And for my doctors and staff who'll be injured. Show me your coach.'

I ushered her down the square stairwell with its polished brass frieze, across the marble lobby and out to the *porte-cochère*. I held the door open for her, and she spoke to the coachman, gathered up her skirt and stepped in with buttoned boots. I passed her my pistol, a handful of percussion caps and a handful of cartridges. She put them in her pockets and turned the pistol in her lap. I tried to show her how to use it, but she brushed me away.

'I know, I know. Same as a musket.' She primed it expertly, then lowered the hammer. 'You don't think I'd let a new weapon appear without learning it, do you?'

'Sorry.'

'Cock, ball, nipple and touch hole. I need no further evidence that guns were invented by men.'

'By Equinnes, actually.'

'Typical men and their typical bloody killing machines. Now I have to discover how to treat gunshot wounds.' She raised a hand to my cheek and I felt her fingertips hover a millimetre from my skin. 'This will fade. In a couple of days the heat will radiate away. That blister might scar, but none of the rest will. It will itch; don't scratch it. Keep putting cold water on it and drink salt-sugar water, too. Do you have another of these?'

'I've got a flick knife.'

'Jant, be careful …'

'The driver's name is Halliwell. He often works for me. He drives like the wind and he'll take you wherever you want.'

'Good boy. I'll see you at the Castle.'

I stepped back and slammed the door. The brake blocks lifted from the great spoked wheels. Halliwell cracked his whip and the coach drew away. I watched them speed to a canter. No rear window, just the anonymous chassis and Halliwell's three-tiered capecoat. At the end of the street they reached a gallop and slewed round the Camber Road junction and out of sight, bound for Fiennafor.

CHAPTER 29

Parkour

Swallow's marksman can't target me the way I move. I drew down, cat-leapt, grabbed the edge of the hotel porch and swung up onto it. Crouched in a puddle on its flat roof and jumped again. With a little height, now I can fly. Went straight up, two beats, landed on the roof of the opposite house. Jumped, three beats, landed on the incline of the hotel roof, ran up over the ridge and slid down the other side, gained speed, jumped the guttering and took off.

I kicked off the ridge of a warehouse, grabbed a pipe sticking out of the next wall and swung round it, into the air, then flapped to the ruins of the Science Department and let its hot air lift me.

It bore me up steadily, like smoothly-rounded hands beneath my wings. Held them out straight, glorying in my strength, though I was breathing smoke again and coughing. I turned inside the thermal and bumped higher. The fire engines shrank away, far below, and the men were tiny now.

I rode the thermal until I spread out the city. Table-tops of smoke beneath me obscured Old Town, blurred Galt and Piteem; far below them, the streetlights glimmered like stars on the earth, more constant between the rising palls.

A bright flash to my right, and boom! Smoke torused out in a patch, and seemed to fall, then I saw the flicker of flames. That's the heart of Fiennafor. The Crescent – it must be the Lawyer's house.

A bigger flash – further off, the afterimage danced on my eyes, and bang! echoed off Fiennafor's rooftops like a whipcrack. Bankyn Street. The Architect's house.

A flash – in the haze on the outskirts. White light leapt – and again! – That was a big double blast! Simoon's mansion in Moren Wells.

I heard screaming from the ones below me, then the reverberations of Simoon's explosions rolled like thunder over Hacilith.

Simoon's and Frost's were two black patches where the lights had extinguished, but Gayle the Lawyer's house was blazing, illuminating the white stone façade of the adjoining houses on the Crescent, the curved road in front of them. Turmoil below me as people spilled out.

What could I do? I had to reach the Castle. I let the fire fall to my right and behind me, streets netting away like black capillaries, and flew on, over Piteem's terraces and the canal a strip of dark reflection.

I dropped Camber Bridge out of sight then, after a while, the last lights of the city, and was over the farmland. The Vermiform hung out of my pocket.

'Shit,' I said. 'Did you see that?'

It flurried affirmatively in the cold air.

There was no breeze and my ruined feathers hissed with regularity. I stretched for the greatest arc each flap. The river transformed from turbid mud into a silver pennant, passing distant on my left between silhouette trees and bushes.

I replayed the conversation I'd had in The Exile Hotel with Rayne. She'll find it difficult to leave Fiennafor now, because Gayle's blast has probably blocked Fienna Road, *and* Ward Twelve was already packed full.

Someone had tried to shoot her from the roof of Milvus Street. Well, you didn't have to be a Rhydanne to climb up there. It was probably one of the gypsies. That street was studenty, shabbily-respectable; the tall, eighteenth-century houses of Awian ex-pats who'd brought their silk weaving to Hacilith. 'The Exile' used to be their workshop for winding gold and silver thread.

'The Exile' was a fifth-century story they love, and he was Elland Gleana, a Morenzian whom a quirk of history turned into a feather-back hero. When the Pentadrica fell, the Morenzians and Awians tore it up between them. The King of Morenzia was first to advance into the country, which is now Shivel, I'm flying over, and Eske a little further on. He seized all the land his army could hold. And he sent Elland Gleana, his finest, most trusted warrior, with fifty thousand men to annexe the very best land, where Micawater now lies.

But Elland saw Awian refugees streaming from the Insects. He witnessed bugs killing them by the hundred thousand, and he refused to fight the Awians who were suffering as the first swarm obliterated town after town. He joined forces with the ragged remnant of their army and turned his men on the ranks of his own king, and forced the Morenzians back to Hacilith.

'The Awians should have northern Pentadrica,' Elland said. 'They need it. They've nowhere else to go.'

Well, such treason couldn't stay unpunished, so one night the

Morenzian king sent soldiers to capture Elland in his camp. They dragged him behind six white horses to Hacilith and threw him before the king. The king exiled him to Addald Island at the tip of the Ghallain Peninsula, where Elland Gleana lived alone for the rest of his days. He built a driftwood cabin in the windswept scrub above the sea rocks and every so often his faithful wife rowed from Ghallain to bring him provisions, for the great warrior was reduced to living on gulls' eggs and seaweed.

The Awians celebrate Elland Gleana as one of their finest heroes. To do the correct thing and then be punished for it seems, to me, to be the lot of heroes in any age.

I picked up the lights of Basilard town, then dropped them off behind me as I brought up the lights of Pinchbeck. Pinchbeck slipped behind and I flew in a trance.

When had I eaten last? When had I slept?

A fire to my right jolted me awake. Was it Shivel manor? The town? I beat rapidly over the lightless farmland, drawing the fire closer, as if reeling it in. As the perspective changed, it split into two large fires, and I saw the light flickering on tree trunks and uplighting the canopy of the woods around it.

The lamps of Shivel separated away to the right, the fires were raging deeper in the forest. The air smelt sweet, the smell of malted barley – it was Tornado's brewery.

Underlit smoke was pouring up, shadows flickered – now and then I saw figures clustering round. The flames illuminated the fronts of their faces and chests, making them look two-dimensional.

I focussed on the fire; it destroyed my night vision. I misjudged my height. Raked over the topmost branches, just one black sheet. I whistled down in a sheer glide into the firelight and crashed into the clearing.

I knelt in the heat, winded, and in front of me the brewery's main building and maltings were leaping with flames. Smoke was writhing out of the granary, through the brewhouse itself, and through the open, sliding gate I saw the vats steaming. The front had blown off Tornado's house – bricks were scattered all over the grass.

The fire throbbed and leant against the darkness. Every time it flared up, it cast a rapid light between the trees, illumined the ground, vanished. Then long, sharp shadows broke in and rushed right up to the fire, as if battling it.

The bunch of people watched without lifting a finger and, though I knew they couldn't do anything, it made me angry.

'Do you want marshmallows to toast?' I yelled.

A gap opened in their midst, and through it I saw Tornado. He was sitting on a chunk of brickwork, head in hands. The flames grew momentarily weaker, the circle of light contracted and cast into darkness his shaved head, broad nose, eyepatch, and huge arm muscles. The flames roared high and brightly lit his bunched-up thighs, ripped jeans, and some little guy behind him, tugging at his back.

'Tawny!'

He emerged from his hands. His round, red face was streaming with sweat. 'Shira.' He tried a smile. 'Strongman Beer's off the menu.'

'So I see.'

'We were making really good stout ...' he coughed, vomited, and jerked his thumb at the wreckage.

I reached him and smelt the powder smoke and his sweat-soaked leather waistcoat. The soldier probing his back was actually a huge man, but Tornado dwarfed him. He moved away to let me see. The back of Tawny's waistcoat and t-shirt had been blown to shreds, and his flesh was a mass of small, deep pits where shrapnel had riddled him. The worst was above his shoulder blade, where the corner of a brick was embedded in his trapezius muscle. The triangular wound was bleeding profusely.

'Can you help?' he mumbled, with a hitch of pain and very morosely. 'Because Lyme's being fucking useless.'

'I'll try.' I dropped my pack and picked out one of my ampoules. I scratched the seal off and tried to give it to him, but I had to crouch and shake him before his hand unfolded. 'Drink this,' I said. 'Half of it.'

The phial looked tiny in his fingers – miraculous how he could manipulate something so small. He knocked it back. 'Tastes of grass.'

'Yes, it does.'

His body relaxed. He slumped forward, elbows on his massive thighs, and the piece of brick jutted further from his muscle. ' 'S amazing,' he slurred.

'Isn't it?'

'Can't feel nothing.'

'Good.'

I flicked my knife and rasped the point on the surface of the brick. You have to do this quickly.

I poured water all over the wound, slipped my blade under the edge of the brick, and levered. Tornado howled. The brick popped out, leaving raw lips of flesh, and bounced off somewhere. I tipped water into the deep, pointed pit it had left, and blood welled up and ran down his back. He flexed his shoulder, which pumped out the blood in the wound, and it filled up again instantly.

'Felt it, then.'

'Don't move until I dress it. Can you feel pain now?'

'No.'

'I might die of the medication, but I sure killed all the pain,' I murmured.

'Jant,' he said. 'I can't hear you. I've been half-deafened ... I think I can ride, though.'

'Yes. Cat will make you think that.' I looked around for Lyme – he'd left us and joined the crowd watching the brewery burn. So I cut off the remains of Tornado's thick waistcoat and t-shirt, and from the shirt made what was probably the worst field dressing of all time, but it staunched the blood.

'They got me,' he said, with asperity. I passed him my waterbottle and he splashed water over his face then drained the bottle dry. A bit of burning sacking landed by his foot and he glanced at it. 'Go away.'

'Did you see the bombers?'

'Ugh. No. I was searching for powder like San ordered. Thought I'd check my place first. Roses must have been watching for me ... Lying in wait, like. I opened the door, saw all these kegs in the kitchen. So I ran.'

He coughed and spat, disgusted. '*I* ran. Me! Never run from anything in my life! But what could I do? It blew me arse over tit, just the same as the coach bomb. And then the office ... blew like a bombard. Fucking ingratitude! There's no need to blow up my brewery. Like, that's just vindictive. I've spent my life knee deep in Insects to rescue mortals and they try to kill me.' His tone of innocent bewilderment gave way to bitter revulsion. 'After the centuries I've fought for them!'

'That's what Rayne said.'

'Rayne! Is Rayne all right?'

'Physically, yes. Mentally, who knows?'

He flexed his shoulder and blood seeped through and trickled down his back. 'I've never run before, Jant. *Never*. Eszai die with their wounds in front. But this ... not this. What good is my strength against gunpowder? What good is my axe?'

He teetered upright like a bear standing on its hind legs, and cast around. The fire highlit scars on his face and chest. 'What a fucking mess ... At least everyone seems okay ...'

He gazed through the flames clinging to the door timbers, at the fragrant steam rising from the mash vats inside. 'God doesn't want Zascai to kill us. That's not its plan ... Why would gypsies put such hard work into something so wrong ...?'

221

'It's not the gypsies. It's Swallow. Saker's old girlfriend.'

'Who? Saker's *dead* girlfriend?'

'Yes. I've no time to explain now, but she's alive. She wants us dead, and the gypsies are just her cat's paw.'

'Well, a cat's paw has claws.'

Swallow was trumping Tornado's strength, Saker's sagacity and my speed, as if she was Challenging us all – and winning, so far.

He gestured at the forest. 'My dray horses fucked off, but I can't say I blame them … I … can walk to Shivel.'

'No!'

'What?'

'No. Swallow will be expecting you to. She might have booby-trapped the manor, maybe the stables, maybe the coach house, waiting for you to walk in.'

'Like, really?'

'Really.'

'Saker's old girlfriend? The one who treated him like shit?'

'Yes.'

'She thinks that deviously?'

'And then some. Because San wouldn't make her immortal.'

'Huh? So she blows up my home? Who does she think she is?'

'Well. That's a very good question.'

He pressed his palm over his eyepatch to adjust it. The weedy flames illuminated half his face and body, wavered as if daunted by him, shrank to a sliver, flickered forth again. Light on the faces of the scattered bricks cast their shadows long, highlighted their grainy red texture, and the narrow grass blades of every tussock.

'Evil,' he said.

'That's the very word she would use to describe us, Tawny.'

He sat down on the broken wall. Despondency flattened his deep voice. 'It never used to be like this. Insects are the enemy. Why are Zasceys fighting us and not the bugs? In the old days we'd team up. You have to, to fight bugs, or Awia's sunk, then the Plains, then Morenzia. So instead they blow my house all over the … fucking … forest. Can I drink the rest of this? My back's killing me.'

'It can't have worn off already.'

'Well, it has.'

'Wow. Okay. Go ahead.'

'Is this what I think it is?'

'Centipede leaf fern.'

He huffed a laugh. 'Always wondered what it felt like, Jant. Thought it must be good or you wouldn't be nodding out all the time.'

'Stay here and I'll fetch you a horse.'

'Jant. Thank you.'

He beckoned his brewery staff but they were too frightened to approach. I left him talking to them, quietly in the crackling light, and flew to Shivel manor house. I landed on the bank of its moat and hollered at the solar turret until Anelace Shivel himself brought from the stables a magnificent shire horse, which hated me on sight, but allowed me to lead him back to the burning brewery.

Tornado looked up and his expression transformed from stoned despair to stoned delight. 'You got me a dray!'

'He's called Gavilan. He'll carry you to the Castle.'

'Do you have any more of these little bottles?'

'Uh, no ... Well, all right. One, you can have one. Go to the hospital. Don't tell Rayne. If she finds out, say "Jant was a pharmacist and he knows what he's doing".'

Tawny shrugged and winced. 'Did he ever screw her?'

'Who?'

'Saker. Swallow.'

'No.'

'Thought not. Less piano, more screwing. She wasn't a soldier. He should have stuck to soldiers. Archers, specifically. He should have given her a good seeing to, like he did Linnet and Savory: had 'em starry-eyed with the earth moving. Had 'em eating out of his hand. Amongst other places ... If he'd screwed Swallow, she'd never be a bomber.'

'Mist calls them "terrorists".'

'Terrorist. Good word.' He stepped onto the brick block, and onto the shire's glossy bareback. It tossed its head, lifted its forehoof and replanted it, braced with his weight. The tips of the flames framed their massive bulk.

I said, ' "Linnet?" The eleventh century Linnet?'

'Yeah. He would have got killed. But I don't blame him. She was hot.'

'Did you beat him up badly?'

'Just enough to save him.'

Tornado spanned his crossbow by hand, clicked his tongue like a drover and headed off on the track leading to the Hamulus Road, chest bare but for bandages and smeared in blood and soot. The shire's tack jingled, its feathered hooves rose and fell steadily, and the wood's darkness closed behind them.

*

All the envy and animosity I used to feel for him had vanished. I even forgave him for sleeping with Tern. We Eszai were beginning to cling together more tightly. We could no longer trust mortals, only each other, you see. There's a first time for everything.

By the time I reached the Castle dawn was creeping up the sky. Yellow at the horizon, then grading through a rare leaf-green to clear, pale turquoise at the zenith. A thin mist lay over the Castle and its meadow, veiling its towers into the illusion of pastel delicacy. The whole Castle looked like a model, on its man-made hill. Its towers and the spire pierced the mist, and regained their stark solidity thirty metres above the ground.

I cut down through the damp mist and it spiralled off the tips of my wings. I flew over the Throne Room, between its pinnacles, and landed on the sill of my Northwest Tower, pushed open the shutters and pounced down into the room.

Tern was asleep in bed. I carefully gathered her locks aside and kissed her cheek. On my desk she'd arranged telegraph slips and newspapers, with a bottle of wine and a chunk of cake (stale), and the Filigree Spider brooch laid out beside them. I sat on the bed beside Tern, and stroked her feathers, reading the slips.

June 28
From: Sirocco Tassy, Lowespass Fortress
Jant, Hurricane got serious. Decided anyone with tattoos is security risk. Rounded up all gypsies in Lowespass, imprisoned them in Main Camp. He beat some to learn their plans. They don't have any, but I couldn't stop him. Hurricane executed a dozen for resisting arrest. Some of them were popular with the Hacilith fyrd, lot of bad feeling here now.

June 29
From: Arlen Hurricane, Lowespass Fortress
Sirocco's dying – burns. I'm wounded – thigh. One of our soldiers – not a Rose – fired the fortress powder magazine. Didn't think the traitors would have sympathisers. Heard word he was screwing one of the gypsies killed yesterday. Armoury obliterated, bugs moving in. Falling back to Oscen. Route more ammo there urgently.

SLAUGHTER IN THE SQUARE

Crown Forces Murder Morenzians

This morning only smashed stone and blood-stained cobbles bear testament to the frightful massacre that took place in Royal Square, Tanager, yesterday. Eighteen demonstrators of the Litanee Rose clan were blasted apart by a volley of grapeshot – a weapon so terrible that it was only ever intended for use against Insects – and countless more are injured, many severely. The gunfire came from within the Palace grounds, where a provocatively large military detachment has been stationed since the beginning of the protest.

As the *Intelligencer* has been reporting, over the last week gypsies of the Rose and Oak clans from throughout Awia have been converging on Tanager to remonstrate with the Queen. Since the unfortunate events in Wrought, caused by the actions of a tiny minority of fanatics, gypsies throughout Awia have been subject to insults, constant interrogations by the authorities, beatings by gangs of ruffians, and arbitrary dismissal from all employment. These impoverished people, rarely paid a living wage and routinely taken advantage of by Awian gangmasters, turned in desperation to protesting outside Tanager Palace, petitioning Eleonora Tanager to guarantee their security and restore their livelihoods. The Palace has remained mute since the demonstrations began. Despite the size of the crowd, estimated at six thousand, there has been a carnival-like atmosphere in the Square, with families of gypsies sharing food, song, and tales of injustice.

Now the sudden outbreak of deadly violence has brought this peaceful vigil to a bloody end. There are conflicting reports about what caused the escalation but many saw cavalry pouring in from nearby streets in an attempt to disperse the protestors. Witness Leyla Rose, her clothes tattered and bloodied, told me, 'We were being crushed up 'gainst the railings of the Palace. We called out to the guards but they didn't lift a finger. Fearing for my life, I climbed over. Some of the boys started pushing the rails down. The guards all yelled and started running away. Then I saw them turning the cannon towards us. It was a twenty pounder, as if we were bugs! I dived to the ground but my brother, he was too slow ...'

This morning, royal servants are washing the cobbles. But now the questions start: who ordered the cannon to be used? What future do any gypsies now have in Awia? And will the stain of this atrocity be washed from the name of Tanager so soon?

HOORAY FOR THE GUARD!

Rose Plot to Kill Queen Frustrated by Tanager's Finest!

Yesterday the Morenzian saboteurs responsible for the cold-blooded massacre and devastation in Wrought, and the murder of Cyan Peregrine, launched their most heinous plot yet!

With their typical disregard for innocent life, these murderous traitors infiltrated the protests which Queen Eleonora – with her usual concern for popular feeling – had graciously permitted to continue in the Royal Square outside her palace for the past week. Within the crowds, these armed villains put aside their usual bombs in favour of distributing cheap alcohol and loose talk. Whipping up the roughest elements into a storm of bravado, over two hundred of them launched an attack on Tanager Palace, smashing the railings with pick-axes, hammers and crowbars.

When the Royal Guard attempted to restore order, they were met with hails of cobblestones ripped up from the Square. The Guard – who wear only dress uniform, not armour – suffered numerous severe injuries and were forced to fall back. At this point a roar of triumph rose from the crowd. Your correspondent clearly heard them scream, 'The Queen! Get the Queen!' Surging through the breaches in the railing, they spilled into the Palace grounds. Windows were smashed, firebrands were thrown. The guards fired a warning volley over the heads of the mob to restore their sanity but they simply raged onwards, knowing they would be on the soldiers before they could reload.

The Captain of the Guard – a decorated war hero – faced a terrible dilemma. As he told me later, he could either watch his men be overcome by the superior numbers of the mob, imperilling the Queen herself, or he could use the last tool available to him – the battery of Royal Artillery who fire the Queen's salute. This brave man took the only possible decision. The roaring cannons stopped the onrush in its tracks. Necessarily there were many deaths. These are to be regretted but the blood is on the hands of the agitators who enraged the crowd, not our outnumbered soldiers who had to do their duty in the face of such aggression. The Square was afterwards cleared by mounted units and a number of ringleaders were arrested. The Floret Gate has been destroyed and fleeing gypsies caused widespread vandalism throughout the Palace Quarter, including looting the Palace Arcade boutiques.

The *Wrought Standard* calls for an end to tolerance for these cowardly criminals in Awia. They aim to murder innocent Awian citizens and nobility – even the Queen! – all alike. Many more bombs are undoubtedly yet to be found. The *Standard* calls for all Roses to be removed from Awia as the only way to ensure our security.

The *Standard* notes with approval that Lady Governor Tern Wrought has offered £50,000 for information leading to the capture of Connell Rose, ringleader of the bombers.

Tern lay with her legs drawn up, wrapped in her wings crossed over her front. Their hands clasped her shoulders and her whole body was cocooned in feathers. She was naked but for panties, their thong rode over her hip. There's delicious black hair and small black feathers behind their white cotton, in the triangle between her thighs.

Tomorrow. Tomorrow I'll deal with all this. I lay beside her, fitting together, and exhaustion washed over me. It made the familiar room unreal. The dark blue velvet curtain across it was drawn back, and down the two steps you could see my desk, covered in the Trisian translations I'd been working on, only a few months ago, when everything was normal. There are bookshelves above my desk, the framed original diagram of the musket, then large monochrome poster pictures of Tern, a rack of pigeon holes stuffed with letters, and my beloved red racing bike, upside-down on its drop handles on some newspaper. Then there's a map of the telegraph lines pinned to the wall, the door with my swordbelt hanging from its hook, and the fireplace, with her perfume bottles on its mantelpiece.

The midnight-blue drapes of the bed obscured my suit of games armour by the window. You can just see Butterfly, my Insect exoskeleton, brown with two hundred year old varnish, which has dried in runs from the ball-joints of its legs. My runner's number 001 from the last Hacilith Marathon was taped on its thorax, and it wore my Wheel flag around its spiky lack of shoulders.

I rested my face on Tern's feathers, smelling her musk and ylang ylang. My breaths began to match the rise and fall of her sweet breathing, and gratefully I let it take me, into sleep.

CHAPTER 30

Twelve years earlier, Connell: radicalisation is a slow process

After the harvest, before midwinter, that's the hardest time. We'd threshed and stowed the grain in the Demesne's barns, and apples in the cotes. I left the Castle's employ and couldn't find work anywhere. I'd been moved on, from manor to manor across the Plains, and all I heard was: 'where are *you* from?'

My harvest money ran out. Freefall. Again. I worked long hours for a week, cutting hedges for a racecourse manager, and when I finished he laughed and didn't pay me. What could I do? If I'd taken revenge he would've run me out of Eske. So I left. As it was, some old bag accused me of stealing a chicken, so they moved me on.

I headed into Awia, desperately hungry and cold. I was down to one meal a day – breakfast, because you need your energy in the morning. I only had porridge, and for the rest of the day I drank water or chicken broth. I had no candles in the evening, and the nights were closing in. I just needed work to tide me over till Midwinter, then I can barista coffees in the Spread Eagle in Rachiswater, they know me there.

Starvation drove me to the Front, where Cloud would employ me to cook and wash pots. If not, I could wire palisades. And as a last resort I'd roll Wroughtwards and pick coal scraps from the spoil heaps to sell in town.

There's always a way, I told myself, trying to fend off hopelessness. Nobody cares about me. Nothing I do is valued. It's true, I don't matter to anyone, but I'll look after myself and find food. Though why they make it so hard!

Savouring the daydream of hot soup at the Front, and possibly enough coins to see me in bread and cheese till Midwinter, I hung the 'looking for work' banner on the wagon and headed up the Broad Road. When I roll to the battlefront I try to take something to sell. I can tinker lamps and knives in Morenzia, but the Awians throw better away. This time I'd no money to buy stock. Life has taught me: if you're hungry, get a job in a restaurant, sandwich stall or market. You can eat the scraps. If your clothes are worn ragged, get a job in a laundry, or sewing jackets for the fyrd. You can nick the offcuts. But lengthy hardship had blackened my optimism. You can't see the long term through it. There isn't any long term, because there's no means of planning. No stability on which to build. You can't invest for improvement. There's no money and no chance to develop – just more of the same repetitive trudge, the day-by-day search for food.

I need something to make me feel good. Anything! You see how desperate existence is, when a mug of soup is a fine daydream? Some people even have fun, I've seen them at it. What's the goddamn point of life when all I can do is focus like an Eszai on getting that cup of broth?

I passed through Rachis into Oscen, steeling myself for the bullshit I'll face at the checkpoint. This country is just people stuck in different echelons, different classes, unable to escape them no matter how hard they struggle, staring at each others' lives in bewilderment and disbelief. When they spread their wings, all they can manage is to fly round and round in a cramped cage.

My goddamn axle was grinding. I couldn't pause to mend it, I hoped I could reach Lowespass before it burnt through. This is the problem with being poor. You struggle against the shrinking world. It's not the day-to-day stuff. It's the unexpected disasters you can't afford to fix, you can't afford to escape. Even something small, that a rich lass would laugh off, knocks you into a spiral and you fall far and fast, accelerating, trying to clutch some support, there's nothing to grab; you can fall to your death.

After Oscen the mud sucked at the wheels, causing more friction and I smelt it scorching. Biddy slipped in the cannon ruts, snorting resentfully.

A fyrd detachment was marching up the road behind me. I could see the first men in my mirror. It looked like a whole division, and the captain started shouting quite some distance back: 'Out of the way! Shitty Litanee!'

I tweaked Biddy onto the verge and immediately the wheels began to sink in. 'Come on, lackeys,' I muttered. 'The slaughter awaits you.'

The soldiers passed, whistling and cat-calling. Behind them, six-horse limber teams were dragging cannon bigger than I'd seen before. Two abreast, the stupid fuckers filled the road and their revolving wheels were set to scrape against my paintwork, so I urged Biddy onto the very edge of the ditch.

All the soldiers passing stuck their arms out against the wagon side and pushed. My left wheels slipped into the ditch and the wagon tipped over. The axle snapped, I slid off the seat into the ditch water, and all my belongings inside crashed into the left wall.

I stood up, waist deep in mud. The traces had pulled Biddy onto her side and she was kicking like mad. The soldiers pissed themselves laughing. They stared over their shoulders as they marched, and their fucking raucous laughter bellowed for ages after the last of them was lost to my glare.

Stinking with slime, I unharnessed Biddy and brought her upright. The wagon was jammed at an angle on the slope. Fuck soldiers. Fuck lackeys. Fuck *men*. I was starving and very, very weak.

I climbed into the wagon. My crockery had smashed and the stove was on its belly. I fetched a rope and yoked Biddy, but the grey mare simply pulled my wagon off its broken axle and gouged it into the grass.

So I tried again from the back, and she gradually hauled my home onto the road, leaving the front wheel behind. I rolled the wheel up to the road and stood with it resting on my hip, wondering with bleak despair how I could possibly refit it, when in the distance came the clamour of hooves going at a fast gallop.

Two horses, a palomino and a black, were racing necks out like the last stretch at Cherrywood. Their riders were high up and forward, with shortened stirrups, and yelling like crazy. I jumped out of their way, they hurtled past and splattered me head to foot in liquid mud from a long puddle.

It was a girl and a young man. The girl's flaxen hair flew, and she had the Castle's sun on her saddle rug. The only person it could have been was Lightning. That made the guy on the gold mare, all in black with the sharp face, Comet.

I stared after them. Mud was soaking into my jumper. They snapped round the curve as the road descends to Calamus Bastion – slammed through the checkpoint without breaking pace – so they were surely Eszai. Comet's racehorse edged ahead of Lightning's purebred as they went like the clappers up the hill. He crested it ahead of her and they disappeared.

I wiped mud off my face, lugged the wheel out of the puddle and turned, to find that Biddy had bolted and my home had slipped into the ditch again.

Nobody was going to help me. I've never felt so desolate. Nothing matters any more. I no longer cared for my life, for myself, for my safety. For anything ... at all. I sat down against the back wheel and stared at nothing, while the grey daylight began to fade, and the cold, to clench.

Stiff, chill and with stabbing starvation, I knew I'd have to force myself up ... Force myself up, to stumble after Biddy, catch her and ride her bareback – to Awndyn, and to Swallow.

CHAPTER 31

Connell: how I met Swallow

When my precarious existence brings me to the maple sap harvest, I roll here, to the wood outside Drussiter, where in a clearing I've made a beautiful hideaway. There's a hearth, and a log seat I've carved, and all around the sugar-maples rustle and the birds sing. I need so little, to be happy – which is lucky, really. I wake with the dawning sky and the first trill of the chaffinches. I dip my white enamelled jug in the clear woodland spring. Every dusk I curl up in my caravan with its doors open, and see the pheasants flying up to roost, and the badgers emerge from their sett to tumble off down their well-worn track.

I have all of February to practise the necessary art of sitting by the fireside and looking at the stars. I repaint the caravan and repair any damage, oil the axles and Biddy's trapping, keep them up to scratch. I sharpen my knives, scour my pans and sew my clothes. You people who are trapped in permanent employment, in needless gain and stress, when did you last have time to think things through?

I pick mushrooms and dry them to sell to restaurants. I pack a cargo of maple sugar, which the soldiers at the Front go crazy for. Then off across the world I go, and by August I've rolled up at the Castle. In we come, in wagons, from the four corners of the world. Their harvest is a reliable three months on which I hang the rest of the year. The steward likes to see me – from experience she knows I'm trustworthy. They never give us important work, just labour plain and simple.

I park my caravan by the river, lower its legs and unhitch Biddy. And there I stay from August till November, longer than I stay anywhere else. You see, I'm free. Unlike the farm hands, who mutter with envy, I'm not tied to the Castle. I'm not tied to any employer, not to this land nor any country at all. The work is menial but it means they can't keep me. I owe them nothing, and any time I want to, I move on. I live on the desperate edge of *now*. You think it's exciting? It's hard.

So, this day that changed my life. I'd been tying sheaves in the most enormous field, from first light till the shadows lengthened, and up at its far end men with scythes were still snicking along. At sundown I joined a queue in the field corner, at the cashier's little desk under the tan awning. I received the day's pennies and walked slowly back to my wagon, my hands glowing raw and warm from the cornstalks.

I opened the rose-painted doors, dropped the coins into a box and smiled when I heard them clink. They'll see me through a month of scarce work. Dozy with fresh air and the fatigue of a day's labour well done, I scooped the jug off the dresser and turned to the steps. And a woman was standing there! Trying to see in!

I yelled, 'Hey, get away!' She made no move, so I picked up my breadknife. That backed her off a few steps, but then she stood as cheekily as before, leaning on her stick. Rooted people have a fascination with the interior of my home. Just because it's in a field doesn't make it public.

I left to fetch water, locked the door pointedly and went to the pump. The damn woman followed me. She carried a guitar under her arm – it was entirely laminated in mother-of-pearl, with dirt between the cracks.

'I heard your party last night,' she said.

I placed the jug on the drain cover under the pump, listening carefully. It hadn't been a party, it was just a normal night. But if any Rooted complain about our music, we stop it straight away. We need their good will – I mean, their money – too much to be accused of making disturbance. But Demesne village, where the Castle's staff live, was three kilometres distant and they'd never complained before.

'A lot of music and dancing.'

I pumped water all over the jug. With my back to her I said, 'If it annoys you, we'll shut up.'

'Oh – no! I loved it! ...I want to learn it.'

'What?'

'Litanee music. I like it. I don't want it to be lost.'

'Lost?' I hefted the jug and turned to my wagon. 'Where'd you think it's going?'

The ginger woman followed. 'I'm Governor Swallow of Awndyn,' she murmured. 'I watched you dance.'

'Did you?'

'From outside the firelight. You played the guitar. You were by far the best.'

'If you're really a governor, what the hell d'you care about that?' I laughed, and she stopped. You see, I'd halted her at the appropriate distance from my wagon. I slipped inside and began to slice bread and make tea. Hunger pangs hollowed my belly – I hadn't eaten since midday, and that'd been just cheese and oatcakes.

When I glanced out she was still there. She seemed the sort who wouldn't take no for an answer. She had great, fiery waves of copper-coloured hair, and a green velvet beret, of all things. Her skin was unseasonably pale and her nose and shoulders freckled. Her velvet dress was so short her stocking tops and suspenders showed, she wore riding boots and held under one arm the shabby guitar. I couldn't place her at all. She spoke Awian with a sterling accent, but she was short and plump, and I wouldn't have given sixpence for her clothes.

'Go ask Allen,' I called. 'Blue wagon with the windmills. He plays the fiddle.'

In answer she swung her guitar to her front and began plucking one of the tunes that we'd played last night – but better. Much better! She didn't change it but she improvised it our way, making it more Litanee. She embellished it with thrills that made me salivate, pedalling notes on the lower strings, with hammer-ons, pull-offs and wide string bends.

It was like seeing a mirror that reflected your image ten times more sophisticated, more beautiful and focussed than your own face could ever be. She stopped with a flourish and I hankered for more. We were mesmerised! I was halfway down the steps before I controlled myself, and out of the wagons all around my friends were pouring.

Allen's kids clustered round her, pulling at her dress, crying out for more.

'Maestro!' I called.

She broke the trance and started towards me, a grin on her face.

'If you want to learn Litanee, start by knowing you should ask permission to approach a wagon.'

'All right. May I approach your wagon?'

'Sure.'

She tromped up the steps and I moved back to make room. She looked shocked at the size of my living space, but only for an instant.

'You can sing?' she asked.

'Pretty well.'

'And you know all the dances?'

I laughed.

A lock of her enormous hair kept falling in front of her face, and she pushed it back. She was looking at my check shirt, open at the throat and rolled to the elbow, showing my arms. She was trying to discern my tattoos through my tan.

No use there. But because we Litanee are used to reading symbols, I saw Awndyn's leaping dolphin insignia, in marquetry, on the neck of her guitar.

She'd figured out how to lower the sofa and was sitting, ginger wings crammed up. Rooted people normally goggle at the pale, varnished cupboards and comfortable bed, but she was looking at the opposite wall, at my painting of Princess Gerygone escaping from her tower of caramel.

'It's a copy,' I said. 'Of Gerygone, by—'

'By Jaeger. I know.'

'Why the surprise? Just 'cause I work in a field doesn't mean I'm a donkey.'

'Sorry. Sorry. It's just that ... I've seen the original. It hangs in Rachiswater.' She nodded at Gerygone, who was fleeing with very sticky plaits. 'It's a good copy. She's beautiful.'

'Oh, yes. It's a great story, too.' Because if your father imprisons you in a tower of caramel, all you have to do is shift your weight to one side and wait for a really hot day. 'Gerygone didn't need any goddamned princes ... If you're really Swallow, what are you doing here?'

'I gave him the slip. The goddamned prince.' She fluttered bitten-nailed fingers in the direction of the Castle. 'So I could hear your music. And, having done so, I want to invite you and your tribe to my festival.'

'My "tribe"? You mean my troupe?'

'No, I mean all the Roses. As many Roses and Oaks as you can find.'

I stared at her. 'But isn't the festival for orchestras?'

'No! It's for every type of music. Blues. Jazz. Awian ballet and Brandoch shanties. Anything you can think of. All music's important ... Um ...'

'Connell.'

'Connell ...'

'Connell Rose.'

'Your music has qualities unattainable by a directed orchestra.'

I laughed.

'That's it!' She wiggled her fingers. 'Vitality! Energy! Spontaneity! ... How much does the Castle pay you to do all this haying?'

I told her and she looked scandalised. 'I'll double it. Come to Awndyn, bring in my harvest. Do you need some sort of contract?'

I just laughed and laughed. I'd never seen a contract in my life! She studied me with fascination – like a piece of opal I was dull and cloudy to her at first sight, but when she turned me in her hand she saw beautiful colours. 'Do you want some tea?'

'Tea? Where did you get tea?'

'I worked passage to Tris on a clipper. Just for the hell of it. Join us for supper.'

'No, no. I have to ...' she gestured in the direction of the Castle again.

'... Dress for dinner. Um. I have to go now, Connell. Old Umbrella Wings will be looking for me.' She sighed and glanced round the wagon. 'But can I see you again?'

'If you want to learn real music, come to the campfire tonight. You have to participate, though.'

She gave me a longing glance and quit the wagon. I carried the sliced bread to the fire where Allen was baking trout.

'How can a Rooted play like that?' he asked.

'Oh, you heard? She's not just any Rooted. She's Lady Governor Swallow Awndyn and she visited *my* wagon. She'll join in tonight.'

Join in! Did she ever! We'd no idea how amazing she was. All my friends' foreboding at having a Rooted join us just melted away. Swallow soaked up our repertoire like a sponge, and spun it into new forms, and played it back. With clever variations, and more songs that thrilled us – we clapped and cheered and shouted for more. Soon she led our best musicians, who were like children stumbling in her wake, and she was so unassuming, in her threadbare pine-green dress, that not even Fullam minded.

The season drew to an end. We'd reduced the fields to stubble, with rooks flying in under an overcast sky, and a chill edge to the breeze. I was dragging my tin bath of water from my awning to dump it in the river, wrapped in a sarong with my hair in a towel.

Swallow was leaning on her stick, watching us tidy the ground and harness our horses. She saw me and broke into a rapturous smile. 'Connell, I'm glad I caught you!'

'I'm leaving today.'

'Half the wagons have gone.'

'The boys have rolled for the Front already.'

Her expression clouded. 'Why?'

'To dig ditches and build walls. I don't fancy that. Too close to bugs.'

She came to my side as I tilted the bath over the riverbank. We watched the water cascade into the Moren. I felt rather sorry for the river – as it circumscribes the Castle in a pretty, man-made meander it has no idea what's in store for it in Hacilith.

'Where will you go?' she murmured.

Water passed us in silver swirls, boating autumn leaves along. I assumed a vague air, as I do when any Rooted asks me about my movements, though in truth they're carefully planned. 'Oh ... I cart firewood to the city in winter. Late spring maybe Awia ... carrying coke to the foundries. Wrought estuary at Samphire Hoe, armpit-deep in silty water, cutting reeds for the thatchers, horsehides from the knackers' yard to the tanners. June is the Great Housekeeping at Tanager Palace … boy, do feathers make dust … we lay all the sheets on the lawn. Then back here for the next haying.'

'You don't have to do any of that,' she said.

I turned to her, puzzled by her tone.

'I want you to come to Awndyn,' she said, hopeful and excited.

'Why? Have you got work for me?'

'I'll think of something.' And she stood on tiptoe and kissed me on the cheek.

CHAPTER 32

Connell: Val and the Grey Rose

That morning the first frost had appeared in the shade of the wagons, tracing their outlines as crisply as a portrait silhouette. Swallow climbed onto the driver's step beside me, bright with excitement, cradling a mug of tea, and her copper hair sparkling over her coat and scarf.

She was a rare thing. Brimming with life. I let her hold the reins and Biddy's back rippled on. She kept her childhood enthusiasm, did Swallow. I don't think she'd ever grown up. It's the source of her music, and one of the reasons I'm coming to love her.

We strained to see the road in the soda-grey light, for when morning comes in November, it scarcely brings the day. The sycamore leaves limned with rime crunched under our wheels. Our breath misted and steam rose from her mug. She was all smiles.

I leant and kissed her cheek, by her ear. She giggled and snuggled up to me. The tip of her nose was cold. I put my arm round her, my other hand taking the reins, and kissed her as we rolled on, under the lowering sky.

'I love the roses,' she said, fingering the giltwork.

'I carved them myself.'

'Really? Wow.'

'I made the whole wagon.'

She blinked at me, and smiled. I shrugged. 'Everyone does. You have to be good at fixing your wagon. The only way to learn is to build your own.'

'Did you build Biddy, too?'

'Silly ...'

Mine is a kite wagon, red and gold. The roof is solid birch, with a mollycroft skylight and a steel chimney on the left. The wheels are widely-braced, against the mud of Lowespass. My pride and joy survives there, where the bowtops perish.

'Did you do the paintings?'

'Yes. Everything.'

'There's a woman with a rose.'

'That's Val,' I said.

Swallow rested her head on my shoulder, tapping a beat and regarding the painting, which was the best I could render, given that it's the whole left panel of the porchwork. 'Teon and Lewin are this side,' I said, tapping the panel on my right.

'Teon and Lewin ...'

'It's a story. A Litanee story.'

'How does it go?'

'Like this ... A lady named Val lived in Diw not so very long ago, as the Eszai see it, and she was beautiful. So beautiful, in fact, such fun and so outgoing, that she had two suitors. One was Teon, a warrior, and the other was Lewin, an ingenious craftsman. Teon and Lewin loved her intensely. Teon was courageous and headstrong, Lewin was quiet and clever, and she couldn't choose between them.'

'She should have both,' said Swallow.

'This wasn't Awia. This was Litanee.'

'She should choose neither.'

'Then it wouldn't be a story. Val said to Teon and Lewin, "In Governor Aver-Falconet's palace there's a garden where a rose tree grows. Its flowers bloom dove-grey. Whoever brings me back a grey rose is the man I shall marry." So Teon set off at once for Hacilith, and during the night he tried to climb the palace wall, and the guards arrested him, mistook him for an assassin and threw him in jail.

'Lewin stayed at home and made a rose from green and dove-grey silk. It was crafted so skilfully that Val was duped and married him. They settled down together in the most comfortable house in Diw, and time passed, and they had five children. And ten years later, Teon was set free from jail.

'He came storming to Diw and said to Val, "I've been locked up for ten long years, for following your wish, and you've married this fraud! Look, there's the rose on the mantelpiece! Hasn't it crossed your mind that a real rose would have wilted by now?"

'And Val said, "Who the hell are you?"

'"I'm Teon! Don't you remember sending me to fetch a rose?"

'Val said, "You've no right to come barging in here, where I'm comfortable with my happy family and growing prosperous and fat. I don't know you. I don't care what problems have beset you. Too much water has flowed under the bridge since you walked away. Have you come to harass me when I hardly remember you and didn't even recognise you? Haven't you got a life? Grow up and clear off!"

'Teon left and neither Val nor Lewin ever saw him again. They lived in affluence and peace for the rest of their days and their children grew up wise and happy, and so on, until the nth generation, because the moral of this story is that no one appreciates a person from their distant past resurfacing and unsettling them, especially if they've wronged them, especially if, in the meantime, they've changed.

'You should never return to people you'd find have altered beyond imagining, and you're no longer welcome. Teon made Val uncomfortable and she threw him out. He should have contemned her and never set eyes on her again.'

'That's what we're doing,' Swallow said. 'Setting out for pastures new.'

'It's a gypsy story. To remind us never to return to Litanee. We travel the world, and it's harsh, my love.'

'Say that again.'

'My love. My love. You don't realise how awful my life was before you came. You've given me stability. You've given me purpose. You're the girl I needed to give me meaning.'

I wanted to protect her. My strong arm will always guard her from the severe world and, in the niche of peace I defend for her, she'll be able to compose, for me.

'Get your guitar. Let's sing that roundelay.'

She sang. And I drove on, over the pale brown leaves, through Eske and into the evening, for these short days of autumn are either dawn or dusk, with nothing in between.

CHAPTER 33

Connell: Love in the time of gunpowder

Swallow wrote to me hysterically, and I picked up the letter at Awndyn post office when I returned from Tris. I retrieved my wagon from Allen and drove to the manor.

I pulled up on the grass, unfastened Biddy and went to the window of Swallow's study. A lamp burned inside. I tapped on the pane and a blurry shape moved within, resolved into Swallow on the other side of the glass. She opened one light of the window.

'Connell!'

'It's all right. I got your letter.'

'I thought you'd left me.'

'No.'

'Abandoned me like the others. Rejected me like San did.'

'No.'

'So where have you been?'

'To Tris, working on a clipper. I brought some tea … all kinds of herbs, actually.'

She stared at me, then disappeared into the room. A second later she unlocked the main door and beckoned me through, into her study. She sat at her desk, and I knelt on the floor at her feet. On the green couch lay a silver flute bent in half, an oboe and clarinet with the wood splintered halfway down their length, as if she'd stamped on them.

I hugged her calves and rested my head on her lap. 'I'm yours, Swallow. I never would have gone if I thought this would happen. If I knew you'd need me.'

'What were you doing?'

'Adventuring.'

Her frostiness melted and she began to play with my hair. 'Oh, Connell. It's the gypsy wanderlust, but I love you for it.'

'I'll never leave you again,' I said, emphatically. She told me her diagnosis. Tears pricked my eyes. She was my love, who loved the world so much, and made marvellous music from it and for it. I couldn't think of her not existing any more. With the sadness rose great fear. Swallow's frightened of death, too. Of ceasing and stopping, because she loves the world so much. There's always something new to put into music. She always embraces the next inspiration, investigates it, throws herself into composing. And now ... I began to cry. I squeezed her calves and pressed my cheek on her warm lap.

'So will you never leave me, now I'm dying?'

'I'll *never* leave you, Swallow. I'm your champion, I'll fight for you.'

'And stronger than ever.' She wound a lock of hair around her finger.

I kissed her knees. She said nothing – her shocking hatred flickered like flames in the very air she exhaled.

'Please,' I said gently. 'Become a Rose, live in my wagon. We can start your tattoos.'

'But the Castle ...'

'Forget the Castle. Give it up and join us.'

She said nothing for a long time. I pressed my lips against her velvet thighs, dedicating myself as her warrior, heart and soul. Then she kind of smirked. 'The outdoor life ...' she said bitterly.

'We laugh at the Castle.'

'... is diminuendo ... a pianissimo.'

'No. Vivace, Swallow. Con bravura, giocoso. If you join us you'll see we disdain the Eszai. Put your hatred aside ... we can live in peace. With your money we need never work again. We can play the guitar. We can party in the forest, dance in the olive groves. You can build up your strength, throw your stick away. We need never touch the Castle's silly world again. Wouldn't that be wonderful?' I looked up, at her eyes deep with genius. She's achieved all this, I thought, and now she has to uncouple herself from it. Unfocussed moments of abstraction, distraction and contradiction passed over her eyes, like fast-blown clouds reflected in the surface of a pool.

'I'm going to kill them,' she said. Her voice was leaden. She went rigid, staring across the room at nothing – into some hell of her own devising. 'All of them.'

'No. Stop trying to be an immortal. Be yourself.'

'I'm going to be the one who kills them.'

'They're going to die anyway. They're just putting it off. Relax.'

Of course it was too late.

I pulled down her wing and stroked the soft feathers. They smelt of almonds and so did her hair. For all her ferocity, she was defenceless. She was so passionate, she feels so deeply. I'd protect her, come what may; I was heady with warmth for her. Round and round her finger looped my hair distractedly. She was embroiled in her anger, it'd been burning too long, but I still believed, then, that with months of perseverance I could quench it.

I wrapped my arms around her, hugging the second shoulderblades of her wings, feeling the warm feathers move in the skin. She held me with her wings' little fingers.

'I'm a thing of their past now,' she said. 'Saker got married, and Jant thinks opera boxes are for debauchery.'

'Forget them. Come and live at peace.'

She tests me this way. She rubs in how closely she lived with kings and Eszai, and what firm friends they'd been. She knew all the details of their lives and predilections, but they're just distant names to me. They rejected her from their circle of friendship as well as from the Circle ... so she said. But I'm not such a fool as to fall for her constructions: did they really reject her or did she tear herself away?

'We'll leave the Rooted People's world,' I said.

She woke. 'Oh! You got a ship tattoo.'

'It's the clipper.'

She bent her head and rubbed her lips on its scabbed surface. 'How long will it take to heal?'

'Not long.' I brushed my hands down her back, over her hips and thighs. Her muscles were tight but she moaned and, delighted, I massaged her legs. She is a precious jewel whom I want to save, but I can't. And she's so very complicated. Two complicated people shouldn't be lovers because it creates too much complexity, which leads to misery. Fortunately I'm straightforward, so I'm well matched with her – I'll try to make everything all right, and show her the way. 'My next tattoo will be your loveheart. They'll shower us with rose petals as we dance.'

'Tornado has a tattoo of the Castle's sun,' she murmured. 'I'm going to kill him.'

'Sh ...'

'All of them.'

'Join us. We can roll anywhere.'

'But San would still exist.'

'Who cares?'

Beyond the windows, the flat cloud base flashed pale with the lighthouse beams. My horse moved to and fro, cropping the lawn.

Swallow's tone hardened. 'San cannot be allowed to exist. He cannot keep going the way he has: never letting in any decent talent. His Eszai are corrupt.'

I sighed, temporarily beaten.

'Oh, Connell ...' She leant to me; her full lips brushed my cheek. One hand went under my breast, and the other around my waist, and

I opened my mouth as she pressed her lips on mine and kissed me deeply. '…We can kill them. All of them. And this is how we'll do it …'

CHAPTER 34

Swallow in Maple Wood, Drussiter

I am overwhelmed by hate. Hatred consumes me. Anger has long since become hatred, and I hate with the intensity of fury.

My hatred of the Castle knows no bounds. I am totally given over to it. I want to tear down the Castle, destroy it, rive it to shreds. I am pure wrath. I am the Colossus of Death. I will stand tall above the earth and pour oceans of black hatred on the land and the seas, and I will sink the Castle. I will flex my fingers and unleash a destructive force as great as the Insects; I will become immortal in my notoriety, and soon people will say, 'Swallow, who destroyed the Circle, did mankind its greatest service.'

I sit here in my wagon, just as I sat alone in my house, and think of the immortals enjoying themselves. In my manor I went about in absolute hatred, not able to concentrate on the running of the place. I moved as if through thick mud, so cloyed and hindered and dragged down was I by hate. When I grew tired, the hatred became despair, and back again to searing hate when my energy revived.

I could think of nothing else but the insults I've been subjected to. They replayed in my mind night and day. I ruminated on them every second – I was trying in vain to understand why San treated me so badly, why I was just his plaything. And my mind dwelt on every affront and eventually I had no other thoughts. I was a broken instrument: the music no longer came to me: I could no longer compose.

So I gave up my manor to direct my hatred. It was easy, and here I am: free – but as free as a gypsy, not an immortal. Time is still passing and my death is drawing very near. Hatred sets my face in a snarl as I think of the Eszai wallowing in decadence: Jant with his needle, Tornado with his feasts, Tern fizzing with fame on the front row watching the catwalk. The hardships of the world never touch them. Well, now they'll learn.

Other people enjoy their simple pleasures: friends and happy families. But that's because they've spent their lives pursuing those successes, while I have spent my life composing, in the hope of getting into the Castle. Which, as it turns out, is a vain hope. Of course, I knew all along that immortality is not for musicians, and if I wanted to be Eszai I should have made myself a soldier instead. Could I have Challenged the Artillerist or the Grenadier? Of course not. A talented musician is what I am, and so I will never gain eternal life. If all my symphonies are played hundreds of years from now, beyond the lifetimes of every current Eszai, so what? What fucking good does that do me?

I hate them. As long as one lives, I won't rest. I'll destroy each and every one, tear down all they stand for. How dare San block me? I'll rend the Circle apart!

The pain in my chest is getting worse and some days I feel nauseous. But my disease won't rob me of my genius. Time won't destroy my talent. I won't die in a sick bed, I'll go down fighting. Bring on the dying faster! The Emperor won't let me fight for him, so I'll snap every link in the Circle. Every Eszai will feel his friends die one by one – I hope it feels like death fifty times over!

Hatred so strong can't last: no overwhelming emotion can. It either drives you mad or with time it metamorphoses and fades. I've nurtured it for ten years and I fear it breaking, so now's the time to act. If I don't act it'll burn itself out and I'll end my days strumming a guitar in the woods with Connell, while my disease eats me up from within.

She's returned to camp, with her troupe, though I didn't see them arrive. They're very good at not being seen, which is why I've employed them.

I put my emotion aside. It sustains me, but I must concentrate and need a clear mind. Revenge is a dish best served cold, they say. Who says that? They're wrong. Revenge is a dish best served at eight hundred degrees centigrade: the temperature at which gunpowder burns.

I jumped out of the wagon and joined their ring around the fire. Connell's arrow wound pains her, but it hasn't slowed her down. My music and my words have convinced her I should be Eszai. I've stoked her with the same hatred, and it drives her great energy.

The seed of such hatred exists in us all, and we were once as innocent as you. And if these events happened to you, you'd turn out the same.

Looking back, the path on which I was set seems inevitable. The Emperor compounded my hatred as precisely as the gunpowder in a mill. A mixture of fury, bitterness and resentment in the proportions of 75:15:10. The bitterness supplies fuel, the fury ignites with a white heat, and the resentment burns long and slow.

The Emperor mixed these ingredients together, not me. I am only the vessel. I used to feel hope, creativity, and a willingness to fight for the Fourlands. I applied to the Castle and San turned me away: again and again he magnified my enmity. He polished it into the lens that sets light to the fuse. I even tried battling Insects to show him I could, and they injured me so much I lost the ability to bear children. I only started to walk unaided when I joined the gypsy life.

So San poured rancour into the mixture, and lastly malice, when he made me a laughing stock in front of thousands. Capelin was accepted, and I was rejected – now see what I can do! All my feelings have been mixed wet and finely ground into a powder that dried slowly, slowly: so that it won't explode at once but, coated with self-restraint, will stay deadly potential until the last.

CHAPTER 35

Back to Jant: Audience with the Emperor

Tern kissed me awake. 'Love? You're back.'

I blinked at her blearily, 'What time is it?'

'Carillon's just struck six.'

'Damn,' I leapt up. 'Your junkie husband has to report to the Emperor.'

She slipped out of bed, brushing the ivy that entwines our four-poster. 'You're covered in bandages.'

'Connell got me, at the cove.'

'Are you badly hurt?'

'Ha ha. What's "hurt"?'

'Oh, god, Jant. Are you on cat?'

I felt her disappointment twist me into hard-heartedness, the only way I could safely go. I didn't want her to know I've been using … but at the same time I needed her to take these phials away. Save me from them. But I couldn't tell her that.

She came to look into my eyes. I gave her the last line first, it saves time: 'Tern, my love, I have an illness, it controls me. I can't stay clean when I'm in this much pain. But if you help me … I can stop before I become addicted.'

'I'm here for you, Jant. Just don't lie to me.' She examined my bandages, ducking all around. I reached out the wing I'd sheltered behind in the explosion and tickled her with shrunken flight feathers.

'They're all burns.'

'Yes. The blast threw me to my knees, like this …'

'Oh, sweetheart.'

'It made me spread my wings … instinctively. Which … didn't work.'

'Telegraphs are pouring in. Did you see them?'

'Yes, there'll be a tsunami waiting for me in Lisade. It's been clicking since first light,' I said, and then I felt Sirocco pull on the Circle so powerfully I cried out. Tern stared at me in concern. 'Sirocco … he just yanked on the Circle as if it's his last breath … Come on, Tassy, it's not elastic. He's only got hours left, I think … No. Minutes. Can you feel it?'

'Not yet.'

'It feels like it's sucking me inside out.' As if it was pulling me out of my body. I looked at my hand, and was surprised not to see another ghostly hand next to it, the sensation of dislocation was so strong.

Tern fastened her dress quickly. 'I'm coming with you. I'll tell San he should've made Swallow immortal.'

'Bet you won't. Ah, shit! It's going to break.'

She ran to me and hugged me. I could tell she was feeling the vertigo now; she clawed her fingers into my feathers. The sensation started to tighten, to a white point of nausea. Our bodies contracted, feeling the Emperor striving to hold the Circle together. To stop Sirocco from tearing it. And you feel it stretching, thinner and thinner, tighter and sicker with anticipation, and tighter and tenser, so thin you can see through it.

I can't breathe!

San working hard to keep it from breaking, thinner still – and it goes. Ripped open. Out beams a flash of light to a plane of infinity. It snapped closed. All was dark. The feeling of safety flooded back. And our bodies relaxed.

Tern was limp, clutching my feathers. She seemed to be on the brink of fainting. I rubbed her shoulders, muttering, 'Please, San, try to be faster.'

'Oh,' said Tern. 'Uh … Poor Sirocco … What a way to die.'

'Fourth degree burns.'

'I hate feeling someone die.'

'You didn't feel him die, love, you felt him break the Circle.'

'It's the same thing.'

'No, it isn't. We didn't go through whatever he felt … thank god.' But then, if Sirocco had been burnt to eschar he wouldn't feel pain. His nerve endings would have been seared away, and his skin sloughed off like black puff pastry. The more burnt you are, the less pain you feel. It's the smallest of mercies.

I released Tern. 'It took San a second to mend it. We're all a second older.'

'Does that matter?'

I stripped off Fulmer's shirt, put on a t-shirt, rifled through the wardrobe for a pair of jeans, then picked my sword belt from the door hook and buckled it on. 'On the battlefield, yes. A second lost in that fucking vertigo is enough for an Insect to grab me.'

'Is everyone else OK?'

'Tornado got hit.'

I explained as she descended the spiral steps ahead of me and out into the bright morning, the colours of the lawns and walls of Carillon so brilliant we shivered. When the Circle breaks it always makes you wonder what your own death will be. If Swallow gets me, I hope it's quick. I'd rather be blown into a cloud of pink meat than suffer burns like Sirocco.

Tern dawdled, staring at the ground, so I took her hand. She gulped. 'I've always known him ...'

'Come on, or there'll be more! Who knows who's next?'

'That sick bitch Connell!'

We passed quickly along the front of Carillon, past its red and white conical towers. The breeze breathed between its ornamented chimneys, the semi-circular pediments, and the cupola of the clock tower.

'Where did you get fifty thousand pounds to offer as a reward?'

'It's the insurance money from Wrought. Some of it.' She glanced at me. 'Yes, Simoon has his uses. But it's been no good so far. No one knows anything about Connell.'

We passed the fantastic, baroque carving around the windows: Carillon's griffons, cobras, storks and seahorses, and turned into the cool shadow of the Breckan loggia, then through the Starglass Quadrangle. The South Façade rose, noble and strong, a symbol of the Emperor's message of concord and resilience, which would be great if the world wasn't falling apart.

The halberdiers in the tympanum portal saw us coming and stepped back. We walked between them, entered the dim narthex and paused, holding hands, smelling the frankincense which always recalls us to the day I brought her here, to be married. We had paused, just like this, beholding each other. Tern had looked incredible in a long, lace dress. I had made a statement, wearing an immaculate copy of Rhydanne clothes my tailor had contrived, fur-lined suede with wolf teeth and its hood draped down the back. She'd been so nervous, it amplified her beauty. It had been the first time Tern had ever set foot in the Throne Room. But she'd spoken to San without a quake in her honey-hued voice, and I loved her the more.

We kissed. 'Are you ready?'

'Ready.'

'Let's do it, catkin.'

We entered, and walked down the crimson carpet like the day we married, Tern sighing, the Throne Room shining around us. We reached the dais and bowed before the Emperor. There were no shadows this early, and the air was like spring water. The mosaic, gold in glass, sparkled all the way up into the octagonal hollow of the spire above the Throne.

San looked most unsmiling. He said, 'Comet, as you know the Grenadier just died. I hear the Roses blew the Lowespass fortress magazine. Hurricane brought it upon us, and Sirocco was the blameless victim. I have been receiving your correspondence, the last letter being that you had lost Connell. What has happened since?'

I related everything. 'So Tornado will return in the next few hours to treat his shoulder, Rayne is on her way, and King Saker is bringing Rax's Roses whom he captured in Awndyn.'

'How is the search proceeding in Litanee?'

'Aver-Falconet telegraphed that he's combed Diw and Vertigo, and the surrounding woods and villages, and found nothing. The people of Vertigo clam up, they don't respond well to being questioned by troops from Hacilith.'

'You go, and speak to them.'

'Yes, my lord.'

'If you catch Swallow alive, bring her to me. She wanted an eighth audience, did she not?'

Tern flinched.

San said, 'Swallow is more important than the bomber troupes. But I wish to speak to them as well.'

'Certainly.'

Tern began quivering with anger and fear. She was staring at the columns in the apse behind the throne. When I agreed with San she burst out: 'My lord Emperor, you're sending him into explosions!'

'Which he described most luridly.'

'What are you doing to protect us?'

I spread a wing and pulled her to me. She shouldn't be questioning San! In the crook of my wing I felt her trembling.

'Lady Wrought,' San said calmly. 'I have tripled the guard on each gate. None of them are Litanee, and we have searched the entire Castle. There are no powder charges here. All the immortals Comet requested to return are safe. He will apprehend Swallow and the risk will soon be ended.'

'One of these fireballs will kill him! Swallow's bombing us because we're loyal to you! Who's next? Your Messenger?'

'Tern,' I said. 'It's what I'm for.'

'No! You swore to fight Insects! Not to track down some mad musician!'

'He swore to help me preserve peace,' said San.

'You always say Eszai are forbidden to fight Zascai. We're supposed to advise them! Yet you're sending him to kill them.'

'I did not order him to kill Swallow. I asked him to bring her here.'

'How can he, without bloodshed?'

'He is permitted to defend himself.'

Tern's dress clung to her body with perspiration. 'Swallow must have been planning this for years! She's turned all her genius to the task. Every bomb sends Jant – Comet – into a trap for three, four, five more!'

'He can out-think her.'

Tern burst into tears.

The Emperor rose, descended the steps, and rested his hand on her shoulder. She raised her face in astonishment, and looked into his eyes, more from surprise than audacity, gave a little nod and stopped crying.

'Follow me,' said San. He walked away, through the last spacious arch of the west arcade, and across the smaller aisle beyond. He went to a door which matched, in mirror image, the one to his private chamber on the right side of the Throne Room, which no-one's ever seen inside.

He pushed this door and it swung open. We followed the Emperor into a dim, cool staircase. As we walked behind him up the narrow curve I sought out Tern's hand and squeezed it. She looked at me with brimming eyes, a look of deep and honest affection.

The passage led into a room above the lantern. It was a large, empty, octagonal chamber, spanning the width of the tower. Its lancet-arched windows were set so closely together the walls were glass. Sunlight shining through made a pattern of bright fangs on the floor. This was the first stage of the spire, with the chalky smell of dust and chiselled fine, white Marram limestone. Above us, a graceful staircase spiralled up into invisible heights.

San went through a plain portal at the end; we followed into the morning light and found ourselves on a balcony overlooking the lawns. The massive Dace Gate, with its portcullises and four heavy barrel towers of grey sarsen, stood directly ahead. The marble-clad Lisade Library was on our left, my telegraph pivoting on its roof and operators visible in the white cabin alongside. There was Gayle at her desk behind the centre window. On the other side of the lawns was the red brick barracks, with the Southeast Bridge high above it, arcing gracefully from the third floor of Simurgh to the curtain wall. Above us, the presence, the splendid solemn weight of the spire. We were seeing the Castle from a new perspective: a private balcony that only the Architect could visit, and the Emperor used.

A warm breeze stirred Tern's feathers and the Emperor's hair. It carried the scent of cut grass and meadowsweet; the dry, rutted smell of the Eske Road. San laid his long, gnarled hands on the quatrefoil balustrade and seemed to be watching the lawn. He spoke precisely. 'Could Swallow be in the Shift?'

'My lord?'

'She may be organising her rebellion from Epsilon, or any of the Shift worlds. Your letter said Swallow writes music that can Shift the listener to Epsilon. Maybe that's where she's hiding.'

I realised the Emperor had brought us out of the Throne Room so the marksmen on the gallery wouldn't hear him. 'Or the drug atheudos might be a gateway. So Swallow has two ways in. I will not allow her in the Shift.'

'No, my lord.'

'There are things there one must *not bring back*. Every time someone Shifts, one of those *creatures* may follow him through.'

'What creatures?' said Tern. 'Insects?'

San moved his hand slightly and left a dark mark of perspiration on the stone. 'Comet has seen one of the *things* that would come through.'

'Yes ...'

'You saw the least of them!'

I became aware the Vermiform was lying motionless, limply in the base of my pocket. It was listening as intently as it could.

'Swallow would bring these miscegenations here unwittingly,' San said. 'Or, perhaps, deliberately. The Gabbleratchet. The Back of the Night Sky ... and the vaster things. The Ribbon. The thing I faced inside it ... the one that waits for me.'

Tern and I looked at each other, and didn't dare ask.

'And that foul being made of worms. I know it's in the soil, but on no account must it show itself in numbers here again. So, Comet, Shift and find any trace of Swallow. Consider it part of your search.'

'My lord,' protested Tern. 'Please, no! Every time he goes there I think he's going to die. He comes so close. It *will* kill him.'

The Emperor raised his eyebrows in an expression that said: *And?*

He returned through the tower chamber, and we followed down the stairs, into the Throne Room. I put my hand in my pocket, feeling the Vermiform lying doggo.

San walked noiselessly up the dais steps and seated himself in the Sunburst Throne. On the arm of the throne his shield still hung, with his Wrought Sword and a musket fully primed. They symbolise his promise that he'll protect the Fourlands until god returns from its holiday – if there ever was a god at all – and we're his expendable weapons.

San doesn't care about any individual Eszai – if he needs to send me into the firestorm or sweet oblivion, what's that to him?

A commotion outside – horses' hooves and a crowd of men's voices – started me out of my reverie. The great double doors of the Throne Room were open, and through them came Saker. He looked up at the bowmen on the galleries and spread his hands, then strode towards us, through fractures of colour cast by the stained glass, past me to the lowest step and described a succinct bow. 'My lord Emperor, I've brought Rax and his troupe of twenty Roses. I apprehended them loading ninety barrels of powder at Awndyn canal.'

'Bring them in.'

'All twenty?'

'Yes.'

He trekked back down the aisle, and through the amber portal. A few minutes later the gypsies spilt into the Throne Room like ink, all dusty, dishevelled and sweat-stained from the ride. As they crossed the threshold they fell into silence and clustered in a blot. In their combats, vest tops and jackets, they stood staring towards us, between the two arcades of arches and past me, at the Throne. Those at the rear gazed up to the vertiginous ceiling; vaulting and ornate bosses: caravels on a churning wave, a hare in foliage, Insect heads with knotted antennae.

They stared at the rose window glowing with saffron yellow, peridot green and peacock blue, and smelt the mauve odour of incense. The gold lamps hanging on long chains hypnotised them; the arcades' perspective to the Throne mesmerised them. So did the battle mosaics glinting on every surface, and some older, duller patches of fronds, a huge variety of animals and ancient buildings, which were the original tesserae still remaining from the Pentadrican palace.

It had the most stupendous effect on these Roses used to the space inside a caravan, and they shrank as if being squashed. Saker and some Imperial guards shepherded the last of them through. They had immense difficulty herding them down the aisle – they'd still be trying now, if the Emperor hadn't lost patience and raised his voice: 'Come here!'

Rax and the Roses involuntarily responded to his tone, filtered down the aisle. Rax limped, supported by his fellows, and I directed them all into the first benches. They stank of horse sweat and road dust. Saker wiped his forehead on his sleeve, making his dirty hair stick up, and bowed.

'Thank you,' said San.

'My lord, I await your advice.'

'King Saker, I suggest you return to Awia. Please stop Queen

Eleonora's wrongful treatment of Roses. Comet, tell him what transpired outside Tanager Palace, then fly to Litanee.'

We left the rebel prisoners with the marksmen in the gallery attentive to every move. The Emperor descended from the throne and began to address them: 'Rax, Roses, my friends, I give everyone a chance to live forever ...'

Outside the Throne Room, Saker received his bow, quiver and sword from the halberdier, slung the bow on his shoulder and tucked a wing through the strap. He buckled on his swordbelt as we trotted down the steps into the Starglass Quad, and checked the blade ran free by drawing a few centimetres and clicking it back.

'You wouldn't believe how weird it is going into the Throne Room unarmed. I had to give up my sword, like any Zascai. Like any fucking Zascai. Humbling, that is.'

His archer's short sword is the same length as the quiver and sits on his opposite hip. He dropped a hand to its hilt, swung it behind him, and walked off slowly, across the square paved with graves of past Eszai, looking without seeing. He was keenly aware of the buildings around us, but repressing as firmly as possible any temptation to dwell on what they meant. He hadn't set foot inside the Castle for fifteen years. The welter of emotions was intolerable, so he did what he always does, and blocked it.

'I can't say it was all great,' he announced, to the smooth, three-storey heights of Simurgh. 'But the war can't stop, you see.'

He pinched his flight feathers closed with tension, and paced off, direct as a dart.

Tern sped after him. 'Listen! This won't be good for you!'

'I want to see my rooms. I mean, Cyan's rooms.'

'Come to the tower and have a drink.'

He kept going, 'I want to see *Lightning*'s suite.'

'Why?'

'I don't know. She's probably wrecked the place.'

We kept up with him, wanting to offer support, but how? There was a vast gulf between the mortal he now was, and the immortal it was possible to be. His past self of fourteen centuries belonged here, but now he was a pale visitor to the Castle, where he once was its deepest heart.

You're a fool to revisit a place you no longer belong. No amount of thinking can square the circle and pinpoint the ways you've changed, the ways you no longer fit, no longer mesh with the cogs. The very shape of the Circle has changed. But Saker, when he's in the mood, can scoop great handfuls of nostalgia and rub it into his very pores.

We walked into the tilting shadow, through the gap between Breckan and Simurgh, and he turned left into the shaded loggia that runs down the front of Simurgh. We strode along with the red flicker of sunlight as we passed every arch, and the smell of old paint from the ground floor windows.

'Need a new ...' he murmured.

I said, 'I don't know what kick you're getting out of this, but you should know that Leon's guard gave the protestors a whiff of grapeshot.'

'They did?'

'Yes!'

'Ah.'

He would remember me climbing through that window with a bottle of champagne in each hand. Tern laughing drunk with marquees on the lawn behind, when we piled into the basket of a hot air balloon and unreeled to view the Castle from the air.

And god knows what other memories he saw: the famous duel between Tré Cloud and Shearwater Mist. The time he dragged himself here in 1007 after his fiancée Linnet was cemented into the Wall, the only occasion he ever fought Tornado – or interring the dead under each and every gravestone. Like ghosts recorded on the buildings, they flitted translucent in the corners of the square, seethed and layered between the beeches of Six Mile Avenue. His memory is seven times as long as mine, cherished to a higher power, and I can't begin to describe its potency.

It stopped him like a blow at the door at the end of the loggia. He looked at the knob as if doubting his strength to turn it.

'I know why Swallow hates you,' he said.

With a weak hand he forced himself to open it, paced through and doubled back along the corridor inside. Here, we reached the doors to the Archer's suite, the brass rail above them simply rings, bereft of the tapestry that once hung there. All his feathers rose up like bristles and he settled them with a shudder. 'Why is this still here?'

'Saker—'

He tried to turn the oval handles. 'It's locked ... of course.'

'The Architect has the key.'

He indicated it, and stood aside. 'Jant, please ...'

I had no qualms about breaking into the Archer's suite, but this was the most unhealthy thing we could possibly be doing. I hesitated, but Tern stroked my arm, and when I looked up she nodded subtly.

'All right,' I said. I took my stiletto from my boot, flicked the blade, and knelt down before the lock with its brass plate. I eased the point in, and rested my other hand on the cold panelling, probing for the sliding bar inside. I pressed my knife point against it, and drew it back a little. Again, and a little more. Again, and on the third time it clicked out of its mortise. I pushed the door, and it swung wide.

Saker walked in and stopped in the middle of the room. Tern and I followed with grave foreboding. It was as Cyan had left it. It smelt of crisps.

On a round central table, tin soldiers, brightly coloured but chipped, marched out of a little straw-filled crate. Cyan had arranged them in a line, some on horseback, some teams pulling wheeled cannon, and a mass of play-worn tin Insects stood poised to attack them.

Behind them, a stack of volumes were some of Saker's archery theses, Cyan's notes on ballistics trials, a half-written report, then a crimping machine and the components of cartridges.

Saker rested the tip of his finger on a toy cannon, and rolled it a little. Its reflection moved in the polished table top.

The walls of celadon green damask showed patches where his pictures had been and, though the paintings had gone, I remembered them all. On the far wall had hung the most realistic Awian still lifes. By the fireplace, a silhouette portrait of a woman with a braid had left an oval patch. Prints had occupied those two large squares; one a plan drawing of his palace and grounds, the other a nautical chart of Tris. Their nails were still projecting and, on the walls instead, Cyan had tacked big signed posters of some rock band called Wagtail.

In place of the chandelier Cyan had hung a regular lamp, dwarfed by the frescoed ceiling. Nothing on the mantelpiece but a vase of Insect antennae; she'd never grown out of collecting them, and samples of rifle locks. Her dirty clothes were piled by the bedroom door and the empty fireplace was full of crisp packets, between the andirons with gilt ends shaped like eagles.

Saker swept a glance around the room, and went to look out of the window, crossing from the grey and violet carpet onto the parquet floor. The series of tall, eight-paned windows corresponded exactly to the arches of the loggia outside; he gazed out of one, across the passage and through the arch, over the striped lawn to the hospital garden.

The carpet was the same apart from Cyan's wine stains, and bore the impressions of Saker's furniture like thousand year old footprints. There had stood the tortoiseshell cabinet full of chess sets. There once stood a pair of silver vases fully my height entwined by lizards: every spine perfectly cast. There, his jousting armour and an abalone-inlaid sea chest he bought back from Lythos. There, the little dimple made by the point of his cello when it rested against the wall, and there, the dents of the piano's feet conjured up its ghost.

Tern met my eye with a grimace. We waited upon the silence and, as Saker said nothing, she tried, 'No one responded to the bounty I offered.'

Facing the window, his reflection on the glass. 'They won't,' he said softly. 'Swallow gave them music. They'll die for her.'

'Will they?'

'I never noticed ... Why did I never notice ... how beautiful a view that is?'

He gathered himself and went to the bedroom as if through thickened air. Tern and I followed, stopped in the doorway. His four-poster had gone and in its place was a simple bed of pine, but the grey lampas silk canopy remained. He looked up to it. 'Who's been sleeping in my little room?'

The covers were thrown back, still untidy from when Cyan rose to ride to the Front. They smelt of her. He smoothed the sheet and sat down. Her muddy boots thrown under the chair in the corner, her quiver of arrows and a bowl of crisp crumbs on the floor. There was the entrance to the bathroom and the long, folding panels of the empty wardrobe. Three rooms is all you get.

He sat staring at nothing, into a private world of grief. Tern took my arm, and we prepared to leave him to it.

The motion made him stir. He flipped open a jewellery box on the bedside table and drew forth Cyan's ruby pendant on its slender chain. He seemed to know it'd be in there. He slid it in his pocket and approached us without seeing us; we drew back and let him pass, eyes blank, with determination he walked out, across the neoclassical carpet, through the double doors and disappeared down the corridor. We hastened after him.

'What are you doing?' I called.

'Finding my feet!'

He plucked open the door to the loggia, slipped out and passed the other side of the tall sash windows. I won't let him get away that easily. I caught up with him halfway down. 'Where are you heading?'

He shuddered to throw me off. As if trying to wake himself. But there are many levels of waking and he was only halfway. 'The gym. I can't have a shower in *there*!'

We reached the end of the Simurgh loggia, across the gap and into the Breckan one. I stopped to let him go. He turned on his heel and, walking backward a few steps, drew lips from clenched teeth. 'The Litanee were followers waiting to happen! They'll die for *her*, and they're coming for us! This place is no fortress!'

He whipped round and hastened down Breckan. One hand on his quiver hanger, his wing joints hooked above his shoulders.

*

I went back to Tern. She was in the corridor, walking to and fro. She said, 'I'm not going in there again. It's horrible.'

'Oh, love. Horrible doesn't begin to describe it.'

'What did he say?'

'Not much.'

'He should never have set foot this side of the Dace Gate.'

I looked through to the ceiling. No wonder he's like a cornered beast. He'd commissioned it in the seventeenth century to be painted as Awia – a beautiful lady barely-clad as an archer, seated on a cloud surrounded by winged victories. They floated up to the limitless heights of the sky in a trompe d'oeil so flawless I've often thought I could take a trip, lie on the carpet and soar among them. The same improbable dawn-pink light shone on romantic ruins ... which I always thought very apt, given that he is one.

His chandelier had been made from raindrops, immortalised on a whim of the Emperor over a thousand years ago. When time had started passing for him again, they'd fallen down and wet the carpet.

I closed the doors but couldn't lock them. Tern led away and we returned across the grass and past the gymnasium.

CHAPTER 36

As we passed the gymnasium, I had a clear memory of Saker, with Swallow, twenty-five years ago when she was visiting for one of her first petitions.

He was lifting free weights at the far end of the weights room and Swallow was watching him, and singing under her breath. I'd just come in from flying circuits, and when I saw her I leant all the way over backwards, put my hands on the floor behind my head, and flicked up my legs in a handstand. Slowly over; I did two more backflips on the spot. She laughed and ran to me. 'This is boring!'

'Yes, but he has to do it,' I said.

'Boring!'

'We're going to fight Insects in the amphitheatre next. Do you want to watch?'

She sighed. 'He never stops.'

'Of course not. One off-day and a Challenger might turn up. We must be our best every single day. There's no such thing as a retrial of a Challenge.'

'Well, this doesn't help me get any closer to the Emperor, or the Circle!'

I flicked my towel into the basket in the corner. 'Then why don't you sing in the theatre?'

'It's empty.'

'Swallow, if you start singing, everyone will stop and listen; word will get round. You'll have half the Castle in there by the time you belt out a barcarolle.'

'Hey ... great!'

I offered her the key.

'Thank you!' She tiptoed and kissed me on the cheek, then left, reflected in the mirrors past the fixed weight machines. I sat down on a bench, unlaced my pumps and, dangling them from one hand, set off for the dining hall. A crack sounded the length of the gym, and an arrow appeared in the wall before me.

Saker was standing with his bow and a handful of arrows, *furious*.

'Hey!' I said. I stepped forward and he shot an arrow into the wall in front of me, another into the wall behind, and a third in front of my toes into the mat.

'*What are you doing?*' I yelled.

He pulled a splay of arrows from a quiver hanging on the weight rack, clicked one to string and held the rest between his fingers. Sweat darkened the armholes of his vest. His eyes were ferocious. 'She kissed you!'

'It was only a peck on the cheek!'

'Don't you dare take her away from me!'

'What? Why would I do that?' Angry, I took a step, and the arrow whacked into the floor at my toe. Another step, another two arrows, before and behind my foot.

'You gave her a key.'

'To the theatre! I'm not interested in Swallow – I'm married!'

'It's never stopped you before!'

'What does that mean?'

'You sleep with anyone!'

'For your information I don't! Swallow doesn't belong to you. You're possessed! Hey! Damn it, watch my feet! Swallow belongs to herself – she's just a friend!'

'Just a friend …?'

'Yes! And together we're trying to convince San to make a place for her – the first Musician, all right?'

He nodded, ugly jealousy subsiding into confusion. He lowered the bow. 'All right.'

I exhaled. 'Idiot!'

'Sorry.'

'Now, can I get out of here without you cutting my toenails?'

'Don't you trust my aim?'

'I quite like my toes!'

'Well … where did she go?'

'She's going to sing in the theatre. I'll run from room to room and invite everyone to listen. Do you see? I'm on her side.'

I'm on her side.

I was on her side back then, and look what she's become. All the women we chase undergo a transformation, caused by our pursuit. It's our fault – if you chase someone you change them. Didn't he know that? Their hearts turn to wood and their arms become the vine.

261

Swallow was the headiest blend, but it matters not which vintage or vineyard, aroma or aftertaste, all wine changes to vinegar when time has its way.

CHAPTER 37

Tern and I entered my tower, and climbed the three hundred spiral steps to my apartment, past the store rooms that filled the lower part of the tower. My suite is at the top, first the Myrtle Room (pale green, empty, the last time I used it was when convalescing after Slake Cross Battle and occasionally for visitors), then another twenty steps to the bathroom (brass and white). Tern ran a shower while, in front of the mirror, I unpeeled the bandages from my neck. The skin was very red, but hadn't puckered, and I supposed that was a good sign.

'Tern, you were brave to stand up to the Emperor.'

She wriggled out of her dress. 'I can hardly believe I did. It was feeling the Circle break. He didn't seem to care about Sirocco and he doesn't care about you … You'll never take Swallow alive, you know.'

'I know.'

She stepped into the shower and her long hair ran with water, snaking above her little breasts. Streams ran down the curve of her back, poured off the tips of her olive-oiled feathers, and her rounded buttocks. 'Come in.'

'I don't have time. I have to go.'

'You never have time. You always have to go.'

'If you think I'm joining you in there, with these burns, you've another thing coming.'

'But I've only turned on the cold.'

'It's cold?'

'Yes.'

'All right.' I hissed through my teeth as the water hit my burns. Then it soothed them. Tern pressed herself to my body and lay her head on my chest. Her nipples pushed up like pink beads against my ribs, and water ran between them. I kissed her forehead, feeling my eyelashes brush over her floating locks. She turned her mouth to mine and we kissed: she pushed her tongue into my mouth, the water running over our faces.

She gasped a breath. 'Oh, I want you ...'

'Later ...'

Her hand went between my legs and held me. Rubbed me slowly and I grew hard in her hands. I walked her a step backwards, pressed her against the tiled wall and kissed her. My erect cock rubbed her belly.

'I never know what state you're going to be in, every time you come home.' She wiped water from her face, framed by ribands of hair – her penetrating eyes, the little sensitive defiance mixed with the love. I rested my head on her shoulder and let the water flow over us. Her tongue flicked my nipples, she took a handful of my feathers soaked back to the quills, and pulled gently like the wind.

I soaped her skin, enjoying my hands slipping over her slick waist and bottom, her luscious soft curves. She rubbed herself against my hard body in the foam, and we let the cool water cleanse us, until we couldn't contain ourselves any more and ran, drip-wet, up the last spiral steps and onto the bed.

She was cold, so I wrapped her in her furs, went down to lick her. She put her legs over my shoulders and rested her feet on my wings.

She was so wet ... She tried to pull me on top of her. 'I want you in me – Ah!'

'I'm in you, now ... does that feel good?'

'More!'

I sank the full length into her, gasped and paused. She pulled my buttocks, separating them, urged me deeper, then wrapped her legs around my backside and pressed in her heels.

I gave her long strokes, almost pulling out each time, then pumped deep. I know her body so well, I can give her fantastic pleasure, keep her on the edge for hours, or make her come quickly with thrusts and words in the right place.

'I'll put armour on my arms,' I said. 'Hard cold steel, soft warm skin. I'll let you lick the edges.'

'And on your chest.'

'Pressing you down. I'll press you down with my armour.'

'Bite my throat ... Ah, yes, there ... I want you to come. Come inside me ... I want you to come. I want your come inside me. Fuck me, come on!'

While she was orgasming under me she cried out and I pumped hard and came into her hot wetness, thrust after thrust, there was so much, and I took her hard and emptied myself. I moved in and out more slickly and stopped.

I rested my face between her breasts. 'Litanee.'

'Right. Don't go.'

'Kitten, I've got to go.'

I left her lying on the bed, and she began to tell me about Wrought as I dried my wings and brushed them, then I threw on some clothes and swigged a phial. What to take to Litanee? Just my wits, my drugs, and my sword.

'Tern, do you know I describe your voice like cocoa?'

'Cocoa …?'

'A bowl of cocoa, like at the Front for breakfast.'

'Mmm.'

'Sweet and chocolately. Like you.' I reconfigured my sword belt into a back harness, buckled it on with the scabbard between my wings. 'I might not be able to have children, but I was a good father to Cyan, wasn't I?'

'Yes, Jant. You were.'

'Briefly.'

I glanced out of the window.

CHAPTER 38

Beyond the gleaming curve of the river there were hedges and flooded fields, black cattle on the water meadows. Something the size of a bull scurried fast across the field. An Insect!

Russet-brown, long legs jointed above its body. It *was* an Insect. Or was I seeing things?

It ran beyond my field of view and I leant out. Yes, an Insect running really fast, and stampeding the cattle into a herd before it. It lunged at the last of them, pincer mandibles bit into hide, and with two quick motions it severed a cow's head and struck at the next.

'Tern!' I yelled. 'There's a bug out there!'

She appeared beside me and at the same time five more Insects tore into view. They tangled into the herd, which pounded away across the meadow. The Insects darted after them and brought down cow after cow until they'd slaughtered them all, then hurtled off, splashing the shallow water overlying the grass. Only then did I notice two herdsmen fleeing. The Insect in the lead grabbed the last man. Its main jaws closed around his waist. He punched the chitin, but it lifted him off his feet and snipped him in half.

Another seized the second man by the shin and dragged him through the standing water, until its jaws sheared through his leg. Blood sprayed up, the Insect ran on, then realised it had dropped its screaming prey. It turned and jumped on his chest with two sharp foreclaws, breaking his ribs. The Insect clutched, cut off the man's head with a single bite, and all five bugs swivelled their antennae, turned and charged in the direction of Demesne town.

All this happened in an instant. I already had my foot on the sill and pulled myself through the window. Half-out, with my hand on my hilt, I said, 'I'll chase them.'

She nodded, horrified.

I spread my wings, jumped, and flew up along the curtain wall, its stone streaming past. I crested the crenellations, above the Skein

Gate, and saw the northern demesne spread out beneath me. Insects were everywhere! How many? Thirty? Forty? Running amok in great excitement, some had slaughtered the fishermen fleeing the bank and were pulling them to shreds. Some, on the far side of the river, were dashing over lines of strawberry plants. The girls who'd been picking strawberries were sprinting for their lives, but Insects grabbed them, one by one, and gashed their stomachs open.

I can save the last girl. I dropped towards her, saw an Insect bearing down on her, mandibles gaping. I couldn't reach her fast enough – it smashed her to the ground. She shoved her basket into its whirling maxillae, turned on one side to crawl, and the Insect shredded the basket, then ripped out her throat.

Her determined expression burnt on my memory. I leant on my right wing, wheeled so tightly the curtain wall slipped into the sky. The Throne Room's North Façade filled my field of vision, like flying into a cliff. I beat hard and swooped up in front of it: long lines of carving raced down past me – the gargoyles topping the wall, then the thinning pinnacles with drooping feathers, and the finials atop each one. From a frieze before me, to spikes below – I was over.

I cupped my wings half-closed and plunged across the cloister towards the balcony where we'd stood with San. I skidded vertically down the air alongside the Throne Room wall, the balcony no bigger than a fingernail, then a matchbox, then I saw the balustrade rail and backed frantically – wings splayed against the airflow so extreme it fingered out all my feathers and popped up the thumb feather.

I whammed onto the balustrade, jumped off it, into the tower, down the staircase, threw wide the door at the bottom, and into the Throne Room.

All the archers on the galleries drew on me in surprise before they recognised me. I halted in front of San, my plumes spread everywhere. 'My lord! There are Insects outside!'

'Here?' said the Emperor.

'In the demesne!'

San left the throne and paced past me. The gypsies had gone and the benches were empty; he must've finished questioning them. I sketched what I'd seen and his brows met in a scowl. 'A breach from the Shift?'

'I don't know!'

'On all sides?' He strode down the aisle. 'I knew they'd break through in more places, one day, but I hoped it wouldn't be here.'

'I'll rally us all!' I said.

'Yes, Comet. Send everyone out! Fly and see where they're coming from! Any tunnels or bridges.'

As we left the Throne Room I turned and beckoned half the Imperial Fyrd bowmen. They clattered down the twin staircases and followed behind us as we strode across the Starglass Quadrangle, behind Simurgh at the foot of all the buttresses, across the lawn and into the southern Dace Gate tower. The dim, stone staircase made me blink. San ascended the cold spiral, gathering Imperial Fyrd out of the guard-rooms at every storey, and onto the tower top.

The view was carnage. People, screaming, were running towards us from all directions, over the moat bridge, disappearing in through the gateway arch below us. On the grass between the moat and the river, bodies lay spread-eagled. Insects were rampaging back and forth, killing in a frenzy, then turning to chase down the next farmhand, labourer, angler, servant, stable boy. I saw ten with carapaces shining: they were slaughtering unarmed Zascai as if in their millions.

Ten more bugs were skirring from traveller to sightseer on the Eske side of the river. They leapt upon the last young man on the road, tore him to bloody strips, then began to converge on the scent of the town.

Our archers immediately started shooting at them, but they were beyond range. San said, 'Guards! Let everyone in, stop the Insects entering. Comet, you must not let them reach Demesne.'

I jumped up and over the parapet, flew with wings pointed, pro-pelled me to my fastest level flight over Harcourt, to the Southwest Tower and Tornado's rooms. Now I could see Insects outside the Yett Gate too, on Six Mile Avenue – people sprinting full pelt and Insects gaining on them!

I landed atop the tower, hurled open its trapdoor, jumped inside, onto the landing of the topmost floor, hurtled down the staircase to the middle floor where Tawny lives, hammered on the door.

Tornado answered. He was stripped to the waist, his shoulder bandaged, cupping a cardboard takeaway container in one hand.

'Insects!' I said. 'There are bugs outside! The Dace Gate, the Yett Gate! Get out and kill them!'

He stared at me, dropped the box, spilling fried rice and peas all over the floor, and dashed back into the room. I followed him in, and he grabbed his battle-axe. 'San's on Dace Gate south.'

'Then that's where I'm going,' he called over his shoulder as he vanished down the stairs.

The window was open. I climbed out and glided down, landed on the grass before Tornado emerged from the tower. The Six Mile Avenue men and women were pouring in through the Yett Gate, spreading out and looking for a refuge, running into the gymnasium, Herst and

Breckan. I grabbed one of the servants tearing past. 'Go to Carillon and ring the bell!'

He nodded and darted away.

I ran into the path of two more servants. '*You*, go to Hayl's room. *You*, to the Blacksmith's. I want them both riding to kill the Insects heading for town.'

Carillon's bell began to toll. I sped towards Simurgh, and the Swordsman and Armourer ran out of its loggia towards the Dace Gate. I headed them off. '*No!* Serein, go out the Yett Gate, people need you there.'

'But the Emperor's on the Dace Gate.'

'Tawny's got it covered.'

'I want San to see me—'

'Serein! Insects! Avenue! Go! ... Sleat, get a horse from Hobson's, kill the Insects in the meadows.'

'Yes, Comet.'

'Who's left? You! Is Rayne back yet?'

'Don't think so.'

'Shit. Run to the hospital, tell them to be ready, because I'm going to be bringing a lot of bodies in ... Snow!' The Sapper was leading a wedge of Imperial Fyrd with the odd servant mixed in. He was pointing towards Carillon. 'Where's the fire?'

'There's no fire. There're Insects everywhere outside the walls. Get Hobson's horses and ride up to Skein Gate, eliminate them, and if you find Frost, ask her too.'

'Okay.'

I nodded, turned away, and was about to take off when I saw Saker running towards me, out of the shade of the last trees in the avenue. He carried rifle in hand and bow on his shoulder. 'Gayle told me the place was crawling.'

'She's right.'

'Which tower's best for me?' He looked about.

I gestured hand and wing at the east wall. 'San's on Dace Gate south.'

We both set off running.

'You didn't leave him *alone*?'

'Of course not! With fyrd archers.'

'*They're* no marksmen! Jant, you kill the Insects in the sun's direction – you can look into the glare.'

I lengthened my stride, left him behind, and climbed into the air, flew over our main gate, and the Emperor standing on its tower top, looking down at Tornado. Tawny was among the Insects on the grass below. He was tearing them to bits. His axe in his right hand, he simply let an Insect run at him, grabbed it by the foreleg and twisted it headfirst into the ground. He stomped the back of its head, driving its mandibles into the soil, and continued twisting its leg up until the ball joint ruptured and the leg came off, with the same oozy crack as pulling apart a cooked lobster.

Then he raised its head by the edge of one mandible, and pulled it back till he rived it off. He dropped the head, hefted the pointed leg like a spear and ran at the next Insect, which jinked and charged at him. I landed, drew my sword from between my wings, dispatched one quickly, and when I next glanced at Tornado he'd pinned the Insect to the ground with the disembodied leg through its twitching abdomen, and he was holding its head up by one soggy palp.

This is Tornado with a shoulder injury and a dose of cat. One rushed at him from the side and he swung his axe against its two forelegs and cut them off. Thrown onto its four back legs the Insect reared. Tornado continued the swing up in an arc, severing head from thorax.

I glanced up to the tower and saw Saker at the battlements. He pulled his sunglasses from his pocket, shook out the arm and jammed them on. He flicked up the sight on his rifle, knelt and steadied the gun on a merlon, leant his cheek to it. I heard the bang. He hooted, exhilarated, and slid the ramrod out of its housing.

An Insect hurtled onto the Bridge of Size. I ran towards it – it could see directly behind and skittered round on the spot. I held my katana with both hands and waited as it careered at me.

You have to let it come at you like this …

Two pairs of jaws wide, antennae swept back, glassy-lacquer almond-shaped head, eyes and thorax reflected the intense sun. I waited till the last second, side-stepped, swept up my sword and lopped its head off.

Took to the air. On the lawn, a man and woman from the fishponds were running zigzag and trying to judge where the next one would dash from. I yelled, 'Go into the Castle!'

They ran over the bridge. Sword in hand I glided over an Insect closing on them. I was about to drop down before it when there was a crack! and it crumpled. Its head had been blown to shards. I glanced back to the Dace Gate tower and saw a puff of smoke rising from where Saker was kneeling.

I flew on further, found an Insect, and the same thing happened. Further still, chased down another and he shot that, too.

'You git!' I said. 'Give me a chance.'

There were no survivors on the Eske Road. Bodies, thirty or so, lay splayed in fans of blood. Just off the road I spotted three carts in a line. The carts were abandoned, no horses in the traces, and each carried a big cage, half-covered with a tarpaulin. They were some of the cage-wagons we use to convey Insects from the Front to our amphitheatres. And the people who ship Insects for us, are gypsies.

I landed at the first wagon. Sure enough, its sturdy, metal-barred hatch was open. Its ramp had been fully extended to the ground. I grasped the bars and climbed onto the cage roof, looked down inside. The steel floor was raked with scratches from Insect claws. The ruckedback tarpaulin had been dented into an impression where a gypsy had crouched as he raised the gate.

Using Insects as weapons!

I stood and counted five more carts on the other side of the road. They'd been carefully positioned to give the released bugs a view of prey – people on the riverbank and cattle on the meadow. Insects had bolted straight at them, allowing the fucking Roses to escape, away down the Eske Road on the horses that had drawn the carts.

I yelled in fury and kicked the cage door so hard it rebounded.

Another bang, and smoke from the tower top. A skittering below me, by the wheel. I turned to see an Insect that had been reaching up the wagon behind me, flexing in death throes. Saker had blown a hole the size of my palm in its head.

I stared at the battlements: I could hardly see him. Light flashed on his lens. I glanced at the dead Insect, then at the tower. He could have fucking hit me! I swept my wings in a beat, feeling my back muscles work, sprang into the air and flapped up, over Tornado and returned to the Dace Gate. The Emperor turned to face me as I landed beside him. Saker was kneeling at the parapet, sighting another shot.

I said, 'They're not coming from the Shift! Gypsies are releasing them!'

The Emperor's face hardened in understanding. From looking concerned, he was now furious.

Saker squeezed the trigger and his rifle cracked. He paused, cheek against the sideplate, watching through the sight, then glanced at me. 'I got it. Tornado's tackling the two in the stables.'

'That one on the cage wagon—'

'Was about to grab your leg.'

'You killed at the greatest distance I have ever seen,' said San.

'Eight hundred metres. ...Um. I've run out of cartridges.'

'What is that gun?'

'Cyan's gadget.'

The Emperor extended his hand, and Saker stood up and passed the rifle to him, letting his grasp slip off it, so San was left holding it. Saker took a couple of steps past us, staring down into the Castle towards Lisade.

Screams started from that direction. The Emperor and I hastened to join him at the inside parapet. Two Insects dashed out from behind Lisade. The lawn was crowded with men and women seeking shelter, banging on the doors of the barracks, Lisade and Simurgh. People had run into the buildings and shut the doors, and weren't letting them in. They fled from one to the next, begging, screaming.

The Insects bolted straight into them. Both latched onto girls hammering on the portals of Lisade – slew them with deep slashes. Everyone raced from them, towards the barracks.

Three more Insects charged from the rear of Lisade, following the foot of the curtain wall, plunged into the crowd. One started scraping at the library's windows, seeing the people inside. One pulled a woman down, she raised her hands to protect her face, but it cut off hands, forearms, head – as her boyfriend watched helplessly. It picked up the head and started masticating it. The boyfriend didn't see – he was running. He carried his young son over his shoulder, and as he reached the barracks he bumped the lad up onto a stone window frame. The Insect pursued him, grabbed his wings, dragged him to the grass and eviscerated him with a scrabble of claws. Antennae waving, it spun and returned for the boy, rode up on its back legs and plucked him from the ledge.

I jumped off the tower, landed behind it, raked my sword over the flexing sclerites of its abdomen, slitting them open, sliced through its neck and collapsed it, dead, but the boy already lay in halves. I ran to the next Insect – when I reached it an arrow point appeared between its compound eyes. I grabbed its antennae, felt their corrugations slip through my palm. It steepled its legs around me, raked down my jeans, and dropped dead at my feet.

I glanced up to Saker. He had already killed the other three Insects, and was rapidly shooting more pouring out from behind Lisade.

The crowd pressed into the barracks. It parted abruptly and Tornado ran through, axe in hand, glaring at the spiny, contracted carcasses, each with an arrow neatly protruding from the triangle of oculi eyes in their foreheads.

Now screams from beyond the Throne Room were telling me the fucking Roses were releasing Insects on the Carillon side, too. I yelled, 'Tawny! Go round behind Lisade and down the west side. There are bugs there!'

He boggled at me. 'Insects *inside*?'

'Go!'

'In the *Castle*?'

'Wake up, Tawny! Saker will clear this side!'

He tore off towards the screeches, hands and battle-axe pumping. I glanced up at the soaring walls and pinnacle-edged roof of the Throne Room. It'd be difficult to gain enough height to clear it, but the Emperor was watching. I sprinted from the crowd, jumped, and flapped hard. I pulled myself up before the buttresses, long stained glass windows, in jerks with each flap. My wings and back muscles burned. I felt their fibres tearing: just when I couldn't stand the pain any more and they started to seize, I made it to the edge of the roof. I clung to a pinnacle, stepped onto the lead, and ran up, across the roof, past two more lines of pinnacles, over the shallow crest and down the other side. I jumped off the edge and glided out over Carillon.

Bodies littered the grass, some curled around their opened bellies, most extended, lacking limbs or heads. Insects dashed about, maybe ten or fifteen. Tré Cloud was standing over one he'd just bisected with his 1978 Sword. The people who'd run in the Yett Gate were sprinting crazily between the servants' quarters and the gym, but Hayl emerged between them, on horseback with her lance.

Good. I'd seen at once where they were coming from: a line of cage wagons parked in front of the theatre and continuing beyond the corner of the North Façade. Most had their gates raised and Insects already released, gypsies racing away to the Skein Gate. Two women atop the rocking cages were opening their hatches, and Insects were thrashing under the rising gates, forcing antennae and foreclaws into the widening gap – then their heads shoved the hatches up – they ran free. Charged down the ramps, straight at me, but I was looking at the women on the cages. The one on the left was Connell Rose.

Connell picked a crossbow from the cage top and levelled it at me. I turned and pelted ahead of the frantic Insects, and took off. I accelerated powerfully, pulling down the air in short, sharp beats, braked hard in the air above Breckan, somersaulted and sped back down the length of Carillon going my fastest.

Connell was on the grass sprinting for the Skein Gate. I stooped like a falcon, half-folded wings pushing me faster. If I hit her at this speed I'll break her spine. Carillon was a blur. I focussed on her back. She raced faster but she had no chance. Her back came closer. Air shrieked over my wings, and she screamed.

At the last second I flared, brought my legs forward and slammed into her shoulder blades with my boot soles. She hurled forwards and landed full length, skidded on the grass. I used my momentum to balloon up over her, and touched down beyond her, bounded twice, and shawled my wings.

She lay prone. Was she dead?

I flapped and bounced towards her like a curious crow. She was breathing. I might have riven the ribs from her spine. I slipped my hand under her, to turn her over. Immediately she burst up and tried to run, but just collapsed with her arms clenched around her chest, groaning.

Above her right breast she had a new tattoo, of an exploding barrel, and on the left, an Insect poised like a mantis. They were bleeding where she'd grazed the grass. Her curly hair straggled, and her eyes blazed with hate. I said, 'How could you release Insects? Of course we'd catch you!'

'Bast'rd ...'

I drew my sword and rested its tip on the ground. She looked from the perfect blade, up to my eyes.

'Why do such a stupid thing?'

She wheezed, and coughed. I grabbed her biceps and pulled her to her feet. 'I'll put you in front of an Insect.'

'No!'

'Oh, you can speak?' I dragged her a few paces and she dug in her heels. 'Hey? Hayl! Save one for me!'

Connell wailed.

'Hayl! That bug! Back it up against the wall. Just ... keep it there ... this lass wants to talk to it.' I hauled her past the empty cage cart, with my swordtip at her sternum, and she screamed, 'Comet, no! Fuck! Not the Insect!'

'Oh, I'm "Comet" now, am I?'

'The noose, not a Insect!'

'If you don't want conversation at breakfast, tell me what the hell you were doing inviting it!'

'All right!'

I paused.

'Swallow. I love her. She loves me. She is our Muse, and I am her soldier.'

'Not good enough.' I started hauling again.

Connell yelled, 'She's my wife!' And yanked down the neck of her vest. There, over her heart, in the shape of love hearts linked together, her marriage to Swallow was writ for all to see.

'Oh ... That explains ... Such a great deal. Where is she?'

'Awia. We set a bomb in Tanager Palace to kill the Queen.'

'An artful response, I salute you. Last time I had the honour, you said Swallow doesn't care about the Queen. *Where is she?*'

Connell spat.

'How did you get in?'

'All men envy immortals! Some flea-ridden featherback on the Skein Gate let us in – because he hates you, too!'

I snarled in frustration. I pushed my sword and its point pierced her skin. She screeched, but I prodded her the other way, back towards my tower. I dragged her through the shadow of the theatre to the tower door, inside, and up the spiral stairs. She tugged and fought like mad. She was as strong as a man; I only subdued her by angling my blade at her throat.

I threw her into the Myrtle Room with such force she bounded off the windowsill and sank onto her knees, with her hands clasped round her ribs. She stared around, at the packing cases and my old skis. As a pendant, just below the notch of her throat, mirroring its shape, she wore a mother-of-pearl plectrum on a leather thong.

'Are you really Swallow's wife?' I said, wonderingly.

'Her music made me live ... I'll die for her.'

'I guess so!'

'We made love tenderly in a way you can never—'

'Great. Describe it at length later. I—' shook the sword at her. 'Have to go clean up your mess!'

'Fuck you, Jant, and fuck the Castle and fuck San!'

'Well, that's quite a lot of fucking; I'd be sore!'

'And fuck immortality, and fuck—'

'Where's Swallow?'

'I'm not telling you!'

'You're going to hang!'

'I'm not scared. Hate banishes fear! I hate your Eszai clique! I hate your contests that San wouldn't let her join. People could have voted on her music! We *can* judge the best music! So she could have been Eszai! But San will never put immortality to the vote ... The buck always has to stop with him. He controls it! Why? Why does he have to control it? He hurt her, so I hate him! I hate *you* – you rode straight past me, when I was starving! You can't intimidate me – I'll die before I say!'

I slammed the door, locked it, and stepped back on the landing, pocketing the key. All this shouting brought Tern down from my study. She paused on the last curve of the steps and raised her eyebrows.

'I've got Connell,' I said, and booted the door. Tern cheered and threw her arms around me. 'Hey, hey!' I said. 'Be careful of the blade.'

'I can—!'

'Sh. She'll be listening. She's Swallow's wife ... Her tattoos say so. Swallow's gay.'

'Oh ... Of course. I know who'll take some adjusting to that.'

'Swallow never liked him because *she loved me*!' Connell yelled from behind the door.

I kicked it. 'The Insects have killed a lot of people, and San's still on the tower.'

Tern released me and straightened her dress. 'The gypsy bitch won't escape. I'll see to it. I'll call some Imperial Fyrd and station them all around. She's mine now ... Do you hear me, gypsy bitch?'

'Fuck your collieries and fuck your forges, you slave-driver!'

'There's a long list of things she wants to fuck,' I said. 'It's very exhausting.'

'I've heard worse language in fashion shows.'

'Fuck your fashion shows!'

'And more imaginative,' I added.

'Oh, indubitably.' Tern kissed me.

'Take good care of her,' I said, and loped down the spiral stairs and out towards Breckan. Hayl, Tornado, and Tré Cloud had between them cleared this side of the Castle of Insects. Tré was laying the bodies of herdsmen, fruit pickers, fishermen, traders, travellers and tourists in a respectful line, in the shadow of the avenue trees. Hayl was riding around jabbing her lance in dead Insects and dragging them into a pile, and Tornado had gone to report to San.

I ran to the Dace Gate, seeing fewer bodies this side, and more Insects that Saker had exterminated. By the barracks one bug had run among the crowd, and left a tangled heap of bodies at the doorstep.

The Emperor was watching from the tower parapet, Saker on his left, Tornado on his right, and he was giving them orders. I ran into the staircase portal, round and round up inside, and emerged into the sunlight to see them turning to me. 'My lord, we've cleared all the Insects, and Hayl eliminated the ones closing on the town. Connell released these by the Skein Gate, but I caught her ... I locked her in the Myrtle Room.'

'What did she say, Comet?'

'That she's following Swallow's plan.'

'And Swallow is where?'

'She won't tell me.'

The Emperor glared. 'Insects in the very Castle!'

'I know, my lord.'

'How did the Litanee get in?'

'The guard on the Skein Gate let them through – spurred by the mortals' usual resentment of our lifespan ... I think the gypsies are the only people who don't envy us.'

'They just detest us,' said Tornado.

I angled my head a little, and looked across the low sunlight so my eyes reflected gold, and watched the Emperor. He said, 'Bring Connell to the Throne Room. She will talk to me.' He strode away, down the steps with Tornado following him, axe in hand, his bandages and jeans clotted with yellow gunge. San approached the people trying to identify the bodies outside Harcourt, and talked with them for some time. They removed their hats in respectful gestures, but he wouldn't let them kneel. Then he walked to the Zascai squatting by the corpses in the shade of the avenue trees, spoke with them, then those at the Yett Gate, and only then did I see him enter the Throne Room with Tornado as his bodyguard.

Saker sat on the inside parapet and fiddled with the sights on his rifle. Far off down the Eske Road, tiny in the distance, my black coach-and-six was racing in, with Halliwell hunched like a hefty rat on the driver's seat. I said, 'Rayne's coming.'

'There isn't a cloud in the sky ...'

'Saker?'

'This thing needs a sun filter ...'

'Hello, Saker? Look, down there; Ella's coming back.'

He jumped up and paced to the battlements. 'In that mail coach? I don't want her to see me! ...I mean, I'm not here!'

'You're the last thing on her mind.'

'Ha, Jant ... I broke her heart.' He watched the carriage clipping along. 'Is she safe out there? Are there Insects?'

'I think we got them all.'

'There could be a bomb.'

'There's no bomb in my Black Coach!'

'But under the bridge. Or in the road.'

'How could there be a bomb in the road?'

'They could have buried it!'

I leant over the battlements and spread my wings. At that distance the coach looked graceful; it glided along like a cannon ball ahead of its cloud of dust. 'We're getting paranoid, and that's what Swallow wants.'

'No harm must ever come to Rayne.'

'Apart from your breaking her heart?'

He huffed, swung the rifle butt to his shoulder and spied through its telescope at the road ahead. 'I'll take Connell to the Throne Room.'

'No! It's very important you go nowhere near Connell.'

'Why not?'

'She'll ... wind you up.'

'She's just a gypsy.'

'Yes, you keep saying that. "Just a gypsy". Strange they've sent us reeling harder than the Insects have managed in a thousand years.' I looked down at the people claiming their dead, and bodies that hadn't been identified, including the little boy, being stretchered to the hospital. 'Insects *inside* the Castle …'

'Well, it's a desperate ploy,' said Saker to the sideplate of his rifle. 'Swallow would have known we'd finish them swiftly.'

'She killed about seventy Zascai.'

'The bloodlust of a psychopath. She'd know Insects would slay innocent civilians, but have no chance whatsoever of hurting an Eszai.'

'Shit …' I said.

He lowered his rifle and looked at me.

'It's a distraction!' I said.

'From what?'

'I don't know! How do you distract Eszai? With Insects! There's no better way!'

My skin chilled. My feathers stood on end. We stared at the tiny figures below, some crouching, some struggling with stretchers. They were peaceful with distance, between our sublime buildings – and the grass, Harcourt Barracks, marble Lisade and my white telegraph grew ominous. A sense of dread weighed colder until the people and the Throne Room, hospital and Simurgh Bridge stopped being real, just flat artefacts of the interplay of light and shade. It was like sliding into withdrawal.

'I need a fix,' I said.

'No you don't, Jant; think.'

'I do … I do … I need a shot. Something horrible's going to happen. We've been acting as she expected us to act … So we'll be right where she wants us to be!'

Saker squinted at Rayne's coach racing in. Infuriated with him, I followed his glance and everything clicked. 'She's been drawing us here! Blowing up our homes! So we return and I recall everyone … Then releasing bugs right on the Berm Lawns, so we ride around like fools showing off!'

'There are no bombs here,' said Saker.

'The gypsies fled! Connell didn't want to be locked in! Swallow's been *herding* us – we've got to do the opposite!' I jumped on the parapet and waved at the coach to stop, but they were kilometres away and plunged on regardless. I yelled in frustration. 'Did any Rose slip in behind our backs?'

'They had no time to lay powder.'

'No, but they could set fuse!'

'San had the Castle searched!'

'The magazine?'

'Of course!'

'The barracks? Armoury?'

'Yes!'

'Cellars of Breckan? Simurgh?'

'Obviously!'

'What is she planning?' I hesitated. Slowly I raised my eyes to the tapering spire of the Throne Room. 'That's what she wants,' I said softly. 'But she can't get in ...'

Saker's expression fell to dismay. A glassiness spread across his face, eyes unfocussed, then screwed up in guilt. 'Oh yes, she can!' He belted to the staircase and down it, and a few seconds later out onto the lawn below. He turned, arms and rifle raised, and shouted up, 'Because of the underground lake!'

He whipped round and sprinted towards the Throne Room. I jumped off the tower, glided down, landed next to him, and ran beside as we hurtled through the gap back of Simurgh and across the quad.

'If you charge in the Throne Room armed to the teeth they'll shoot you!' I yelled.

'I know! I trained them!'

We dashed up the steps into the portal. I waved my arms wide and the guards uncrossed their halberds. We raced past their terrified faces, across the narthex and into the Throne Room. Immediately all the archers on the gallery drew on Saker. We heard the creak as fifty longbows took tension simultaneously. He held up his hands, a gesture countervailed by the rifle in one of them, but he didn't break pace and they tracked him halfway down the aisle until the Emperor stood from the throne and bellowed, 'Lower your bows!'

Tornado was standing beside the throne, his hands resting on the butt of his axe and its double head on the carpet between his feet. He watched us, but said nothing. We halted before San, and Saker cut in straight away, 'The cistern! Did you check it?'

'Of course,' the Emperor said.

His calm voice didn't soothe Saker. 'How long ago?'

'Two days.'

'No ... No ... We must go down there now.'

'What's *wrong* with you?' I said.

He shook his head and gulped. 'It's the "Hall of Faces".'

'What?' I said. 'The cistern of Pentadrica Palace?'

San spoke evenly, 'Pentadrica Palace is long gone. The cistern is the

Castle's water supply. I kept it so we could withstand a siege. What of it?'

Saker hunched his shoulders and wrapped his arms around his waist, so the rifle's muzzle protruded from behind his back. He looked faint. 'Swallow will be down there. She could have brought powder barrels on the barges ... via Awndyn ... Oh, god, we saw the barges leaving Awndyn! They come up the river, to provision the kitchens ... on the river spur where it feeds into the moat – there's a way into the cistern through the arch ... the little archway by the postern gate.'

'Swallow won't know that,' I said.

'Yes, she does ... Because I showed her.'

The Emperor passed us, striding down the steps. He took a key from his coat's inside pocket and beckoned us. Saker lagged for a second, then followed me, and Tornado behind.

The Emperor went to the door of his private room. It was a plain door, into part of Alyss' palace, and no one but San had been inside since the day Alyss left for Lazulai.

Behind him, I hissed at Saker, 'You *showed* her? Are you *insane*?'

'It was twenty-five years ago ... when she first came to petition for a place. I—'

'What did you do, climb down a well?'

'No. It's not like that. It's beautiful ... I ... I gilded a boat ... and filled it with orange blossom. I hung it with lanterns, set a harp at the bow. I thought she'd love it. We stooped, to slide through the arch, then ...'

'You're warped, you know that?'

'It's the only gesture I ever made she truly loved.'

'How come I never noticed you were floating around in a gold boat?'

'Jant, you were dying of drug abuse in the spring of twenty-fifteen.'

'Belt up!' said Tornado. He was staring over our heads as the Emperor unlocked the door. San's hand turned the key, pushed it ajar, and beckoned us through. But trepidation stopped us, and we looked at each other. In sixteen centuries nobody had seen what lay inside. No Eszai, no servants, no one. We based our lives around the fact that the Emperor emerged at six every single morning and returned through the door to nowhere, at midnight, when the Castle's clocks began to chime.

We all had theories. I declared the door led to a sumptuous Shift world filled with sizzling women and delicious food. And, on my bleaker days, I say the Emperor steps through the door into nothingness, a profound space without end, only the faintest stars glimmering in the distance. Saker says it's the Pentadrican royal bedchamber, untouched since the year 411, and Tornado believes it's the very site where god left the earth.

I bit my lip and stepped inside. It was a small room with a futon bed on the floor. The bed had a simple pillow and one sheet. The walls were just plaster, painted white, and somewhat greyed with age. It smelt faintly of cotton, nothing else, and there were two plain doors, one in the left wall and one in the right.

'Is this all?' I said.

'Yes,' said the Emperor.

Saker and Tornado crowded in behind me, but I couldn't shuffle forward because the bed was at my feet. We stood pressed together while the Emperor unlocked the bare door in the left wall, with the same key. He opened it, and behind was only blackness. Tornado and I gazed at the forbidding, pitch-dark rectangle, while Saker stared at the Emperor's bed on the tatami-matting floor.

San said, 'There's a lamp inside.'

Saker shook himself. He walked in, and found a shutter lantern in a recess. He flicked Fulmer's lighter and the flame flared in his cupped palm. He opened the hatch, lit the wick, and the lengthening flame scooped his face into hollows. He altered his grip on the handle of the lamp and held it out – illuminated monumental granite steps curving down into darkness.

'At the water's edge a boat hangs from the wall,' said San.

'My lord, I *will* stop Swallow Awndyn.'

The Emperor nodded and drew back. He left the room, to return to the throne, with Tornado accompanying him. Saker and I were alone at the top of the stairs leading into the void. It was like standing high in the night air.

'Twenty metres down,' I said.

'How do you know?'

'I saw Tré's son fishing, through the kitchen floor.'

'Ah … Yes … This goes under the kitchens, all the way to the moat.' He started down the steps and I pursued, to keep within the sphere of light. On our left the stones slipped by: gigantic, smoothly-chiselled to fit together so ingeniously you couldn't slip a knife blade between them.

'It's the foundations of the east wall,' I whispered.

Saker swung out his arm and the lamplight revealed how the other edge of the staircase dropped like a cliff, and faded. I couldn't see the bottom. The action made his shadow starve and arc up the wall behind us, bristling with spines from quiver, bow and rifle on their crossed straps. The sense of an enormous space around us pressed our skin and our feet felt leaden as we descended carefully into a chamber so vast the lamplight couldn't penetrate it. I sensed an immense space with the faintest air currents circulating; I smelt stone, and water, like a cavern pool, and heard indistinct drips in the distance, but they gave me no idea how far the chamber stretched: I couldn't grasp the scale.

I opened my wings as if to brush the surrounding walls, but the cistern scorned me. I could fly in it, I was sure, but I had no means of gauging how many wing beats would cross it, no way of seeing any obstacles – I couldn't even glimpse the ceiling.

'It makes me feel small,' Saker whispered.

'Evocative. You should be a poet.'

'It extends to the inner side of the Postern Gate. Just within the curtain wall.'

The groundspace of a quarter of the Castle seemed much vaster here beneath, with no walls to block the view or lend it proportion. But I assured myself that the blackness reaching to infinity was just an illusion. 'So are we still under the Throne Room?'

'Probably that end's roughly under the throne itself.'

'Uh-huh.'

'San sleeps on the floor,' he added, acerbically.

'What did you expect?'

'I don't know ... riches.'

'He doesn't need riches.'

'The room has nothing to occupy him.'

'We're his chess pieces, and the world's his board.'

Saker nodded. 'Then Swallow has us in check ... One sparse meal a day, and he sleeps on the floor. For sixteen hundred years. What sort of life is that?'

'The most finely-honed.'

'*You* said San's room was a gateway to the Shift.'

'So it might be. All he needs is a place to meditate.'

The staircase made a hairpin bend, and we descended. At last he stepped onto a paved floor, and turned to illuminate the last step for me. The edge of water glimmered at our feet, as if it was a beach with the tide creeping in. Saker raised his wing to shield the lamp. Its halo slipped over the inky water that lay motionless, not so much as a ripple. Its surface was like a sheet of metal; it could be fathomless. But at the edge of the lamplight, where it illumined layers of water into the green depths, a white carp curved and swam away from the light.

'How did you know about this?'

He raised a hand before his mouth to whisper. 'After the Games, we explored the Castle. Carillon, the kitchens, the moat weren't built then. It was fed by an aqueduct from the river.'

'But you don't remember it being built?'

He smiled faintly. 'This is five hundred years older than I am.'

He gave me the lantern and went to the wall of solid bedrock. Hanging on it was a slender kayak, with a paddle propped against its hull. He lifted it off the hook and set it on the water with the merest ripple. He placed the lantern on its middle plank and laid his weapons down, then stepped into the stern and held the bank with the paddle blade. I folded myself onto the bow seat.

'I used to lay in my boat down here,' he said. 'Whenever I needed to think. When I needed to disappear.' With a quick motion he pulled the paddle, and we were away.

The paddle lifted; water ran from it like liquid glass, swirling into the ripples. Gold bubbles formed and popped without sound. The space around us was completely black; I stared into it until my eyes stung. Then, out of the darkness, a column loomed. It was rooted in the water and stretched up; following it I at last made out the ceiling. The column, topped with ornate latticework, supported a vaulting high above, as pristine as the day it was carved. Behind it was another, with scrolls, and another, which wasn't a column at all but a giant marble arm.

They seemed to be evenly-spaced; the rows beyond faded into darkness. Their white grew from the gloom as we approached, and they were blanched clean to half their height, where the water rises.

Here was one with a surface carved to resemble bark. We passed another, with serried scales. The next was upside-down, and our bow wave rippled around its half-submerged capitol of leaves. Some columns were wedged atop blocks of masonry to increase their height, and they were haphazard fragments of gigantic buildings, delicately-carved cornices, jigsaw sections of friezes with inscriptions running their length, sometimes lodged vertically or upside-down, in a language I didn't know. And if I didn't know it, it was pre-Pentadrican ... early Pentadrican ... no word of it had been spoken for two millennia.

'Where are they from?' I whispered.

'No one knows.'

'But they're masterpieces ... and they're just supporting the ceiling.'

'Like Eszai and the Empire.'

'The Pentadricans used pieces of ... older ruins? Made by who?'

He shrugged.

We passed a burnt column with a cracked and reddened surface. It had been plucked from a building destroyed in an inferno. Maybe, millennia ago, a family had watched crying; maybe silent crowds gathered in a public square seeing smoke billow between the columns. Now it stood above pure water, with only the scent of our lamp oil.

'But ... they must have been made before god left.'

'Stop asking what no one knows.'

'You showed Swallow.'

'She wrote "The Hall of Faces".'

It was one of her most famous concertos, I've often heard it, shelving into the low and tingling trepidation of chill water and deep time. Strings plucked slowly dripping in the unseen distance, and gradually, gradually, crept up the crescendo of tympani, and you stood on the brink of two thousand years. How many lifetimes, and what were they *doing* back then, before god left the world? The churn rolled your stomach like the slow approach of a thunderstorm, and then came the refrain, and it was the repeated dipping of the paddle, water peeling off the keel, and Swallow's rejection of love, because love will not gain you the Circle.

We passed a column placed on a gigantic woman's face, taller than I am, with wild eyes the span of my hand. Water slipped into the curls of her stone locks and her stretched-open mouth, reflected in ripples from teeth and tongue.

'Swallow said she was singing.'

'No. She's screaming.'

Then there was a gargantuan male face. I saw the stippled surface where it had once joined a building, perhaps an entire body in high relief, or lone faces screeching above a gateway.

'No trace of Awians,' said Saker. 'Some human civilisation ... The Pentadricans used any ruin they could lay their hands on. Any massive stone.'

'Before the Insects came.'

'When they had time to carve ... She'd have fitted in well back then. Shh ... We're nearing the centre.'

We passed in silence an arm used as a column. Its muscles bulged seemingly in the effort of supporting the vaults. Maybe theirs was the age of the Emperor. Was he from the time of the sculptors? Did he also come here in his boat, to be with them?

We skimmed through a forest of columns from the same edifice, then huge statues; a naked man's body with a powerful torso and gracious face. He was wingless and so was the next; his partner a willowy woman dancing, drapes flowing out around her. She'd lost her arms so long ago that the broken surface was smooth and brown.

Saker quickly pressed a lever on the lantern and its lens cap irised shut. Our light winked out. Darkness pounced back. I gasped a breath then felt his hand on my shoulder. He leant to my ear and his breath was hot – he smelt of gunpowder. 'Our prow, one o'clock. Do you see?'

A speck of light danced ahead. I nodded.

'Keep your fingers inside. Don't look at her lamp, your eyes will glow.'

'How can you see?'

'I can't … I know my way around the Castle in the dark.'

We darted swiftly between the statues. I felt cool air pass my face, heard the slick as he dipped his paddle and smelt the broken water but saw nothing. Velvet blackness beat the surface of my eyes.

The speck grew. In the dome of light I made out a figure, hastily crossing a platform, and behind it a freestanding wall of wood, like the side of a ship. Then I realised the light came from several lanterns on a free-floating platform of tied-together punts. That the corrugated wall was a charge of gunpowder barrels that stretched up into the vaulted ceiling. The figure returned into the pool of light, a stocky woman in a short green dress.

Saker jammed in the paddle and halted so abruptly I was thrown forward. He stirred it and reversed us into the shadow of a column. 'It's *her*.'

'Yes.'

'We're near the west wall. Under the kitchens.'

I glanced up as if to see the chink of light where the floor tile was missing, and Gabby's fishing line slanting into the water. Blue specks prickled in my vision, and of course I saw nothing.

Swallow walked across her stage, past her loaded crossbow standing on its two props. She walked without her stick, but limped. She bent down, the lantern light illuminated her wide, freckled face and copper hair. She started pulling some brown paper fuse from a big reel. She was laying slow match … and singing quietly to herself.

Soundlessly, Saker picked up his bow and slid an arrow out of his quiver.

Swallow cut the length of fuse, taped it expertly to the cable sprouting from the barrels, and reeled out another length.

Saker bent his bow.

Swallow started. 'Who's there?' She picked up her lantern and its pool of light swung towards us. Suddenly we were bathed in light: the canoe, the pillar base, Saker beside me holding his bow at full span with the shining arrowhead aimed at her.

She cried out, glanced to her crossbow and then a smile came over her face. She began to sing. She flowed into an eerie aria and began to reverberate the air. It was transcendent, melancholy, supremely powerful, as if her wisdom distilled from all her terrible experiences could tumble a fortress before it like tinder. Tears sprang to my eyes. I felt as if she was reaching into my chest and stroking my heart; surely such talent should be made immortal and I cried for its inevitable loss. I cried for our inexorable death, for mine, and yours, and I hated her, but I yearned for more. And that was nothing compared to the effect she had on Saker.

He wavered. His jaw tensed, and I thought he would loose his arrow. Then tears flowed down his cheeks. He lowered the bow. He placed it on his lap with the arrow at string and wiped the tears from his face, hunched as if he couldn't bear to look at her, as if his bow was too heavy to lift. I tried to pull it from him but he held it tightly. Swallow smiled at us struggling, raised her voice and sang till she rang the air.

'Shoot her!'

'No ...'

'Shoot her, *Archer*!'

'... Can't.'

'Then let me!'

Swallow picked up the linstock around which her taper sparked. 'Go now,' she declared, in a clear voice. 'Do not look back.'

He seized the paddle. With a quick pull he whisked the canoe away from the column, but as it tilted, I jumped out, beat my wings and flew onto the platform, and drew my sword. Saker in the canoe flashed into the darkness.

I leapt forward to stab Swallow, but she crouched down, hovered her taper over the end of the quick fuse. Saker's canoe slipped swiftly before an arch of daylight no bigger than my thumbnail. When he reached it I saw the low archway was three times wider than the boat. He ducked down, shot through it and was gone.

Swallow looked up at me. 'So music *is* mightier than the bow ...'

'Swallow ...'

'Back off! More! If you come a step closer, I'll light this!'

'All right!'

She tapped the taper over the fuse like a conductor's baton.

I said, 'Swallow ... please ... give me it.'

Loathing mangled her face. 'No! I said not to look back! But you *always* look back, don't you? It's your worst goddamn habit, Jant Shira. Well, here you are, at my last performance. A solo performance!' She bent to light the fuse.

'No!'

'I can't take Saker with me, but I will take you!'

'Please, Swallow! He showed you this place out of love.'

'Love! Love, you say? Well, what a fucking fool! He brought me here in a skiff full of flowers. At first I thought it'd be the usual Lightning boreathon but – yes, yes – you must admit, it turned out quite interesting … The acoustics are superb.' She struck a note, and the chamber resounded.

Then she gradually stood up, and gestured with the linstock to the fuse roll on its stand. 'The slow match would've given me time to walk out, but … never mind.'

'You still can.'

'No.' She rubbed her strong face, then the little feathers on the membrane of one auburn wing, then fixed me with her piercing green eyes. 'I'll finish my act. In this, the perfect auditorium. I wish I could fill it with every Eszai. Every one of you fuckers for my last encore. But sadly, I only have you.' She dipped the taper to the fuse.

'Don't! No! No! Please … please, Swallow … It doesn't have to be this way.'

'It does … It does. San never came to his senses. You don't *know*. All you Eszai are so self-absorbed, none of you have any idea.'

'What do you mean?'

'I mean I have cancer.'

'Oh.'

She touched her left breast. 'San could have stopped time for me and prevented it developing. I could have lived forever with the tumour at an early stage. I could have survived! But no, the bastard won't listen. The Circle is only for *warriors*, he says. Warriors! No warrior's worth saving while a musician lives. And my cancer's getting worse. Spreading. Soon the music will end. And I see you for what you really are. I hate you for it – *I hate you all!*'

'I can take you to the Shift,' I said. 'You can live forever there. Painlessly – you can make music, for eternity – the inhabitants of Epsilon will love you.'

'Ah. The afterlife you peddle. Has it made you rich …? Once, maybe, but it's too late for that, Jant. All I want is to kill San.'

She raised her lantern high and the shadows of the statues tilted over the water. For an instant the ceiling reflected in the still pool. 'Look at it! Lightning said it was a song in stone. How right he was …'

She illuminated the immense stack of barrels. There must be three hundred of them – fifteen tonnes. Fuses were taped to their sides, in careful lines. They'd blow the ceiling up, the columns out, and the whole northwest quarter of the Castle would collapse into this space.

Her mother-of-pearl guitar leant against the kegs. Fragments of it would be the first to pierce our bodies. The thick fuse at her feet ran a few metres and split into two, then four, eight, sixteen, and ran into the barrels at the base of the stack. I couldn't reach them before Swallow could drop her taper and light them. And the taper was sparking too slowly, and wrapped around the wand, was too long for me to keep her talking until it burnt out.

'I'll sing Gerygone, like I did just now. The aria I sang when I first saw Lightning. He was leaning out of the box, and he dropped his programme fluttering down to the limelights. So I turned and sang to him. Love at first sight, on his part, but not as beautiful as this ... It's my instrument, Jant, don't you see? The sound of my rage. More colossal tympani than I could ever score. The most fortississimo drum to play ... in the history of the world ...'

I leapt to slash her again and she crouched to the fuse end. 'Back off, you cunt! Back off, I mean it!'

'Please!'

'I hate you! I hate you all! I won't fade out quietly; that's what the Emperor wants! I'll kill him with his own fucking toy, the powder I replaced with sand from Awndyn beach. How fast can you run?'

'Not fast enough.'

'Good.' She looked to the fuse.

'Connell!' I cried desperately.

What about Connell?

'Connell – your wife,' I said, trying to speak slowly and calmly. 'Is locked in the Northwest Tower.' I pointed in that direction. 'If you detonate your bomb, it will collapse the tower and kill her.'

Surprise crossed Swallow's face, but hatred overswarmed it. I said, 'Do you remember your marriage dance? Did they throw rose petals over you? Did you spin arm in arm, in the ring of gypsies?'

She glanced to the north wall and set her expression. 'She was prepared to die for me.'

'She—'

'Shut up!'

'Loves you.'

'Oh, I know. Yes, we married at the festival, but so what? The drive to be immortal purges love.'

'The gypsies—'

'Do the real work of the Empire! It sits on their shoulders, not yours! Can you even understand I found peace there? In her wagon, in the woods ... I found a place at last where it was natural to write, to perform, where my music was appreciated and not squeezed dry. Appreciated by "the raggle-taggle gypsies, oh", and not by your stupid fucking Circle.

Not through San's stupid fucking contests. By Connell, whose beauty wasn't rotted by the Circle's envy. The gypsies are spontaneous, they're free, they don't strive till they're drained dry. They aren't spent and thrown aside, like San does with you. I lived with her, living music every day ... There was no longer any need to write it down.'

'Don't kill her.'

'Oh, Jant, stop it! I'm not giving Saker chance to save San. Connell dies. We all die! ...Yes, I loved her ...because she said what she meant, not the weasly bullshit you Eszai spout, the craven crap you think you ought to say. She had nothing to lose.'

Swallow contemplated her taper. '...And I have nothing to lose. Coda. At last. I will not cry. The world is crying for me.'

In the distance she had distinguished, with her conductor's hearing, water drops tinkling into the lake. 'I'm a cripple. I can't run. But better this, than a slow death from cancer.'

'No!'

'Oh, yes! As I'll take you, too! The very Castle walls say, "we're in, and you're out". They must fall.' She nodded, contemplating the truth of it, and licked her lips cracked by gunpowder. 'Doesn't it taste bitter?'

She looked into my eyes. Her green eyes brimmed, and tears ran down her freckled cheeks. 'Here's my Challenge.'

And she lit the fuse.

A white flare raced along it. I jumped to stomp it out, but it had already reached the connection, split into two flames, and tore to opposite ends of the platform. They split again: four, eight, sixteen.

I dropped my sword and sped for the daylight. The opening, too far! I *ran*. I pounded along the prows of the punts. Somehow I pushed harder, faster, legs and arms pumping, I opened my wings.

Behind me, Swallow began to sing. She sang out her heart, resounding in the darkness with the baton sparking in her hand – the flames behind her split sixteen; thirty-two.

I ran faster still, anticipating the shockwave throwing me forward, the fireball overtaking me. Come on! Faster! Daylight ahead, the end of the platform, and before me just water. I jumped, smacked my wings on the punts, on the columns, four, five beats, battered the water.

I pulled my wings in and cannoned through the arch, and beat straight up. My field of vision was the blue air, then a tremendous force thumped the breath out of me – threw me high into the sky. I passed out, for seconds, and caught myself falling. Below me, spinning, the curtain wall. A solid jet of flame spurted out of the hole in the wall – the archway erupted – fire spewed out ten metres wide. Blocks were breaking from the wall and shooting across the moat, hitting the bank and bouncing. The whole wall cracked and blew out.

Then silence. I fought for breath. This was no silence. A raging storm of noise is going on. I was deaf. My head was ringing. I steadied my flight; the whole Castle swung into view below. The roof of the Throne Room began to buckle. The roof of Carillon was starting to dent, the kitchen and dining hall tilting into themselves. The great expanse of the Throne Room roof creased like paper, its west wall pinnacles disappeared straight down in clouds of stone dust – the east wall pinnacles began to fall outwards. Blooms of flame blew out every kitchen and hall window.

The Circle broke.

I cried out.

The Throne Room, the Carillon wing, Mare's Run, the dining hall and kitchens simultaneously sank down and disappeared into billowing, surging, clouds of smoke and dust. The immense spire dropped ten metres – then began to tilt towards me.

I dived and accelerated out of its way. It tilted more and more, to an angle you wouldn't believe possible, and then the coherence of the stone blocks started to yield. They stepped, like dominos for a second, dust spurting out between them. The spire bent at its base and then laid its seventy metre length into the swelling fumes and smoke, falling out of view. Pulverised stone billowed up, hiding everything, and the last I saw was the shining gold sunburst atop the spire fall into the clouds of dust.

An enormous rumble broke around me. I can hear it! I can hear it! Oh, god! It crescendoed louder than cannon as the buildings crumpled into the ground. Where the dining hall had been boiled solid clouds of brick-red dust.

The Circle hadn't re-formed.

I felt stripped naked. No safety net of the Circle, part of me ripped away. I tumbled, out of control. The dust cloud hurtled over my head, down behind me, spun over my head again. I was raw. The shockwave had blasted my body and every joint of my arms, legs and wings felt pulled out.

Where was Tern?

I skimmed the rising cloud, whipping it up around me. I had no strength to gain height. I fell through the surface and my next breath was cement particles and caustic smoke. Retching uncontrollably, I emerged to see the treetops of Six Mile Avenue way too close. People were running away from the Castle, up the road – they turned, aghast, to look at me.

I came down at full speed onto the branches, rolled to miss them, flapped frenetically, slowed only a fraction, then smashed into the grass arms out and propelled head over heels. My arms, collarbones, shoulders, jarred with agony. I balled-up on the damp grass, coughing and panting.

The Circle had stopped. I couldn't feel anyone. I couldn't feel Tern. The loneliness was overwhelming – time was passing – for all of us. The Emperor must be dead, squashed in the Throne Room, directly under the great spire's base, under thousands of tonnes of rock.

But where was Tern? Was she dead too?

My mind flashed back to Swallow, singing her loudest in a hall of statues when, from behind her, the blast lit them.

Hands tried to lift me. I was dimly aware of voices babbling, but all I could think of was Tern, flattened underground. I must find her, if I have to dig her out with my fingers.

'Comet?' said a voice.

'Tern!'

'Get out of my way!' It was Rayne's voice and I went limp with relief. I flapped my wings, shook everybody off, then I leant to one side and vomited. Faces crowded in, all strangers, wide-eyed servants and some Imperial Fyrd. They glanced up at the Castle, then tore away down the avenue, leaving me alone.

I saw Rayne on a Black Coach horse and, behind her, the dust cloud was fast approaching – over the grey tiled roofs of Breckan and Simurgh – they were pulverised to rafters with fallen masonry. They disappeared into the cloud – it rolled towards us and over the solid Yett Gate, then kept rolling in a rounded wave up the avenue, swallowing beech trees, and everyone was fleeing downhill towards Demesne. I jumped up, and ran from Rayne, *into* the smoke.

It was dense dust and infinitesimal fragments of marble and mortar, and scraps of cloth. It coated me, the gatehouse invisible, the trees vanishing into it on either side. My mind was full of the image of Tern bleeding under the masses of rubble. Stones were still falling, thumping into the grass around me. I coughed and reeled, clamoured over the drawbridge and into the dust-filled arch of the gatehouse, and passed out.

I fought back to consciousness in the hospital some time later.

CHAPTER 39

The Hospital

My first sensation was moistness, my skin all sticky. The ward was intensely hot. Then someone squeezed my hand, and I looked to the bedside, to see Tern. She had clasped her fingers into mine, and I melted in relief, brought her mortal hand to my lips and started kissing our interlocked knuckles, to assure myself she was real, that this was really happening. I burst into tears. 'I thought you were dead!'

'I thought you were.'

'The Circle stopped.'

'I know, I know!'

'It's night …?'

'No …'

The room was a hubbub, and extremely dim. People were just grey silhouettes: Eszai, all kinds of servants, some Imperial Fyrd and hospital staff. I couldn't hear over the loud buzz in my ears, and couldn't make them out.

Tern's hair was plastered with dust, her dress was solid with it, her legs and feet were bare, cut ragged and daubed with blood. Her hands were grazed; I could feel their heat against my palms. She'd sponged her face clean but the dust remained, smeared around her hairline. I was encased head to foot in it, too. I said, 'How did you get out?'

'Jant, shh! Rayne's …' She began crying. I reached my wing and pressed its fingers against her face and she looked at me gratefully.

'What happened?'

'… Everything collapsed. The noise … I was outside the Myrtle Room. The stairway jumped up, then – way down. I ran out. The bowmen did, some of them. Some of them … were behind me …'

'Yes?'

'I ran for the north wall. It took forever … Forever! When I reached it I squeezed against it … seemed right. I looked back and saw … oh god, Jant, I couldn't see anything. Just this dust cloud. This huge wave of *dust* coming at us.'

'Quiet!' Rayne called, from the front of the ward.

'Then what happened?'

'We ran but we couldn't run fast enough, and it rolled over us, and we couldn't see anything.' She coughed. 'I couldn't see the bowmen. I couldn't breathe. So I felt my way along to the Skein Gate. I ran through but the dust rolled with us, so we kept running. Aigret tower was blocks, the size of ... this ... this whole ... My throat's full of grit. I coughed so much I was sick. Look. We ran all the way round to Dace ... and I saw you zip out of the smoke—'

'Quiet!' Rayne yelled.

'But I couldn't tell where you'd crashed. Rayne appeared on a post nag. She—'

'Everyone! Quiet!'

Tern whispered, 'Was it a bomb?'

'Yes. It was Swallow. Have you seen Saker?'

'No Saker. No Tornado. No Emperor.'

Rayne climbed onto her desk and bellowed at us individually until we simmered into silence. 'Eszai!' she said. 'There's no time to talk! There's a lot of people buried. We must act fast! Kay Snow, I want you to start digging for the Emperor. Split everyone into teams, they'll follow your orders – every second's vital! Architect, tell us what buildings are unstable. Is the West Wall going to collapse? What about Jant's tower? I need to know, because I won't endanger the rescue teams. Simoon, you're in charge of them. Bring injured *here*. These wards will fill up. Messenger, get Snow everything he needs, and we need manpower. Take Lisade, if the telegraph's still working.'

'The Emperor is dead,' said Simoon.

A mutter of agreement roved among them.

'No! We're digging him out and everyone trapped, including Tornado, including Tré Cloud, so, my fellow Eszai, get to it!'

Kay Snow the Sapper beckoned them; they were about to leave but the Treasurer said, 'Ella—'

'I'm Rayne,' she said, firmly.

'You're not Rayne any more. I'm not Simoon. The Circle broke. It hasn't mended. So San must be dead. He *must* be, if he's under that. We're mortal and our oath's over.'

'I don't care! People are injured – move!'

'We don't know what happened!'

'Jant will tell us *while* we dig!'

'But there might be another explosion!'

Everyone looked at me. I stood up, wincing with pain. 'No,' I said, and described Swallow's bomb as briefly as possible. When tears

293

involuntarily started from my eyes, with pride I let them flow. Then a sensation of somehow being closer to everybody in the room brought me to pause. Rayne, standing on her desk, closed her eyes in pleasure as if she was gently being floated.

'It formed ...' she said softly. 'The Circle. San repaired it.'

'San's alive?' said the Treasurer.

'Can't you feel your link?'

I could. There was a hush as those of us cognisant of the Circle tried to sense it. I felt the flow of time break around me, raising me from it, suspending me above. I could feel presences again! But, no, the Circle was smaller ... I felt Rayne's personality as if she was holding my hand. I felt the cinnamon flame of Tern, the low-level aggravation of Hurricane, and, yes, the intelligence of Fulmer – and Saker! Saker was there, too, crimson and gold ... though he can't be. I couldn't tell whether the sensation was a product of shock and my injuries.

I breathed out. Everyone was staring at each other.

'I feel San!' said Simoon. 'Can you?'

'He's very, very faint,' said Rayne.

Simoon looked to the window and clenched his arms round his chest, his muscles rigid. 'He must be conscious, underground.'

'I can't feel Tré ...' said Rayne. 'There's about ... thirty of us gone. If the bomb killed Tré and knocked the Emperor unconscious at the same time ... that would explain it. If San's just regained consciousness and linked the Circle ... but he's faint ... he's dying.'

We gazed at each other in rising panic. Rayne added, 'Tornado's unconscious ... He's dying, too. He's fading out.'

'They were both in the Throne Room,' I said.

'They're buried alive,' said Kay Snow. 'Maybe in a pocket ... that masonry is big.'

Rayne announced, 'Everyone, if you relish staying immortal, do what Kay tells you!'

He gave her a significant look. Then he yelled at us. 'All right! Hayl, bring all the horses. Simoon, stretcher teams. Everyone else, follow me. You're going to work harder than you thought possible!' He swept out and the room emptied after him. Their boots left grime on the tiling. I realised the clamminess all over me was the same thin mud; someone had tried to sponge off the ash and now it was drying, tightening my skin.

I said to Rayne, 'I think I can feel Saker. Am I going mad?'

'No. San linked him into the Circle.'

'But that's against ... Why? Why would he ...?'

'That man is the least of my worries,' she said darkly. 'Can't you feel how many of us are dead?'

'You're better at it than me. Tré's gone ... The Blacksmith ... Mistral ... Serein's wife. Gayle wasn't here ...'

'And more! I – I need to make a roster. We need to find everyone. San might only have minutes!' She pointed at the door. 'Go help Kay. He knows we've no chance. And, Jant, you were hit by the full shock of the explosion. You're lucky you were airborne. If you cough up blood, any blood in the urine, come straight back. I've seen blast casualties drop dead three days later.'

'*What?*'

'Tern, watch him closely.'

'Of course, Doctor.'

'Patient compliance at last!' She turned to an orderly. 'Quicker! We need it spotless! These beds will be full in thirty minutes!'

When Tern and I reached the door we stopped dead. The dust cloud completely blocked the light and a rain of ash was sifting down, through a white false twilight. Everything was covered in it. The vast space where the Throne Room had been, was pale grey smog. Only the South Façade still stood tall, like a monolith, blurred through it, the pinnacles gone, the apex destroyed down to the Rose Window broken in half. From a circle, it was now an arc, the top and right side gone – it hooked the sky. Muted light opaqued the two shattered panes remaining in its tracery, and drifts of ash were building up on all the statues' plinths.

Smoke was rising from a hole in Simurgh's roof, this end, in the Swordsman's rooms. Every single window in Simurgh was smashed, great patches of facing stone blown away. And, beyond it, fading into the thick whiteout, the rubble of the Throne Room peaked like a mountain range. Some entire pinnacles lay embedded in the lawn – they'd ripped it up like spears. Scattered blocks lay here and there, and some recognisable fragments ... a flying buttress toothed with crockets, the snout of a gargoyle, ball flowers along a rib, pieces of pilaster. Ash snowed on them, and on the rubble summit three metres high. The stalks of buttresses projected snaggle-toothed from it, broken off at uneven heights.

The dust fell and velveted the roofs. I kicked off my boots, gave them to Tern and waited while she put them on. Kay Snow was blaring orders at the far end of the Throne Room rubble, nearest to where the throne should be. His short figure silhouetted through the dust, high on the debris like the lead role in a battlestress nightmare.

'Kay needs me,' I said.

'But it's impossible!'

We crossed the grass thick with masonry and followed the swathe of footprints towards his team on the Berm Lawn.

'San's under *that*?' Tern's voice shook with shock.

'Yes.'

'How could she …?'

'Sh …'

'How could she …?'

'Don't think about it, kitten. None of us can think, yet. We've got to dig.'

Because if you stopped to think, you'll realise we can't shift thousands of tonnes of stone. I was aware the shockwave of rumour would be expanding at great speed in a ring across the Empire. I had to catch up with it. I had to ride the front of the news and make my mark for the Castle. Whatever's going to happen now, will take more than a generation to sink in, and the dust may never settle.

CHAPTER 40

Kay Snow takes charge

Kay was poised on the ridge of the rubble close to the base of the spire. The Throne Room's east wall was upstanding to about two metres, covered in a huge slope of broken freestone. He was yelling, 'You: get horses from Hobson's. Pickaxes, shovels from the Blacksmith's yard, timber for shoring. You: get me the cranes off the barges. You: pull those stones together to make a bed for them. Here! In a square! You: bring me every horse, pony and rope in Demesne! Jant?'

'Yes?' I called.

'Get me all the manpower, horses, carts and tackle in Eske, Shivel and Fescue.'

'Eske fyrd can arrive in an hour.'

'They'll have heard the explosion, but they won't believe it!'

Hayl came through the Dace Gate with ten horses roped together. She halted, gawping at the stump of the tower. Kay roared at her but the Master of Horse couldn't move. She simply couldn't. She gazed in shock at the dust-filled sky where the spire had always been. Tern took her arm gently and prompted her to walk.

'Where's the sunburst?' she said.

'Hayl?' Kay bawled. 'Drays good! Wagons better! Go fetch them! You! Run with her to Hobson's and bring all the rope you can find for block and tackle. You! Put out the fire in Simurgh!'

Tern and I climbed the steep jumble of masonry to his side. As we crested the ridge, the immensity of the task hit us. It was a panorama of destruction – white hills of scree giving onto the crumpled lead escarpment of the Throne Room roof, below us. It looked as if a gigantic hand had pressed the entire Throne Room into the ground.

Kay bit his nail. 'What are you thinking?'

'It reminds me of Darkling.'

'Ha! More like Valley Twenty.'

The gradient of the east wall's rubble ran down to the roof, and under it the glory of the nave had vanished into a gigantic pit. The marble floor and the scarlet carpet, the ebony benches, the monumental gold candle holders, the gleaming onyx columns of the arches had fallen into the cistern. In a couple of places the rubble left black gaps at the edge of the roof, one almost directly below us. Kay pointed at it. 'I think that drops into the east aisle.'

'Hasn't the floor fallen in?'

'All of it but this edge, or we wouldn't be standing on it.'

'I saw the wall's foundations underground. They were solid.'

'I won't know until I climb in.' He scraped his fingernail inside his ear. 'Look. The base of the tower. The octagon lantern above the throne was a strong cage. Its columns had to be, to hold up seven thousand tonnes of spire. The tower rested on four pendentives. They've peeled out ... there ... and the base of the tower's come straight down. All that ... is solid stone. But the columns of the vaulting might have preserved an airspace underneath. I'm going in ... there. I'll see how far I can crawl.'

The roof was broken like a crust from the fallen spire, angled into a powdery grey metal awning. 'We have to widen that gap. Jant, how long it takes depends on how quickly you can bring me men and lifting equipment. I need *everything*. I need you to *know* everything. This is like the Front. I can do it, but I need Lowespass-capacity.'

'You've got it.'

'I'll send you a runner with orders every ten minutes.'

'The Emperor ... crushed ...' Tern murmured.

'He doesn't have long. We don't have long. Tern, there's no water or food. Will you ride to Demesne and tell Auburn we need *everything*? Every milk churn of water, all their medical gear. Bring it to the servants' quarters, that's our mess hall now.'

'She'll ask what happened.'

'Aye, she has Insects chewing her arse one minute, bits of spire falling on her next. Tell her all.'

Tern gave me a kiss, then left.

'How long can they survive in there?' I said.

'Depends how mangled they are.' Kay redoubled yelling.

The massive roof-lead panels looked like a still lake. Pieces of the pinnacles lay on it like broken icicles. Along the centre, in a spine of rubble, the huge ridge of the fallen spire stretched back towards the South Façade. Its nearest blocks had been torn asunder by the collapse but, further up the tower, further south towards the bookend of the still-standing Façade, whole sections lay complete. Gargoyles had smashed off them, and lay petrified in mid-escape.

I flew up and sailed above it. Crevasses split the lead sheets, then the roof ended, sheer, and I looked down into the pit. I glimpsed dark rubble far below – the west side of the Throne Room had vanished underground. So had the north end of Carillon and Mare's Run, all of the kitchens, dining hall and theatre; the pit gaped all the way to my tower. This end of Mare's Run had shorn off, revealing sudden interiors: the purple wallpaper of the Sailor's room on the first storey, a huge, gold-framed painting dashed to the floor, water pipes jutting from the bathroom below.

I flapped over the ruins of Carillon. They stepped as if kneeling, then corniced into the pit. By the curtain wall, the storerooms were nothing but a range of rubble. Food and dead bodies dotted, half-buried amongst the bricks. Simoon's search team crested one heap into a valley, heading towards the source of horrific screams.

My tower had broken open with a crack two metres wide, starting at the lintel above the doorway. It spiralled around the tower like a fracture in bone, and through the wide fissure I glimpsed our corkscrew staircase, before it curved out of sight. The inner half of the whole tower had fallen a metre. The blast had undermined it, carved the front off it and dropped it a metre lower, smashed the Myrtle Room and bathroom windows. The wall was soaking where a broken pipe had spewed before all water pressure ceased.

It might fall down any second. Tern had been lucky to escape. Fuck Swallow. Fuck Swallow! This was my home!

I landed at the ruined doorway and ran up to the Myrtle Room. Its door had been ripped from its hinges when the front of the tower fell. Connell had gone. Whether she lay under the rubble, or deep in the cistern, I couldn't tell.

I flew to Lisade, landed on the library roof and ran down to my desk.

CHAPTER 41

Communications

I sent telegraph messages and fast riders to Eske, Shivel, Fescue and Hacilith, requested their Select Fyrd, equipment and medical supplies. Then the news that the spire no longer dominated the skyline must have flashed across the Empire from Demesne to Summerday, because the telegraph crashed.

I don't mean it physically broke. There were so many messages backed up on the lines that the terrified senders couldn't prioritise. The Hacilith line jammed, then Eske to Tanager, and the whole lot went down. One minute the boy delivers an armful of pink slips, and the next there was ... nothing.

I was dropped out of my window on the world and brought to myself, blinking at the desktop wood. Then I became aware of the sound of rubble crunching and Snow yelling. All my lines are dead. My picture's blank.

I climbed to the roof and yelled at Jackdaw. 'I told them emergency protocol! It's my code and it's red! Tell them *again*! Nobody talks except me!'

'Yes, Comet.'

'Well?'

Jackdaw, his watcher and I stared out of the viewing pane, emptied of shattered glass, through the white murk, to the Binnard tower, which had lowered its arms to the receiving position. Which they'll all have done, by now. 'Well, go on. Give it a kick!'

'Comet ... is the Emperor ... is the Emperor ...?'

'Dead? He will be soon, if you don't knock all that shit off the line!'

He gulped and started sweeping the knobs of the levers across the sloped desk. I stood in the doorframe and watched him describe the code to clear the line and give the senders chance to recover.

I said, 'Shut down the Peregrine line. I want to talk fastest to Eske.'

'Yes, Comet.'

'If I ask Eske a question, I want a fucking answer, not a question in return.'

'Yes, Comet.'

'Ah. That brought them back.'

'Brome two keeps tacking on he's tired.'

'Already? Ha! Have him relieved; there's six in Brome one.'

Looking down to the rescue site, I saw Kay's men digging like ants to widen the gap at the edge of the roof. He had fifty wagons already – Imperial Fyrd carts and fruit pickers. A team of drays was ploughing up the lawn, dragging a chunk of facing stone the length of the telegraph mast. Jackdaw leant forward until he was bent over the powdered glass on the sill. 'He's setting up floodlights ... You can actually see the sunburst ... there.'

'Keep your eyes on Binnard.'

'Sorry, sir.'

Search teams swarmed the rubble. The only place free of them was the Throne Room roof. Down its centre the spit of spire debris tapered to a point, and the sun boss on its golden lance shone like a shield of flame. In comparison with the searchers, it was twice the height of a man.

I returned to my table and arranged the slips in importance, category, manor, and it looked like a colossal game of patience. In five minutes, the runner brought down another handful and the rescue jacked up a notch.

From: Eske. Sending Select cavalry ETA one hour.
From: Hacilith. Doctors requested leaving now coach ETA three a.m.
From: Fescue. Heard it. Sent horsemen.
From: Shivel. Select dispatched.
From: Carniss. Miners preparing ETA four days.
From: Hurricane, Lowespass. What the FUCK is going on??

I scooped the Vermiform from my pocket and dumped it on the table. The Fourlands were buzzing, now let me see if the Shift will help. Its worms huddled in a flaccid lump until I poured a sachet of sugar over them. They scoffed it with a high-pitched chomping, and twirled up into a tiny version of the beautiful woman.

'Feel better?' I asked it.

She unravelled and fronded at me vigorously.

'Can you see the cistern? Can you see the Emperor? Do you have worms in the Castle's foundations?'

She sagged into a swarm, streamed across the table and lifted my fountain pen. The worms spiralled around it and deftly spun it unscrewed. They dropped the steel barrel, wound around the rubber reservoir inside, and squeezed a shining blot of black ink onto the table top. Then they split, and half the worms crawled through the ink while the others dragged over one of the telegraph slips and held it down. The inky worms crawled across the paper, writing: We can see the Emperor

'Is he badly injured?'

VERY!

'And what about Tornado?'

Both dying on the throne

'Will you help us? Can you help dig them out?'

Dunlin EXTREMELY angry about this!

'I'm not asking Dunlin. I'm asking you … Vermiform, I know you could rebuild the Throne Room instantly if you wanted to. I know you can raise San up. Please help us.'

There's a little man down here now

'That's Kay Snow.'

We like him

'Will you help him?'

Yes

The worms enthusiastically bathed themselves in ink, splashing it everywhere. Your world will fall apart without San. Insects will overwhelm you. So we dig. Flowing through ~~~

They trailed off, and I could see the throng was thinning rapidly as worms disappeared from it, back into the Shift and presumably into the Throne Room collapse. 'One more thing!' I said. 'Where's Gayle?'

Buried deep. We show Kay.

'Where's Saker?'

STEPS

'What steps?'

The few remaining worms whirled in spirals, beaming frustration that they lacked the correct term. They hurled themselves through the ink, raced across the paper and drew with uncanny precision the outline of the South Façade, complete with ruined Rose Window. Then they dwindled to five worms. Three worms, and were gone.

I was alone.

I went looking for Saker.

CHAPTER 42

Saker in the portal

I could feel Saker in the Circle but he wasn't pulling on it. Gayle the Lawyer had begun to pull violently, and I thought her rooms midway along Carillon's ground floor must have become her living grave.

I ran down the grand staircase of Lisade and out into the ash, and turned to glance at the building. Its polished marble cladding, salmon pink, green and grey, had been pocked with holes and gouged in great scrapes by falling pieces of Throne Room.

Kay had built a crane atop the rubble, with a trough for a bucket, and an operator was spilling stone down the outer slope. On the far side, on the mound that used to be Carillon, a stretcher team was lifting a body with a sheet over it.

I climbed to the excavation, and found that Kay had wriggled down into the East Aisle. He was shifting debris between the last column of the arcade and a huge fallen ceiling boss, the final one before the throne, which lay like a coin on its side. Beyond it the tiled floor ended abruptly, hanging over the black abyss of the cistern. Kay came to the wall and looked up at me, his hair full of dust and a kerchief over his mouth. I explained the Vermiform as best I could. He was too desperate to be daunted, he sagged in gratitude when I described how it was digging towards us from the throne.

Behind him the timbers of the roof space jutted in a jumbled forest. Two thousand years ago the hardiest oaks of the Pentadrica had been felled, suspended above the ceiling for millennia and now ripped down in a mass of rafters.

I climbed down to the roof and walked along it, grating the dust beside the spire towards the South Façade. The ledges crusted with pigeon shit lay segmented along the same lines where they'd been built, and the separated surfaces of the blocks revealed the iron staples that had bound them together since before the Insects invaded.

I'd often landed on the spire. I'd been familiar with every crevice, every toe hold. I knew that cluster of moss in the corner of that arch, when the arch had been upright. I'd perched on the gargoyle with the bat wings, when it had reared into space. And now the impact had scattered its fragments of weathered limestone and lichen onto the lead.

Higher up, the spire narrowed. I'd spent hours standing high on the arcade course, looking out at the Demesne, washed by scolopendium and the breeze, while guardsmen in red walked tiny the wall tops below. That gargoyle with the Insect eyes, I'd tried to land on it once in the lashing rain, slipped off and fell all the way to *that* pinnacle. And now they were all on a level.

The octagonal-pyramid point of the spire lay cracked in half, a fissure running right-angle by right-angle down the surface of the stones. I passed the sun boss, its smooth gold disc embedded in the lead with the force of its fall.

I reached the south end, clambered down the roof and saw Saker sitting in the nested arches of the main portal, his back to me. I scrambled over tiles and slabs where the narthex had been, but my crunching and sliding didn't alert him. There were the carved amber drapes of the doorway lying broken under immense beams and fan vaulting. The guards were flattened under them too, and reeked of scorched flesh. Only one bare lower leg and a glimpse of jacket projected.

I dropped into the portal. Saker was huddled with his knees drawn up, his head resting on the wall under the plinths. The statues had fallen from their niches and lay with rigor mortis on the steps. Dust covered him so thoroughly he looked like one.

His wings were burnt. All his golden flight feathers were reduced to their central shafts, no vanes remaining. The barbs had melted and shrivelled, leaving just the splay of quills which looked like long, thin claws, scraping the step with his every breath. Some had stuck together with ugly black blobs of keratin. The molten, bubbling gunge had dripped onto his trousers and set there, too. It stank like burnt straw. His singed feathers had curled, revealing bands of muscle, and scratches from flying debris smeared them with blood.

I took his shoulder but he nestled into the stone. 'Saker ...'

Silence.

'San made you Eszai.'

He opened his eyes. The red rims stood out ghastly as the only flesh colour. 'Why ... when I did this?'

'Swallow did it.'

A whisper like breathing: 'I couldn't ...'

'Did you try to warn him?'

'I ran. I got here and the fire ... burst out ... in front of me. The hall fell ...' He spread his wings reflexively and the quills were like spiders' legs. One laceration yawned and bled. God, I thought. Two more steps and he'd have been inside.

'Why? Why make me Eszai?' He came alive and punched the stone. 'San *knows* I walked away! He *knows* I left the Circle! Why taunt me? When I'm to blame!'

'You're not to blame.'

'For this!'

'Swallow lit the fuse.'

His eyes widened and for a second I almost saw the blaze reflected in them. Then he gave a horribly unhinged laugh and rested his head against the wall. 'Fire like a torrent. Like a flame thrower.'

'I think you should see Rayne.'

'No! It ... folded up ... before my eyes. *Before my eyes*, Jant! Where's San?'

'Snow's digging him out.'

'Is this some punishment?'

'No. San must want you to take a lead. He knew you were waiting for a competition.' But Saker was in no shape to hear it. He was shaking with shock.

'How'm I going to tell her?'

'Tell ...?'

'Eleonora!' he cried. 'He didn't join *her* in! He didn't make *her* immortal! Just me!' He punched the wall so hard I winced.

'Saker,' I said. 'King Saker. San never joins anyone to the Circle he hasn't met and questioned. Come sit with us, at the rescue site.'

'Oh, *god, how will I tell her?*'

I tried to help him up, which was impossible. He stared vacantly for quite some time and then stood up abruptly. He fanned out his wings and looked at the melted feathers as if they belonged to somebody else. 'I lost my array,' he said. 'See? Every single one.'

'Come on,' I said.

'I can sense you ... and Tern ... and Ella ... and ...'

'Good. Let's go.'

'I left my bow in the boat.'

'You don't need your bow.'

'Left ... also ... the rifle.'

'You don't need the rifle either.'

'... I lost my array.'

'We've established that. Come on.' I pulled at his scorched sleeve and he moved in the direction of the pull. I led him down the steps and into the Starglass Quad. I'd rather have led him behind Simurgh but the path was shoulder-height with rubble.

305

When we were far enough into the square for him to register the whole South Façade he stopped dead and gazed up at the broken Rose Window. He stared for so long I thought he'd lost his tenuous grip on reality altogether. Then he murmured, 'How could I …?'

'*Swallow* did it.'

'I … I … killed San. I've broken the Empire. What will happen …? I could've shot her, Jant; why didn't I? I don't understand … I just loose the string nothing easier why not why didn't I?'

He rubbed his eyes and cleared patches around them, though the dust stayed in the spider-web lines of his skin. '…I showed her the lake and I brought her here, like a, me, I did it, I showed her, what for? Why do that?' He stepped back and gazed at the stained glass filmed with grime. 'Some idea, some wrong idea: love. Why? Well, why? I just roll the string off my fingers and she's dead and didn't do this …'

'You did shoot her,' I said. 'You shot her, and with her dying breath she lit the fuse.'

'Ah, don't furnish me with a lie to live with … Is San … under that?'

'Yes.'

'Shit.'

'Come on, soldier.' I pulled his sleeve again and he followed. He said nothing along the front of Simurgh, though wet smoke was billowing out of Serein's attic window. He was silent past the barracks, but when we sighted the cranes he shuddered, rattling his quills. 'Why did you jump from the boat?'

'I tried to talk Swallow out of lighting the fuse.'

'So much hate … Your sharp tongue won't cut …'

'It doesn't matter now. She's gone. She was blown to—'

'The heat's her hatred.'

I walked him to the base of the rubble, and he looked up to the winch. The man standing above us clicked a hook onto the bucket's base. His mate on the grass led his horse forward, tipped the bucket, and with a crash cascaded the debris down the slope. I saw a twinkle of tesserae, and a piece of mosaic the size of a shield slid to rest against Saker's boot.

It showed the forked tip of a banner, superimposed by a raised silver sword. Saker stared at it. Then he suddenly shook himself, hurtled up the slope, crested the top and cried out. I followed. There was the adjoining piece of the mosaic. Its surface slanted to the sunlight: it showed the rest of the soldier on horseback, carrying the pole of the banner and the hilt of his upraised sword, the horses' heads of a division of cavalry ranked behind him.

Saker crouched and wiped his hand over its surface. The dust smeared away and gold tesserae glittered. 'This was above the first arch.'

'Yes.'

'But it was my friend. All the hours I spent looking at it!'

'I know them by heart, too.'

'She did this!' He glanced down into the excavation where you could see part of the east aisle blocked to the ceiling. A worker was hurrying bits of vaulting into the bucket. 'It's a ... It's a ... mass grave. Look. Someone's squashed! One of the gallery archers ...' He pointed to a hank of hair, broken feathers, tail of a red coat, sandwiched in the debris above long drips of drying blood. 'The poor man.'

'We can't dig them out yet, or it'll undermine the rubble.'

By the winch a number of tools were spread on a blanket. Saker selected a pair of pliers. Then he sat down on the mosaic, pulled his wing in front of him, and with his left hand pressed it strongly onto his knee.

'Oh, no,' I said. 'You're not doing that.'

'I am. I want my array back.'

'Hadn't you better help with the rescue?'

He was too traumatised to reply. I said, 'I'm going to answer the telegraph. I'll tell Leon you're all right.'

'Don't tell her I'm immortal!'

He rubbed the skin hummocked over the quills, to stop it sticking. I could see them all the way up, lying parallel, like pens in a rack. Then he clamped the pliers to his first primary feather, and pulled it out. Agony flared on his face but he made no sound. He dropped the carbonised plume, fastened the pliers to the next, and pulled experimentally. Then with all his strength and a little twist, rived it out, and swore.

Each flight feather has a nerve, and is connected to the bone. They sit through a band of tough membrane, which keeps them stiffly in place and will also turn them, like the tape on a window blind, depending on how you hold your wing. If he plucks them out, new feathers will start to grow back, which is faster than waiting a year for them to moult through. But pulling them off the bone and through this membrane really fucking hurts.

He squared up to the pain. Like some catharsis it brought him round, woke him up. 'And I'm not riding through Awia looking like this!'

'Through Awia?'

'To the Front. I'm going to secure the Castle. Then I'll lead the fyrd to reinforce Hurricane. Ah, *shit*, that hurts! We must show everyone the Castle hasn't fallen! We still fight for them. We're not beaten!'

He pulled one out and threw it down, wiped his hand across his eyes and reverently pressed his palm to the mosaic. In the dust he left a handprint wet with tears. He clamped the pliers to the next feather so firmly it squashed the shaft, rived it out smoothly and dropped it on the pile. 'Ah – shit! We have to show our purpose! We have to stop the Insects … And Eleonora is there. I have to explain … don't I?'

He plucked a quill and flinched. Every feather was twice the width of a pen, nearly a metre long and burnt free of barbs. Their ends had curled, but every tip was like a clean, fresh nib, hollow with white lines inside, where the pulp had dried in its early growth. They were mature and didn't bleed, but his wing twitched with each one, and its hand must be numb by now. Damn it, he was making *my* eyes water.

He yanked a feather out that still had a bit of vane adhering, held it up and spun it between thumb and forefinger. 'Here's enough to fletch an arrow. With it I'll shoot Connell.'

'She's gone from the tower. I don't even know if she's alive,' I said.

He threw it down. 'Then we might never know. Can you imagine the devastation on its way …? The factions that'll arise the second this sinks in? We'll never deal with them. The Circle will never work together, without San!'

Since he has forty flight feathers in all, he was giving himself a long ordeal and it made me squeamish. The sensation's awful – like drawing teeth – the pain shoots up the nerve. 'Ah – shit! That hurt even more!'

'You're not pressing hard enough.'

'The skin's burnt.'

'At least—'

'No! No drugs. No brandy.' He paced the crest of the rubble and sat down again, set his teeth and pulled the last primary, then started down the arm on the secondaries in a rhythm. Then the tertiaries one after another; they came out more easily, but he had to twist round to reach the last.

He threw down the pliers and flexed his wing. It looked stumpy, and the burnt covert feathers hardly hid the empty follicles – a line of hollow skin tubes like the round holes of a harmonica. He looked down into the pit while he tucked it behind him and spread the other wing across his knee. Then he picked up the pliers, leant his strength onto the ruined flight feathers, and began tearing them out.

At length there was a grunt and a scraping from the crevice leading to the throne. Another grunt, and a flash of light. One filthy and deeply-lacerated hand emerged from the tiny hole and with precision placed a mining lamp on the ground. Then another hand … both arms bent and pressed palms against the column and ceiling boss, pushed, and Kay Snow slid himself out of the passage with the fluidity of a squat octopus unfurling from its lair.

His workmen stopped, while Kay sat cross-legged and turned off his lamp. His calm and factual voice belies a great energy: 'Jant. Go fetch Rayne, because I saw the Emperor.' He shook his head. 'I hope she'll tell me how to move them without killing them. If you could only see!'

Saker tossed a stone into the pit and immediately had Kay's attention. 'Describe it,' he said.

Kay stood with balletic grace and assumed a position like a bear hug. 'Tornado saved the Emperor. He's bent over San in the throne, protecting him. He placed his arms around the Emperor as the roof fell on them. San's squashed between Tornado's body and the back of the throne. The blocks of the ceiling, the spire, bent the flames of the throne, caging them in. It looks like a claw. It made an airspace, only eighty centimetres clearance, but above the flames and all around is solid rubble. Their legs are buried in it. Your Shift worms are moving it quickly, Jant. They're dumping it in the cistern – they're amazing – they're working like a living net.'

He pulled himself into a crouch. 'There's ... less space than this. No room to move, no air. If I dig rock out, more will fall, so I'm letting the worms carry it away. I was breathing all the Emperor's air, so I left.'

'What injuries?'

He hesitated. 'Tornado has a broken skull. Blood is weeping from his eye. San has a crushed arm, maybe. I can hardly see him. But their legs ...'

'What do their legs look like?'

'Jam, gentlemen. Jam.'

CHAPTER 43

Raising San

It was midnight by the time Kay had cleared the roof fall sufficiently to move the Emperor. By that time, Mist Fulmer had arrived, and Tern had ridden back from Demesne.

At midnight, Rayne and I were watching on top of the rubble. Saker and Kay were down in the pit. The sky brewed an unsettling dark purple, clogged opaque with smoke and dust, and the black Berm Lawns milled with lanterns like fireflies.

A queue of carts formed a chain of lights, moving one by one away to the Dace Gate, through the crowd that Mist had cordoned back from their path. Their lamps illuminated fractions of cartwheel and horsehide. As they emerged into the floodlights on the Dace Gate, they segued into whole horses and tumbrils, each with a man on the driving seat and a full load of limestone rubble glimmering with fragments of mosaic.

There was Halliwell, driving a cart carrying one of the moulded bases that once held a column. I recognised curved fragments of the aisle lierne ribs, a piece of the quatrefoil piercing that had topped one of the windows above the gallery. They were carting it out and dumping it in a huge pile by the river.

Rayne and I looked down into the part of east aisle that had been cleared. The marble floor slabs jutted over the great drop into the cisterns, covered with grit and dust. Our attention was fixed on the passage leading to the Throne, in which a single lamp flickered.

Kay slithered out of it and blinked up at us backed by the floodlight. 'Jant! You should have seen the Vermiform bend back the rays of the Throne!'

'Do you want stretchers?'

'Don't stand so close to the edge. Bits are falling in. No, no stretchers. Watch this!'

A thick tendril of woven worms erupted from the passage, wrapped around a fallen column, and more worms crawling onto it caused the cable to reel, and carried out the huge form of Tornado, completely encased in worms as if sewn into a net. The cable grew strands, braced them against the ground and raised Tornado's body to us. His bulk reflected darkly on the shattered mosaic as it rose. It crested the edge, curved towards us, and the Vermiform deposited him carefully on a backboard stretcher that Rayne had specially made.

Rayne picked up the glass drip bottle that Kay had fixed into Tornado's rotund arm, and held it high. The Vermiform drew back like a shrivelling vine, seemed to suck itself into the passage, and emerged a few seconds later, bearing as if in a seed pod the broken body of our Emperor.

It raised San to us, deposited him with utmost care on a back-board, and drew away. Rayne and I gasped. Kay had pinned a cloth over the Emperor's face, but the rest of his narrow body, brown with dried blood, tapered to his legs. They were crushed to a thinness I'd not thought possible. His trousers were flat and his white riding boots mangled where slabs of the mosaic had smashed his fibulae into minute fragments. Kay, following Rayne's advice, had tied tourniquets at the top of both thighs and affixed a needle and drip bottle into the Emperor's arm.

Rayne lifted the cloth covering his face and recoiled. 'Jant? Go! Go!'

I raised my carriage lamp and strode down the rubble. Her men, behind me, lifted San's stretcher and followed. Rayne walked swiftly beside them, and through the crowd we passed.

The cordon restrained them but faces leant in. Gibbous faces pressed together. A solid wall of faces shocked, faces terrified, bloated into my narrow ellipse of light. They loomed parchment-yellow, palisaded, and passed into darkness. Men and women had come to watch and help. Journalists, Demesne townspeople, everyone who could find a horse had raced for a chance to glimpse the Emperor's body, to say they were present on this night San might live or die, as the ink of history scrawled across the page. They'd pushed their children forward of the crush and my light reflected on their hair, on eyeglasses in the crowd. Lanterns glimmered and, as we passed, separated into feeble glows in anxious hands. I swept on with half-spread wings, ahead of the stretcher-bearers. Their feet whisked the grass and San's blood pattered off the taut canvas.

Once I rode ahead of San's glorious entry into Lowespass. Now I lit his way to the grave. The terrified crowd seemed the host of those who had died before, reconstituted from the soil of Lowespass or scraped themselves out of the Insect Wall to crawl here, to catch one baleful glimpse of the Emperor who'd sent them to their fates for fifteen hundred years.

We passed Harcourt in a meteor-trail of light. Rayne ran ahead and called to Fulmer, who hooked open the hospital's double doors, illuminating the garden of dust-shrouded flowers. I stood back as the stretcher team angled up the ramp.

'Don't hit the walls!' Rayne yelled.

They handled the Emperor's stretcher into one of the white wards, dazzling bright, and slid it onto a table. Rayne bawled at her orderlies without taking her eyes from San. 'Boiling water! Cold water! Antiseptic! Gauzes!'

They flew about.

'Jant, Fulmer, out of here! Stop idiots coming in!'

She pulled the cloth from the Emperor's face, flung it at me, and closed the doors. Alone in the tiled corridor, Fulmer and I regarded each other. The cloth was stained with blood, in a vague imprint of the Emperor's face. I shoved it in my pocket.

Some of the crowd had ventured into the hospital garden. We shooed them out and I set my lantern on the wall. Fulmer lit a cigarette and paced back and forth, guzzling it.

Saker arrived, bearing the front of Tornado's stretcher, with two strong soldiers on the rear poles. As they passed I saw stained glass glittering in Tornado's skin, and clear fluid running from his ear. They carried his body into the hospital, then Rayne ejected Saker the same way we had been.

He approached; the mortar dust that clung to every dewy grass blade had left cement streaks on his boots. 'What are you doing?' he said.

'The fucking foxtrot,' said Fulmer. 'What do you think?'

Saker put his hands in his back pockets, looked up at the starless sky and exhaled one of those long Awian sighs where you empty your lungs, then the airsacs in your back and long bones.

'Rayne will revive the Emperor,' I said.

'If there's any chance.'

The night breeze pulsed and cooled us. The lanterns of the vast and silent horde speckled the ground to the foot of the curtain wall. The great monolith of the South Façade stood solitary against the plum-coloured clouds. A faint anaemic reflection of light twinkled high in the hook of the great rose window. On the Dace Gate the floodlights, like sprigs of laburnum, cast an amber glow on the heads and shoulders of the sentries beneath their steel stalks. In the arc of my lamplight, carefully-tended pansies had been trampled thick with damp grey ash, the crushed grass gave off the scent of scolopendium and San's blood drops timed the path. The white doves of the Throne Room tower huddled together on the hospital roof, homeless and traumatised. Rayne's nurses had drawn the curtains and figures moved purposefully behind them, but we'd no way of knowing what was happening inside.

'Fuck it,' said Saker.

'The *mot juste*,' said Mist.

I said, 'What are we going to do?'

'What we're best at. Jant, send out news that the Emperor is safe.'

'No. He's dying. Do you want me to lie?'

'Since when did you have qualms about that? And tell these rubber-neckers they're better off in bed. Leave the fyrds to me. Mist, ask Hayl to arrange horses – can she manage a thousand? – I'm taking the warriors north tomorrow and we'll look the part. I want every flag flying that isn't covered in this grey shit.' He set off, and glanced over his shoulder. 'I'm going to pick up my other rifle and I swear to god, if I find even a half-decent bow in this wreckage, I'll give you Micawater.'

'Saker—'

'Lightning. Call me Lightning.'

CHAPTER 44

San's Ward

At dawn, I watched from the telegraph cabin as Lightning assembled the Eske Fyrd on the Berm Lawn. I'd been awake all night, driving the semaphore as fast as it would go, relating the news. Tern and Jackdaw were asleep in the room below, and the deeply-shadowed pit of the excavation lay silent, but over in Carillon, Kay's team was digging deep for Gayle the Lawyer, with the help of the Vermiform.

Lightning watched the troops filing out of the gate and then he strode towards the hospital. I brought the control knobs together and down, folding the paddles to rest, and saw Binnard do the same. I slipped out of the cabin, jumped off the roof and glided over the soldiers' lines. I landed beside Lightning, halfway down the hospital path. He wore travelling clothes, his coat covered his wings; he still reeked of burnt feathers.

He knocked on the hospital door. We waited, and the first blood-red arc of the sun began to show above the Dace Gate. Without a breath of wind, the smoke still drifting out of Simurgh rested in a hammock haze between the towers of the curtain wall.

The door opened and Rayne tottered out. She looked up at Lightning and recoiled as if struck. Then she peered closely at his face and the lines on her forehead pulled together. 'You look different,' she said. 'Look at you, Saker; you've changed.'

'It's been fifteen years,' he said softly.

'Fifteen years ...'

'It doesn't matter now,' he said. 'Tell me how the Emperor is.'

She slapped him hard across the face. 'Doesn't *matter*? Of course it does! *You* did this, you arse. This!' She thrust a finger at the ruins. '*You* brought Swallow here. *You* lent her hope. You gave her a taste of our lives. Of course she'd want more! So look at the devastation! San's ... San's ... Oh, god! Why did you show her the cistern? Just because you like red-haired amazons! Just because you liked the racket she made!'

'That slap,' he said. 'I deserved it.'

She slapped him harder. *'You deserve two!'*

'Very well. I deserve two.'

'Are you accepting the role San's given you?'

'Yes. Yes, Ella ... I'll do what I think San would want.'

'It's the only way,' she said.

'If I uphold the Empire and San regains consciousness, he'll make Eleonora immortal.'

I said, 'Zascai will question your place.'

'Then I'll run a fucking tournament ... sometime.'

Rayne raised her hand to the wrinkles at the corner of his eye. 'Saker. Do you remember when I pulled you from under that chariot?'

'... Yes ...'

'I told you then, we didn't belong in the mortal's world any longer. I said they would never understand us again. They *couldn't*. But ever since, you've tried to be part of it. Tried to play the prince! *I'm* the only one who understands you; *you're* the only one who knows me. You were my only solace, my only confidant, my best friend. For fourteen hundred years! And what did you do? Walk away!'

'Ella, I—'

'Without a backward glance! Without a thought! Chasing your stupid ideas! A life alone stretched out ahead of me – you left me alone forever.'

'I'm not clear what "forever" is, now.'

She really tried to slap him, but he caught her hand.

'Didn't I save your life?'

'Twice.'

'Yes, twice! I revived you from the brink – but you walked away! You left to waste yourself for a dumb idea! I didn't! Now your stupid ideals have destroyed the whole Empire!' Completely exhausted, she started crying, and he hugged her close, like a contrite son.

'Our Emperor,' he said gently. 'I need to know before we leave.'

'You're leaving?'

'For Lowespass.'

'As Lightning?'

'Yes.'

'Yes ... yes ... you must.' She pulled a cloth from her smock pocket and dried her eyes. Then she walked back against the door and opened it. 'Boots off. Coats off. Wipe your hands with phenol. Come in.'

The Emperor San lay alone in a small ward, with a silk sheet tabled over his legs, his arms by his sides and a rubber tube leading from a big glass bottle on a drip stand into the crook of his uninjured arm. His head was bandaged, his left eye and cheek. A lurid bruise covered that side of his face, but his eyes were closed.

Being so close to him for the first time I saw the details: the white hair on his dented old man's chest, which hardly rose and fell. The liver spots on his ridged hands had coalesced into an archipelago of brown patches. Half-moons waned on his nails, which Rayne had cut short because he'd scraped them ragged on the roof fall. His cheeks were hollow, face tapered, lips dried to plaques, skin alabaster-pale, and none of his hair was visible under the bandages. He was keeping us immortal, but he was just a man.

'He's in a coma,' said Rayne.

'What do we do?'

'Wait.'

'How long?'

'I don't know.'

'Rayne,' I said. 'The world's crying out for news.'

'Tell them "soon". Tell them I'm doing all I can!'

'Can he hear us?'

'No.'

Lightning said, 'If the Castle can't run Challenges ...'

'We can run them, all right,' said Rayne. 'We just can't make victors immortal.'

'Zascai will protest.'

'Well, they should have thought of that before they destroyed the balance.' She picked up the antiseptic cloth and ran it along the sidebar of the bed. 'There's nobody in and nobody out. And think of this when you're fighting in Lowespass: if any one of us nineteen remaining Eszai dies, San can't mend the Circle. We'll all stay mortal. And that's the end of us.'

'When do you think he'll wake up?' I pressed.

'Jant, I can't even guess.'

'But *will* he wake up?'

'Maybe not, forever.'

I couldn't discern his breathing. The indentations of his chest and withered wrinkles of his neck were so acutely clean they looked carved. You could see the capillaries in his delicate eyelids. They covered the perfectly round hollows of his eye sockets, into which his eyes had sunk. Their purple contrasted with the pure white hair of his eyelashes and brows.

'My lord Emperor,' said Lightning. 'I am here ... the flotsam of your system. I'll do what you will.'

'Hypoxia caused it,' said Rayne. 'No air in the rubble.'

'And Tornado?'

'Also in a hypoxic coma, but with a fractured skull to boot. He's stirring, though.'

'If he wakes up, San might wake up?'

'Jant, our Emperor is an old man.'

I went to Tornado in the next ward and found him asleep. He was swathed in bandages, with medical notes on his bed for bicarbonate saline drip at a litre an hour. It was unnerving to see the giant so still.

Through the wall, I could hear Rayne and Lightning talking. 'I'm expecting another wave of casualties,' she said. 'The really complicated ones. Suffocation, settled blood, rotten blood, dehydration, heart attack, kidney failure ... Gayle's still unaccounted for. And upstairs I have eighty patients including Serein. If any of you die at the Front it'll be the end of the Circle.'

'If we don't fight Insects it'll be the end of the Empire.'

'I see that, but ...'

'We must reinforce Hurricane and Capelin. We must keep the manors working together; remind them we're still their advisors. Try to keep our legitimacy or the mortals will turn on us. All kinds of bastards will rush into this vacuum. I can't predict who, but I'm ready to slow them down.'

'Is Jant staying?'

'Yes. He's dealing with the press and the manors, keeping everyone in contact. Kay Snow's staying, of course. So's the Architect, she's working on getting the bodies out and some water restored before the heat ... I'm leaving you Hayl, to take charge of security. She's recruiting all the reporters arriving, into rescue parties. She has the Imperial Fyrd, she'll protect you. The rebels might attack again.'

'Rebels? Swallow died. It's over – and she won.'

'What about Connell?'

There was a pause. I imagine Rayne sighed. 'Forget Connell! Lightning, are you the soothing oil that'll heal the Empire, or one of the faults along which it will break?'

'San knew I have the greatest chance of holding it together.'

'All right. Jant will keep us in touch. I'll tell you everything about San ... and Tawny.'

'The Circle is in your hands, Ella; I trust you ...'

'San could die any second.'

'You'll bring him back to life.'

'Even if he wakes up, he won't be in any state to govern.'

'You'll save him. You will. Come here.'

As I entered the room I saw him hug Rayne, with strong arms, then wings that looked stubby without the long flight feathers. Rayne wrinkled her nose, took one wing and raised it to peer under the coverts at the line of empty feather tracts.

'Ouch. How are you?'

'Sore. Stressed. I keep having flashbacks of the explosion … And I'm afraid of how Leon will react when I tell her.'

'This will take five weeks.'

'I know.'

Out of the window, I could see Kay hurrying in, across the rutted lawn, bringing another casualty on a backboard stretcher. It must be Gayle. The Doctor looked up, and leapt to action. 'Out! Jant, Lightning. Goodbye – for now.'

'Goodbye, Rayne.'

The stretcher bearers passed us, and we glimpsed the Lawyer's unconscious body. Thankfully Gayle's a Morenzian. None of the Awians will have survived being buried.

The sun, like an oil drop, oozed its way clear of Dace Gate South and hung, looking unnaturally large, as if sticking to the battlements by a run of colour. The Castle, like a bowl, continued to fill with smoke. Lightning and I walked across the splay of brown earth, more deeply furrowed and hoof-pocked as the tracks converged into the Dace Gate. I glanced back at the hospital, but the newly-cleaned windows reflected only the billows of rubble and I couldn't see Rayne inside.

Saker looked back, too. Sometimes he does.

CHAPTER 45

Leaving

A light rain began to fall, washing the dust, soot, and the blood of our Emperor from the grass blades into the soil. It smelt of nitrate and petrichor; the sun shone a diffuse pewter blur through the white layer of cloud.

The grey stone gatehouse backed the scarlet of five hundred pennants that wound their poles above the heads of the cavalry. Lance points gleamed under films of condensation. Raindrops ran down the chestnut flanks of shivering horses and starred their hooves; shallow plaster-white streams braided from the spoil heap into the river, and dragonflies glided between us on the Vs of their wings.

Every roll of kit on the back of a thousand saddles darkened with the rain until the colours were crimson and moss-green against the washed-out pastel of the Castle's round towers.

The rain, backlit by sunlight dazzling from a gap in the clouds, sprinkled on oilcloth coats over stirruped legs, across the path and over the roof of the Bridge of Size. A sudden gust blew it to a curve, drops spattered against my leather jacket, then all was still. The shower stopped as abruptly as it began.

Lightning stepped up onto Balzan. His rifle butt jutted from the saddle holster and a bow from the armoury slung on his back. He took his place at the head of the column, next to Mist.

Mist had just finished kissing Tern's hand. The rain had wet his shirt and through it you could see his taut muscles and many small, brown feathers overlapping on his shoulders. He'd been digging out survivors; his curly-topped hair was bedraggled and his fabulous clothes, filthy.

Lightning threw him the cigarette lighter and he caught it, went straight for his case, lit one and exhaled a cloud of smoke. His hand tipped back in a dandy gesture. 'Listen.'

'To what?'

'To Carillon bell not striking the hour.'

The bell of Carillon was lying in the cistern with the stones of its belfry, water lapping into its bronze mouth, carrying the settling sediment. It was silent for the first time in seven hundred years.

San on his throne had kept order, now everything is chaos. Men and nature had an order; now it's swung out of control. Father will bury daughter, and the sun spire no longer shines on high. We must try to keep the world together – strains will soon begin to widen the cracks and tear it apart. But the sunburst remains on our pennants and our shields.

I said, 'Keep watching the telegraph. Any sensitive news, I'll bring word of mouth.'

Lightning smiled thinly and waved his arm forward. His horse high-stepped; Tern and I moved back as he began to lead the column over the bridge towards the woods. The grind of hooves and clink of tack overcame the chirr of grasshoppers switched on by the heat.

The rain on the warm ground began to rise as mist, as their backs led away and the last forked tongue of the Castle's banner licked the air. It was ten a.m., on Monday the first day of July, in the Year of Our War 2040.

Connell

I hid behind a tree trunk and watched soldiers pass. First came Saker and Mist, tall on their warhorses. Riding out like bats from the ruin of the Castle on the hill. They looked confident, not in any way broken. I dropped to the soil – they're searching for me.

The telegraph said that the Emperor lives, so they're still freaks, aren't they? Jant's going to drop in everywhere, interrogating all and sundry. But the Emperor's in a coma and we've decimated the Eszai, so who knows what'll happen?

I've told you these events because I want to set the record straight. I want to say what truly occurred because there'll be too many inaccurate versions published and all kinds of crazy rumours will start flying around. I won't let Jant distort it for the Castle's purpose, because Swallow had a point. She had a very valid point and she wasn't as black as he's going to paint her.

Swallow tried to kill San because he killed her. That's the true version of events and I hope it'll clear your mind.

After San finished speaking to Rax's troupe, he let them free. None of us Roses were caught in the collapse and, after his parley with the Emperor, Rax and his troupe are changed men. He's hiding out in the Demesne, declaiming how wonderful San is, and our oath has broken down. No Rose cares to help another – it might lead to his arrest.

The spire has gone. San's palace is destroyed, the Castle undermined, and blood's soaking out of the Eszai's corpses into the underground lake. I'm glad, but scared – there'll be repercussions. We're a very discernible group to blame and my tattoos are condemning evidence. So while the world's still reeling, I'm nicking a horse and riding home to Vertigo. If they find me, they'll have to fight.

I wish I'd never met Swallow, but I loved her with a passion. She's made the world a powder keg. If the surviving Eszai can't quench this burning fuse the Empire will soon blow itself apart.

She had the biggest ego of all. More than any Eszai. She had the greatest sense of entitlement and yet, all she's managed to do is extinguish her own immortality. No one will ever want to play the operas, symphonies and concertos she's left for posterity. All the art she's produced in her lifetime will sink into the oblivion of the past. Because now, nobody will remember her as the greatest musician. They will tar her character and remember her, for all time, as a monster.